THE SECOND BOOK IN THE
INVERSE SHADOWS UNIVERSE

SUFFICIENTLY ANALYSED MAGIC

THE SECOND BOOK IN THE
INVERSE SHADOWS UNIVERSE

SUFFICIENTLY ANALYSED MAGIC

CHRISTOPHER G. NUTTALL

Elsewhen Press

To everyone who asked me for a sequel, with many thanks.

Author's Note

Dear reader.

I must apologise for the long and unintentional gap between *Sufficiently Advanced Technology* and its planned sequel, *Sufficiently Analysed Magic*.

To cut a long story short, my life was going through its ups and downs and while I did have a plan for a second novel in this series I thought it would be better, at the time, to concentrate on other projects. It was not until recently, when I attended the WorldCon in Glasgow, that I felt encouraged to return to this universe – a great many people asked me what had happened to the series and told me they would be very interested in the second book. I dusted off the original plot, updated it, and sat down to write.

Given that there was a long delay, I made the decision to concentrate completely on newer characters rather than return to the characters who starred in the first book. I hoped it would make it easier for new readers to get into the story, while readers who read the first novel can easily draw lines between the first set of characters and the next. All you really need to know is this:

Sixteen years ago, the Confederation, a hyper-advanced human society stretching across thousands of light years, stumbled across a world – Darius – in which magic appeared to be real, with witches and wizards casting spells that appeared to have very real effects. Baffled, the Confederation dispatched a team of observers to investigate the society, eventually discovering that the source of the magic was the Darius Machine, an alien artefact at the heart of the planet that appeared to control local reality itself. The machine went critical shortly afterwards and had to be shut down, seemingly ending the magic … but leaving behind a number of babies and infants who had strange abilities of their own.

Now, the children are reaching adulthood and attracting attention from alien factions that are very far from friendly to the human race …

I hope you enjoy this book. If you do, please let me know. Hopefully, the gap between this novel and book three will not be so long.

PROLOGUE

Pandora dreams.

She doesn't know how she knows she is dreaming, but she is.

It is odd, for one such as her to dream. The Darius Children sleep together, their minds touching gently as they relax, lulling each other into a deep relaxing slumber that leaves them rested when they open their eyes once again. Pandora knows it is rare for humans to communicate on such a deep and primal level, almost impossible without crossing hardwired ethical lines, and yet she accepts her life as normal. It is all she knows.

And yet, she dreams.

Her mind explodes out of her body, out of the mental nest, and out into the universe. She finds herself drifting high above the galaxy, watching the stars as they circle the Great Attractor at the heart of the Milky Way. She sees life in all its many and manifest forms, from aliens practically akin to humanity to creatures so strange that communication is almost impossible; she sees life flowering across the universe, flowing out of rocky worlds and gas giants; she sees civilisations rise and fall, coming into existence briefly and then fading away, as if they had never been. She knows that some destroy themselves, or are destroyed by others, or stagnate ... or go on ...

As if the thought changes everything, the universe seems to dissolve around her. Her thoughts are pulled onwards, deeper into the reality of the cosmic all: she sees ancient entities flittering in the darkness between the stars, or peeking out of dimensions that exist at right angles to her own; she senses, more than sees, giant eyes peering down at the universe, watching and waiting for something to happen. The universe shifts, growing darker. Some civilisations are wondrous beacons of light, others are stagnant ... still others, she realises numbly, are cancers, poisoning the reality around them. She feels unwell as she stares down, her stomach queasy. It bothers her at a very primal level, ancient instincts warning her she needs to run. It is the first time she has ever felt unwell.

The universe shifts again, pulling her mind towards the Great Attractor. The immense black hole at the centre of the galaxy reaches for her, yanking her into a darkness that seems endless. She falls into the singularity and sees ... light. Light everywhere. Her mind's eye is almost blinded by the sheer brightness, at the heart of the black hole. It shouldn't be there ... *she* shouldn't be there. This is not a human place. Powerful waves of pure thought buffet her, battering at her mind. She grits her teeth and tries to force her mind to accept, closing her eyes briefly to impose some kind of order on the reality around her. She understands, now, what it feels like to be a fly, buzzing through the human world. Here, *she* is the fly. The minds around her are so big, so immense, that all she can see is just the tip of the iceberg. It really is not a human place.

She opens her eyes and sees ... gods. Humans ... no, entities that *look* human and yet are so much more. They are almost caricatures of humans, from men so old and wise their wisdom shifts around them like a shroud to muscle-bound brutes and women so beautiful it is hard to look them in the eye. They are huge, towering above her ... she feels her mind try to expand, try to understand what she is really seeing, but recoils helplessly the moment she catches a glimpse of what lies beneath. They are not human. They are ... gods.

What you are seeing isn't real, a voice whispers. It is

quiet, so quiet she cannot tell if it is real or just a figment of her imagination. *It is merely a way to visualise the world in a manner you can comprehend.*

Pandora swallows, hard. She is drifting in the centre of a towering chamber, a council chamber … a chamber built for entities that exist in multiple dimensions, a chamber so strange that trying to look around makes her head hurt. The gods pay her no heed. They do not seem aware of her presence, or perhaps they simply don't care. She is little more than a fly on their scale, perhaps even less. She cannot touch them. She cannot talk to them. The deafening racket around her drowns out anything she might say, or think …

An entity walks into the light, passing *through* her as if her body – her mind – simply doesn't exist. And yet, she has the brief impression of a wink before he walks on … she stares, trying to comprehend the entity's true nature. It is impossible. She sees aspects of the whole, but not the whole itself.

"The Children of Darius are nearing adulthood," a voice says. The speaker is an old man, wearing a tattered black cloak and a wide-brimmed hat that conceals his eyes. Two ravens rest on his shoulder, their eyes seeming to peer into Pandora's very soul. "They pose a threat to the Cosmic All."

The voice buffets Pandora, battering her like a gust of wind. She feels her mind threatening to snap and grits her teeth once again, trying to keep her awareness from spreading too far. The words are simple and yet, she is almost painfully aware of undercurrents she cannot even begin to comprehend. The gods are whispering … no, they are having multiple conversations at once, the words spinning around the chamber in hopes of consensus.

"The Confederation does not know what to make of them," the newcomer says. His voice is smaller than the rest … she doesn't know why. "It will be many years before they are ready to make the jump into the light."

Loki, a voice whispers. *He is Loki. Watch him.*

The conversation hums around the chamber. "The

Confederation cannot be allowed to make full use of the Children," someone – many someones – says. Pandora realises, to her horror, that they are talking about *her*, her and the rest of her family. "They must not become a …"

Pandora shudders as *something* crashes into her head. A word … no, a *concept*. A meme. The gods speak in riddles … no, it is something so dark and disgusting and dangerous that she cannot force herself to look long enough to understand it. The gods themselves recoil, waves of horror rushing through the chamber and buffeting against her mind. Pandora feels sick, her stomach twisting painfully even though it is in another world. The gods are disgusted … they are scared. Their fear is a physical force … Pandora stares at the entities, so powerful that she cannot even begin to grasp the true scope of their power, and wonders what could scare them so. And what it has to do with her.

"They will not," Loki says. His voice lacks the undercurrents, the whispers of contextualisation that aid comprehension, she hears from the others. She doesn't know why. It crosses her mind to wonder if he is lying to the gods, or if he is merely trying to prove his sincerity to his peers. "The matter is well in hand."

"The" – the meme flashes across the chamber again, battering her mind – "must not be allowed to come into existence," the gods say. Pandora couldn't tell which one was speaking. They all seem to be talking, their words blending together into a perfect – and terrifying – harmony. "You will ensure it doesn't."

Loki bows. Loki doesn't.

Pandora feels her head twist again, the reality spins around her as her awareness opens up to encompass the godly realm. It is huge beyond comprehension, the laws of reality shattered beyond all hope of repair, held in place only by the purest thought … sheer terror shoots through her as she realises they know she is there, and they don't care. She isn't alone, either. There are smaller entities all around her, creatures that brush against her awareness and push her back into the darkness …

She sits up in bed, drenched in her own sweat. The bedchamber feels ... *wrong*. She reaches out with her mind, her awareness brushing against the other minds. They jerk awake too, snapping out of their nest. It strikes her that she is the only one who has had the dream. The others were sleeping peacefully, until she woke them.

"Pandora?" Henri's voice is quiet, trying to be considerate of his peers. "What happened?"

Pandora shakes her head. The dream is already fading, the memories falling into the abyss. She can no longer recall what she saw, save for the sense of overwhelming dread. Something bad is going to happen. She knows it in her bones. Henri crawls over and wraps his arms around her, holding her gently; she feels his thoughts brushing against her, lulling her back to sleep.

And yet, when she opens her eyes a second time, she recalls little of the dread too.

CHAPTER ONE

Pandora stood on the platform and looked down at the world below.

She floated miles above the ground, high enough to take in the planet's curve. It was a remarkable sight, a reminder that the Confederation could produce planet-encompassing Rings and star-encompassing Dyson Spheres and Ringworlds and yet, no matter how advanced humanity had become over the years, they couldn't match the work of mother nature. Clarke had never produced an intelligence race of its own, nor had it been discovered until well after the Confederation had mastered the art of living permanently in space. The surface was almost completely natural, the small town surrounding the research station the only place where the landscape was marred by technology. The blue-green orb was utterly enchanting. She had wondered, as a child, why some folk remained on planetary surfaces, but she got it now. The landscapes her family took for granted simply didn't exist in space, even on the largest Dyson Spheres.

Her eyes drifted upwards. She couldn't see the network of automated defence platforms overhead, or the entry station, but she knew they were there, pressing against her awareness like deadly thorns. The Darius Children weren't precisely prisoners, she had been assured, yet they weren't exactly free to go either. It had been understandable when they had been children, when the two hundred babies had been brought to the isolated research station, but now … she was torn between wanting to explore the Confederation, claiming her legacy as a child of the greatest civilisation that had ever existed, and remaining in the nest, where she was loved. And safe. She found it hard to comprehend the nervousness outsiders felt, when they encountered the Children, but she couldn't deny its existence. Who knew how they would be treated, when they finally left the research station behind?

She looked back down. "On my command, drop the outer shield."

The air rustled beside her, a solid-light hologram fluttering into existence. "I hope you're not planning what I think you're planning."

Pandora grinned at the avatar, a direct link to the AI overseeing the settlement, even though she found it a little disconcerting. She could *feel* her peers – and the researchers – in her mind, and she *knew* they were real, but it was impossible to be sure with the AI. There were times when she was *sure* it was an intelligent being, its thoughts brushing against hers, and times when it was nothing more than a machine – or a hologram. She didn't pretend to understand it. It veered between giving the settlers whatever they wanted, the fabbers churning out everything from food and drink to extreme sports gear, and putting seemingly arbitrary limits on what it was prepared to give them. The one consistency was its refusal to produce a genuine spacecraft.

"You make it sound like a bad thing," she said. "Don't you trust me?"

"You children are extremely honest," the avatar said. It had chosen to manifest as a bird, something that sent a shiver down her spine. She wasn't sure why. "But we do worry about your safety."

"I'm eighteen," Pandora protested. "Old enough to make up my own mind."

"A common delusion, shared by many," the avatar said, dryly.

"There's no danger," Pandora said. "Deactivate the force shield."

The bird seemed to hesitate, a rustle of lightning-quick thought brushing against her mind before the force shield snapped out of existence. Pandora smiled, stepped up to the edge and jumped, the gravity field wavering slightly before the planet's greater mass took control and yanked her downwards. She threw out her arms and whooped as she fell faster, the blue-green blur slowly giving way to mountains and rivers and the tiny settlement, resting on the edge of a tropical beach. She felt a rush of warmth and gratitude for the researchers, who had worked so hard to craft a wonderful place to grow up. She had never had a day of illness, or deprivation, or poverty, in her entire life. It was hard to believe, sometimes, that previous civilisations had lacked the Confederation's post-scarcity economy, the technology they needed to satisfy the needs and demands of their entire population. It seemed impossible to accept that anyone would willingly live that way.

Her mind expanded rapidly, brushing against a handful of her peers on the beach below. Francis was on the water, surfing on a board that appeared marvellously flimsy; Joanne was lying on her back, the warm sunlight lulling her to sleep; Andrew and Janet were playing a game of chess, a difficult task when each player was very aware of the other's feelings, perhaps even their thoughts. And several others were brushing against each other, exploring their bodies in a manner that would have shocked even the most sybaritic pre-space society. Pandora gave silent thanks to her ancestors, for developing the technology they needed to overcome the limits of their bodies and the demands of their society. There was no risk now in sexual contact, no reason not to share bodies as well as thoughts. It truly was a paradise. It lacked only one thing.

The freedom to leave, she thought.

She pushed the idea aside as the beach grew below her, then shaped a thought and *stopped* her fall, bare millimetres above the sand. There was no shock, just an instant halt. She hovered in the air for a long moment, then lowered herself the rest of the way. The sand was hot against her bare feet, the air warm and welcoming without being too hot. The first researchers really *had* done a good job, she reflected. It was a shame they hadn't stayed around. But outsiders really did find the Children disconcerting.

"Hey," Henri said. He was sitting on the beach, wearing a pair of trunks and nothing else. "Nice landing."

Pandora smiled. The researchers didn't pretend to understand *quite* how she could stop herself with the power of her mind, or any of the other strange abilities she and her peers had inherited from their parents. The Confederation could build planet-sized starships, and hurl them across the galaxy at speeds beyond her comprehension, and yet it was completely mystified by the Children. It was galling, in so many ways. The Confederation had developed the technology to break laws of physics her ancestors had regarded as immutable, yet they couldn't understand how the Children did what they did. It was almost as strange as their parents, back on Darius. No one had understood them either.

"It was fun," she said, finally. "How was your meeting with the researchers?"

Henri frowned, his emotion colouring the mindscape. "It went poorly. She had trouble even *looking* at me."

Pandora winced. There were few secrets amongst the children. It was very hard, almost impossible, for any to lie to their peers, when their emotions and most of their thoughts were open books. There was simply no way to maintain the lie without the awareness that they *were* lying shading their thoughts, betraying the truth. She had no concept of privacy because she had none, nor did her peers. Henri wasn't even trying to hide his concern and bitterness, and fear. If the researchers had never managed to get used to the Children, despite working alongside them for nearly eighteen years, how would the rest of the Confederation cope?

She felt a wash of pure sympathy for the outsiders. They would never know the sheer joy of sharing thoughts and emotions. They would never understand it wasn't something to be feared. The Children had no bullies, no dictators; there was no way for any of them to use fear or force to keep the others in line, not when they could all *feel* each other's emotions. There were no outsiders amongst the Children, no one ostracised by the rest. They were individuals, true, and yet they were also linked together.

And yet …

The Confederation had few taboos, let alone laws. There was little reason to be a criminal in a post-scarcity society, and the few that existed could normally be tracked down very quickly and placed in isolation, if they refused to be treated for their condition. A society as old and mature as the Confederation could overcome almost anything, rehabilitating criminals and accepting that the young and immature made mistakes, mistakes they could acknowledge, accept, and put firmly in the past. But one taboo remained unbreakable and that was that you did *not* violate someone's privacy without a very good reason. You did *not* go into their minds.

And yet, that was exactly what the Children *did*.

Pandora felt cold, despite the heat. It was difficult, if not impossible, to keep from reading the researchers' minds. Every word they spoke brought a wave of emotions with it, every touch opened – however briefly – a channel into their minds. Pandora had seen thoughts and memories from a hundred researchers, learnt their secrets – the little shames that were embarrassing even to those born and raised in the Confederation – and felt their shock and horror as they realised their minds had been read. She thought, sometimes, that the researchers would have been happier if they'd remained on Darius, a world populated by witches and wizards out of a children's fairy tale. It had been absurd, and no one understood how the Darius Machine had given some people magic powers, but …

Henri leaned forward, his mind brushing against hers. "You want to spy on their meeting?"

Pandora hesitated, then allowed him to lead her off the beach and through a maze of foliage back to the research centre. No expense had been spared to make the centre look as homely as possible, although expense was relative when one realised there was no reason the researchers couldn't have built themselves a giant castle each and still had plenty of resources for everything from medical labs to defence stations. The buildings looked wooden, blending neatly with the tropical foliage; she smiled, briefly, as they walked around a swimming pool and a small bar before nearing the research centre itself. Her mind reached out, gingerly. There were no Children inside the complex.

"In here," Henri said.

He opened the door to a small hut, still empty after the last occupant had left two months ago, and led the way inside. The AI's drones had cleaned the interior from top to bottom in preparation for a researcher who had never actually arrived. It was a curious blend of primitive chic and modern technology, the latter worked carefully into the walls to keep it as concealed as possible. Pandora didn't know why they bothered. She had studied history. The primitive chic, the pretence that the researchers were roughing it, was insulting to her ancestors, the ones who had truly lived in a primitive environment. They had had no choice, back then. Now … sure, there were people who chose to *really* rough it, to live in habitats where nothing more advanced than a horse and cart was permitted, but they could quit at any moment. Her ancestors hadn't known it was possible. To them, it *hadn't*.

Henri lay on the bed, large enough for three or four full-grown adults. Pandora lay beside him and took his hand, his thoughts flowing into hers. She saw his urge to leave the centre, to explore the universe; she tasted his fear that they would *never* be allowed to leave, that they'd be nothing more than prisoners for the rest of their lives. She saw herself through his eyes, a beautiful young girl shining with life and love, and tasted his attraction to her, just as he tasted her own attraction to him. The urge to roll over and make love was almost overwhelming, but she resisted as his awareness drifted out of his body and floated across the chamber. She followed, her head twisting oddly as she passed through the walls and out into the open air. The world itself bent around them …

… Something nagged at her mind, gone before Henri could sense it …

… And then they were in the conference room, hovering invisibly over the table.

She felt a flicker of guilt as her mind surveyed the chamber. Professor Exurban, the *de facto* head of the research team; Professor Aliya, a paraphysical researcher; Professor Alexis, a xenospecialist who studied ancient alien technology; someone she didn't recognise, a young-seeming man with old eyes, his thoughts calm and intensely disciplined. Colonel Truman, she picked up from Henri's thoughts. The man had presented a blank face, but the agitation behind his mask had been blindingly obvious. Pandora didn't know why he'd bothered trying to hide it.

"The blunt truth is that their abilities shouldn't exist," Aliya said. She was one of the longest-serving researchers, a brown-haired woman who had spent the last five years on Clarke. "They defy everything we know about how the universe works."

She spoke with quiet intensity. "Telepathy. Telekinesis. Astral projection … a bunch of other abilities, none of which make much sense. They really shouldn't be able to do half the things they do, certainly not in the manner they do."

Truman leaned forward. "In what way?"

"They can communicate telepathically with each other, at least to some degree," Aliya said. "This communication appears to be instantaneous, faster than hyperwave signals. We put one of the Children on a spacecraft and punched it up to just below the speed of light, yet they were still able to communicate even though the time dilation effect should have rendered it impossible. Their telekinesis is even stranger ... frankly, I think the only thing limiting their abilities is their own lack of belief. The more they learn to combine their abilities, the more they'll be able to do."

"You have the finest sensors in the Confederation," Truman said. "Can't you tell what they're doing?"

"No," Exurban said, flatly. Pandora tasted his frustration. "The attempts to monitor their brainwaves have proven futile. We should see *some* activity when they use their abilities, but ... very little. Certainly not enough. The environmental sensors see nothing. We can pick up tractor beams easily, but their telekinesis simply doesn't register. There are some very faint flickers on the quantum sensors, when they push their abilities to the limit, yet ... not enough to determine what they're actually doing. As far as we can tell, their abilities are not rooted in science."

Truman's brief flicker of amusement lit up the mindscape. "Magic?"

Exurban looked irked. "The Darius Machine was not magic. It was nothing more than a piece of highly-advanced technology. We don't understand how it worked, let alone how to build our own, but given time we will eventually solve the riddle. If we start thinking of it as magic, as something inexplicable, we will effectively be giving up."

"Our ancestors might comprehend that the tech we use here is not magic," Truman pointed out, "but it would still take them years to duplicate it for themselves."

"Yes," Exurban agreed. "And given time, we will unlock the secrets of their abilities."

"If we have time," Truman said. The cool urgency coloured his thoughts. "How long can we keep them here? Should we keep them here?"

"They lack for nothing," Exurban snapped.

"Except freedom," Alexis countered. "We call them Children, but the youngest amongst them is seventeen. It is just a matter of time before they attain their full majority and demand the right to leave Clarke. What do we do then?"

Truman's thoughts were cold, hard. "Do they pose any danger? Their powers ..."

"Don't think of them as *powers,* but abilities." Exurban sounded very firm. His emotions told a different story. "It's hard to be sure. Their abilities could be very dangerous, but there's no reason to think they're sociopaths. Their empathy is off the scales. Their ability to be aware of how their fellows are feeling makes it very hard for them to jump onto the slippery slope. To be honest, I'd say they were more mentally stable than most teenage humans. Far too many of us need to hit thirty or forty before we stop indulging ourselves and develop the maturity to grow into fully-rounded human beings."

He paused. "That said, their telepathy is going to cause problems. *No one* likes having their mind read."

"And it won't be long until the first lawsuits get filed," Alexis put in. "It'll be an interesting legal case, that's for sure."

"Quite," Truman agreed. "So ... what do we do?"

The question hung in the air. Pandora held her breath, tasting the surge of emotions running through the air. What could they do? What *would* they do? The Confederation couldn't legally keep them prisoner, but ... it would be difficult to leave the planet if starships weren't permitted to pass through the system. She honestly didn't understand the problem. But then, she was used to a life without privacy. The researchers weren't. She could feel their unease at having their minds read, their skin crawling even though they *knew* the Children weren't doing it deliberately.

"We keep studying the Children, and helping them to develop their abilities," Exurban said, finally. "And hopefully we can find a way to teach them control before it is too late."

"They don't want to learn," Aliya said. "To them, their existence is natural. It's the way things were meant to be. They no more want to shut their telepathy down than the average child wishes to be isolated from the datanet. Or have his eyes poked out. And frankly, I'm not convinced they *can* learn. There are just too many things about their abilities that don't make sense."

Henri's mind slipped back into his own body. Pandora followed, her awareness flickering back in the blink of an eye. Her chest heaved as she took a breath, suddenly very aware of her own body once again. Henri let go of her hand and sat up.

"They're never going to let us out, are they?"

"That's not quite what they said," Pandora reminded him. She could feel his anger – and desire to be free. Henri wanted to travel the stars, to explore the universe ... he wanted the freedoms enjoyed by the rest of the human race. "If we can figure out how to control ourselves ..."

"Yeah," Henri agreed. "If."

CHAPTER
TWO

The research team had originally intended to give each Child a private home, a chamber that would be theirs and theirs alone. It was fairly standard in the Confederation, at least in places that didn't follow a specific cultural template, and few questioned the need for children and teenagers to have a place where they could let down their hair and just be themselves, unburdened by their extended families and the greater society beyond. The Darius Children hadn't bothered to move into private rooms, instead preferring to share several large chambers in close proximity. The researchers had written extensive monographs on why that might be so, but Pandora had never been impressed by any of their explanations. The Children just felt comfortable in each other's company.

She smiled to herself as she sat on the giant mattress and tried to see the chamber through an outsider's eyes. It wasn't easy. She had grown up sharing her thoughts and emotions with her peers and the idea of being trapped in her own head, unable to understand what her peers were feeling, was terrifying. The outsiders had to find it hard to determine who was telling the truth and who was lying, or to work out who might be interested in becoming friends or lovers without reaching out, exposing their feelings openly in hopes they might be reciprocated. She didn't have that problem. She could feel the emotional tides flowing around the chamber, sense the astral presences of the Children who couldn't fit into the compartment. The Children were not all of one mind – they were individuals, and they often disagreed – but they shared so much it was impossible for one to dictate to the rest. Their arguments were more about seeking consensus than dominance.

Her lips twisted in amusement. A researcher had once compared their sleeping arrangements to a permanent sleepover, something that had amused her even as she acknowledged the older woman had had a point. There were fifty-seven people in the chamber, their minds huddled together even when they were physically separate, doing everything from reading books and accessing VR sims to physically grooming each other or making out. They looked as fit and healthy as any other set of teenagers in the Confederation, where a combination of genetic engineering and their every need being met ensured they had plenty of time to develop – free of the curses that had plagued earlier generations – but there was a unity to them that their peers on the nearest habitat lacked. Their shared understanding ensured disagreements were minimised, that jealousies and resentments weren't allowed to fester and mutate into something vile. The Confederation was fairly good at dealing with the problems of adolescence, and most were worked through before they led to something truly dangerous, but the Darius Children had never needed assistance. The counsellors who had been brought in, when they'd entered their teenage years, had found themselves twiddling their thumbs, doing nothing. Some had resented it, their feelings all too apparent to their supposed charges. Others had made more practical use of the time and written extensive articles on the development of the telepathic nest, ranging from the plausible to the downright insane.

But it shouldn't be surprising that they don't understand, she mused. *How does one explain colour to a man born blind?*

She felt a stab of sympathy, once again. She had seen the world through Henri's eyes – and those of nearly everyone else in the small community. She knew what it was like to be a young man, just as he knew what it was like to be a young woman. An outsider would never have that instinctive empathy, nor would she be able to fall back on the comradeship of the nest. She had been told that outsiders who embarrassed themselves often migrated, moving halfway across the explored galaxy to escape their past; *she* would never need to do anything of the sort, not when her peers wouldn't rub her nose in her failings. Wouldn't it be so much better, she asked herself, if *everyone* could share their thoughts and feelings with the rest of the community?

Her thoughts darkened as Henri cleared his throat, mentally requesting a few moments of their time. She understood, intellectually, why the Darius Children disconcerted the researchers. She understood ... but she didn't believe, not really. The idea of having a true secret, something minor or something that would see her permanently ostracised if not isolated from the rest of the Confederation, was alien to her. She found it hard to understand why so many secrets *were* secrets, or why their holders tormented themselves so, dying a thousand metaphorical deaths before the secret was ever revealed. There was no rhyme nor reason, no real sense what would get someone ostracised if not isolated; she wondered, sometimes, if humanity was nowhere near as mature a species as it claimed. The Confederation was fantastically advanced, and yet its collective feet were still firmly planted in the mud of Old Earth.

Henri opened his mind, spreading out the memory of the meeting they'd watched. A flood of emotions ran around the chamber, from unconcern to outright alarm, even anger. They had near-complete access to the datanet – they hadn't found it hard to circumvent what few barriers had been placed in their way – and they *knew* there was a towering civilisation out there, just waiting for them to mature before they took their place amongst the stars. The idea of being trapped for the rest of their lives was infuriating, even for those who would be content to remain on Clarke forever. A spark of alarm followed, a thought that refused to go away. If the Confederation thought the Children dangerous, would they destroy them?

"The Confederation isolated a handful of worlds with dangerous races," Pandora pointed out, verbalising her thoughts while allowing them to sense the emotions behind them. "They have no reason to actually commit genocide."

"We're not exactly a dangerous *race*," Charles countered. He had dreams of joining the Peacekeepers, flying across the stars and covertly protecting the younger races from those who would harm them. Some sentients were too strange, too alien, to be allowed to come into contact with their neighbours; some were too primitive, too undeveloped, to be permitted to spread across the stars. "They can't isolate us forever."

"They don't need to do more than blockade the high orbitals," David offered. "They can treat us as prisoners, forever."

Pandora felt the wince running around the chamber. The Confederation was too enlightened to use the death penalty, and the idea of deliberately committing genocide was anathema. A criminal who refused to undergo personality redesign would be permanently exiled from society, kept in an isolated location that had all the luxuries they could desire save one, freedom. A dangerous or incompatible alien race, such as the spider-like entities no one – not even the AIs – had been able to communicate with on any meaningful level, would simply be blockaded, kept alive and yet prevented from harming others. The Confederation saw no reason to destroy them completely, particularly when they weren't understood. It was a mystery how they'd managed to develop technology with mentalities so alien ... she wondered, suddenly, if the Children might be able to communicate with them. Or if trying would be devastating to the nest.

"So what do we do?" Charles's frustration filled the air. "If we could get out of here …"

"Our parents were able to do all sorts of magic tricks," Jane said. "If we could do the same …"

Pandora shook her head, even as a surge of grim despondency ran through the air. Their parents had largely abandoned them, partly because they had been struggling to come to terms with the existence of the Confederation – and the sudden shift from an isolated and very primitive society to a technological paradise – and partly because they had experienced a deep and very profound loss. The magic they'd studied so extensively no longer worked, the powers they'd taken for granted no longer at their beck and call. Pandora understood, all too well. The idea of losing her abilities scared her, no matter how dangerous others found them. It didn't help that so many of their fellows had moved on, forsaking their old culture and embracing the new.

And why, she asked herself, *should they not?*

She had been born shortly *after* the Darius Affair. She had never seen the planet. She certainly hadn't grown up in a world that only respected the powerful, a world that looked down on those who couldn't wield magic. It was hard to understand how such a society could even exist, but easy to grasp why the powerless would want to leave. The Confederation had shipped nearly all of the population to a Ring, and spent the last seventeen years preparing them to integrate into the greater civilisation. It wasn't a difficult task. Just time-consuming.

Henri pointed a finger at Jane. "Abracadabra," he said. "You're a frog."

Nothing happened. Pandora rolled her eyes.

"Of course not," Jane said. "We just don't know how to do it."

"Nor does the Confederation," Charles pointed out. "That's what scares them."

Pandora nodded, slowly. Most civilisations moved along a predictable tech tree, often taking two steps forward and then regressing a little – or sometimes destroying themselves, if their technology moved too far ahead of their maturity – and discovering more advanced technology existed was often good for development, even if the advanced technology wasn't something they could duplicate in a hurry. A warp drive civilisation might be astonished to encounter a race that used hyperdrive, which allowed travel several orders of magnitude faster than any warp starship, but it wouldn't be beyond their comprehension. Given time, they would adjust their theories to account for hyperdrive and then build the technology to turn theory into reality. There was nothing in the technological marvels around her, the environment they took for granted, that could not be eventually duplicated by another race, no matter how far behind they were on the tech tree.

But Darius was different. Had *been* different.

The Confederation couldn't turn a man into a toad with a snap of their fingers. It was impossible. No amount of matter reformatting could trap a human mind in a toad. Nor could it turn a woman into an obedient slave, nor harm someone without inflicting very visible damage ... the sheer magnitude of impossibilities that had been possible on Darius, at least until the Darius Machine had been disabled, were daunting even to a star-spanning super-civilisation. If Pandora hadn't seen the records, and sensed the thoughts of those who had visited the planet before the end, she would have wondered if it was an elaborate practical joke. There were people on the datanet who thought that was precisely what it was, a hoax that had somehow slipped through the legion of fact-checkers who prided themselves on spotting and calling out misinformation and outright lies. She knew better. Darius had been real.

"But we don't have the same powers," Henri said. "We are ... telepaths. We have mental powers."

"Abilities," Pandora corrected, mildly. *Powers* had some very negative connotations. "Perhaps our ancestors had the telepathic gene, allowing them to make contact with the Darius Machine and use it."

"If that is so," Jane said, "where is it?"

Another ripple of frustration ran through the chamber. The researchers had ensured the Children could study what they liked, everything from spacecraft design and manufacture to medicine and genetic engineering. They had the same grounding as every other child growing up in the Confederation, and then they'd been allowed to follow their interests wherever they led. The Children who had chosen to specialise in medicine and genetic research were unpractised – they hadn't been allowed to work on real patients – but they weren't inept. They – and the researchers – had spent nearly two decades looking for a genetic explanation for their abilities. They had drawn a blank.

"We have explored every last atom of the human body," Jane continued. "We understand the causes of every disease and genetic abnormality, and we have written them out of existence through careful genetic modification. The days when genetic engineering was little more than hackwork are long gone. We can alter everything from skin and eye colour to gender and sexuality. And yet, we don't understand how our abilities work. The power seems to come from nowhere."

Adam leaned forward, his thoughts tightly controlled. "If you click on a light switch, the light appears to fill the room instantly. It doesn't, but the light moves so fast the human mind cannot perceive movement. If our abilities work so fast they simply cannot be detected."

"An AI could track the light as it lit up the room," Pandora pointed out. "There should be *something*."

"Professor Weasley wondered if our powers were a con," Gavin said. "He was on the team that cracked the super-stardrive hoax."

Pandora smiled. A primitive race, new to star-travelling, had tried to move up the ladder by claiming to have invented a new kind of stardrive, a technology that allowed FTL travel in realspace. Their ships had moved so fast they passed through the detection webs without being detected … or so they'd insisted. They'd actually been running a complicated con, with one ship vanishing into FTL and another, completely identical in every way, decloaking moments later on the far side of the galaxy. The final report had noted there was no way the deception could last indefinitely, but it had very nearly succeeded in its goal. If the race *had* been recognised as higher up the tech tree, it would have been granted access to technology that would have allowed it to leapfrog several centuries of slow development in a single bound ...

Ice ran through her mind, a spike of emotion that spread rapidly through the nest. No one knew who had built the Darius Machine or why, but ... had it been intended to push a subset of humanity forward, to evolve in a manner unsupported outside the machine's influence? Were the builders trying to help, or to hinder, or simply eager to see what would happen when humans gained seemingly-magical powers. Or was it an accident, a device left behind and accidentally cannibalised by the planet's original settlers? Or ... or what?

Henri hugged her, then addressed the nest at large. "What do we do?"

The conversation spun around, a babble that would have been confusing if she hadn't been able to sense the thoughts behind the words. Some wanted to wait, to gain their majority before asking for their freedom; some wanted to leave now, to use their abilities to escape the planet and vanish into FTL. If they could get their hands on a ship, with the right command codes ... the majority squashed that idea, pointing out that they *were* young, and the Confederation wasn't given to genocide. They could appeal for their rights once they were old enough to stand alone ...

"We can't change our nature," Naomi said. "If they are scared of us reading their minds ... we can no more stop than we can keep ourselves from breathing."

"Perhaps there is another option," Pandora said, slowly. "Why can't we bring them into the nest?"

A ripple of astonishment ran through the mental communion. The researchers had always assumed the children were genetically different in some way, even though they hadn't been able to find any physical source for their abilities. There had been no reason to believe the Children could bring an outsider into their mental network, but … was there any reason to think they *couldn't*? It was a strange thought, yet it refused to go away. If they could open someone's mind, and welcome them into the shared awareness, they could show them there was nothing to fear. And who knew how far it would go?

Her heart twisted. The Confederation was immense, billions upon billions of humans living on giant megastructures or flying on starships that could easily be mistaken for small planets, and yet … it was made up of individuals trapped in their own minds, unable to communicate with their peers on anything other than a very basic level. Even humans who uploaded themselves into datacores and became electronic personalities, or bonded to a starship and effectively *became* the starship, were individuals. The AIs were different – they were both individuals and a hive mind, something that worked for them even as their human allies found it contradictory and impossible to comprehend – but they weren't human. They lacked human weaknesses.

"We can read their minds," Jane said. "Why can't we open them?"

Pandora nodded in agreement. "If we can get it to work …"

The conversation flared around her for a long moment, the different minds contemplating the problem from a dozen different angles. There would be risks – they had never tried to adjust someone's mind, let alone open it up – but the rewards would be worth almost any price. She had no doubt they'd get a volunteer or two, once they took their proposal to Professor Exurban. The Confederation had millions of people who were bored, despite – or perhaps because of – the luxuries surrounding them, people who could be relied upon to take almost any risk if it meant they'd have something to do. And others crazy enough, she reflected, to do anything.

"It might work," she said, once the Children had come to a rough consensus. They'd have to work out a way to do it, if only to determine if it were possible. If not ... at least they would have tried. "And if we can do it ..."

She smiled as she stood and walked outside, feeling another little twinge of pity for all those isolated minds. The night sky was bright with thousands of twinkling stars, each one orbited by planets and moons and space megastructures, the latter inhabited by countless men and women trapped in their own minds. If they could bring them all into the mental link ...

It would change the universe, she told herself. For the better.

CHAPTER
THREE

Parnassus was a fairly unremarkable planet, as planets went. It was the second world from its primary star, fortunate enough to be in the rough centre of the system's life-bearing zone; fortunate, too, that there were no asteroids or other pieces of space junk in the same general region, rocks that might eventually be drawn into the planet's gravity well and pulled down to the surface, inflicting damage that might be lethal, or at least incredibly damaging, to the newborn ecosystem. The biosphere had grown more and more complex until one species had made the jump into sentience, rapidly spreading out to inhabit every last corner of their world and develop the technology that would eventually allow it to climb into interstellar space, if they didn't stagnate or destroy themselves first.

The Confederation hadn't noticed anything particularly remarkable about the Parnassusians either, when the first and second survey missions had passed through the system. They were humanoid, like the vast majority of intelligent races, although they couldn't have passed for humans except in very bad light, and they were progressing along a completely predictable tech tree that offered few, if any, prospects for surprises or potential threats. The xenospecialists and psychohistorians studied the race intensely, projected its development until it reached interstellar space, and advocated a strict policy of no contact. There was little disagreement. The Confederation had learnt the hard way that direct contact between a hyper-advanced race and one still struggling out of its gravity well was utterly disastrous, giving the former a dangerous delusion of inherent superiority and the latter an inferiority complex that would keep them from developing into a spacefaring race in their own right. The Peacekeepers placed a handful of surveillance platforms around the star, to keep an eye on the locals while warning off other – less enlightened – factions that might have plans of their own for the system, then moved on to other matters. There was little reason to be concerned, they told themselves. Parnassus was a typical developing world, differing only slightly from others in the same category. Its future was, at least in general terms, entirely predictable.

In that, they were dead wrong.

X floated in the centre of his starship, surrounded by holograms depicting the planet's remorseless march to war. It had been a stroke of luck finding the world before its maturity caught up with its technology, a dangerous point in any world's development ... a bottleneck that not all intelligent races, despite the Confederation's occasional quiet interventions, managed to surmount without blowing themselves back to the Stone Age or outright destroying all life on their homeworld. He'd studied the files extensively as he'd sneaked into the system, locating and subverting the surveillance platforms one by one, and then made covert contact with the planet's five major powers. It was a situation tailor-made for malice, particularly when the locals barely had any concept of alien life. The planetary crisis would have been unpleasant even without his intervention. With it ...

His lips quirked darkly as he plunged his mind into the starship's datacore and studied the updates from his drones. The planet had three major powers that had effectively ruled the world for the last century, and two more intent on challenging the hegemony before it was too late. The former had the manpower to keep the latter down, according to his projections, but the challengers had moved ahead to develop newer and better weapons, threatening to counter a quantitative edge with qualitative superiority. X had supplied the challengers with advanced technology, pushing them ahead, then made the same offer to their rivals. He knew there were locals who wondered about his motives – the story of a Galactic Federation, just waiting for the planet to unify itself before making open contact, was difficult to believe – but it hardly mattered. They knew their enemies were developing their technology, and that meant they had to keep developing their own or face certain defeat. And *that* meant they needed him.

That means I get to watch them destroying themselves, he thought. *And so do my fans.*

His lips quirked. He had grown up on a perfectly normal megastructure, born to a perfectly normal set of parents and an extended family that ensured he lacked for nothing; he had had the same education, the same opportunities, as everyone else born to the star-spanning civilisation. He had developed an interest in engineering, first mechanical and then social, and mastered the art; he had devolved into simulations that allowed him to explore the lives of kings and emperors, dictators and politicians, generals and spies. He had played and won countless games and yet … none had been real. What did it matter, he asked himself, if he won a simulated war with countless simulated battles? The men didn't die, the women weren't raped, the children weren't marched off to be raised as war orphans … it was meaningless. The Confederation itself was meaningless. When you could get anything you wanted, and explore any kink you pleased with someone who shared it, what was the point? He wanted power, *real* power, and that was lacking. He had drifted into the underground darkweb of citizens who wanted to explore pleasures denied even to the Confederation, and that had led him to …

He smiled. Parnassus was real. The Parnassusians were

real. And the war he'd spent so long cultivating would be real too. His awareness flittered across the planet, peering through countless nanotech drones too small for the locals to have a hope of detecting and removing, noting the rockets being fuelled for launch even as the politicians gamely tried to calm the tensions at the eleventh hour. They had little hope of success, he was sure. The armies were already clashing, their masters unwilling to withdraw and yet unwilling to order an advance; their air forces and navies were brushing against each other, all sides increasingly convinced that the key to victory, or merely survival, lay in striking first. He could practically sense the orders flickering through the telecommunications network, the troops being assembled at their bases as their civilian counterparts were urged to prepare to hunker down and pray for peace. The latter were doomed, X was sure. Parnassus had never used nukes in war. They had no comprehension of the devastation they'd wreck, when the rockets were launched. The living would envy the dead.

An alert flickered into his mind. The Prime Minister of the Northern Confederation was trying to contact him, to beg for the Federation's help. X ignored the message, and the signals from the other four world leaders. He'd spun them a line of crap about a non-interference rule that prevented open contact with a disunited world, and then another about their rivals being unrelentingly hostile to any sort of planetary unity. He wasn't sure how much of the crap they'd actually believed, and his surveillance suggested there were quite a few who doubted what they'd been told, but it didn't matter. The crisis was gathering steam. He placed a mental bet with himself that the first rocket would be launched within the day. The rest would follow shortly.

His lips twisted nastily. The planetary intelligence agents, the few that knew about alien contact, hadn't been able to understand his motive. What was the point, they'd asked themselves, in helping their nations to improve their technology? If he was bent on conquest, why would he make his life harder; why would he try to start a war that could easily destroy the entire planet? There were easier and safer ways for him to exterminate the entire population, if he wished. None had understood the truth, and how could they? It wasn't about conquest, or slavery, or raw materials that were far more plentiful in interstellar space than any planetary surface; it wasn't even about the sadism of a primitive warlord who had somehow managed to get his hands on a modern starship and set out to hack and slash his way across the cosmos. It was ...

Art. The impending war was art. And X was the artist.

It didn't bother him that he had sentenced billions of intelligent beings to death. They were nothing to him. Their deaths would serve him better than they ever could in life, the live feed of their planet's final moments flowing into the darkweb and convincing his fans of his true greatness. The Confederation would be horrified, when they worked out what he'd done, but that was part of the appeal. He would make them feel something, all the sheeple who were little more than pets in a society that granted their every wish, and in doing so feel something himself. It would be art, painted on the canvas of a destroyed world with alien blood for pigments and ...

"Interesting," a voice said. "But very ... limited."

X froze. The starship was a *long* way from anything that could possibly harm it, protected by a powerful cloaking device as well as force shields and teleport jammers. There was nothing on the planet below that could so much as *find* his ship, let alone scratch the paint, and his sensor drones would have alerted him if a modern starship entered the system, well before it could track him down and open fire. Parnassus was effectively off-limits, thanks to the Confederation. There was no reason to think anyone would locate him before it was too late.

He disconnected his mind from the datacore, opening his eyes. A man stood on the far side of the chamber, his face ... X's eyes narrowed as he studied the intruder. He was dark and handsome and a little *too* perfect, his face so uncanny that X *knew* he wasn't human. His mind reached out through his implants, checking the internal sensors. They insisted he was alone, that the figure was nothing more than a figment of his imagination. X felt cold as he ran through a series of internal checks and sensor sweeps, looking for traces of the intruder. There was nothing … it was impossible. Even if someone had managed to hack his datacores, or slip a projection into his systems, it should have triggered his sensors. He should not have been caught by surprise.

His eyes narrowed. There was a tiny – tiny – flicker on the quantum sensors. And that meant …

"A very limited display indeed," the intruder said. His voice seemed to reach X's brain without passing through his ears. The tone was dispassionate, as if he were discussing the weather rather than a planet-wide war. "Why do you think this will matter, in the long run?"

X ignored the question. "Who – what – are you?"

"Call me Loki." The intruder smiled, revealing too many teeth. "And as for what I am …"

There was a long, chilling pause. X swallowed, hard. There were stories of strange encounters with god-like alien entities, stories that never quite made sense, or alien artefacts that defied everything humanity knew about the limits of technology. He'd seen all sorts of things on his wanderings, when he'd obtained his ship and set out on a cruise to obscure his first destination, but nothing quite so … alien. And now … one was standing in front of him. He wanted to believe it was an illusion, but it was impossible. The entity – Loki – was real in a manner that could not be denied.

Loki strode across the chamber, moving in a manner that suggested his body was bending in all the wrong places. "I bring a warning," he said. "The Peacekeepers are on their way. You might want to leave."

X blinked, honestly shocked. "And how do they know where I am?"

"Your live feed has been traced," Loki told him. It was hard to doubt the entity. "I'm afraid not all of your fans are friendly, and some are hoping for a happy ending."

X swore under his breath, leaning forward to check the long-range sensors. They were clear, but that was meaningless. The starship was fantastically advanced to the locals down below, yet she would be hopelessly outmatched by even a lone Peacekeeper cruiser. X had purchased a dozen fabbers and downloaded plans for all kinds of weapon systems, but if it came down to a straight fight he was doomed. His art would remain uncompleted for the rest of time. Worse, he would never achieve the notoriety he sought. If the Peacekeepers were sneaking up on him, he was about to run out of time. He'd be lucky if he merely spent the rest of his days in isolation.

He looked up. "And what do you want, in return for the warning?"

"We will discuss that later, if you escape," Loki said. He leaned against the bulkhead, resting as if he didn't have a care in the world. "You might want to hurry."

X said nothing as he took one last look at the live feed from the planet below. The crisis was moving faster than he'd predicted, the first wave of nuclear-tipped rockets blasting their way out of the silos and up into the skies. His projections updated hastily, as the rest of the nations launched their own rockets, a cavalcade of devastation that would wipe out thirty to forty percent of the entire population in the first hour. The blasts would throw tons of radioactive dirt and ash into the atmosphere too, raining poison on the remainder of the planet and sentencing the rest of the population to death. He'd seen the files, from worlds that *had* killed themselves, the planet-sized graveyards discovered, too late, by the Confederation. Even if a handful survived the explosions and the poison, it would be decades before the planet recovered ... if it ever did. It was truly a work of art.

But there was no more time.

He linked his mind back into the datacore, dispatching a set of drones into hyperspace even as he brought the warp drive online. The Peacekeepers would expect him to jump into hyperspace, he was sure, and they'd deploy their forces accordingly. The drones would keep them busy long enough for warp drive to take him away, putting enough space between his starship and the planet for him to slip into hyperspace without being detected. Probably. The Peacekeepers couldn't have deployed more than a couple of hundred ships at most, and they wouldn't be able to cover all the possible escape routes. Or so he hoped.

His mood lightened, slightly, as the warp drive came online, folding space around the starship. The planet was doomed. His sensor platforms would keep the live feed going as long as possible. The datanet was designed to be impossible to take down – the system regarded censorship as a fascist nightmare and made certain that any attempt to censor the net was broadcast as widely as possible – and so the Peacekeepers would have to destroy the platforms to keep word from spreading any further. By the time they located and destroyed them all, it would be too late. His infamy would be broadcast across the entire Confederation. Everyone would know his name.

"The missile submarines are launching now," Loki observed. He spoke as if the issue was of no concern to him, which made a certain amount of sense. A timeless entity wouldn't care if a planet of mortals destroyed itself. They were mayflies, of no importance to the greater galactic civilisation. "Another planet destroyed by its own people, with a little help."

X shrugged, studying the datafiles. *Loki* was a very old name, one that dated all the way back to the Norse Gods. The original had been a trickster god, sometimes a mentor and sometimes a menace: the stories suggested he'd been a giant who had joined the gods, a genderfluid shapechanger who had birthed monsters, and also a prince who resented growing up in the shadow of his older brother. X felt a flicker of kinship with the mythological Loki – he hadn't fitted into his society either – although he suspected the entity in front of him wasn't the original god. There were worlds that *had* been influenced by alien visitors, including some who had posed as gods, but Earth wasn't one of them. Unless it had happened in a manner that left no traces behind.

He took a seat and studied the display, bracing himself for pursuit. The Peacekeepers were good at their jobs, and if they tracked him down … he had a feeling he was already clear. Loki wouldn't have warned him unless he wanted something in return, and that meant he had an interest in ensuring X escaped. He wasn't sure how many of the stories about godlike alien entities were true, but Loki was clearly powerful. What did he want, that he couldn't get for himself?

X felt a thrill. Finally. Something *new*.

He looked up. "What do you want from me?"

"I have a task that needs doing, for which I will hire you," Loki said. His tone never changed. "You will name your price."

"Oh, I will, will I?" X raised his eyebrows, irked at the presumption. "Are you sure?"

Loki looked back at him, evenly. Up close, his face was so perfect it was hard to make out any details. It was just … there.

"Yes. You will."

X conceded the point without rancour. Loki could offer him a reward that he couldn't get anywhere else, not even in a Confederation. It was worth almost any risk, to gain a prize that could make him the most important person in the known galaxy. He could ask for almost anything and get it. His dreams were on the verge of being fulfilled. And the entity knew it.

"Very well," he said, finally. "What do you want from me."

Loki smiled. It was a deeply inhuman – and unnerving – expression.

"Tell me," he said. "Have you ever heard of the Darius Children?"

CHAPTER
FOUR

Archangel Mari exploded out of hyperspace, too late.

She cursed, mentally, as her awareness expanded rapidly, brushing across the planet and sweeping through datafiles that might have been secure by local standards, but may as well have been unencrypted when faced with modern technology. Parnassus was on the verge of committing suicide ... no, it *was* committing suicide. The rockets rising through the upper atmosphere might be painfully slow by her standards, but they were still deadly; the fleets of nuclear-armed bombers, making their way through enemy air defences in a bid to reach their targets before it was too late, were almost as dangerous. There was no way in hell the locals should be this advanced, let alone on the verge of total destruction. X had clearly been working overtime to boost their technology far ahead of their morality.

He could have spent his entire life in a simulation of incredible personal power, she thought, with a wave of disgust. There was little crime in the Confederation, not when most citizens could get whatever they wanted just by asking, but the handful of sociopaths were utter nightmares, nothing more than serpents in the garden. *And instead, he condemns an entire planet to death.*

She reached out with her mind, looking for X's starship. There were a handful of craft slipping into hyperspace … too many to be real, if any were. It was vanishingly rare for two sociopaths to work together, thankfully, which suggested all but one of the contacts were nothing more than decoys. She was fairly sure she was faster than any drone, yet she didn't have time to track them down and the rest of the task force was still light-hours away. Intentionally or not, X had created a situation that effectively forced her to let him go. The only other option was to abandon the planet to its fate.

Her mind reached out again, merging with the datacore so completely it was hard to tell where one ended and the other began. There were nearly five *thousand* missiles in flight, her sensors noting that all but a handful carried nuclear weapons. Her subroutines threw up a picture of what was likely to happen in the next half-hour, as the warheads started detonating. The planet would be devastated beyond any hope of recovery. Worse, perhaps. A handful of warheads appeared to be loaded with biological weapons instead, ensuring the deaths of anyone who survived the nuclear attack. Madness, she thought numbly, as her awareness slipped through more datanets on the planet below. The locals were likely to destroy their entire race, unless she intervened.

She sucked in her breath, hastily plotting out firing solutions. The Peacekeepers believed in keeping their distance from primitive worlds, as much as possible, but if the locals were going to destroy themselves the Peacekeepers had permission to intervene. It had happened several times, the effects almost as devastating – in the long run – as the threatened nuclear war. That wouldn't be the case this time, she told herself firmly. If the locals had any idea how much nuclear tonnage had been launched, they'd know her intervention was all that stood between them and complete devastation. She hoped their society would recover from the combined shock of near self-annihilation and contact with vastly superior aliens. If they didn't …

At least they'll be alive, she told herself. X had set out to murder an entire race, through convincing it to commit suicide, and she was damned if she was giving him the satisfaction of watching their world burn. *They can recover from the shock afterwards.*

Her weapons systems came online, hurling tiny pulses of energy through hyperspace. The locals had no awareness that hyperspace even existed, let alone the technology they needed to shield their missiles from hyperspace attacks. From their point of view, the missiles had simply started to explode one by one, the flashes of energy powerful enough to vaporise the warheads before they could be detonated. Even if they had enough realtime data to realise the energy pulses were literally manifesting *inside* the missiles, there was nothing they could do about it. They didn't have time to detonate the missiles themselves, and even if they did the damage would be a self-inflicted wound. Mari allowed herself a moment of relief as the last of the missiles vanished from her awareness. The entire engagement – if it could be dignified with such a term – had lasted less than ten seconds.

There was no time to congratulate herself as she plunged onwards, hastily scanning the network of orbital satellites surrounding the planet. Some were pointing outwards, watching for interstellar visitors ... an oddity, in a planet that was supposed to remain in quarantine until it developed FTL itself. X must have revealed himself, she noted as she scanned the remaining platforms. They were primitive, and didn't seem to carry any actual weapons, but a handful were designed with enough manoeuvring thrusters to be turned into makeshift kinetic killers that could be pointed at enemy satellites. Clever, if futile. They might be able to see her coming, but there was nothing they could do about it. X had probably ensured it.

She swept into orbit, bringing her teleporters online. The bombers were still crawling towards their targets, thankfully not too fast to make it impossible for her to yank the crews out of their seats before blowing the bombers to atoms. She ignored the fighters as much as possible. Their missiles weren't dangerous to anyone, and their targets had been destroyed anyway. She dumped the crews on a handful of isolated islands – there was no time to sort out who was on what side – and allowed her awareness to sweep across the rest of the planet. A number of tank battles were already developing, her analysis subroutines noting that the soldiers didn't seem to understand the full potential of their technology. Their tactics were wasteful, the sort of tricks a child might use in a war simulation rather than a real general commanding a real war. She hacked their command networks and ordered a full withdrawal, commanding the fighters to separate. If everyone was trying to retreat, the fighting would die away. For now.

Whew, she thought, as she completed her scans. The locals had expended most of their nukes. She wiped out the remainder, just to be sure the job was done. *And now ...*

She ignored the confusion on the planet's surface as she hunted for X. There was no trace of him, beyond a handful of stealthed sensor platforms. They were broadcasting back to the Confederation, the signal relayed through a set of hidden stations until it made its way into the darkweb, where the perverts and cowards could get their kicks watching an entire civilisation destroy itself. She hoped they'd enjoyed watching her save the civilisation instead, although she feared otherwise. It was the great downside of the Confederation. There were so few taboos now that it was hard, almost impossible, to feel a naughty little thrill without doing something that did break those taboos. And there were people who would do anything for that thrill.

And X wasn't content to play his games with his own people, she reflected, as the rest of the task force dropped out of hyperspace. *He came here to sentence an entire race to die.*

She sent a quick update to the task force's commander, then watched the reaction on the planet below. They wouldn't have seen much more than a glowing blur when they spotted her – the Archangel looked like a sphere, from the outside – and it was quite possible they'd written her off as a meteor, but the task force's planetoid was impossible to miss. The starship was easily the size of the planet's moon, far larger than anything the locals could hope to design and build for themselves. Hopefully, the sheer size would keep someone from doing anything stupid. The uneasy peace might just last long enough for the planet to be introduced to the galaxy properly.

A message entered her awareness, a signal request. She nodded.

Commodore Roger's hologram appeared in front of her. "X?"

"He made it clear," Mari said. She would search the rest of the system, once the task force had opened communications and talked the locals out of killing each other, but she would be astonished if X was anywhere closer than a light year or so. The rat bastard might not know everything her ship and the rest of the task force could do – the Peacekeepers had done their best to keep their full capabilities secret – yet there was no denying his intelligence, or his ability to take public information and extrapolate what might have been kept secret. "There was no time to chase any of the sensor contacts, and by now he could be hundreds of light years away."

"No," Roger agreed. He would have already reviewed the datadump. Very few would argue that she should have chased him, and if she had tried the odds were good she would have lost both the planet *and* the sociopath. X had out-thought them ... somehow. "How did he know you were coming?"

Mari said nothing, hastily reviewing the sensor data. There should have been nothing to betray her presence, nothing to suggest she was bearing down on him. X had his fans, damn them, but she didn't *think* he had any in the Peacekeepers. The people who signed up for naval service didn't tend to be the type who were drawn to sociopathic acts; they were rarely inclined to commit them or to watch, swearing all the time their hands were clean. It was possible she was wrong, she supposed, and there *would* be an investigation … she shook her head slowly. She hadn't detected any message from the task force to the planet, nor had she done anything that would alert him to her arrival. Archangels were *designed* to be stealthy, even in hyperspace. Perhaps she'd simply got very unlucky …

No. The odds of X simply deciding to leave at just the right moment were impossibly low.

"I don't know," she admitted, finally. *She* would be investigated, of course. It would be immensely irritating, even though it wouldn't take long for her to be cleared. The task force's analysts would note she hadn't tipped X off, accidentally or otherwise, and leave her alone to search for other suspects. Perhaps someone had noted the task force's departure and sent an alert through the darkweb. Nothing had been noticed, but a prearranged code phrase was almost impossible to detect without advance warning. "He did it, somehow. I just don't know how."

She pulled up a starchart and glowered at it. The Confederation didn't have a border, not in the old sense. It was more of a fluid society, an ocean of starships and megastructures that paid little heed to the islands – planets and star systems – inhabited by other races. Given a relatively modern starship, X could be quite some distance by now, either sneaking back to a megastructure or simply finding a hiding place amongst races that were as advanced as the Confederation, sometimes even more so. Some were friends and allies, others were rivals or simply unconcerned about human affairs. She wanted to believe she could track him down, but with each passing second the odds of finding him got lower.

Her heart sank. How the hell had he been warned?

"Stay here, for the moment," Roger said. "The cruisers can sweep the system."

"Understood." Mari understood the underlying message all too well. She would be investigated. "I'll be here when you need me."

Roger vanished. Mari let out a breath she hadn't

realised she'd been holding and disconnected, mentally, from the Archangel. Her mind fell back into her own body, her breath coming in fits and starts as she tried to remember how to breathe. It was hard, at times, to recall she was both a human *and* a starship, that she was a combination of man and machine … she sat upright, her thoughts painfully slow as she gathered herself. Her tunic was drenched in sweat, her arms and legs aching despite genetic modifications and nanotech helpers in her bloodstream. She forced herself to stand on wobbly legs, thinking dark thoughts about psychologists who insisted she and her peers couldn't let themselves merge permanently. Apparently, being human kept her grounded. She couldn't help wondering if that was wholly a good thing. She was as enhanced as anyone and yet, compared to her ship, she was as weak as a newborn babe.

She closed her eyes for a long moment, her link to the ship withdrawing to the back of her mind. It felt odd, as if she were twinned with herself …. her thoughts endlessly talking to herself, repeating everything time and time again. She felt uneasy as she summoned a mirror field and stared at her image, feeling almost as if her reflection was actually part of her. The Confederation frowned on duplicating people – it wasn't precisely taboo, but it was relatively rare – and yet there were times when she wondered where she ended and the starship began. They were the same person and yet they weren't … she shifted, suddenly very aware of her stench. The air scrubbers were working overtime, but …

The thought made her smile as she stepped into the fresher and washed, then checked her appearance again. The Confederation prided itself on its body-sculpting techniques, from the incredibly handsome or muscular to the weird and wonderful if not downright bizarre, but most naval personnel preferred to keep their appearances as simple – and traditional – as possible. She had stayed female for most of her life, with a simple body, blonde hair and a face she knew to be as close as possible to her natural face. It was hard to be sure, when there was so much genetic engineering in the family true, but ... she shrugged and stepped into the next compartment. A meal was already waiting for her on the table. The datacores knew her, knew she'd need to eat.

She sat and ate quickly, barely tasting the meal as she looked around thoughtfully. The Archangel was cramped compared to a cruiser, let alone a planetoid, but she was alone and the lack of space didn't bother her. She spent most of her time linked to the datacores, wearing the starship as if it were a body ... in a sense, that was exactly what it was. There was no need for decoration, no need for anything beyond a simple living space and a datanet terminal. Her body might be held in suspension, but her mind was free.

The terminal bleeped as she ate. She keyed the console and scanned the report. Roger and his diplomatic staff had held the first meeting with the alien governments, discovering – in the process – that X had opened contacts with all five superpowers. Mari had to admit he'd done a good job of manipulating them, telling them a great deal of nonsense they'd needed to take seriously even as their doubts grew. They had been competing for his favour without ever being truly aware of it, without ever having a hope of success. The cold-blooded bastard had been very clever, but their own lack of understanding of his motives had ensured their doom. X hadn't wanted power, not in any sense they'd understood. He had wanted to watch their entire civilisation destroy itself.

She sighed, cursing him under her breath. It would be a long time before the planet recovered from the twin shocks. The sight of a starship that could pass for a small moon would scare them to death, then give them one hell of an inferiority complex. Mari had studied history. Direct contact between advanced and primitive societies rarely ended well, even when the two societies were from the same race. Parnassus's normal development had come to a crashing halt, the world left in an uneasy limbo ... effectively under the Confederation's sway without truly being part of it. They might never accomplish anything more for themselves, no matter what they did. She had studied those history files too.

Her heart sank as she flipped through the reports. The planetary damage had been minimal, thankfully. A few hundred deaths at most ... tragic, for the dead and their families, but the entire *planet* had been at stake. They'd feared they would need to rescue what few aliens survived, after their civilisation destroyed itself, yet instead ... she shook her head. In a sense, the civilisation *was* destroyed. It would never heal from the wound X had inflicted.

Because they allowed themselves to be manipulated, she thought. There were all kinds of ways to turn someone into an unwitting spy, or a double agent, ways that were effectively undetectable unless you had the same technology yourself. X could have infected the planetary leaders with nanite swarms that turned their victims into puppets, but he hadn't even tried. There was no hint he'd deployed anything of the sort, even when it made a certain kind of sense. He'd wanted them to have free will. *They let themselves be fooled, and pushed into destroying themselves.*

She shuddered. A civilisation brought to the verge of self-destruction. A civilisation shattered by alien contact. The Confederation embarrassed in front of its peers, forced to devote resources to cushion the disaster as much as possible as well as hunting X down before he struck again ...

I am going to kill him, she promised herself. She understood the importance of rehabilitative justice, but there were limits. X was too dangerous, both in himself and in the example he set to others. His career had to come to an end and quickly, before he inspired someone to follow in his footsteps. *The next time I get a shot, I will end him.*

CHAPTER
FIVE

"In a formal bulletin, Peacekeeper HQ confirmed the near-destruction of Parnassus," the newsreader said. "The fleet stepped in at the last moment to save the population from their self-destruction ..."

X tapped the panel impatiently, turning off the babbling ninny. The Confederation News Service was renowned for its honesty, although it was also well known for lying by omission from time to time. There were no direct lies in the statement, he noted coldly, but the speaker had left out most of the important details. She certainly hadn't mentioned *him*. He allowed himself a moment of irritation as he scanned the rest of the hyperwave broadcasts, from understandable and sensible commentary to insane conspiracy theories that – surprisingly – were quite close to the truth. They'd be ignored, he was sure. Surrounding the truth with a bodyguard of lies was one thing, but it couldn't beat burying the truth in a pile of batshit insane nonsense. The idea the planet had nearly died because the entire population had spontaneously decided to commit suicide was absurd.

He paid as little attention to the entity as possible as he calmed himself and walked into the fresher, trying to show that he was unmoved and unthreatened by the presence of a near-omnipotent being. He took his time washing and drying himself, then eating a scrumptious meal that rested uneasily in his stomach. It was impossible to escape the irritation at watching his wonderful work of art be spoiled, or the sense he'd been betrayed by one of his followers. He could just imagine the traitor, someone brave enough to immerse themselves in the darkest parts of the darkweb and yet too afraid of their true self to get their hands dirty. He would track the sneak down, given time, and turn their body into a work of art too. There were others who would spend the rest of eternity screaming, because of him. The betrayer would join them soon enough, he promised himself. There was nowhere he could hide from a man determined to find him and make him pay.

Loki showed no visible reaction to X's delays. The entity stood by the console, his face so unmoving it was easy to believe he was nothing more than a statue. There was something utterly timeless about his expression, something that suggested there was no way X could delay matters long enough to crack the entity's composure. X supposed, rather sourly, that it was true. Loki was effectively ageless, perfectly capable of waiting for years without so much as twiddling his thumbs. Hell, he could probably send his awareness elsewhere and leave running the body-image in the hands of a subroutine, something that would alert his core self the moment X broke his silence. A cosmic answering machine, waiting on hold ... his lips twisted at the thought. Loki was such an advanced being that it was hard to believe he wanted, or needed, to focus *all* of his awareness on a single problem. Talking to X might take up as little of his attention as breathing.

X was tempted to wait longer, but there was no time. Loki's expression might be unchanging, and his body unmoving, yet his presence was growing stronger. It felt almost as if there was a black hole in the compartment, something drawing his attention towards the entity ... something clawing at the fabric of reality itself. He blinked hard, feeling as if he'd been given a very brief glimpse behind the curtain. There was something there, scratching on the other side of his awareness … he closed his eyes and centred himself, then opened them. It felt almost as if he'd awakened from a nightmare, although he knew he hadn't been asleep.

And Loki was still there, waiting.

"You mentioned the Darius Children," X said, finally. "What do you will of them?"

He leaned forward, trying to hide his curiosity even though it was probably pointless. He knew of the Children, of course, although he had never been sure how much of the rumours were actually true. The datanet wasn't known as the web of a billion trillion lies for nothing, not least because anyone could say what they liked without fear of professional or legal consequences. The price the Confederation paid for free speech was free speech, although most of the more insane concepts died away when subjected to rigorous analysis by people willing to engage with the ideas *before* dismissing them. He was fairly certain the Children couldn't perform acts of raw magic, but strange powers and abilities? The entity in front of him was clear proof there were things in the universe unimagined by limited and mortal humanity.

"You will kidnap one of the Children and take her to the Life Sphere," Loki said. He spoke with an odd certainty, as if he *knew* beyond a shadow of a doubt that X *would* take the commission and he *would* succeed. "You will name your price when you hand the Child over to the researchers there."

X didn't bother to hide his irritation. He was tempted to refuse the commission, if only because he found the presumption he *would* accept annoying … but he couldn't. The prospect of a reward from a near-omnipotent being was too tempting to pass up, and even if he gritted his teeth and said no the danger was too great. Loki could vaporise his ship or toss the vessel halfway across the universe, so far from the Milky Way that there would be little hope of so much as *finding* a way home before it was too late. The Confederation's fastest ships could fly at unimaginable speeds and yet it would still take centuries to reach the nearest galaxy. If he found himself so far away he couldn't even *spot* the Milky Way …

He frowned, inwardly. He had no idea why Loki wanted – needed – him to serve as an agent, not when he could presumably kidnap his target for himself, but it suggested a certain need for a deniable asset. It was an oddly encouraging thought – perhaps Loki wasn't truly omnipotent after all – and yet it was also worrying. The more vulnerable the entity was, the greater the need to cover his tracks, suggesting X wouldn't be allowed to survive once he outlived his usefulness. And yet … the prize was just too great to pass up. Loki knew it too.

"That will not be easy," X said, carefully. Clarke would be heavily defended by the most sophisticated technology the Confederation had to offer. As technology advanced, the tech needed to fool it advanced too – X had plenty of experience circumventing sensor arrays capable of tracking an atom light-years away – but there were limits. The slightest misstep would land him in hot water, arrested and hastily transported to an isolation cell. "Are you willing to assist me?"

"I cannot be seen to act openly," Loki said, calmly. "You must complete the mission without supernatural assistance."

"Supernatural?" X was almost amused. "Are you *really* a supernatural being?"

Loki smiled, in a manner that suggested he was a hunter, closing on his prey. "A mortal such as yourself cannot be expected to understand a being such as I," he said. There was no condescension in his tone, which somehow made it worse. "Such terms are imprecise, but … suffice it to say there are those who *will* notice if you receive such help and react … poorly. You must act without open assistance from me."

"I see."

X did, surprisingly. There were ways to use psychohistorical analysis to determine if a planet's development had been influenced, openly or covertly, by an outside force. If the conditions for a specific technological advance didn't exist, for example, it was possible – although not certain – that someone had been meddling, pushing the planet's development in an unnatural direction. He'd been very careful to keep his meddling as subtle as possible, just in case the Peacekeepers chose to inspect Parnassus before the brewing war finally exploded into outright conflict, and he'd worked hard to create the conditions that would make the advancements seem organic, but a careful examination would reveal that someone had been playing games. One advancement was acceptable – freak developments weren't unknown – two or three were highly suspicious, particularly if there was nothing linking them together. It was as good as a calling card.

"I will give the matter some thought," X said. He was a brave man, but bravery had its limits and he wasn't going to throw his life away for a reward he couldn't claim if he were dead. He'd have to work out a way to get onto the planet, snatch a Child and then get away before the defences targeted him. "And what do you *want* with a Child."

"The researchers will determine if the Children represent a threat to the greater community," Loki told him. "And they will proceed from there."

"What a vague answer," X said, dryly. "Don't you know?"

"I do, they don't," Loki said. "The greater community must be informed if there is a threat."

X considered the matter for a long moment. The galaxy was alive with intelligent life, from races very close to humanity – the humanoid form was easily the most common in the known universe, if only because it was such a simple solution to the problems of evolution – to entities so strange, so *alien*, that they had little in common with the human race. There were giant sentient gasbags drifting the stars – no one was quite sure if they were starships, entities in their own right or some combination of the two – intelligent viruses and *things* so weird that it was difficult to believe they were genuine intelligent life forms. Or even life forms at all. Races evolved, climbed into the stars, and then …

No one knew.

Some had vanished, leaving their worlds behind. There were empires built on wreckage left behind by long-gone races, their new masters unsure how their technology actually worked and unable to repair or replace it when the tech finally failed. Others had stagnated, reaching a point where they were able to meet their every demand and found themselves deprived of any reason to reach further. Still others played petty power games, or let themselves die out, or … he shook his head. The Confederation was odd, a galactic power on an unprecedented scale. X had long suspected a great many Galactics weren't happy about the human race's predominance. They had achieved the kind of immortality and influence most races chose to deny themselves. And if they came to fear the human race …

He looked at Loki. Did *he* fear humanity?

The thought was absurd. X had run every sensor scan he could while refreshing himself, pushing his gear to the absolute limits, and he hadn't been able to get even a *hint* of Loki's true nature. The majority of his sensors didn't register his presence. The audio monitors couldn't hear his voice, nor did he show up on any visual sensors. A tiny flicker on the quantum sensors … that was all. If he hadn't been able to *see* Loki with his own eyes, he would have dismissed the flicker as nothing more than a random fluctuation, the kind of energy surge that came and went without being noticed. And yet, anyone capable of manipulating the quantum foam underpinning the universe like that would have no trouble swatting his ship like a bothersome fly.

His thoughts darkened. The Galactics hadn't been threatened by the giant human fleets that had fought a handful of interstellar wars. It hadn't mattered how many millions of starships the human race had deployed, when a lone starship from a hyper-advanced race could obliterate them practically effortlessly. The modern-day Peacekeepers could slaughter the fleets of a bygone age and never even know they'd been in a fight. And yet, if that was changing … a great many other things would change too.

It was rare for an advanced race to feel threatened by their lessers. There were few primitive races, even spacefaring powers, that could do *anything* to a megastructure. The defenders could just sit back and wait for the attackers to give up, rather than destroying them. There was rarely any need to intervene more openly, nor any belief they should do so. And yet, if they were thinking they could be threatened …

If they think they can be threatened, he thought coldly, *they may well be right.*

A flicker of anticipation ran through him. Perhaps he didn't *have* to hand his captive over at once. Perhaps he could see what, if anything, the Child could do first …

"Very well," he said. "I accept your commission. I'll claim my reward on the Life Sphere."

Loki vanished. X blinked, the compartment seeming to shift oddly around him. The quantum sensors bleeped an alert a second later, reporting that the flicker in the quantum foam had disappeared. X let out a breath he hadn't realised he'd been holding. The image he'd seen had been little more than the tip of the iceberg, a tiny fraction of something much greater that had been poked – however briefly – into the universe. He felt cold as he considered the possibilities. A child might feel nothing if he pushed his hand into a rock pool and felt around, but his movements would be astonishingly disruptive to anything that lived in the pool, creatures too limited to understand a human child. A five-year-old would be incredibly – impossibly – large to them, the idea of a human parent even more so. They couldn't even begin to comprehend what they were seeing.

His eyes narrowed. The Confederation had crafted countless perceptual realities for its population, everything from simple habitats to worlds of magic and mystery, universes determined by very different physical laws. Those worlds were very believable, and yet it was difficult – almost impossible – for someone to lose themselves so completely they forgot the universe was little more than a shadow, created by a giant datacore and held in place by processors that could be hacked, or shut off, if someone gained access to the network. But if Loki and his peers could create their own universes, *real* universes, the possibilities were endless.

And if I can get my hands on such power, he thought, *the art I could create ...*

He allowed himself to dream, just for a moment. There were those who argued that the universe was itself a giant simulation, that the laws of physics were held in place by programming rather than natural chance and evolution. X didn't believe the theory – he certainly didn't believe in a God, a cosmic force great enough to love and care for each and every human who had ever existed – but if he could build entire universes for himself, would he not be a god in truth? He could visualise himself tossing a few thousand humans into his universe, leaving them trapped in a place of utter insanity ... a real hell, perhaps, or a place beyond their comprehension. It would be great, a work of art beyond any he'd ever attempted. And he'd have plenty of volunteers to take their place in his worlds.

His eyes opened as his datacore pinged him. There was a file waiting for him, a file with no discernable origin. Loki might have refused any form of overt assistance, but the details on the planet's defences would be very useful. Clarke was surrounded by automated weapons platforms and a lone orbital station, yet there was only one actual starship. He wondered, morbidly, if the researchers had planned to evacuate the planet, if the Children had turned out to be monsters or simply beyond their comprehension. There were alien life forms so alien that any sort of contact, no matter how controlled, was damaging. They weren't malicious, as far as anyone could tell. They were just too different. To see them was to risk losing a part of your sanity.

He sent a handful of commands into the ship's datacore, ordering the vessel to alter course and sneak towards Clarke. It was unlikely the Peacekeepers were close enough to spot him – hyperspace was a difficult realm to navigate, and even modern sensors had trouble tracking any starships more than a few light-hours away – but there was no point in taking chances. He'd switch his IFF beacon to something harmless once he was a long way away, making sure there was no way he could be identified. There were millions of starships crossing the Confederation at any one time. He'd go unnoticed long enough to build up a proper cover story. A handful of ideas had already occurred to him.

His lips twitched as he sent his mind roaming through the network, reminding him his stasis cells were online. He'd kidnapped a few hundred Parnassusians from their homeworld, intending to sell them to collectors as the last survivors of a dead world and doomed race. The trade was highly illegal, to say the least, but that was at least partly why the collectors wanted them. When any normal thrill could be had just for the asking, the thrill tended to vanish very quickly. But there was no point in keeping the aliens now. They were hardly rare.

He tapped a code into the system, feeding the Parnassusians into his matter reformatter. Their faces went wide with horror, a second before their bodies dissolved into dust and fell into his storage tanks. The raw matter could be reformatted into anything, from food and drink to the tools he'd need to complete his mission, ensuring there was no hope of anyone managing to get the evidence they'd need to convict him. Not, he suspected, that it would matter. The Peacekeepers wouldn't bother with a trial if they caught him. They'd throw him into an isolation cell and toss the key out the airlock.

But if there was no risk, he reminded himself as he set course for Clarke, *there would be no fun at all.*

CHAPTER SIX

The farm lay to the west of the settlement, a small cluster of farmhouses surrounded by fields worked by human farmers, the majority determined to embrace the primitive life as much as possible. Pandora knew through mind-reading that some were genuinely in touch with the soil, some too set in their ways to consider any other lifestyle, and two more than a little resentful their partners had chosen to become farmers. One was tiredly waiting for his wife to give up on the lifestyle, the other had already determined to leave at the end of the year, the resentment poisoning her relationship to the point she no longer cared if her partner chose to stay with her or remain behind. Pandora's heart ached for the couple – she knew the partner didn't have the slightest idea his lover was increasingly bitter and resentful – but there was nothing she could say or do that wouldn't make it worse. The Children had learnt *that* lesson the hard way.

She walked down the path, her eyes flickering from side to side. She didn't pretend to understand the satisfaction that came with growing fruit and vegetables with your own bare hands – she was apparently too young to understand – but she could feel the emotion wafting through the air as the farmers worked the land. Mostly. A young man was staring sullenly at a patch of ground, his thoughts irked that his efforts weren't paying fruits. He really *was* young, she noted absently, too young to devote himself to full-time farming. He raised his eyes and caught hers, a rush of complicating feelings running through his head as he looked away. Attraction and arousal, shame and embarrassment ... a combination that left her mourning his blindness, his inability to share anything with his peers. She didn't know why he felt so guilty for being attracted to her – it was natural – or why he was ashamed. They didn't live in the dark ages. It wasn't as if she had anything to fear from him. Or vice versa.

The air shifted, blowing the scent of grapes towards her. The vines had been genetically engineered to grow almost anywhere, to the point she was surprised the farmers had been allowed to plant the seeds on Clarke. The planet's ecosystem was weaker than its earthy counterpart, like nearly every other world that had failed to produce an intelligent life form, and an infestation of crops from a stronger biosphere would lead, almost inevitably, to the destruction of the native ecosystem. It had happened several times, when mankind had started the expansion into interstellar space. Procedures were better now, and laws were tougher, but it was still difficult to prevent ecological collapse once the intruders took root. She supposed the farmers had engineered their crops to be vulnerable to a specific compound, if the Confederation decided to leave the planet fallow. It was the simplest solution to the problem.

She spotted Professor Exurban kneeling in front of a potato bed and walked towards him, making sure to stay on the path. The professor wasn't a farmer in any sense of the word, but he apparently found tending his garden to be relaxing after a long day of battering his head against a seemingly insoluble puzzle. Pandora could taste the frustration pervading the air, the dark moods of researchers who found themselves at a loss; she understood, all too well, the true cause of their feelings. They were amongst the smartest minds humanity had ever produced, heirs to a scientific tradition dating back thousands of years, proud possessors of hyper-advanced technology and near-limitless resources ... and yet, they couldn't even *begin* to understand how the Children did what they did. The Confederation could do so much, from teleporting someone halfway across a star system to uploading them into a datacore, but there were limits. The Darius Children were beyond their ken.

Professor Exurban looked up as she approached, his calm thoughts drifting on the wind. Pandora tried to mentally pull back, to leave the older man what little privacy she could. He *was* old, easily old enough to be her great-grandfather, yet ... his mind was strange, sometimes flexible and sometimes not. She had read in the files of people who thought themselves too old to live, people who had destroyed every last back-up of their existences and then killed themselves ... the concept was alien to her, and yet she was young. How would she feel, she asked herself, when she was older than the professor? Would she still have a zest for life? Or would she seek the next great adventure and accept her death?

"Pandora," Professor Exurban said. She could sense his surprise at being sought out. It was rare for any of the Children to look for the researchers, when they weren't at their lessons or being poked and prodded by scientists who didn't have the slightest idea of what they were doing and didn't want to admit it. "What can I do for you?"

"Professor," Pandora said. She had read his monographs. The professor had more than earned his title. He'd had a gift, as a younger man, for explaining himself in ways a novice such as herself could understand. It wasn't quite comparable to the Children, who could make themselves understood perfectly, but ... in some ways, it was better. The Children could only explain themselves to their peers. Professor Exurban could explain himself to the entire universe. "We have a proposal to put to you."

The professor stood, brushing down his tunic. "Should we go to my office?"

"If you wish," Pandora said. They weren't supposed to discuss anything of significance on the farm. She had been told the farm was more for therapy than growing produce, which made a great deal of sense. The farm couldn't hope to match a single food processor when it came to putting together meals from raw energy or compressed matter. "I don't mind if you want to talk elsewhere."

The professor shrugged and turned away, leading her back to the research town. A handful of researchers were gathered around the open-air bar, chatting about something that had happened a few hundred light years away. Pandora wondered why they considered it important, although she had to admit that anything less than a thousand light-years away was disturbingly close to Clarke. The planet was supposed to be isolated and protected, and very few races would risk picking a fight with the Confederation, but who knew? History had hundreds of examples of wars starting because of idiocy, or someone calculating they could fight and win ... and discovering, too late, they were wrong. She made a mental note to check it later. The affair might impinge on them after all.

It was not the first time she'd been in the professor's office, and – in truth – she found it hard to believe it was an office at all. Professor Exurban had decorated his chamber with dozens of plants, from earthly breeds that dated back thousands of years to saplings he'd collected during research trips to particularly interesting and alien biospheres; she knew, without having to ask, that he found it relaxing to spend an hour or so a day tending to his plants. It wasn't something she shared, but she could feel his thoughts relax as he worked. If it was good for him, then good.

Professor Exurban sat behind his desk, an enormous piece of bio-sculpted wood that was somehow tied into the local biosphere. The feeling of life was almost overwhelming, drawing her mind into a network of tree houses that had been carefully engineered to grow into something a human could turn into a living space. The Children had been offered such accommodations for themselves, but they'd resisted. The homes felt oddly unwelcoming to the nest. They weren't sure why.

"So," he said. He nodded to the food processor, looking faintly odd amidst the tangle of plants and saplings. "Would you like a drink, or would you like to get to the point?"

He was admirably direct, Pandora noted, although there was little point beating around the bush. Most significant conversations started with sweet nothings or insignificant chatter about the weather, brief exchanges designed to build up a rapport before genuinely important topics were broached. The Children had never developed such patterns, not least because they were already in near-permanent rapport. There was no point in pretending otherwise, when it would be blindingly obvious that was what you were doing. They couldn't hide the truth from each other for long.

"The Confederation is … uneasy … around us," Pandora started, flatly. "First because of the mystery of our origins, and second because we are telepaths. We read minds."

"Correct," Professor Exurban said. His face was calm and composed. His emotions weren't much different. "Your existence is an unexpected challenge."

Pandora nodded, slowly. The Confederation didn't have many laws or customs. One stated, put simply, that grown adults could do what they liked, as long as it was done between consenting adults in private. No one really cared if consenting adults wanted to explore the most perverse forms of sexuality, and everything else for that matter, as long as they *were* adults and they kept it to themselves. She didn't pretend to understand why the latter rule even existed, although she had felt the disgust a researcher had felt for another's bad habits. Perhaps it was yet another problem caused by closed minds, by people who felt unable to be themselves …

Her mood darkened, briefly. The Children imposed on

outsiders simply by existing. Their ability to read minds wasn't something they could turn off, which meant … she groaned inwardly. They were breaking a very important taboo, quite by accident. And *that* left them caught between two fires, unable to avoid causing a serious miscarriage of justice that could lead to everything from bad feeling to all-out war. If they kept reading minds, outsiders would be angry; if they were isolated for the rest of time, *they* would be angry. It was all a horrible ghastly mess.

"We have discussed the matter," she said. "Are we correct to believe that there appears to be no physical source of our abilities?"

"Yes, as you know very well," Professor Exurban said. His thoughts were patient, but wary. "If there is a telepathic organ somewhere in your body, we have been unable to locate it."

Pandora cocked her head. "You've never tried sequencing our DNA into a volunteer?"

"It was tried," Professor Exurban said. He didn't make any attempt to lie to her, even though the attempt was brushing up against some very strict laws. "There were no visible results. It was concluded that we simply didn't know what we were doing."

She heard the frustration in his tone and nodded shortly. The Confederation knew every last inch of the human genome. It could modify the baseline human body in any way it chose, determining everything from height and weight to sex and gender. The average citizen changed gender at least twice in their lifetimes, as well as reformatting themselves in a hundred lesser ways. Indeed, the *reason* there were so many ethical rules and guidelines surrounding the whole affair was that it was easy to create a slave race – it had been done – or turn people into puppets, helplessly triggered by seemingly-random stimuli. Wars had been fought to stop people who thought that was a great idea, who wanted to turn humanity into an insect colony with themselves the only ones possessing any kind of free will. And in their desperation, the researchers had come very close to crossing the line.

"We have a proposal," she said. "We think it should be possible to bring one of you into our nest."

A flash of alarm shot through the air, all the more striking because it was so unexpected. The professor was old enough to have few regrets, and enough maturity to understand his secrets were hardly war crimes, yet ... she winced inwardly, recalling some of the secrets that had drifted across her mind over the last decade. They had been strange, almost silly; they hadn't deserved to be treated as true secrets, let alone soiled with the emotions that had tainted them. It was heartbreaking to know that such silly issues were bottled up, poisoning minds instead of being examined and overcome.

Professor Exurban gathered himself. "How do you believe it so?"

"If there was a telepathic organ, we would have found it by now," Pandora said. "That suggests there isn't one, that the only real difference between you and I is that I was born slightly more attuned to the telepathic field than you and that opened my mind ... and that once I had learnt to use my abilities, there was no going back. If that is true, we should be able to open your mind and invite you into our nest."

"If," Professor Exurban said.

"People are scared of us because they feel violated," Pandora said. It hurt to admit it, but there was no escaping the truth. The Children couldn't hide from themselves. "We can read their minds; they can't read ours. They have no way to understand how we see the universe and ..."

She broke off, wishing the professor could just touch her mind. It was easy to feel the conviction, the sense she was right; harder, much harder, to put it into words. The feelings were ... *feelings*, not reasoned arguments. How many debates throughout history had turned poisonous, she asked herself, because the people on one side were blind to the feelings of the people on the other? How many had believed their opponents were evil, instead of merely having a different point of view? If some of the chatter she'd seen on the hyperwave datanet was representative of the whole, almost any number would be too small.

"If you send us out into the galaxy now, you will infringe on the rights of everyone we meet," she added, after a moment. "If you keep us here, you will infringe on *our* rights. But if we can open someone else's mind ..."

"If," Professor Exurban said, again.

"If," Pandora agreed. "We think we can do it."

"We thought we could solve the riddle of your existence too," Professor Exurban said. "So far, we have drawn a blank. Your abilities do not appear to exist, as far as our sensors are concerned, and yet they do. It is simply impossible."

"Or maybe your sensors aren't designed to handle our existence," Pandora said, wryly.

Professor Exurban kept his face blank, but she sensed his annoyance. "Your body is a combination of bone, muscle and flesh, steered by electronic pulses that pass through your nervous system. When you move your arm, for example, your brain sends out electric pulses that give instructions to your arm, while your arm sends feedback all the way back to your brain. It's a little more complicated than that, but that's the basic idea."

"It's a great deal *more* complicated than that," Pandora pointed out.

"It will suffice." Professor Exurban shrugged. "Point is, we can read the electric signals your brain sends and receives. We can tie a prosthetic arm into your nervous system, to replace an arm you might have lost, and install processors that will allow you to move the arm as if it were your own. We should be able to tell what your brain is doing when you use your abilities because we can monitor the electronic pulses in your brain. But we can't. As far as our sensors are concerned, you're not doing anything at all."

"Yeah." Pandora hid her amusement with an effort. The

researchers had come very close to breaking the rules banning direct brain scanning, no matter how hard they worked to get informed consent. If they'd done it to almost anyone else, they would be looking at permanent ostracism. At least. The Children didn't care. "That's another reason to think we can make it happen."

"Yes." The Professor met her eyes, evenly. "There's no way to qualify the risk. Are you prepared to go ahead on those grounds?"

"Yes," Pandora said. "If we can get a volunteer …"

"I'll see who might be interested," Professor Exurban said. "I can't order anyone to take the risk."

Pandora nodded. The researchers hadn't signed away their rights when they'd joined the team. They could be asked to volunteer, but not forced … she wouldn't want to risk forcing anyone anyway, no matter the cause. She wondered, suddenly, if a volunteer would truly volunteer … if they would truly wish to do it. She'd known her peers walk up to a cliff and stop, unable to convince themselves it was perfectly safe to step over the edge and let themselves fall. A person's conscious mind might say *yes, yes*; a person's subconscious might have other ideas. It was something that, quite frankly, had never occurred to any of them.

But we cannot fool our peers into thinking we really want to do something, if we really don't, she mused. The idea of informed consent was a joke if someone lied about consenting. She recalled the unwilling farmers and sighed inwardly. *That* wouldn't happen amongst the Children. How could it? *And it is impossible for someone to insist he was tricked into believing there was consent.*

She stood. "Thank you for your time," she said. It wouldn't happen immediately. The professor would need to ask for volunteers, then get organised. The Children would have plenty of time to work out the rest of the details themselves. "If this works …"

"There's too many unknowns," Professor Exurban cautioned her. She could sense his conflicting emotions, the eagerness to proceed balanced with fear of the consequences if the experiment failed. Or worse. "If we knew how your abilities worked, we would be a great deal happier."

Pandora nodded. She couldn't disagree.

CHAPTER
SEVEN

"Here we go," Henri said. "She'll be here in a moment."

Pandora nodded, feeling torn between anticipation and apprehension. They had done everything in their power to plan the experiment, working out the details as precisely as possible, but they knew all too well that they were messing with forces they didn't understand. It was impossible to put any real figures on the risk, different to tell just what might go wrong let alone work out how to contain it if it did. The chamber was both extremely comfortable and heavily protected, sensors and shield projectors worked into the walls; she wasn't sure, not really, if the precautions were overkill or not enough kill. Or if they'd be effective in any sense of the word. The researchers had experimented with everything from tinfoil hats to hyperspatial disruption shields and nothing had proven effective at blocking telepathy. It was deeply frustrating.

"If any of you want to back out," she said quietly, "you can do so now."

A mental rustle ran around the chamber, but no one chose to leave. They had debated the matter extensively and wound up with more volunteers than they thought they needed. Pandora and Henri had chosen carefully, picking Children who were committed to the experiment rather than Children who wanted to leave the planet as soon as they reached their majority. She wished, at times, that they genuinely were a hive mind, although she thought that would be dangerous as well as boring. A hive mind was uniquely vulnerable to meme warfare.

The door opened. Pandora looked up, tasting someone else's nervousness as she stepped into the chamber. It was such a strong emotion that it pulled her forward, a whirlwind of thoughts and feelings slipping through her mind … she had to bite her lip, hard, to keep from being sucked into the maelstrom. Professor Cleo was naked in every sense of the word, her mind as open to view as her body … body modesty was rare in the Confederation, where everyone could have the body they wanted, but it bothered the older woman here. Pandora tasted the surge of emotions that ran around the chamber, flickers of lust and attraction mingled with pity and a grim determination to help as much as possible. Cleo was tall and striking, with long dark hair, light brown skin, perfect breasts and a single small triangle of dark hair between her … Pandora gritted her teeth as the surge of emotion and thought yanked her onwards. They weren't her thoughts, but …

She forced herself to stand, her legs suddenly wobbly. "Are you sure you want to do this?"

Cleo nodded, clearly not trusting herself to speak. Pandora felt Cleo calming her thoughts, the fear of exposure being slowly replaced by something more focused. The researcher wanted to make a name for herself, but she also wanted to be part of something greater … Pandora could almost taste her envy, her desire not to be alone in her own head. Perhaps that was why she'd been chosen, from the short list of volunteers. She genuinely wanted to join the Children.

"Lie down on the mattress," she ordered, as she pulled her robe over her head and tossed it outside the circle. The others followed suit, their faces calm and composed as they took their places. "We will begin shortly."

She sat herself, feeling the tension rising. They'd recovered hundreds of books from Darius, all depicting magic rituals that appeared, at best, utterly absurd. The researchers had joked some had clearly been devised by teenagers, particularly the ones that required nakedness and sexual acts disturbing even to the libertarian Confederation. She had tried some of the simpler rites and rituals herself, roaring and chanting words in a language that had no link to any known human tongue, but she'd accomplished nothing beyond making herself feel ridiculous. The magic was gone. And yet …

"The sensors are online," she said, more to centre herself than anything else. There was almost no privacy within the compound, and the chamber itself was being monitored so thoroughly that a stray atom couldn't move without being detected … on paper, at least. The researchers had added a whole host of monitoring systems, but none were able to detect telepathy. "It is time."

She reached out, joining hands with Henri and Clara. She was suddenly painfully aware of their bodies and minds, the latter brushing against hers in a manner that was both welcome and oddly overbearing. Their thoughts radiated the same impression right back at her, an odd little contradiction that puzzled her. Normally, their thoughts merged together effortlessly. Maybe the presence of an outsider was confusing them, or … she pushed the thought aside as her mind kept expanding, touching the rest of the group. A series of thoughts and emotions ran through her – ran through *all* of them – with no clear source. They were so closely attuned they thought as one.

Her awareness expanded still further as she closed her eyes, brushing against the edge of Cleo's thoughts. A barrage of memories shot through her mind, none hers. Cleo had lived a fairly boring life, she noted coldly, with little in the way of secrets. Her parents had been researchers and so she'd gone into research too, dividing her time between her studies and a handful of lovers … none particularly interesting. Pandora felt a wash of pity as she realised Cleo had always felt alone and unloved, unable to understand her parents or make them understand her. No wonder she wanted to be one of the Children, she reflected. She wanted their shared awareness for herself.

The awareness reached out, slipping further into Cleo's mind. Her memories faded, replaced by the very core of her being. Pandora felt the shared awareness recoil as it tried to understand what it was seeing, to put it in terms they could understand. Cleo was standing in the core of her own mind: her arms and legs chained and shackled; her head hidden behind a hood that both blinded and deafened her. The mental image was a metaphor, an illusion used to display a reality in a manner she could understand, and yet … there was something about it, something very wrong. She couldn't put it into words. Was that how Cleo saw herself, or was it how they saw her? She didn't know. A flicker of doubt ran through her as the awareness reached out to remove the hood, to open Cleo's mind. It wasn't enough to convince the rest to stop, not when they were united in sympathy for the trapped woman.

They touched the hood, and pulled it away, and …

***

Cleo hadn't been *that* bothered by the Children, although she had to admit they were a little creepy. The original researchers had proved they weren't a group mind, that they were as individualistic as any other random sample of humanity, and yet they tended to think and act in a manner that suggested otherwise. She knew she envied their shared connection, even as she was also a little scared of it. She had never been able to form any real relationships with anyone, a weakness she hated. There was supposed to be someone for everyone, yet … for her, there was no one. The handful of lovers she'd had, both male and female, had always left her. They knew she wasn't quite normal.

She felt oddly silly as she lay on her back, stark naked. She had never felt any of the Children reading her mind – she had been assured they couldn't help it, and unlike some of the other researchers she actually believed it – and part of her wondered if it was an elaborate trick intended to humiliate her. She had been the victim of too many pranks for her to easily put the impression out of her mind, although the Children were never purposely cruel. They felt the pain of the researchers, as well as their own. In some ways, they were as mature as humans in their second century. In others, they were strikingly immature.

Something *brushed* against her mind. She felt tickled, her entire body twitching uncomfortably ... she was suddenly very aware of every last atom in her body. It was as perfect as modern cosmetic surgery could devise, the result of a desire to try to put her childhood behind her, and yet it was suddenly imperfect to her eye. The world spun around her suddenly, her eyes somehow both open and closed; she gritted her teeth and tried to understand what she was seeing. *How* she was seeing. The Children were all around her, the minds perfect webs of thought; she sensed their pity and compassion, strong and unyielding, and shivered inwardly. Her awareness was expanding, her mind sweeping through the walls and sensors as if they were nothing more than ghosts. It was funny how she'd helped to set them up and yet she could now see every imperfection in their design.

The world shattered around her, the walls and chambers crumpling out of existence as her mind flowed *beyond*. She saw ... *things* ... scuttling along the edge of reality, strange creatures her mind refused to comprehend, poking and prodding at the dimensional walls, looking for a way into the human realm. They raised their eyes as she looked at them, questing mandibles reaching out for her; she looked up and away, seeing more and more *things* that existed in worlds and dimensions she couldn't even begin to comprehend. Great eyes peered down at her, *things* so large she couldn't grasp the scale ... it wasn't a human realm. Her mind opened and opened and opened and ...

Shattered.

***

Pandora recoiled, the sheer shockwave of pure horror crashing through her awareness and shattering the nest. She felt as if she'd been hit badly, something rare in a community where everyone could feel everyone else's pain. A tidal wave of disgust washed over her a second later, a seething mass of nightmarish sensation that left her staggering backwards, mentally if not physically, until she crashed into a wall that felt oddly insubstantial to her touch. The ground heaved a second later, something crashing and exploding ... she squeezed her eyes shut and hugged herself, feeling as if her mind had gone blind. The others were gone. She was alone ...

Someone screamed ...

Pandora jerked upright, her eyes snapping open. The chamber had been devastated. The sensors had been destroyed, the walls cracked and shattered by an almighty force. Her body ached, as if she'd been brutally beaten; she looked down at herself and saw no traces of any bruises, nothing to suggest she'd actually been hurt. Her head felt worse ... she looked up and stared at Cleo, her fingers digging into her eyeballs. The woman had crushed her own eyes ... Pandora felt her gut heave, the sheer shock making her retch painfully. A team of medical drones popped into existence a second later, their fields hastily scooping Cleo up and depositing her in a stasis tube. Pandora knew, without being sure *how*, that it was already too late. The damage to her body might be healed – at worst, the medics could grow her a new body and perform a brain transplant – but her mind was broken, beyond all hope of repair. She was gone and ...

"Fuck," Henri muttered. He staggered to his feet and grabbed her, holding her tightly as he struggled for some trace of the intimacy they'd once treated as their birthright. "What happened?"

Pandora shook her head as the rest of the group joined them, huddling together so tightly it hurt. Cleo was dead ... guilt shot through her, the guilt of knowing it had been her idea to try to bring her into the nest. Where *was* the nest ... her mind wavered and cleared slowly, her awareness expanding gingerly. A wave of relief – his relief – shot through him as she made mental contact with Henri, followed by another surge of pain. It was his headache … she felt as if he'd slapped her in the head, at the same time as she'd slapped him. A series of confused thoughts shot through her, unsure what had happened and why. Her memories of Cleo's thoughts reached a certain point and stopped. Dead.

She went somewhere we couldn't follow, Pandora thought. It was strange, as if they'd freed Cleo from her trap only to see her jump blindly into another. *What happened to her?*

The drones returned, helping them back to the nest. The remaining Children gathered round, their faces sombre. Death was unknown on Clarke. There were no dangers that could threaten a human, certainly nothing capable of ending someone's life in the blink of an eye. And yet … Cleo was gone. Her body might survive. Her mind wouldn't. Pandora washed and dressed, her head spinning uneasily as she and Henri made their way down to the research station. The mood was grim. No one had expected Cleo to die.

"She not only took out her eyes, she drove the tips of her fingers into her brain," Professor Exurban said. Pandora didn't need telepathy to sense the horror running through his mind. "The nanotech in her body did the best it could, as did the medical team, but it seems unlikely she will ever return to us. Brain damage is tricky to repair at the best of times, and this …"

Pandora nodded, sombrely. The researchers would want a report, of course, and she didn't have the slightest idea what to tell them. The experiment had started well and then gone spectacularly wrong. She didn't even know what the sensors had picked up, before they'd been destroyed. There should have been a live feed to somewhere a long way away …

Henri was thinking along the same lines. "Did the sensors see anything?"

"Nothing," Professor Exurban said. "One moment, everything was normal; the next, the systems are exploding in a manner that, frankly, defies logic. A plasma blast, a bomb, even a nanotech dissembler … they'd inflict damage in a manner we'd be able to understand, to follow. Here … the last sensor readings suggest the damage was completely random. There was a flicker in the quantum foam and that was it."

He met their eyes. "The experiment will not be repeated."

"But we must," Henri said. "If we can't expand our nest …"

"We just lost a young woman with a promising career ahead of her," Professor Exurban said, sharply. "There is no way we can restore her. The personality transcripts cannot be replayed into her mind to resurrect her. Her body may be alive, but her very *self* is gone. There is no way we can repeat the experiment."

"We could bring children into the nest," Henri said. "Real children. I mean. They'd become part of us …"

"And there is no way in hell anyone would authorise such an experiment," Professor Exurban said. His tone matched his emotions. "The Oversight Committee is going to have kittens about the first disaster. They'll argue that Cleo didn't know the risks, that *we* didn't know the risks to explain them to her. They won't be wrong, either. None of us expected such an outcome."

Pandora swallowed, hard. Cleo had been so alone, trapped in her own head. She had wanted to help the older woman, and instead she'd killed her. It had been a colossal accident and yet … guilt tore through her mind. They should have known. Cold logic argued otherwise – there was no way they could have known – and yet, logic meant nothing in the face of her guilt.

Henri cleared his throat, dull resentment poisoning his words. "What now?"

"I'm referring the matter to the Security Council," Professor Exurban told him. "They will determine how best to proceed …"

"We have *rights*," Henri said. "You can't keep us trapped on this planet forever!"

"Right now, I don't know what we can do," Professor Exurban snapped. "I understand, really I do. But we don't know what happened and we don't know how best to proceed ..."

"And then ... what?" Henri's anger grew stronger. "How long will it take for them to come to a decision?"

"I don't know," Professor Exurban said. It wasn't entirely true and they all knew it. "The council is not known for moving quickly. They will want to study the files carefully, perhaps dispatch a few representatives to investigate personally. I don't believe they will imprison you permanently."

"But they will keep us here for years," Henri said. "That isn't fair!"

The professor met his eyes, evenly. "The universe is rarely fair. It isn't fair that your abilities are at best disconcerting and at worst dangerous. It isn't fair that your movements will be restricted because you have little control over them. It isn't fair that you are feared because of something you were born with, something that is a part of you. But the universe isn't fair. You can look forward to five or six centuries of life, most of which you will spend elsewhere. Wait."

Henri glowered. "Is that all you can say? Wait?"

Professor Exurban glowered back. "Right now, I have to call Cleo's family and tell them what happened to her," he snapped. "And that isn't fair either."

Pandora put a hand on Henri's arm. "Come on," she said. "There's nothing we can do here."

Henri kept his thoughts to himself until they were back in the open air. "They're just going to keep us prisoner forever," he said. "We need to get off this mudball."

"You don't know that," Pandora reminded him. The professor had been hurting, but there had been no hint he was actively planning to imprison them. Or kill them. "Give him time."

"Time?" Henri was unimpressed. "Why?"

"Cleo is dead," Pandora reminded him. "She might not have thought very highly of herself, but she did have friends here. They're still shocked by what happened to her."

And so are we, she added, silently. *What the hell went so badly wrong?*

CHAPTER
EIGHT

If there was one great advantage to the Confederation's interstellar communications network, it was that it was about as leaky as a sieve.

X smirked to himself as he studied the display, silently calculating the best interception vector for a snatch-and-grab. Something had clearly gone badly wrong on Clarke, something that had drawn attention from the Security Council itself ... curious, all the more so for the lack of any real hard data. It was normally impossible to keep people from leaking, no matter how hard the authorities tried; it suggested, to someone like him, that there was general agreement that whatever had gone wrong *needed* to be kept secret. That was unusual, almost unique. He couldn't wait to find out what had happened, what was so secret that the secret was actually being *kept*.

His drones pinged an alert, informing him that his target's ship had entered the same region of hyperspace as himself. It hadn't been easy, even for him, to calculate the precise vector Councillor Marla Noonan would take, on her flight to Clarke, and the slightest mistake would ensure they missed each other by hundreds of light-years. Hyperspace was both an alternate dimension *and* a fold in the fabric of space-time, an oddity that had never been fully explained even as humanity took ruthless advantage of its nature to speed starships across the galaxy at many thousands of times the speed of light. The Councillor was flying nearly seven hundred light years from her home, but at such speeds it was little more than a walk down the block. She didn't need a full-sized cruiser or planetoid, merely a tiny little ship. She certainly felt no need for an ego-boost. She was already one of the most powerful people in the known universe.

X smiled, rather coldly, as his drones crept forward. The primitives wouldn't be very impressed with a starship a mere seventy metres from bow to stern, but it didn't really need to be larger – or military. Her defensive screens were enough to keep out anything less than Confederation weapons, her drives fast enough to outrun anything that could threaten her hull. The sensors would be civilian, he was fairly sure, but it was rare for anyone to *need* military-grade sensors so deep in friendly territory. Sure, the Confederation didn't assert any authority over the planet-bound races in the region, yet everyone knew it could if it wished. Better to avoid poking the sleeping dragon than risk having it wake and come for you, crushing your military and reshaping your society before it went back to sleep. X rolled his eyes at the absurdity of choosing a deliberate policy of non-intervention. What was the point of having so much power if you refused to use it? The entire *galaxy* could have been reshaped by now.

He pushed the thought out of his head as he allowed his mind to reach through the quantum link, probing the edge of the defensive screens. It would be almost *laughably* easy to destroy the tiny ship, to leave the Peacekeepers with a disturbing mystery, but he needed to take the vessel and its lone passenger intact, and undamaged. Clarke was a security zone and if anyone, even a Councillor, arrived in a damaged ship, the defenders would ask some pretty searching questions before they allowed her to land. X knew better than to think he could bluff his way past an alert force, no matter how carefully he prepared. Given the nature of the Darius Children, the defenders would certainly be more wary than usual. And if he were exposed ...

The thought nagged at his mind as his awareness moved onwards, the quantum link delicately synchronising itself to the defensive fields and slowly inching *through* them. There was no overt threat – he dared not do anything that would alert the lone passenger, not until it was too late – but piece by piece, he reached through the shields and pressed his drone against the hull. The Councillor, thankfully, didn't hold with AIs. The datacore controlling the ship might be incredibly smart, in some ways, but it was quite stupid in others. Once X was inside the datacore's outer screens, without setting off any alarms, it would mindlessly assume he had every right to be there and do nothing, not until it was too late. He smirked, again, as his awareness penetrated the starship itself, slowly undermining the internal security network and deactivating the protective screens. The datacore came awake, too late. X's subversion software took control before it could alert its charge, let alone crash the starship out of FTL or send a distress call. X breathed a sigh of relief – he had known it would be close, that he could do everything right and still fail – and then moved on to the second stage. A stream of sub-nanotech was teleported onto the starship, searching for its target. It didn't take long.

X felt a flicker of contempt as he spotted the Councillor. She was nearly five hundred years old, according to her public biography, and her career had been one of public service and selflessly sacrificing herself to the needs of her people. A military career, followed by a period as an elected civil servant ... she didn't seem to have done anything for herself at all. She hadn't even bothered to alter her body, not beyond a handful of flourishes and genetic tweaks to ensure a long and boring lifespan. She would have been attractive in an earlier age, he noted, but nothing special now. Her life made no sense to him. She could have obtained a starship and set out to sail the stars, building something that would be unique to her. Instead ...

The Councillor had no warning before the stream

slipped into her body, the tiny machines rapidly overrunning her internal defences and implanted datacores and taking control, subverting her mind before she even knew she was under attack. A handful of implants remained closed, at first, only to be opened after the subversion overwhelmed the rest of the defences and started telling the implants a set of comforting lies. X was almost disappointed by the results. He'd always assumed the Security Council had access to information denied to the rest of the population, no matter how much the government denied it, but it seemed they were largely telling the truth. The only big secret was just *what* had happened on Darius.

He smiled as he brought his own ship into alignment with the Councillor's vessel, then teleported over and looked around. A handful of chambers, a small fabber … the Councillor hadn't bothered to decorate, beyond a handful of pictures hanging from the bulkheads. A quick scan of the public database revealed they showed a handful of her former partners, the men and women who had sired or carried her children. X shrugged as he turned to study the Councillor herself. Her face was blank, her intellect banished. She was now nothing more than a mindless husk. He wondered, idly, if she'd bothered to back herself up, the last time she went through a regeneration cycle. If so, she would live again. And she wouldn't know what had happened to trigger a resurrection.

His implants activated, checking that the datacore had been completely subverted and that no distress call had been sent. There hadn't been time to investigate the entire system without triggering alarms and there was a very real possibility that the internal self-monitors might have managed to damage the datacore, or activate a beacon, before they'd been subverted themselves. Or that there was a completely separate monitoring system … it didn't appear so, thankfully, but he checked time and time again, just to be sure. The Councillor was a very important person. It was a surprise the Peacekeepers hadn't put a cruiser at her disposal.

"And now," he muttered, "let us see if we can get this to work."

He altered the implants, activating a quantum field link. The Councillor's body jerked once as the link formed, her eyes opening wide. X found himself in two places at once, staring both down at himself and up at himself … he took in a breath, the action making his head spin helplessly. He was in her body, and also in his … he stepped backwards, feeling his awareness spinning in a truly disconcerting manner. He really *was* in two places at once.

"The miracle of quantum magic," he said, addressing himself. "I can wear her body like a costume."

"And remain completely undetected," he answered himself. The Councillor's voice sounded odd to him, even though he was the one speaking. It was her body, but his manner of speaking. "They can't detect our presence before it is too late."

X nodded as he despatched his original body back to the ship, then started exploring the Councillor's implants. There were no unpleasant surprises, which suggested she'd had the military-grade implants removed after she'd left the Peacekeepers. *That* was unusual. Most Peacekeepers preferred to keep their implants, just in case they wanted to rejoin a few hundred years after their first retirement. X closed his eyes and explored the Councillor's memories, feeling a twinge of amusement at how … *boring* … she'd been. He'd hoped for scandal, for something that could have been used to destroy her reputation, but there was nothing. She hadn't crossed the line. She hadn't even come *close*.

Boring, he thought, as he accessed her muscle memory and forced himself to practice manipulating her body. He couldn't afford to stagger around like a drunken idiot, not when the Peacekeepers had the entire planet under heavy guard. They'd smell a rat and take steps to confirm her identity before allowing her to land. *Why couldn't she have done something more interesting with her life?*

He sent a command to the datacore, ordering it to

resume their voyage, then kept practicing as the starship accelerated. It wasn't the first time he'd been female, but that had been *his* body. The Councillor had never been *him*, in any sense of the word, and even with her muscle memory – and her real memories, as boring as they were – he had to keep walking back and forth to get the hang of it. He could feel his other self, part of him and yet separate … sort of. His lips twitched in dark amusement. Very few would risk using a quantum field link to be in two places at once, even if the links were – in theory – unbreakable. It was incredibly disconcerting. There were people who would do almost anything for a thrill, but they wouldn't do that.

And after everything else I've done, he thought wryly, *stealing a person's identity is nothing.*

He sat back and ate a hearty meal, reviewing the files carefully. A person had been killed when the Darius Children tried to make mental contact, tried to bring her into their mental nest … killed in a manner that made little sense. The sensor records were incredibly confusing, so completely contradictory X wondered if the researchers were trying to lie to their superiors. The trick to telling an effective lie was to make it plausible, and this … *wasn't*. Perhaps they were out of practice, or … perhaps they really *didn't* understand what they were seeing. It had to be galling, he reflected. The Confederation had been the master of the known universe for so long that coming face to face with something beyond its collective understanding *had* to be annoying.

The reports grew a little more focused as he read on. The Children could read minds, as naturally as breathing … and they didn't have much, if any, control over the ability. X doubted *that* was true. If he'd had the ability to read minds, he would have used it all the time and sworn blind he couldn't help it too. The researchers insisted the Children were telling the truth, but … X looked down at his stolen body, guided by stolen memories, and told himself the researchers had been tricked. If the Children could read minds, and they *could*, they could easily tell which lies would be believable, and how to angle their conversational approach to achieve the desired result. X prided himself on his deep understanding of human nature, and the coiled serpent at the heart of every single human being, but the Children would be his superiors. How could they not? They would *know*, beyond a shadow of a doubt, how their tactics were working – or not – in realtime.

He felt a dull shiver running through the starship as she neared the Clarke System and mentally prepared himself. The Peacekeepers had set up a network of stations to alter the hyperspace currents around the system, making it difficult – if not impossible – for a primitive starship to gain access. Anyone advanced enough to get through the outer layer would know there was someone inside who didn't want to be disturbed, someone who would have more lethal ways of dealing with unwanted visitors if they refused to take the hint. X knew there were quite a few systems that were sealed off, the alien inhabitants choosing to isolate themselves from the galaxy so completely little was known of them. The Confederation had never been so isolationist. He suspected, as the shaking grew worse, that the Peacekeepers were actually attracting attention from outsiders. They had to be wondering what was concealed within the system.

His other self followed him as they flew through the currents and out into the system itself. The currents were always stronger around gravity wells, making navigation near a star surprisingly tricky, but here they were disturbingly treacherous. X allowed himself a tight smile at just how determined the Peacekeepers were to keep out unwanted guests, even though it had at least one weakness. They hadn't anticipated *him*. He steered his stolen ship back into realspace and waited, all too aware his disguise was about to be tested. If he'd missed one little detail, he'd would be exposed, too close to the system to escape. His mind-twin would have bare seconds to get clear before it was too late.

The system opened up in front of him, the display

showing a boring star surrounded by boring planets. Clarke itself was surrounded by a handful of orbital structures – an entry station, a fabber, a network of defence platforms – but the remainder of the system's planets were all alone in the night. The Confederation didn't need to mine gas giants for fuel or pick through asteroids for rare ores, not when it could draw power from the fabric of space-time and construct nearly anything it required from pure energy or a relative handful of raw materials. There was no suggestion anyone lived on any of the other worlds, something that made him smile coldly. Normally, such a system would be left to the races that depended on rocky worlds, asteroids and gas giants. This one had been reserved for the Confederation and no one else would be allowed so much as a peek into the system. It was something else, he reflected, that would draw attention from the outside universe. But it was hardly *his* problem.

The datacore pinged, beginning a series of IFF exchanges with the entry station. X waited, bracing himself. There didn't appear to be any starships in orbit, something odd for a Confederation base, but he was far too close to the orbital defences for his peace of mind. There'd be no way to get clear if they opened fire … he put the thought out of his mind, wondering if the lack of starships was a way to make sure the Children could never leave Darius without permission. They shouldn't be able to hijack a starship, but there was no way to be entirely sure. They had mental powers. For all the researchers knew, those abilities might include mind control.

And if their abilities are effectively undetectable, he mused as he waited, *it might be impossible to determine what truly happened.*

A hologram appeared in front of him. "Councillor," a man said. The datafiles identified him as Professor Exurban. "Welcome to Clarke."

"I thank you," X said. He activated the personality overlays, ensuring his conduct matched his stolen body.

Councillor Noonan preferred to be blunt, although she was also unfailingly polite. "I came as quickly as possible."

"And you are very welcome," Professor Exurban said, again. X had no trouble recognising a man who was hopelessly out of his depth, trying to remain calm while hoping and praying someone would come along and take the responsibility away. "We have much to show you."

"I'll enter orbit shortly," X said. "I take it none of the others have arrived?"

"Not yet," Professor Exurban said. He managed a faint smile. "They seem to keep changing their minds."

"I'm sure they do," X said. The memories he'd stolen suggested the councillors didn't want to come face to face with mind-readers, something that hadn't bothered Marla Noonan much ... another sign, he supposed, that she had lived a boring life. She had no guilty secrets, nothing genuinely criminal or even merely mildly embarrassing. "I'll proceed on the assumption they're not coming."

The professor smiled again. "I look forward to seeing you," he said, weakly. "You are cleared to enter orbit. You can teleport down once you arrive."

X nodded, then closed the connection. The professor was a weak man who had been badly frightened ... good. He didn't know Maria Noonan either, not personally. That was a relief. There were limits to how perfect a personality overlay could be, and that meant ... if he met someone who knew her personally, it would be hard to keep up the pretence. As it was ... his thoughts blurred, just for a second, and made contact with his twin. He'd be ready, when the time came. It wouldn't take long to prepare. And then all hell would break loose.

CHAPTER
NINE

Pandora could feel the impatience – and fear – echoing through the mental nest.

The entire universe seemed to be holding its breath, waiting for something to happen. The researchers had signalled for orders, and visitors were supposed to be on their way, but no one knew what would happen after they arrived. Some researchers expected to be told to continue their research, perhaps repeat the disastrous experiment with a second volunteer; others, more worryingly, thought they'd be ordered home, leaving the Children isolated on Clarke for the rest of time. Or destroyed … Pandora didn't think it likely, but humanity had a poor track record when it came to dealing with things that scared it. The fact she didn't understand *why* they were so scared didn't keep her from realising they *were*.

She found herself wandering the town and research station, feeling the seconds ticking away one by one. It was hard for the Children to come to any real agreement on what to do. Henri wanted to demand their rights or simply find a way to escape, Darren wanted to remain on the planet; they both had supporters and detractors, their arguments so loud it was hard for anyone else to think clearly. They both believed their words too, something that made the arguments even worse. Pandora didn't want to believe either of them, but … she felt her heart twist every time she thought of the dead researcher. It was hard, almost impossible, to look past the horror they'd unleashed. What had gone wrong and why? She didn't know.

No one did.

"Pandora!"

She looked up and spotted one of the younger researchers, a young man only a handful of years older than herself. Peter was attracted to her, his feelings tinged with embarrassment and a certain degree of guilt … she felt pained, inwardly, at just how trapped he was in his own head. She didn't think poorly of him for being attracted to her, and she might have welcomed him if he'd invited her on a date, but she had no way to *tell* him so. Henri and the rest of her peers had no trouble reading her emotions, and telling if she was interested in them; *he* could not. It was yet another reminder of just how different the Children were, how they were more stable and yet …

"That's me," she said, dryly. Someone had joked the Children should all look alike, citing an old novel she'd never read, but about the only thing they had in common was being human. "What can I do for you?"

"We have a visitor, from the Council," Peter said. There was a hint of relief in his feelings, a hope the whole affair would be over soon. "The director was wondering if you would like to meet her."

Pandora tried to smile, but it was hard for her to fake any emotion. "Does *she* want to meet *me*?"

There was a flicker of hesitation in Peter's feelings, a sense he wasn't quite sure of the answer and yet feared it was *no*. Pandora felt her heart sink. The newcomer probably didn't want to meet someone who could read her mind, like so many others who had passed through the planet and then left again. And yet … she wanted to turn and walk away, but she knew she shouldn't. If she had the chance to make her case directly …

Her heart sank. She could talk to her peers, allowing her emotions to colour her words and let them taste her sincerity, and she knew how to speak to the researchers, but an outsider? She didn't know the newcomer, didn't know how to address them … it was going to be embarrassing for both of them, particularly if she accidentally read the newcomer's mind. Or worse.

"I'll come," she said, reluctantly. It was probably better she went, instead of Henri or one of the others who feared the worst. "Where is she?"

Peter turned away. "The auditorium," he said. "I'll take you there."

Pandora opened her mouth to point out that she *knew* where it was, that she'd been on the planet longer than any of the researchers, then closed it without saying anything. Peter wanted to spend time with her … she felt another surge of pity for the young man, barely in his second decade. It might have been wiser to ensure the researchers were in their second centuries, with the experience and maturity of humans who had lived longer than their ancestors could ever have dreamed, but there weren't that many volunteers. And besides, Peter was old enough to set a good example and serve as an older brother figure without being too old to be relatable or too young to take seriously. Or so he'd been told.

She followed him instead, her thoughts a conflicted mess. It was easy to get along with her peers, when she *knew* what they were thinking and feeling, but outsiders … she could feel his desire for her, his desire to be one of them, and also his fear of what might happen if they repeated the experiment. He hadn't volunteered the first time and he was both relieved and ashamed … Pandora wanted to reach out and give him a hug, to tell him it would be alright, and yet she knew better. He wouldn't thank her for reading his emotions. Or his thoughts. He was trapped in his own mind.

The thought haunted her as she reached the auditorium, a lecture and display hall that had seen very little use since it had been established. The Children didn't need to attend lectures in a body – one or two could attend, then spread the knowledge to the rest of the nest – and there were few unique artefacts on Clarke. The vast majority of the *magical* things the survey crews had discovered on Darius had lost their powers, to the point the researchers insisted they'd become little more than props for a low-budget fantasy production. Pandora had once spent an hour waving a wand around, in hopes of producing a spark of raw magic, but it had been nothing more than a waste of time. If the so-called Objects of Power hadn't been crafted using techniques that defied explanation, they would be of no interest at all.

Peter's thoughts shifted as they stepped inside, passing a row of display stands. It was easy to see the artefacts through his eyes, objects so dull and degraded it was hard to believe they'd ever been important. They lacked the sense of age that pervaded artefacts dating all the way back to the pre-space era, when mankind had assumed it was all alone in the universe; they lacked, in many ways, the sense they'd been put together by someone who had spent years developing the skills they needed to do it. They were part of her heritage, she supposed, and yet it was hard to take them seriously. If she hadn't seen the records, she wouldn't have taken them seriously at all.

"Ah, Pandora," Professor Exurban said. He stood next to an older woman, who was studying a jewelled casket with every expression of interest. "This is Councillor Noonan. She's here to consider the situation …"

And help us decide what to do with you, his thoughts added.

Pandora looked up and studied the Councillor thoughtfully. She was clearly old, her features and dress plain rather than the mature youthfulness so many others preferred; her face was so bland, to Pandora's eyes, that she couldn't help thinking it was instantly forgettable. She held herself calmly, with an authority so profound she had no need to throw her weight around. Pandora had met others who were so trapped in their own heads they *had* to prove their power by pushing others around, driven by their own insecurities, but this one was different. There wasn't a single doubt in her mind that she was in charge.

And yet …

"Pleased to meet you," Pandora said, holding out a hand. The Councillor shook her hand gravely. "Welcome to Clarke."

"Thank you," the Councillor said. "It is good to be here."

Pandora felt a flicker of … *something*. Something *new*. She couldn't put it into words and yet … it was there. A faint edge, a sensation that crawled at the back of her mind and made her eyes ache … she wasn't sure if she was feeling the Councillor's emotions, or she was reacting to something else, something her instincts were telling her to avoid. It was … she wanted to open her mind, to try to read the Councillor's thoughts, but she knew better. The woman in front of her would be making a decision, *the* decision. She could not be given any reason to order the Children confined for the rest of time.

"Pandora is one of our success stories," Professor Exurban babbled. He wasn't trying to hide his nervousness. "We have learnt a great deal from studying her."

"But you still don't understand how their abilities actually work," the Councillor said. A flicker of odd amusement ran through the air, as if she was amused for reasons beyond the obvious. "Why not?"

Pandora didn't need telepathy to sense the professor's sudden annoyance. "When faced with something new, we can normally use sensors to monitor its development and devise theories to account for it, then devise newer and better sensors to gain a fuller picture of what is happening. Those theories can then be adjusted to fit our better understanding, or discarded if it becomes clear they are worthless. There is no such thing as settled science and anyone who says otherwise is, at best, severely misinformed. Many of our technological developments have come from observing the seemingly inexplicable, at least at first, and then developing ways to duplicate it."

He paused, controlling his feelings with an effort. "Much modern science would seem magic, to those of a bygone age. Quantum field theory, for example, would be completely bizarre to our ancestors. They would certainly have no way to detect a quantum communications network, let alone figure out how to shut it down or duplicate it. This" – he nodded to Pandora – "may be something that appears magic, until we find a way to analyse it properly."

The Councillor's emotions seemed to shift, just slightly. "Are their brains linked together at the quantum level?"

"That was one of the theories we considered," Professor Exurban said. "It's certainly possible they are linked together in some way, although they are individuals … no more or less so than any other human. They may understand their peers, and even us, better than most …"

He frowned. "Given time, we will understand them. Given time, we will figure out how their abilities work and how to duplicate them. Given time."

"Time is the one thing we don't have," the Councillor reminded him. She looked at Pandora. "What do your people *want*?"

Pandora hesitated. "Some want to explore the universe," she said. "Others want to stay here."

"Of course they do," the Councillor said. There was a flicker of *oddness* surrounding her, a sense that reminded Pandora of a solid-like projection. But they'd shaken hands … no projection, no matter how advanced, could mimic the sense of a human being attending in person. Not to fool her, at least. "What about you? What do *you* want?"

"I don't know," Pandora admitted. "But I do want the freedom to decide for myself."

***

Under other circumstances, X might have been fascinated with the Darius Children.

They represented a remarkable scientific puzzle, from

their inexplicable and frankly bizarre abilities to the weird and wonderful artefacts recovered from their homeworld. The objects might be broken now, the magic – or whatever it really was – long gone, but that didn't keep them from being interesting in their own way. They'd been made on a primitive world, in ways that should have been impossible without modern technology … he understood, even if not all the researchers agreed, why they'd been kept on Clarke. Perhaps the Children would be able to make them for themselves, one day. Or perhaps they'd remain an enigma for the rest of time.

He studied Pandora thoughtfully, noting all the ways she was slightly disconcerting … even to him. There was nothing special about her face or body – the researchers had declined to give her unrestricted control over her biology, changing her appearance or gender at a whim without reference to anyone else – and yet, there was something odd about the way she carried herself. It was a strange combination of maturity and immaturity, self-confidence and insecurity … it wasn't the security that came with growing up in a post-scarcity society, or the desperate quest for meaning that consumed so much effort once someone grew old enough to want some meaning in their lives, but something else. He supposed it had something to do with their abilities. A person who could sense the thoughts and emotions of their peers would have fewer insecurities, and what they did could be addressed openly. And yet …

Pandora was young. And yet there was something *old* about her.

He kept the personality overlays firmly in place. Professor Exurban suspected nothing, from the way he was wittering on, and he'd been careful to keep the Councillor away from the other researchers until he'd finished babbling about the importance of finding some kind of solution to their problem. X hadn't argued, although he knew Marla Noonan would … if she hadn't been reduced to a set of recordings guiding his actions. She wanted the opinions of just about everyone else, X wanted to limit the number of people who met him – in her body – before it was too late. He didn't mind leaving her with the blame for the crisis, but he wanted to get away before it was too late. All he had to do was delay matters a little longer, until everything was in place.

"Maybe they have some kind of access to hyperspace," he said. He'd heard the possibility discussed, before he'd excluded himself from society. "If they can manipulate the world around them …?"

"It has been considered," Professor Exurban said. He wasn't trying to hide his frustration. "The energy involved would be off the charts, so … where is it? And where is it coming from?"

X cocked his head, playing his role. "They cannot produce the energy for themselves?"

"There is no way a lone human could produce the energy they'd need to access and manipulate hyperspace," Professor Exurban said, bluntly. "We have monitored their food intake and tried to determine how their bodies use energy, drawing a complete blank. As far as we can tell, their abilities don't use any energy at all. Which is impossible, even for a full-fledged genie. There should be *something*."

"Yes." X looked at Pandora. He needed to play the game a little longer, and if that meant pretending to be someone who thought she could figure out something the scientists had missed that was what he would do. The act would annoy the researchers, but it was the sort of thing they'd expect. They were very used to visitors who considered themselves experts, just because they'd accessed a few files. They wouldn't look past it to see the truth. "Do you grow tired, when you use your abilities?"

Pandora stared back at him, her eyes so dark they were almost pools of shadow. They were well within the range of normal human variation, and yet … he frowned inwardly, suddenly all too aware she could read his thoughts. If she saw through the personality overlays … he put the thought out of his head as best he could, choosing to examine her instead. She was tall and thin, but not scrawny. That too was understandable. Her genetics would have been tweaked at some point to ensure she shared all the advantages of the modern human race, from perfect health to automatic adaptation to new environments. And yet ...

"Not really," Pandora said, finally. She sounded distracted, as if her mind was somewhere else. In her case, that might be literally true. "It ... it just happens."

She spoke with a hint of frustration. "How do you explain colour to a man born blind?"

"There are programs that will let you see the world as an alien sees it," X pointed out. A flicker of excitement ran through him. His mind-twin had everything in place now, ready to make his move. It was almost time to push the personality overlays away one final time and gamble his life on a single throw of the dice. He couldn't wait. "If we could do the same for you ..."

Professor Exurban frowned. "That would require direct brain access," he pointed out. "It would be illegal ..."

Pandora stared at X, her eyes going wide. X *knew*, beyond a shadow of a doubt, that she had just read his mind, that she'd realised the personality overlays were all that reminded of a dead woman ... worse, they were the smile on the face of the tiger. Professor Exurban looked dull and stupid – he hadn't realised that the fact a Councillor had suggested something overtly illegal was a huge red flag – but even *he* would twig that something was wrong within seconds. The young man behind him, his eyes falling constantly to Pandora's rear and then rising again, was even worse. Too old to be considered a child, too young to be wholly mature ...

"What ..." Pandora staggered, as if he'd struck her. "What *are* you?"

She retched a moment later, her hands clutching at her temples as if she intended to rip out her own brain. Professor Exurban stared at X, his face twisting in horror. He knew now, too late. Far too late.

X opened his hands and let the sub-nanotech fly.

CHAPTER TEN

Commodore Jason Lehman knew, without false modesty, that he was a throwback.

It was rare to find a ruthless Peacekeeper. The Peacekeepers rarely *needed* to be ruthless, not when they enjoyed a massive advantage over nearly all of their potential foes. The fleet was advanced enough to suppress a primitive race without a single casualty on either side and numerous enough to intimidate any peer power without actually needing to fight. The only real threat was an angered Elder race, or an alliance between the Confederation's peers, and both were extremely unlikely. Jason had assumed it was just a matter of time before he was quietly discharged from the service, if he wasn't asked to put himself in suspension until the human race had need of his ruthlessness. Instead, he'd been asked to take command of the defence forces orbiting Clarke. It hadn't taken him long to realise why he'd been picked for the job. If the Darius Children proved extremely dangerous, and their abilities made them dangerous even if they weren't actively hostile, he had the willingness to destroy the entire settlement and obliterate the Children before their threat could reach beyond the planet's atmosphere. It would be a hell of a thing – mass murder, perhaps even genocide – but he would do it without hesitation if there were no other choice. The Confederation had to be protected. And that meant he might have to get his hands dirty.

He sat in his command post, surrounded by a handful of holographic displays. The vast majority of the defences were completely automated, giving him near-autonomous control over the system … free, as far as could be determined, from any interference from the planet below. He wasn't afraid of being alone, nor of being overpowered by any threat capable of making its way through the hyperspace wall. The Peacekeepers had deployed a network of sensor platforms covering every possible angle of approach, ensuring that nothing could move within five light years without him being aware of its existence. The only excitement had been the arrival of Councillor Noonan and *that* hadn't been more than a minor incident, allowing him to run a handful of tracking simulations. It was almost a shame the councillor hadn't had a chance to speak to him personally. But …

An alarm sounded. Something was moving … a flicker of alarm shot through him as he looked up, his implants linking him into the defence network. There was a small fleet of starships flickering out of nowhere, each one a five-mile long dealer of death and devastation … lethal, if pointed at a world without modern defences, but nothing more than a handful of easy targets for him. Except … how the hell had they got so close? The sensors were extremely sensitive. Even if they had been cloaked with modern technology, and directed into the system on ballistic trajectories, they shouldn't have gone unnoticed. His sensors should have picked them up hours ago.

Alarm shot through his awareness as more and more defences came online. The enemy ships were far too close, and there was nothing in the warbook to suggest who'd sent them. Most races started out with crude and blocky designs, then let their imaginations fly free once they reached the point they could build craft with almost any design, no matter how seemingly absurd. There were starships that looked like giant birds and others that resembled flying saucers, but … these craft looked like spears, plunging towards Clarke. They were bizarre, technologies from several different eras blended together into a patchwork mix that made it impossible to determine their true potency. Perhaps their builders had discovered and reverse-engineered tech belonging to a much older race. It wasn't uncommon. Quite a few races had become local superpowers – briefly – through piggybacking on a piece of technology designed by someone else.

He sent a brief signal, ordering the newcomers to stand down or face the consequences. He dared not assume they were harmless, or that he could take chances with them. They were already far too close to the planet, close enough for modern weapons to destroy the entire biosphere. (He was not far gone enough to wonder if that would be a neat little solution to their problem.) If they didn't stand down, he would open fire without further warning. He waited, torn between Peacekeeper precepts and his growing fear for the planet behind him. The ships made no reply. Instead, they brought their weapons online.

Jason scowled, then triggered his weapons. The enemy ships had hypershields, as well as realspace defences, but no hyperspatial weapons of their own. More proof, he supposed, that they were using technology they hadn't developed for themselves. Their missile pods opened fire as his weapons started to pound their shields, their missiles absurdly fast on a human scale yet practically crawling on his. He had no trouble settling up a counter fire pattern, wiping out the hundreds of thousands of missiles before they could get remotely close to the planet he was charged to defend. Their shields started to fail moments later, bursts of energy manifesting inside their hulls, setting off chain reactions that blew their ships into atoms. Jason had hoped for captives – he was ruthless, but he took no pleasure in slaughter for its own sake – but the ships were loaded with antimatter. The moment their hulls were hit, they exploded. There would be no captives, no surviving examples of tech to take apart and trace back to its makers. The attack would remain a disturbing mystery.

An alarm howled. The councillor's ship was moving, picking up speed so rapidly Jason *knew* something was wrong. It was too late. The tiny craft slammed into his shields, its drive fields adjusting to form a shaped pattern an instant before it drew a tidal wave of energy from hyperspace and sent it boiling through the inky blackness of orbital space. The shields failed completely, the ravening blast tearing through the outer edge of the defence station and ripping it apart. Jason sent a desperate command into the network, signalling for help he knew wouldn't arrive in time. The first attack had been a diversion, and now …

The station exploded. Jason barely had a second to teleport himself into a secure lifepod before it was too late.

***

Pandora staggered, suddenly aware of her vulnerability.

The person in front of her – the Councillor; no, something wearing her flesh – was a monster, nightmarish cluster of thoughts and feelings that pervaded the air. She couldn't understand how she'd missed it, when she'd shaken her hand … she couldn't understand how she'd got so close without being repelled. She had grown up in a safe place: amongst adults who treated her kindly even as they grew afraid of her abilities; surrounded by medical science that could cure anything, as long as it wasn't immediately fatal. She knew, intellectually, that the children of earlier generations had been lucky to grow into adulthood; she didn't really believe it, not deep inside, not where it mattered. And now …

The Councillor's body shifted. For a moment, she thought she was growing fur … and then the fur exploded outwards, brushing against Professor Exurban and Peter. They hadn't realised … not yet, not ever. She could sense their minds dying, snuffed out so completely they were dead before they even realised they were under attack. Their bodies shambled backwards, already growing fur of their own. Nanotech, part of her mind whispered. Her history lessons had covered monsters who'd unleashed Grey Goo on entire planets, nanotech intended to murder or enslave billions of people before they could escape. The technology was heavily restricted for a reason and that meant … she retched, helplessly, as the Councillor's body reached for her. The fake emotions were gone. Instead, she was staring at a nightmare in human flesh.

She tried to scream, but her body refused to move. Her panic bled into the mental field, the warning flickering around the planet … she reached, desperately, for the rest of her peers, yet it was hard – almost impossible – to think clearly. The air shifted, her perceptions blurring, as the Councillor's body caught hold of her arm. Pandora was young and strong, but the Councillor had enhanced strength. She tried to kick the older woman somewhere it would hurt and succeeded … she didn't seem to notice. The mind behind the body wasn't harmed. It didn't care how much damage the Councillor took as long as the body succeeded in its mission.

The body pushed a terminal against her head. No, it wasn't a terminal. It was …

Pandora screamed as pain shot through her head. The others were screaming too, their minds howling in shared agony. They had always felt each other's pain and yet … this was too much to handle. The pain shattered the nest, a second before the blackness reached out and claimed her.

It felt like the end of the world.

***

X allowed himself a moment of heavy satisfaction as he lowered Pandora to the ground, careful to keep the nanotech fibres from touching the young girl. Nanotech was closely regulated for a reason, and very few would dare unleash it without making damn sure the swarm couldn't evolve or mutate in any way. He'd thrown caution to the winds when he'd created his sub-nanotech swarm, unleashing a nightmare right out of the darkest days of human history. The subverted slaves would spread it further and further, forcing the local defences to deal with it. X didn't care if it swallowed up the whole world or not, as long as it did its job. As a diversion, it could hardly be bettered.

He removed the teleport beacon from his arm and snapped it onto Pandora, keying the switch to override the security precautions. It wasn't uncommon for people to carry beacons when they expected to be teleported, and no one had been suspicious when Marla Noonan had appeared wearing one, but the defensive fields surrounding the planet would make teleporting difficult even if the high orbitals hadn't been filled with antimatter explosions. The destruction would make it harder for the Peacekeepers to work out what was actually going on, if he'd calculated everything correctly, yet it would also fuck with his ability to get Pandora offworld before his time ran out. She needed the beacon, which rendered Marla Noonan's body surplus to requirements.

He concealed Pandora under a blanket, then made his way outside. The warm summer air was rent with screams, the researchers having seen what remained of their comrades and realised what they were facing. It didn't sound as if they had any real plans to deal with an attacking force, not one that somehow got through the orbital defences. There weren't many humans who had the ability to switch to a warfighting mode and fight, even in self-defence, these days and those who had those abilities tended to go straight into the Peacekeepers, where they could put their skills to work defending the human race. The panic would provide all the cover he needed, he told himself, as he shambled towards the lone power plant. There didn't seem to be anyone close by, anyone close enough to notice the fur flaking off his face. The researchers really weren't ready for trouble.

There was no guard on the power plant, but the door was locked. X pressed his hand against the metal, allowing the nanotech to eat its way into the structure. The defensive fields flickered and flared, confused by the combination of authorised access codes and free-floating nanotech; he snickered, inwardly, at the failure to bump the question up to a human mind. Or even an AI. The AIs had taken an interest in the Darius Children right from the start, after discovering Darius itself, and *they* should be watching ... too late, he thought, as the door crumpled. An operator stood, one hand holding a primitive firearm. Good thinking, X acknowledged as the bullets cracked into his chest. Modern weapons were restricted, but it wasn't that hard to convince the fabbers to churn out the components for a more primitive firearm without setting off any alarms. It wasn't enough to stop him, no matter how many times he was hit. The nanotech had absorbed most of his stolen body.

The operator staggered back, too late. X brought up his arm, now a writhing mass of dark fur, and slammed it into the other man. His body started to shift and change a second later ... he tried, desperately, to bring up the firearm and point it at his own head, taking his own life before it could be subverted. X watched without interfering, curious to see if he would make it. He didn't, his face dissolving into a black mass that spread rapidly, tearing through the remaining defences as if they weren't there. X didn't bother with anything special as his stolen body started its final collapse. He merely shut down the entire datanet, then the power plant. There would be some autonomous systems on the planet still active, he was sure, but most civilians never considered even the possibility of losing power. Their access to near-infinite power was a right ... one they were about to lose. He smiled, then felt the body finally give up the ghost. The nanotech swarm ran out of control ...

His eyes snapped open, a sense of utter disorientation running through him. He had been on the ship. He had been on the planet. He had been in two places at once ...

he snarled a command, ordering the teleporters to find the beacon and bring its wearer up to the ship, then brought the drive online. He dared not assume he had taken *all* the defences down, not when the Peacekeepers had gone to extreme lengths to protect the planet. For all he knew, they'd sent a distress signal the moment they'd seen the dummy fleet. It hadn't posed any real threat to the planet itself, or the defences, but sending a signal anyway would have been smart. They hadn't known for sure the fleet was harmless.

He shrugged as Pandora's body materialised on the teleport pad, the biofilters confirming she was both alive and free of nanotech. X allowed himself a moment of relief – he didn't have time to search for a second victim – then ordered the drones to secure her, just in case. His medical sensors confirmed there was nothing particularly odd about her brain, nothing that might be the source of her abilities. He hadn't *thought* Professor Exurban had lied to him – the man had thought him a Councillor, and he'd been desperate besides – but it was good to have it confirmed. It suggested the rest of the data he'd harvested from the planetary network would be accurate too. It would bring a hefty profit, on the Life Sphere. The entities who wanted Pandora would want the data too. Who knew? He might be able to sell it to multiple interested parties. It wouldn't be the first time.

His hand darted over the console, running one last scan before he brought the warp drive online and fled. The rest of the nanotech was slowing its advance now, suggesting it was being successfully contained and countered. Perhaps he'd underestimated the defences after all ... or maybe it was the Children. Their power was inexplicable, which meant they might be able to stop the nanotech, nipping its spread in the bud without ever having any clear idea of what it actually was. Not, he supposed, that it mattered. There was little to be gained by destroying the entire world. His mission had been completed ...

And now it was time to leave.

***

Jason felt his head spin as the lifepod spun helplessly. The secure structure had been deemed a panic room, a display of both paranoia and safetyism that had always made him roll his eyes, but it had saved his life. His station had been shattered, effectively destroyed, yet he was alive. He forced himself to gather his thoughts, to link into what remained of the planetary defence network. The incoming starships were gone, and ….

Alerts flooded through his mind. Nanotech. Free-floating nanotech, loose on the planetary surface. The power was largely down … he cursed under his breath, directing the establishment of a foldspace link to the surface, followed by the deployment of emergency defence drones and teleporters. The nanotech had to be confined quickly, or the entire planet would dissolve like a sugar cube in water. It had happened before, when the universe had gone mad. Whoever had attacked them … the attacker had to be mad. Nanotech, hyperspace energies, entire starships crammed with antimatter … madness.

"Launch the distress drone," he ordered. The attacker had taken out the hyperwave relay node, isolating Clarke from the universe. Thankfully, the drone – another display of Peacekeeper paranoia – hadn't been mentioned on any outside files. Jason and his superiors were the only ones who knew it even existed. The attacker certainly hadn't tried to destroy it. "Get it to the nearest base as quickly as possible."

His mind raced as he rebuilt as much of the network as possible. He could get the fabber online and rebuild the settlement, then try to recover data from the compromised datacores. If the attacker hadn't finished the job … ice ran down his spine as he realised the truth. The attacker could have scorched the entire planet and the defences couldn't have stopped him, which meant … he *had* completed his mission. Jason wanted to believe the operation had failed, but he was too realistic to convince himself. There was only one thing on the planet worth taking, certainly only one thing that couldn't be obtained elsewhere, for far less effort and risk …

And *that* meant that one or more of the Children had been kidnapped.

CHAPTER
ELEVEN

Pandora felt … cold.

Her mind was drifting, caught in a cold grey ocean that surrounded her, waves of … *something* … pulsing around her. It was hard, almost impossible, to think clearly. She couldn't feel the nest, couldn't feel the thoughts of her peers … for a moment, a terrifying moment, she thought she was truly alone in the universe. The sudden burst of fear yanked her forward, dragging her mind out of the grey ocean and back into her body, She thought she sensed, just for a second, someone talking – the words so quiet she couldn't make them out – before her eyes snapped open, the shock depositing her mind back into the real world. Her body felt dull and degraded, as if it were a set of clothes she had outgrown long ago. It was so disconcerting she wondered just how long she'd been asleep, trapped in a nightmarish vision that was already fading from her mind. It was …

Memory returned, a flash of insight that drove the remnants of the drowsiness from her mind. The Councillor hadn't been a councillor, but … someone else. She had unleashed something nasty, then knocked Pandora cold and … and what? The Darius Children had excellent memories, practically perfect recall of everything that had happened to them since they gained self-awareness, but her memories were blank. She had been on Clarke and now she was somewhere else, a faint hissing at the back of her mind making it hard to think clearly. The nest was gone ... she told herself, grimly, that she had to be a very long way from her peers. No one was quite sure how far they could reach with their telepathy, but she had to be outside their range. It wasn't a pleasant thought, yet she clung to it with a passionate intensity. The alternative was worse.

Clarke could be gone, she thought, numbly. The last war had been truly terrifying in scope, entire planets blasted to atoms and stars sent supernova to wipe out enemy fortifications that had been too strong to reduce with lesser methods. Given a fabber, plenty of time and a complete lack of scruples, her mystery captor could easily churn out enough antimatter to scorch the entire planet, or build a gravity-compression device capable of blowing up the entire star, or simply snuffing it out so completely it collapsed into a black hole. *They could all be dead*.

Her heart sank. Death was a stranger on Clarke, but ... Professor Exurban might be dead. He'd been right next to the fake Councillor when she made her move. Peter too, the young man with so much promise ahead of him ... dead and gone, or wishing he was. There were fifty-seven researchers and two hundred Children ... they might all be dead. She felt sick as she forced herself to concentrate on the universe around her. The world was dark and yet ... she could feel something covering her eyes. A blindfold? She tried to separate her mind from her body, to inspect her surroundings through astral eyes that she knew from experience were effectively undetectable, but her astral projection refused to separate itself from her body. Ice trickled down her spine. The researchers hadn't been able to find a way to shut down her abilities, despite centuries of experience studying and modifying human genetic patterns, but if her captor had solved that particular mystery ...

She gritted her teeth, trying to parse out as much as she could of her surroundings. She could barely shift her body, her arms and legs restrained in a manner that made it impossible to move more than a few millimetres in any direction. She thought she was naked, naked and vulnerable ... the shock and panic boosted her telekinesis, tearing the blindfold away. Bright light – cold light – stabbed into her eyes, seeming to drive needles into her brain. The entire chamber was glowing, her skin crawling as she was suddenly aware of the radiations pulsing through the air. She couldn't tell what they were, or what they were intended to do, but ... she thought they were dangerous. The sensation of *something* nasty crawling over her skin grew stronger with every passing second.

Her head ached, painfully, as she risked opening her eyes again. The light was bright ... too bright. Her vision should have adjusted by now, her eyes – like the rest of her body – engineered for near-immediate adaptation to new surroundings. She didn't like the implications of her eyes failing to adapt, either her captor had meddled with her genetic code or his datacores were adjusting the light to ensure it was always painful. She closed her eyelids as much as she could without blinding herself, then tilted her head to examine the metal bands around her left wrist. It was held in place by a clockwork contraption, a mixture of levels and wires that made little sense. She forced herself to study it carefully. If she pushed down with her telekinesis at just the right spot ...

Her hand came free. Pandora chuckled, despite herself, and turned her head to look at her other wrist. This time, the lock was hidden inside a metal casing ... her heart sank as she tried to shift to push it clear with her free hand, only to discover she was secured too tightly to move past a certain point. Despair flickered at the back of her mind, before she closed her eyes and carefully reached out with her power. The locking system unfurled in front of her, identical to the first in every way save one. She pushed down on the right place and freed her other hand.

She tried to sit up and nearly choked herself. She had a

collar around her neck, one secured to the table. She closed her eyes again and concentrated on finding the lock, undoing it with a careful application of her abilities. The collar left her neck aching as she sat upright, her entire body groaning in pain as she looked around, covering her eyes to make it easier to see. There were two more lockboxes covering her ankles, binding her to the table. She could barely reach them with her hands, and when she reached out with her mind she saw the locking mechanism shifting constantly. It was easy to see how to unlock it, harder to free herself without jamming the clockwork and trapping herself permanently. It was just odd.

Suspicion flowered in her mind as she looked around. The chamber was empty, save for the examination table. Her captor could have kept her unconscious, or put her in a stasis tube, or even injected her with subversion nanites. Instead, she had put her in a trap that she could escape. It worried her, on a very primal level. It was possible she was dealing with one of the sociopathic sadists, monsters who couldn't get their kicks unless they came at the expense of someone who hadn't consented, but ... why would such a monster risk attacking *Clarke*? The odds of being caught were staggeringly high, and that meant ... what? She didn't know. Perhaps the risk was part of the thrill for her captor, although she found it hard to comprehend. She couldn't imagine pleasuring herself through hurting others, not when she was part of the nest. Hell, one didn't have to be a telepath to know hurting others was wrong. There were so many people in the Confederation that there was a fetish for practically everything. If you wanted something dark and dangerous, you could find someone who shared your desires ...

Unless inflicting yourself on someone is part of the point, she thought, numbly. She knew some of the researchers wondered, deep in the deepest darkest recesses of their minds, what it might be like to make love to a telepath. The idea of having a partner who could literally sense your desires and respond to them ... she wondered, suddenly, if her captor had the same thought. Or something worse. *I have to get out of here.*

She closed her eyes, studying the closest lock through her astral vision. It was a complex piece of clockwork, but the more she looked the more she realised that two-thirds of the ever-shifting interior were intended to do nothing more than confuse her. The remnants were moving too, yet … as she parsed it out, she realised the four-digit combination that had to be entered to open the lock. It was hard to open it with her mind, but … she reached out and held the mechanism still, just for a moment, as she used her hand to enter the code. The wheels spun once, then the lock clicked open. She pulled her leg free, then studied the last locking device. It was the exact opposite of the previous mechanism, utterly unmoving. The whole system had been locked in place, then carefully jammed. She couldn't free herself.

Anger shot through her as she tried, and failed, to turn the lock. The mechanism wasn't just broken, it had been deliberately sabotaged, Someone had locked her up and literally damaged the lock to ensure it couldn't be opened, even with the proper key. She felt her anger building as she let her astral presence float through the mechanism, examining it from the inside, then split her attention in two, telekinetically shaping a replacement part composed of her thoughts while carefully entering the right digits. The lock clicked open, allowing her to pull herself free and stand upright. A faint sensation vibrated through the floor … no, the *deck*. She was on a starship.

Which isn't really a surprise, she thought, dryly. *If I can't feel the nest, I have to be quite some distance away.*

She checked her appearance as best she could, frowning inwardly as she realised her hair hadn't grown out much, if at all. It suggested she hadn't been asleep for very long, although it was meaningless. Her captor could have put her in a stasis tube, as soon as he got her onto the ship, and she wouldn't have the slightest sense of time passing until she was taken out again and left to recover naturally. A flicker of panic ran through her mind. How long had she been kept in stasis? Days? Weeks? Months … or years? Her captor could be halfway across the galaxy by now, his ship – no matter how large – nothing more than a grain of sand on an infinite beach. The Peacekeepers could deploy every ship in their fleet, the millions of vessels from tiny one-man transports to planet-sized warships, and never catch a glimpse of their quarry, unless they got incredibly lucky. The thought made her panic worse, the sensation gnawing at her mind. She had grown up in a universe that was safe, by and large, and help would always be available to those who needed it. And that left her ill-prepared to be on her own.

Her thoughts hardened as she forced herself to survey the glowing walls. There had to be a hatch somewhere, didn't there? The light made it hard to think clearly, so she closed her eyes and allowed her awareness to wander through the metal. The starship was larger than she'd thought, although she wasn't sure why *that* was a surprise. There was no inherent reason why a private citizen couldn't own a starship large enough to pass for a small city, not when a datacore and a small army of autonomous repair systems could keep the starship running. For all she knew …

Her thoughts brushed against a hatch. She stumbled forward and pushed it open, finding herself in an airlock. Her mind reached ahead as she stepped into the tiny chamber, finding another corridor on the far side of the outer door. The hatch slammed closed behind her a second later, trapping her. The air grew heavy, difficult to breathe. She couldn't tell if it was being pumped out or if there just wasn't much air in the tiny chamber, but it hardly mattered. She gritted her teeth and reached out desperately, trying to open the outer hatch. The mechanism wasn't complex, but it was primitive and stiff. She pushed down hard, forcing the hatch to open through sheer force of will, and stumbled forward into a second airlock. The gust of fresh air that greeted her was a relief, but it didn't last. She was on the verge of running out of air for the second time.

Something crossed her mind and she kicked herself, mentally, for not putting the pieces together earlier. She'd been through quite enough tests of her abilities, from the simple and pointless to the complex, deeply frustrating and even *more* pointless, and she knew the signs. The researchers had managed to put together a fairly good picture of what the Children could do, but they hadn't found an underlying theory that explained it … hell, they hadn't tried to put the Children in very real danger to force them to reveal their abilities. She doubted *she* was in any real danger now, not if she'd been kidnapped … there were better, and more reliable, ways to keep her under control if that was what her captor wanted. She was being tested, and that meant …

She sat down on the deck, cross-legged. "I don't know who you are," she said into the empty air, "but I am not going to play your game any longer."

The air grew thin, making it hard to breathe. She closed her eyes and reached out with her mind, trying to pull every last air molecule towards her … touching, as she did, a cold and calculating presence watching her. Her body screamed in protest as it gasped for air, demanding she move, demanding she did whatever it took to appease her captor. Pandora kept herself from moving through grim determination and a cold-blooded awareness she had probably left it too late to save herself. The second airlock was closed and locked and she hadn't bothered to take more than a glance at the mechanism, let alone try to open it. Her vision started to blur, despite her best efforts. Her body wanted to live, even if she didn't …

A rush of cold air brushed against her, jerking her out of her stupor. The second airlock was open. She forced herself to stand on wobbly legs, staggering through a third and final airlock chamber before finding herself in a simple – if large – compartment. It looked disturbingly like the nest's bedroom, a cluster of comfortable chairs, sofas and mattresses strewn around randomly … proof, as if she'd needed it, that her captor had managed to access the planetary datacore and download a number of files, perhaps even everything the researchers had learnt over the years. Her lips twitched at the thought. The files wouldn't be *that* helpful. The researchers hadn't managed to solve any of the *important* questions.

"Greetings," a calm voice said.

Pandora looked up. A man was standing on the far side of the chamber, wearing a simple dark outfit that betrayed no trace of individuality. His skin was dark, his eyes darker still ... ice ran down her spine as she realised the darkness surrounded him, making it hard to get a clear idea of his true appearance. It was almost a physical force, dominating the compartment ...

She reached out with her mind, intent on reading his thoughts ... perhaps even killing him outright. The researchers had speculated on just how easily a telekinetic could kill a man, simply by reaching inside his head and *pinching*; Pandora had been horrified at the time – if she felt whatever she did to her peers, even something as simple as treading on their toes, she dreaded to think how it would feel if she killed someone – but now, now she almost wanted to do it and to hell with the consequences. Her peers might be dead, either through the destruction of their homeworld or simple old age, and if that were true she might be the last of her kind. No one knew if her abilities would breed true, if she had children with her peers or someone who had no abilities of their own. For all they knew, there would be no more Children after they were gone.

Her mind touched something cold and dark and horrifying beyond words, the sheer shock throwing her back into her own body so quickly her legs buckled and she hit the deck. She had expected a sociopath and braced herself for desires so disgusting their bearers dared not speak their thoughts out loud, but instead ... her captor was worse. He didn't see her as a pretty young girl, someone he could abuse at will until he finally tired of her; he saw her as an object, something that could be used and discarded, or traded, without a single flicker of remorse. She had wondered, years ago, how such pathologies could exist in the Confederation, a state that could satisfy most reasonable and unreasonable demands from its inhabitants, but … her gut churned, her skin crawling once again. The person in front of her cared nothing for her. It was …

Her captor spoke with quiet firmness. "We have a great deal to explore together, you and I," he said. "I do hope you'll cooperate with me."

Pandora glared, struggling to her feet. "And if I refuse?"

The air shifted. A tractor beam picked her up and pressed her against the nearest bulkhead. Pandora scowled. Ask a silly question … her captor had complete control of the ship, backed up by datacores that were probably as insane as himself. Even if they weren't, it would be difficult to out-think one … or shut it down before it was too late. If her captor had read the files, he could have taken steps to prevent her escaping …

"My name is X," her captor said. He smiled, a strikingly unpleasant expression. "We are going to have *lots* of fun."

CHAPTER
TWELVE

"But who could do such a thing," Professor Gallus whimpered. "Who?"

Mari felt a stab of sympathy as the recovery drones pulled him from the wreckage, transferred him to a stretcher, and prepared to activate the stasis field. The professor had grown up in a universe where outright violence was rare, the few young children who showed a tendency to bully their peers consoled and carefully steered towards maturity before their tendencies turned pathological or outrightly sociopathic. The relative handful of mature adults who could handle violence tended to drift into the Peacekeepers, although even *they* had problems when they realised the push-button wars they fought involved the deaths of countless sentients. There shouldn't have been any real danger on Clarke, certainly nothing that killed at least ten people and threatened a number of others with death. And yet …

"We'll find out," she promised the older man. He would need years of therapy, she was sure, before he could return to his post. If he ever did. Most people had a pathological fear of wild nanotech and she couldn't blame them, not when it represented a danger on a planetary scale. "I'll see to it personally."

The stasis field snapped into place, freezing the professor in a timeless moment. He'd be released once the stretcher was transported to the planetoid, where he could be treated for both physical and mental injuries … after, she acknowledged coldly, he was scanned thoroughly for any traces of hostile nanotech. It was unlikely he'd been infected – he was still alive and reasonably intact – but no one took any chances, not with something that could turn into a full-blown grey goo. If he was infested …

She looked away, her eyes slipping across the remnants of the research station. The files she'd downloaded during their hasty flight to Clarke had noted that the research station was as much a small town as anything else, the kind of long-term settlement that provided plenty of diversions as well as resources for its inhabitants, but the scene in front of her was a twisted nightmare. The epicentre of the nanotech outbreak was an eerie furry mass, the nanotech somehow confined and then frozen in its tracks; the buildings outside the structure were warped and twisted, in a manner that made her head hurt when she looked at them too closely. They were twisted works of art from a psychopathic artist … she thought, suddenly, of X, and the broadcasts he'd uploaded to the darkweb. He thought of himself as an artist, she recalled, and whoever had attacked Clarke had the same basic mindset. She closed her eyes for a long moment, uploading a query into the tactical network. Was it the same person? There was no reason X couldn't have travelled from Parnassus to X. He certainly had a starship capable of making the flight.

Although attacking an incorporated world is a little out of character for him, she thought. The psychologists had put together a profile on their target, noting that he considered flesh and blood intelligent beings as little more than raw materials for his twisted artworks. *Why would he take the risk?*

Her mood darkened as she turned away, passing the remote force field projectors carefully isolating what remained of the research station – and the hostile nanotech – before wrapping it up into a zone of force and throwing it into a matter recycler. The remnants of the bodies were somewhere in the mess, but there was no way they could be recovered safely; the dead researchers would be resurrected, once their deaths were confirmed, yet it would take years for them to overcome the shock. And the endless angst that came with being a clone of a dead person, wondering if sharing the same DNA and memories made you the same person or nothing more than an imposter …

She shook her head. It wasn't her problem.

The Peacekeepers had set up a small bivouac several miles down the beach, providing temporary accommodation for the Children and the remaining researchers. Mari felt her thoughts harden as she walked across the sand, tempted to teleport even though she'd been cautioned not to risk using the teleporter unless it was urgent. They dared not risk anything that might disrupt the force fields, not when the nanotech could easily turn even *more* hostile if they accidentally triggered a final protocol. She was mildly surprised the mystery attacker *hadn't* programmed the nanotech to run wild, ensuring that all evidence of the kidnap victim was lost in the devastation. It bothered her, although she wasn't sure why. X hadn't destroyed Parnassus either. It had been well within his power to devastate the planet so completely that nothing short of a miracle could save it.

A Child met her as she reached the small cluster of prefabricated buildings. "Hi," he said. "I'm Henri."

Mari studied him thoughtfully, feeling a twinge of unease. Henri looked like just about every other eighteen-year-old young man in the Confederation, wearing a face a little *too* handsome to be believable, and yet there was something about him that was more than a little disconcerting. He could read her thoughts … she was used to sharing her mind with a starship – in a sense, she was the ship – but having a stranger know her most intimate thoughts was unpleasant. Was he reading her mind now? She was tempted to connect herself to her ship, to see what the mind-reader made of it. But would that hurt him? She didn't know.

"The Commodores are waiting for you," Henri said. He had a nice voice, without any real trace of an accent. "Would you like me to show you to their tent?"

"Please," Mari said.

She allowed him to lead her through the maze of buildings, her eyes lingering on his movements. He moved like a real human … which was, she supposed, something of the problem. He *was* a real human, yet … his abilities were inexplicable. Mari knew people who turned their faces into ugly nightmares, or bio-shaped their bodies into creatures that alternatively shocked and excited their fans, yet … none of *them* were quite so disconcerting. She told herself, firmly, that she was being prejudiced. And yet … her lips twisted. There was a race that was shunned and abhorred throughout the known galaxy, because they stank. Every other race found it hard to be in their presence for more than a few moments. They couldn't be blamed for their smell, she reminded herself, but nor could the other races be blamed for not wanting to have anything to do with them. How could they?

She pushed the thought aside as she stepped into the tent. Commodore Roger and Commodore Lehman were standing together, the latter looking mad as a march hare. Mari didn't blame him. The attack had come without warning, and involved technology advanced enough to be a fair match for the planetary defences … and yet, there was no way in hell Lehman's career wasn't going to take a blow. He'd let one of the Children be kidnapped, perhaps more than one. And there was always someone, sitting a safe distance from the incident, who would insist the disaster had been the result of incompetence …

Commodore Roger motioned for her to take a seat. "We have completed the preliminary assessments," he said. "Most of the sensor platforms, and planetary nodes, were damaged or destroyed, but we have been able to put together a fairly complete picture of what happened."

"It looks as if Councillor Noonan either betrayed us or

was subverted," Lehman growled. "Given the nature of the attack, I tend to believe the latter."

Mari nodded, curtly. The Security Council was the single most powerful gathering in the Confederation. The Councillors were put through extensive checks to ensure they were of sound mind and body, giving up a degree of their freedom and privacy to preserve their independence of mind. It was hard to believe *any* of the Councillors could be induced or blackmailed to turn traitor, not when they lived in a post-scarcity civilisation and any deep dark secrets would have been uncovered long ago. She shuddered as she considered the implications. The attacker must have captured and subverted Councillor Noonan during her flight to Clarke – the subversion nanotech would have been noticed, if she had been infected earlier – and then …

"The attacker deployed a sizable fleet to distract me," Lehman added. "It was quite successful. I was caught by surprise when the Councillor's ship rammed my platform."

Mari nodded, again. A modern starship with a fabber could churn out a cluster of much larger fabbers very quickly, then put together a small fleet of slaved starships … they wouldn't pose any long-term threat to the Confederation, not unless they had modern datacores and weapons, but any lesser civilisation would find itself in serious trouble if it was challenged by such an enemy. A lone planetoid could put together a full-sized battle fleet very quickly and even if its tactics were limited, a result of datacores purposely designed not to develop intelligence, would still have the numbers to crush any opposition with no loss of life. Not human life, anyway. The Confederation did everything it could to avoid killing anyone, but there were limits.

"Quite," Roger agreed. "We went through the recovered data very carefully. Thankfully, the livestream from the sensor network was relayed through a foldspace link to a stealthed sensor datacore some distance from the planet, so we have data records covering the period between Noonan's arrival and the nanotech destroying the sensors themselves. It appears that one Child was kidnapped."

"Pandora," Lehman said. "Her name is Pandora."

Mari leaned forward. "No others?"

"Everyone who was on the planet during the attack has been accounted for," Lehman said. "The last sensor records are badly degraded, but it is clear Pandora was teleported out seconds after the attack began. We traced the teleport back to a starship that vanished into hyperspace moments after the nanotech overwhelmed Councillor Noonan. It's a ship we've seen before."

Mari grimaced. "X."

"Yes," Roger said. "It seems so."

"Odd, for him," Mari said. "Why?"

"We don't know," Roger said.

"We might," Lehman said. "The Children represent many things, from an insight into abilities that may lead to transcendence to a potential weapon against our enemies. We fended off a great many enquiries after the news about Darius broke, and only the fact the Darius Machine was destroyed beyond any hope of repair – past any point of figuring out its secrets very quickly – kept our peers from demanding access to Darius. Or Clarke. We kept the truth about the Children as quiet as possible, but you know how leaky our datanet is. Someone might have figured out the truth and chosen to act decisively, rather than making contact and demanding access to the research project here."

Mari grimaced. Open war amongst post-scarcity societies was rare to the point of non-existence, if only because there was no reason to fight. The galaxy was big enough for a million such societies, and if the galaxy turned out to be too small there was no reason they couldn't send colony missions to the Clouds or Andromeda or one of the countless other galaxies dotting the night sky. The Peacekeepers had simulated such conflicts and noted there was a brutal simplicity about them, although no one knew for sure. The tactics had never been tested in complete unrestricted warfare. But if the Children turned out to be potential weapons …

She felt her mood darken. What would happen then?

"We need to track him down, and quickly," Roger said. "We *have* to recover Pandora."

"Of course," Mari said. The Confederation did not tolerate the abuse of its citizens, but even the most advanced material society known to exist had its limitations. If X was being backed by a peer power, it would be difficult to hold them to account. Better to catch him before he handed his prisoner over to someone else. "But where is he going?"

She shook her head. The galaxy was vast, and two human beings – although she wouldn't have willingly conceded any *humanity* in X – tiny. There was no way to be sure of tracking them down, nothing they could use … certainly, nothing X would overlook. He wasn't a primitive who had no idea hyperspace existed, or that FTL communication was even possible, but a citizen of the Confederation, heir to the most advanced technology in the known galaxy. He might not be able to duplicate top-of-the-range gear, not yet, but he still had a much better idea of what was possible than any primitive race poking its way into space for the first time. And if he was working for a peer power, he wouldn't make any careless mistakes.

"We don't know, but we do have an idea," Lehman said. "Henri has volunteered to accompany you."

Mari hesitated. "How does that help me?"

"The Children share a mental connection," Lehman explained. "It is possible Henri will be able to steer you towards your target."

"And if this is true," Mari mused, "can he not do it already?"

"They have tried, but they are still very drained," Lehman said. "They stopped the nanotech without quite knowing what it was …"

Mari sucked in her breath. "They stopped the nanotech? How?"

"It's hard to say," Lehman admitted, in a tone that suggested he hated admitting ignorance. "The sensors were badly degraded, and they have never been able to … to detect what the Children are doing, when they're doing it. They can track the effects, but not the cause. I think they simply created a telekinetic barrier that prevented the nanotech from spreading."

"Fuck." Mari shook her head in disbelief. "If they can do that …"

She recalled wargames, exercises designed to study how newer and better weaponry performed in combat. They'd concluded that most modern engagements would be little more than trials of strength, mighty starships blasting at each other in a manner that left little room for subtle tactics and one-shot tricks that would be easy to counter, once they'd been seen in action for the first time. The weapons were just too powerful and the defensive fields too comprehensive … but if the Children could reach *through* a defensive screen as though it wasn't there … she felt her heart sink. Stopping rogue nanotech was one thing. If they could take out an entire planetoid through force of mind alone …

"Yes," Lehman said, bluntly. "You see the problem."

He looked down. "The truth is, we don't know what's really going on," he admitted. "The Children are human, to ten decimal places, and what little deviation they show is well within the known limits of human variation … but they have strange powers – *abilities* – that we don't understand. Are they the next step in human evolution? Are they a fifth column, a subtle attack on human society? Or are they nothing more than genetic freaks, no different – at base – from anyone else with genetic modifications spliced into their DNA? And if the news gets out before we have a clear answer to the question …"

"I see your point," Mari said. Some of the possibilities were borderline paranoia, but they weren't wholly unfounded. A person could be infected with subversion nanites and turned into an unknowing spy. They would pass undisturbed through most basic tests because they didn't *know* they were spies. "I'll do my best to bring her back alive."

"And if you can't, she must not be left alive," Lehman cautioned. "Do I make myself clear?"

"Yes, sir," Mari said, grimly. She suspected Lehman had orders – very secret orders – to blow up Clarke himself, if the Children proved to be actively dangerous. "I won't let you down."

"Henri will meet you outside," Lehman told her. "Good luck."

Mari nodded, schooling her face into a blank mask as she stepped out of the tent and looked down towards the shore. The Children – odd, she reflected, to use such a word for a group nearing the age of maturity – looked like any other group of Confederation teenagers living their lives, save for one thing. They were surprisingly quiet, what few words they exchanged almost monosyllabic. She shivered, helplessly, as she realised they were talking, just telepathically. She simply couldn't hear them. It left her feeling oddly excluded, even though she wasn't one of them and she hadn't been a teenager herself for quite some time. It was …

Henri looked up, then hurried over to join her. "Is it time to go?"

Mari looked back at him for a long moment. "My ship isn't a pleasure cruise liner," she cautioned. "I have a fabber and food processor, but living space is cramped and comforts are minimal. You will not have any real space from me, or vice versa, nor will you have any real privacy. If you want to back out, now is your chance."

"Pandora needs us," Henri said. He spoke with all the bravado of a young man just starting his career, unaware – yet – of the true meaning of military service. "I can use VR, can't I?"

"Yeah, but there are limits," Mari said. She suspected a telepath would have problems losing himself completely in the sim. "Like I said, it will not be a pleasure cruise."

Henri nodded. "I understand," he said. "It doesn't matter, as long as we get her back before it is too late."

"If you have anything you want to bring, grab it now," Mari said, as she called her ship into the atmosphere. She doubted there'd be very much. If she was wrong, she'd simply veto whatever he brought. "We'll be boarding in five minutes and leaving in six."

Henri smiled, although there was a worried edge to it. "I'm ready now," he said. "We can go when you like."

"Good," Mari told him. "Because we have no idea how much time we have left."

CHAPTER
THIRTEEN

X studied Pandora thoughtfully, his mind racing.

She was physically in her late teens, although that was largely meaningless. Too many youngsters made themselves look older and prettier than their physical ages, a perverse sign of the immaturity they had yet to overcome; she hadn't taken body-shaping to its extreme, turning herself into a goddess, which suggested a certain level of self-acceptance denied to most teenagers. She was tall and slight, her dark eyes betraying her fear as she looked back at him … he felt a twinge of pleasure, bathing in her fear, even though he worked on a much greater scale than any mere sexual deviant. The idea of hurting just one person wasn't *art*. It was just pointless sadism.

He said nothing, letting the silence grow and lengthen. He'd gone to some pains to test her, carefully trapping her in a set of chains and lockboxes that could only be opened by someone with supernatural powers, or the kind of enhancements that would be impossible to miss. His scan had revealed nothing particularly special about her, certainly nothing that suggested a physical source for her abilities. The files had said as much, but he'd thought it wise to check while she was unconscious. A person who wanted to be normal, and who had mind-reading abilities, might be able to alter minds too. If she could convince the scientists there was nothing different about her, to the point their minds simply skipped over whatever their sensors were actually showing them ... he shrugged, mentally. It didn't look as though she'd been tricking the researchers, intentionally or not. Pity.

She stared at him, her face pale. She'd touched his mind then, touched the sociopathy that was the core of his being. Too many citizens couldn't bring themselves to believe such people existed – and too many others gloried in his art, even as they refused to admit they were very much like him – and she was clearly one of the former. It would take her time to accept the reality, accept he was a real person ... perhaps less time than others, given that she was a mind-reader. She couldn't deny the evidence of her own eyes.

X spoke with quiet amusement. "I should tell you that this starship is completely under my control," he said. "The control datacores are linked to me and me alone. If you make any attempt to take control, the internal defences will knock you out and hold you. If anything happens to me ... well, let us just say there won't be a second chance."

He paused. "If you behave, and cooperate, there's no reason this trip has to be unpleasant. If not ... well, I can keep you under control."

"I got out of your chains," Pandora said. She was trying to be brave, but he could hear the fear in her voice. The fear ... and the isolation. He had figured that there was a limit to how far she could communicate, telepathically, but there had been no way to be sure. They were already a few hundred light years from Clarke, the distance growing wider with every passing second, yet ... he'd taken a few other precautions, just in case. "Take me back home."

X snorted. "No."

"Take me back!"

X felt it, a powerful shuddering compulsion that brushed against the edge of his mind. It was strong and yet unfocused, as if he were a small boat bobbling in the wake of a far larger vessel; it pushed him to do as she wished, yet wasn't strong enough to overcome his free will. He gazed on her with new respect, stroking his chin as he studied her. If she could push him, a free spirit, to obey her ...

"*Take me back!*" Pandora's eyes bored into his. "*Take me back!*"

X stepped forward and slapped her, hard. She stumbled back and collapsed to the floor, a nasty red mark appearing on her face. Physical violence was rare in the Confederation, and very few would think to smack a child. He would bet half his starship that she wasn't used to physical pain, let alone actual danger. The researchers might have poked and prodded at her – the files made very clear they'd brushed against ethical guidelines time and time again – but they hadn't actually struck her. He doubted they'd ever seen the need. The Children might be strange, with unearthly abilities, but they weren't sociopaths. They weren't unwilling to explain their true nature, they just didn't know how.

"Try that again and it won't go well for you," X said. The experience had been a little odd, a torrent of feeling that felt disturbingly alien ... no, not *alien*, simply not part of him. She had tried to steer his thoughts, just like a thought-leader ... the monsters who had inflicted a bitter war on humanity, thousands of years ago. "There will be no further warnings."

Pandora stroked her cheek, her eyes wide. "What do you want with me?"

"For the moment, I want your full cooperation," X said. "And if you want anything to eat, you will cooperate with me now."

He turned and led the way into the next compartment, deliberately exposing his back even as he watched her through the starship's internal sensors. Was she broken? It was hard to tell. She wasn't remotely normal, no matter what his scans indicated. A regular civilian wouldn't be able to stand the idea of being so helpless and alone, but a Peacekeeper could put up a fight ... or watch and wait for the best moment to strike, to kill him or make a bid for freedom. She tottered after him like a dog on a leash, too scared to do anything. For now. X knew he would have to keep an eye on her. He'd done everything he could to secure his ship, but her abilities were a dangerous unknown. It might be better to keep her in stasis until he reached the Life Sphere, yet he needed her awake. It was the only way to run the tests he wanted to try.

The next chamber was a medical lab, with every piece of medical gear a fabber could produce and several he'd obtained through covert contacts with the seedy underside of interstellar civilisation. He heard Pandora draw in her breath as she saw the collection of scanners and smiled inwardly. He hadn't made any attempt to disguise the lab's true purpose, let alone make it comfortable for her. She was far too used to labs and test chambers that looked like spas. He wondered, idly, if that was why the researchers hadn't got anywhere …

"Lie down on the table," he ordered, curtly. "Do I have to tie you down?"

Pandora shook her head as she stumbled to the table and clambered onto it, her every movement betraying her fear and confusion. It would have been alluring if he'd been interested in anything more than his art, he considered, as he slipped the first sensors into place. The researchers hadn't used nanites to explore their bodies, if the reports were to be believed. He'd make up for that lack now. His lips twisted in dark amusement as he considered the possibilities. It would create an interesting ethical dilemma for the researchers if he solved their problem, using blatantly unethical methods. He wondered, idly, how they'd reconcile the answers with the methods used to gain them.

"Hold still," he said. There was no real need for her to do anything of the sort, but he needed to train her into obedience. "Let us see what we see."

He triggered the first set of scans, watching thoughtfully as a three-dimensional image of her body appeared in front of him. Pandora moaned, as if she were in pain, although he was fairly sure she was faking it. The sensors didn't even *touch* their subject as they performed their scans. She appeared to be a fairly normal human female, lacking the tell-tale signs she'd grown up outside the Confederation. Her parents might have been born and bred on Darius, but she had been born after the Darius Machine had been destroyed. Nine months afterwards, according to the files. He had a feeling that wasn't a coincidence.

"Tell me," he said. "Do you remember your parents?"

Pandora glowered at him. "They chose not to stay on Clarke."

X smirked. "Was that what they told you, or was it what you want to believe?"

"They told me they couldn't stay," Pandora said. "They admitted they found us uncomfortable."

X studied her vital signs for a long moment. Interestingly, she didn't appear to be lying ... either to him or herself. And yet, she didn't show any traces of resentment at being abandoned ... odd, for a young human child. X would have expected something more than mild bemusement. It was the first trace of something inhuman about her, something that didn't quite add up. Even in the Confederation, children resented it when their parents had to go away.

He cocked his head. "Why do you think that might be so?"

"We could read their minds," Pandora said. "And they knew it."

X kept her talking as the nanites swarmed through her body, studying her cellular makeup. She genuinely *did* appear to be a pureblood human, although there were some glitches in her DNA that suggested her ancestors had left Earth thousands of years ago, before genetic engineering started purifying the human genome. The files weren't clear on just when Darius had been settled, or why. The planet was so far from Earth he wasn't even sure how the original colony ship had travelled so far. Had someone helped it along the way? The files suggested the Peacekeepers thought so ...

His eyes narrowed. The nanites were dropping out of his network, one by one. It was strange, almost impossible. The nanotech was nothing like the wild swarm he'd unleashed on Clarke. He'd designed them carefully to carry out an invasive examination and nothing else ... and yet they were dying. Interesting. He triggered the sensors and scanned her body again. The nanites were breaking down, their last traces fading into nothingness as they fell into her bloodstream. It made no sense.

"Interesting," he said, out loud. "Do you know what you're doing?"

"I'm lying on my back, stark naked, being examined by a desperate doctor," Pandora said, sarcastically. Her tone was light, but he could hear the fear lingering in her voice. "What are *you* doing?"

"Nothing that need concern you," X told her. Her vitals suggested she was telling the truth – or, at least, she thought she was. Very interesting. Very interesting indeed. If her body was somehow rejecting the nanotech, she wasn't aware of it. "I'm adding to the sum total of human knowledge."

Pandora turned her head to look at him. "Every year, we get a handful of researchers who think that they, and they alone, have the genius insight to determine how we do what we do," she said. "Every year, they come and try their experiments – no matter that they're the same experiments every time – and discover, to their frustration, that they can't crack the mystery so easily. Every year, their thoughts are tinged with bitterness because they're not as smart as they think, and crazy ideas about just what they could discover if they threw aside all ethical restraint and dissected us. Every year ..."

Her lips twisted. "You're not Teufel in disguise, are you?"

X raised an eyebrow. "Teufel?"

"He was one of those doctors," Pandora said. "Nastier than most. He told Professor Exurban that we recognised no rights, because we read minds despite being told we shouldn't, and therefore had no rights of our own. He had a whole series of experiments planned, telling himself it was fine because we weren't quite human. The professor told him to leave the planet at once and not come back. He was a petty, small-minded little person, trapped in his own mind."

"Most people are," X said. He checked the datacore thoughtfully, trying to determine if he'd recovered a list of proposed experiments. It didn't look like it. "If you don't respect others, it is hard to convince them they should respect you."

"But we can't help it," Pandora protested. "Why should we …"

X shrugged. "There have always been obsessive people who throw away all restraint in pursuit of their dream," he said. He supposed it was true of him and his art, as well as Teufel. "And the fact you break the rules just by existing would be galling for them."

He pointed to a small device at the far side of the chamber. "Pick that up with your mind."

Pandora scowled, then did as she was told. X felt ice shivering down his spine as he saw the device wobble into the air. His sensors insisted it was moving of its own accord, yet there was no motive power … nothing that could prove just *how* it was moving. He suddenly felt as dull and stupid as a primitive astronaut, coming face to face with a giant starship lacking rockets or any other obvious drive systems. He could use gravity fields and tractor beams to duplicate the trick, sure, but that would be instantly detectable. Whatever Pandora was doing, it couldn't be detected.

"Interesting," he said, out loud. "Try that device instead."

Pandora lifted it too, without putting the first one down. "I can juggle if you wish …"

"Be quiet." X studied the display for a long moment. Her brain activity was normal, for someone who was effectively a lab rat as well as a prisoner. Suspiciously normal. Was she concealing her true brain activity, or was the whole act so minor her brain didn't respond at all? "Do you know what you are doing?"

"I'm moving two objects with my mind," Pandora said. Her voice was light, betraying no strain. "Can't you see?"

"How are you doing it?" X's eyes bored into hers. "How?"

"I just *do* it," Pandora said. "How do you breathe?"

X scowled. "I know how my lungs work," he said. "I just don't think about breathing."

He felt a surge of frustration as he pushed more sensors into place. No change in her brain activity. No decline in her blood sugar. No suggestion she was doing anything more than lying on the bed, yet ... she was doing something. It was deeply frustrating, if not impossible ... he picked up a brain probe and pressed it against her head. She squeaked and tried to inch away.

"Stay still," he ordered. The nanites couldn't get inside her head. "This might be more revealing ..."

He triggered the probe. A sudden flush of data rushed into the datacore, followed by a surge of pure *panic*. X jumped backwards in shock, letting go of the probe; it retracted safely, even as he fell and hit the deck. He had never been so scared, never. It was ...

Pandora sat upright. X sent a command through his implants to the compartment's security systems. A force field flickered into existence, pushing her back down again. The panic grew stronger, alarms sounding as his devices started to flicker and flare ... he thought he saw, just for a second, a near-invulnerable force shield begin to crack and shatter. The compartment shivered ...

... And then the panic was gone, as if it had never been.

"Stay there," X growled.

"I'm not going anywhere," Pandora managed. She sounded as shaken as himself. "Just ... stop."

X ignored her as he pulled himself to his feet, deeply shaken. The sensors had collected all kinds of data, but his datacores were having very real problems analysing it. Their algorithms insisted the data was clearly in error, and glancing at the live feed he feared they had a point. The data was just … bizarre, as if two plus two was suddenly fifty-nine billion. For a moment, the compartment had been larger – stretched, somehow – and then shrunk to almost nothing. He'd been lucky the safety protocols hadn't triggered, in a desperate bid to contain an explosion that hadn't really taken place. They could have easily killed both himself and his captive, quite by accident.

"For a moment, everything changed," he mused. Pandora broadcasting her fear at him was one thing, but … the incident, whatever it was, was clearly far more than *just* a telepathic broadcast. The simplest explanation was that she'd somehow subverted his sensors and even that wasn't anything like enough to explain the chaos, the moments when the laws of physics seemed to have taken a running jump into sheer insanity. "What were you thinking?"

Pandora glared. "I was thinking you were about to ram your little toy into my brain!"

"And your panic did more than just strike me," X said. He'd had an idea. A wonderful awful idea. "It actually damaged the compartment."

"Oh."

X smirked. "Don't do that again," he added. "You came very close to accidentally killing us both."

Saying it was a risk, but … he doubted she had the nerve to commit suicide. It was unlikely she was backed up. Children rarely were, and Clarke hadn't had the facilities to resurrect a grown adult. Even if she was, would she be the same afterwards? Would her new body have the powers of the old? Or would she be blind, trapped in her own head, for the rest of her life?

He felt his smirk grow wider as his idea took shape and form. It would mean a short delay, but he doubted his clients would mind. His art came first. And who knew? It might give him everything he needed to truly change the universe. If his idea worked … he might not even need to fear Loki.

"You know," he said, "in the wrong hands, abilities like yours could be truly dangerous."

CHAPTER
FOURTEEN

Mari didn't need telepathy to know Henri wasn't impressed with the Archangel's interior.

She tried not to roll her eyes as he made a show of exploring the ship. It was pretty much the finest instrument of destruction in the known galaxy, capable of taking on even a planetoid and coming out ahead, yet the interior resembled a teenager's living suite rather than a starship bridge. There were none of the service droids who could be relied upon to clean up after a real teenager, none of the displays showing everything from live recordings of the latest here-today-gone-tomorrow sense-o-video act to images of interstellar views, naked people or whatever else the modern teenager chose to decorate their private room. There was no holovid bridge, carefully designed to allow dramatic proclamations from the captain and fitted with exploding consoles to add drama – as if the designers had never heard of fuses and circuit breakers. The interior was just a handful of small and rather cramped compartments. The Archangel didn't need anything more.

Henri glanced at her, his eyes wide. "I thought starships were bigger?"

"There are some smaller designs," Mari told him, dryly. The craft Councillor Noonan had used was smaller than the Archangel, designed for hasty conveyance rather than a home for a wandering citizen. They would have to upgrade their security precautions, after losing a councillor in such a manner. "It doesn't need to be anything bigger."

She shrugged at his astonished look. The Archangel's drives, sensors and weapons were carefully built into the hull, and controlled through a combination of direct mental link and datacore subroutines. There was no need to install a manual command and control network – no human ever born could handle such combat *without* a mental link – when losing the datacores would mean certain death. The Peacekeepers had never lost an Archangel in combat, they'd never even come close. Mari hoped it would stay that way, although she feared otherwise. The advanced races, the ones that had seen Archangels in operation, would have put their own models into production by now. If they hadn't come up with something more advanced …

"Take a seat," she ordered, bluntly. There was no need to sit when the ship's internal compensators could easily handle any sort of acceleration, and ensure the crew didn't feel anything, but it was important he listened to her and obeyed. The Archangel wasn't a planetoid or CityShip, with all the space the crew needed to compensate for mistakes and misjudgements, and the slightest mistake could get them both killed. "We'll be taking off in a moment."

She linked her mind into the task force datanet and requested permission to depart, then plotted a course out of the atmosphere and into hyperspace. They didn't have a good idea where X was going, or where he was taking Pandora, although the psychologists and xenospecialists had come up with a list of possible destinations. Mari wasn't convinced they'd put their finger on the right answer. X was a crafty bastard, no doubt about it, and he was working for an unknown alien race. The researchers couldn't tighten their list of possible destinations until they knew which one, and they weren't likely to find out in a hurry. Even the most advanced of the material races would think twice about picking a fight with the Peacekeepers. They'd keep their involvement as quiet as possible.

Henri sat, looking irked. "Can we see outside?"

"In a manner of speaking." Mari sent a command to the chamber's processor, which displayed the live feed from the exterior sensors around them. Henri gasped as the bulkheads seemingly dissolved, realising – a second later – that it was nothing more than a holographic projection, if a disturbingly realistic one. "Let us be off."

She sent another command into the network. The Archangel took off smoothly, the holographic image updating rapidly as the tiny craft flew up and out of the planet's atmosphere. Henri tilted his head from side to side, as if he was trying to feel some hint of acceleration. There was none. The flight was just a little *too* smooth. Mari hid her amusement at his confusion, although the dirty look he shot her suggested he'd sensed it regardless. Most starships and transport pods were designed to give a little hint of acceleration, when the ship got underway, but the Archangel's designers had never seen the need. The pilot was so closely tied into the ship's datanet that they couldn't convince themselves they weren't moving at all.

Her lips twitched. There were people who believed they were trapped in a simulation, a virtual reality so perfect they couldn't find their way out, and others who believed the entire universe was a simulation. Mari had considered it when she'd been younger, and concluded there was no point in worrying about it. If she were trapped, she still had to treat it as real; if the entire universe was a simulation, whoever had crafted it was so far beyond her reach that they might as well not exist. She supposed that explained X and some of his peers. If they believed the universe wasn't real, and nothing they did was real either, they might as well go nuts. What did it matter if they killed or raped or tortured someone who wasn't real? They weren't *real*!

Henri leaned forward. "I can still feel my family."

Mari cocked her head. "Can you send a message to them? Telepathically?"

"Yeah," Henri said. "What do you want me to say?"

"Goodbye, if you haven't already." Mari brought all her sensors online, from the simplest passive devices to the most advanced and complex designs humanity had devised. "Anything you like."

Henri nodded. Mari watched the sensors, sucking in her breath as she saw … nothing. She had believed the reports – she'd scanned every report the researchers had written, from the first encounter with Darius to the disastrous experiment on Clarke – and yet it was hard to convince herself the researchers had drawn a big fat nothing. They could track things smaller than atoms, including nanotech and sub-nanotech, and practically read a person's mind … but they couldn't pick up even a hint of how telepathy worked. Mari would have wondered if it was a complex trick – as technology advanced, the tech to fool it advanced too – if she hadn't scanned the reports covering the brief period when the researchers had tried to convince themselves that the Children *were* tricking them, even though they'd been literal children at the time. They'd gone to huge lengths to disprove the evidence in front of their eyes, only to admit defeat. The Children had abilities and those abilities were real – and inexplicable.

"They say good luck," Henri reported. "When do we go?"

"Now," Mari said. "Remain seated. There may be a slight shock."

Henri frowned. "I thought hyperspace transit was supposed to be smooth."

"How many of your peers have left the system on a hyperspace ship?" Mari split her attention in two, half preparing to leap into FTL and the other half watching Henri through a multitude of sensors. "Just one, Pandora. And she didn't leave willingly."

"It wasn't fair," Henri added. "We all want to explore the universe."

"And when I was young, I wanted to jump into adulthood before I had the maturity to appreciate it," Mari said, dryly. Children weren't stupid, but they were dangerously ignorant. And naive. The downside of growing up in the Confederation was that you didn't learn to be suspicious of a stranger's motives until it was far too late, and not everyone outside the Confederation could be trusted not to take advantage of it. She had had to rescue citizens who had let themselves be lured into a blindingly obvious trap, blindingly obvious to those who had the cynicism to be just a little wary. "How long is your expected lifespan?"

Henri blinked. "Two hundred years, without rejuvenation."

"And right now you're eighteen?" Mari smiled. "You have a long way to go."

She braced herself as hyperspace opened up in front of her, a twisting vortex of light and energy that battered her senses even as she steered her ship into the folded dimension. No one had quite come up with an explanation for hyperspace's existence, with theories ranging from it being a higher dimension to the inevitable result of a starship folding space and time around her hull ... a theory that didn't explain, in her view, how two ships flying in close formation could interact. She knew scientists who spent most of their lives in hyperspace, and others who could barely stand any contact with the alternate dimension. It was ...

Henri made a pained noise. "Ouch."

Mari frowned. "What happened?"

"I'm not sure," Henri said. "I just ... I just felt everything. Everything ... like I was suddenly very aware of the ship around me."

"Interesting." Mari checked her sensors. If anything had happened, it hadn't been recorded. "I wonder if hyperspace somehow enhances your senses. Or extends their range."

Henri closed his eyes. "It's odd," he said. "I can sense the rest of my family, but I can't talk to them."

Mari considered it. They were already seventy light years from Clarke and accelerating rapidly, following the course X had set when his ship had dropped into hyperspace. She would be astonished if they somehow ran him down, if only because changing course the moment you were out of detection range was lesson one in the tactical manual. X hadn't survived so long without being very good at looking after himself, and that meant she might be fifty or sixty light years off course already. Was Henri having trouble keeping in touch with his peers because he was so far from them, or because they were back in realspace? Her mind raced as her sensors struggled to pick up something, anything. Radio waves were picked up and scattered across hyperspace – she had intercepted transmissions from the First Expansion Era, or signals from races that had been and gone before the human race learned to make fire – and it was possible it did the same to telepathy. Who knew?

"We'll see how things go," she said, carrying out a quick scan. There was no sign of any other starships, odd for somewhere so deep in civilised space. She turned off the displays and put the craft through a series of manoeuvres, altering course several times before straightening her flight path out again. "Can you get a sense of direction? Can you point at Clarke?"

Henri glanced at her. "Can I stand?"

"Now? Yes." Mari was surprised he'd asked. Perhaps he was more aware of the realities of spaceflight than she'd thought. "Stand up and point."

She watched as Henri stood, turning in a circle before pointing in precisely the right direction. Mari sucked in her breath. She was flying parallel to Clarke, insofar as the term had any meaning in hyperspace, and if he'd merely pointed towards the rear of the Archangel he would have been pointing in the wrong direction. But he'd got it right … a chill ran down her spine. She was an experienced spacer, and she knew countless Peacekeepers who had been serving for far longer than herself, and yet she couldn't have pointed in the right direction, not without access to a datacore and the live feed from the ship's sensors. It was inexplicable …

Henri looked at her. "We don't mean to scare people."

The earnestness in his voice, surprisingly child-like, left her torn between amusement and dismay. He could read her emotions, he could read her thoughts … she felt a hot flash of anger, even though she knew she had been warned. It was one thing to read about it, quite another to experience it. She understood, now, why so many races had trouble coming to terms with the sheer size and power of the hyper-advanced civilisations surrounding them. They were so advanced their abilities were effectively inexplicable, at least at first. The Children were just the same, a mystery that might never be solved. If the reports from Darius were accurate …

Given time, there is no mystery that cannot be understood, she told herself, firmly. The human race had known FTL travel was possible a long time before it had worked out how to create warp bubbles or open gateways into hyperspace. *We can and we will figure out how their abilities work too.*

"People are often scared of the unknown," Mari said. There were a tiny number of humans who chose to step boldly into the unknown, following invitations left behind by long-gone races, but the vast majority choose to stay in their homes, unwilling to take a risk their forefathers would have regarded as perfectly acceptable. "Or the inexplicable."

She studied him for a long moment, then shook her head. "Can you point to Pandora?"

Henri closed his eyes and turned in a circle again, his hand outstretched … Mari frowned as she checked her datacores, mentally drawing a line through interstellar space. Pandora – and presumably X – was somewhere along a line leading out of the Confederation's territory, although the term had little meaning for a society that didn't depend on planets and stars. She made a mental note to triangulate as soon as possible, to try to get two bearings on the assumption Pandora had to be where the lines met. If she wasn't moving … she felt her frown deepen as she studied the line. There was little along it that caught her eye, certainly nothing of considerable importance.

But that's meaningless, she told herself. *A peer power could hide an entire battle fleet somewhere along that line and we wouldn't have the slightest idea it existed.*

"I can feel her, but I can't reach her," Henri said. The frustration in his voice was evident. He was young, too young to accept that you could do everything right and still lose. "She's out there somewhere and …"

"We will get her back," Mari said, hoping the universe wasn't about to make a liar out of her. She slipped her mind back into the datacore, altering course so they were flying directly along the line. She would pause long enough to triangulate in a few hours, adjusting their course once they had a better idea of Pandora's location. It wasn't a perfect system, and her flight path would become erratic, but it would have to suffice. "He can't be expecting us to be on his tail so quickly."

Henri looked unconvinced. "Why did he even do it? Why take her?"

"Research, I suspect," Mari said. "Maybe not for him, but for his backers."

She scowled. Henri had already displayed inexplicable abilities. She couldn't help finding them worrying, simply because they *were* inexplicable. She supposed it explained some of the reactions to Darius, when the researchers had discovered what looked like real magic. Advanced technology was one thing, but something completely inexplicable – something capable of producing results that defied the laws of physics as humanity knew them – was terrifying. She knew how primitive races reacted to hyperspace weapons – to them, their ships were being destroyed by an enemy they could neither see nor kill – and wondered, numbly, just how the Confederation would react to psychic or magical weapons. Perhaps there was something in humanity that feared the unknown, the thing that defied everything they knew about how the world worked. Perhaps the fears that humanity had laid to rest weren't dead after all, just lurking in the back of the human mind, waiting to come out again.

Henri rubbed his forehead. "But why?"

"You're too young to understand," Mari said. Henri might have grown up on an isolated world, but he had lacked for nothing. The idea of someone killing for food, because the only alternative was starvation, or raping because it was the only way to get sex, was utterly alien to him. The idea some people would do it for fun, commit horrible crimes because it was the only way to get a thrill, was even worse. "Some people hate and fear what they don't understand."

She led the way to a smaller compartment. The automated systems had cleaned the section out, then fabricated and installed a bed, a wash basin and a tiny sonic shower. The chamber was tiny, compared to the average bedroom, but it would have to do. Henri would have to lose himself in VR, if the tiny space started getting to him. The Confederation *could* produce ships and structures that were technically bigger on the inside, but the power demands were staggering even by their standards. It wasn't worth the risk.

Henri looked at her. "How do I sleep alone?"

Mari opened her mouth to give a sharp answer, then closed it as she realised the question was sincere. The reports stated the Children slept together in one huge nest … it sounded like a foretaste of hell for her, but they apparently found it normal.

"You'll have to learn to cope," she said, finally. It was hard not to feel a little sorry for him, but … "Right now, there are no other choices."

Henri nodded, then scowled. "Is there anything I should do, while waiting?"

"Study the files," Mari said. In the flicks, a young student could master everything he needed to know to fly a starship within days, a training montage that somehow left out practically everything. The real universe was rarely so obliging. Henri would need weeks, at best, to learn something useful, and even if he mastered the skills in simulations it would be a far cry from the real world. "Do what you can to prepare yourself. We don't know what we're facing."

Henri nodded, slowly. "Got it."

Mari patted his shoulder. "It does take some getting used to," she said. Her first cruise had been on a Peacekeeper cruiser, and she'd had a much larger cabin all to herself. "But it can be done."

CHAPTER FIFTEEN

Pandora felt torn between moments of boredom and moments of absolute terror.

Her captor was a very persistent researcher, with none of the ethical guidelines honoured by the researchers back on Clarke. He made her do all kinds of things, from demonstrating her telepathy and telekinesis to answering all kinds of questions, while poking and prodding at her in a manner that would make Teufel blanch. She suspected he was trying to slip nanotech into her head to take control of her body, and her abilities, perhaps even to trigger them against her will. She couldn't think of any other explanation for some of his odder acts, or the weirder questions he asked. Or perhaps he was just trying to get on her nerves. It was quite possible. Most of his tests appeared largely pointless.

She gritted her teeth as he pressed another hypospray against her neck, her body shifting uncomfortably as something dangerously cold was injected into her bloodstream. It felt as if her neck had suddenly turned to ice, the sensation spreading through her body as her blood carried it onwards. X bent over her, holding a scanner in one hand; his face, cold and hard, betraying none of his thoughts as he studied the results. Pandora tried to shrink back as he came closer, his scanner brushing against her bare skin. It was hard to keep from recoiling in horror. His thoughts were as cold as his face, his mind coolly assessing her as though she were nothing more than a lab animal. She felt a wave of fear …

Her body tensed. No one had ever hurt her before, not deliberately. She had felt pain – she had stood on sharp objects, and once she'd fallen down a hill – but no one had ever set out to hurt her. The moment when Francis had stood on her foot, quite by accident, hadn't been stained with malice – and she knew it, because she had sensed his horror and guilt even as he'd helped her to recover. X was different. He'd slapped her to put her in her place and it terrified her, even though cold logic insisted he should be scared of her. She had enough power to hurt him, perhaps even to kill him … and yet she knew her every action was being watched by a datacore. If she tried to kill X, she would be unconscious or dead before she could finish the job.

In truth, she wasn't even sure she *could* kill him. She had never hurt anyone before, not ever, and she had no idea what would happen if she tried. She could sense him in a manner he couldn't sense her, and that meant … could she hurt him without feeling his pain? Could she kill him without dying herself? No one had ever died on Clarke, not completely; no one knew what would happen when someone inevitably did. Would the Children feel it …

"Curious," X observed. "You have no biological differences from the average human female."

Pandora snorted. He'd poked and prodded every last inch of her body. He'd injected her with strange compounds, flashed odd little lights in her eyes, taken samples of her blood, urine and stools … crossing the ethical guidelines as if they didn't exist … and found nothing. She didn't know if the researchers had analysed her bodily fluids, but they hadn't found anything either. It was … she wondered, grimly, if he was still trying to come up with something, or if he was torturing her for his own sadistic amusement. It was hard to be sure. She didn't want to touch his mind any closer, even if it was the only way to find out.

"Let us see what this does …"

He pressed another injector against her neck. Pandora felt her thoughts start to fade away, the world shifting around her … she gritted her teeth, trying to bite her lip before it was too late and she drifted into unconsciousness. The injury might let her know how long she'd been asleep … she wasn't sure, in all honesty, just how long it had been since she'd been kidnapped. He'd drugged her time and time again, ruining her sense of time as well as making it hard – almost impossible – to contact her peers. It was as if something was blocking her from making open contact with the nest. She'd thought it impossible. Somehow, he'd cut her off from her peers.

The darkness washed over her, the utter blackness sucking her into its gaping maw. She was asleep. She was dreaming. She knew it, and yet … the universe seemed to be breaking apart around her, as if her mind was standing on very thin ice. *Things* were scrabbling on the far side of the ice, looking for a weak spot they could use to break through … she felt absolute utter terror as she saw them in all their horrific glory, *things* so alien they were beyond her comprehension. One looked at her and the terror grew worse, somehow, her legs shambling into motion even as she couldn't tear her eyes away. The dream made no sense, the world cracking into nothingness. It was hard to open her eyes …

"Interesting," X said. "Very interesting indeed."

Pandora stared at him. Her body was drenched in sweat, her muscles aching as if she'd truly been running from something ghastly, something that was already fading from her mind. It was rare for the Children to have nightmares, but … she swallowed, hard, as something nagged at the back of her mind. Something … something she'd forgotten. X was studying his sensor feeds, his mind sparking with triumph. Pandora felt cold, despite the warm air. He'd found something. It had nearly killed her, but he'd found something.

"You may stand," X told her. The sensors were already

retreating, folding themselves back into their alcoves. "We have learned enough for one session."

Pandora grunted as she forced herself to sit upright. The aching wasn't going away. She looked down and sucked in her breath, noticing the odd little scars all over her body. It looked as if he'd beaten her, yet … somehow she knew it was something different. He turned away, his back to her. A surge of anger shot through her and she lunged …

Her body froze, her muscles locking painfully. She tumbled forward and hit the floor hard enough to hurt, pain searing through her body and banishing all rational thought. She couldn't even scream! X paid her no heed as he finished checking his sensors, as if he hadn't even noticed. She didn't need telepathy to know that wasn't true. He knew what had happened. He didn't even feel amused at her situation, merely … coldly satisfied. She struggled helplessly, her muscles refusing to budge. She wasn't even sure how she was still breathing. It felt as though she was trapped in ice.

"I permitted that, as a demonstration of futility," X said. His mind sparked with amusement, as if there was something funny about the whole situation. "The old jokes are still the best."

Pandora tried to say something – anything – but she couldn't move. The datacore held her firmly in its grip, supplying oxygen to her bloodstream to keep her alive even as it kept the rest of her body helplessly frozen. She couldn't move a muscle, and yet …

"You may do as you please, as long as you remain in this section and make no attempt to escape," X continued. "If you do …"

He shrugged and left the compartment, leaving her alone. The datacore let go of her a second later, her body collapsing into a heap as a second wave of agony shot through her. Pandora felt tears prickling in her eyes as she struggled to banish the pain, to focus her attention on staggering to her feet. It was hard to do anything, but gasp for breath. Every moment caused twinges of pain to dart through her system, an agony she had thought the human race had left in the past. And yet ...

She staggered to her feet, feeling dirty and grimy. X had passed through a sealed hatch ... she wasn't surprised to discover it refused to open for her. The bastard had a whole isolated section of the ship to himself. She tried to reach out with her mind, only to sense nothing. She wasn't sure what he'd done, but it was effective. She was trapped mentally as well as physically. She turned away and slipped into the next room, shaking her head in disbelief as she saw the giant bedroom, complete with a food processor and portable fabber. The hatch on the far side led to a bathroom, as well outfitted as anything she'd seen on Clarke. It was a surprisingly comfortable prison.

The fabber lit up when she touched the terminal. "I want a gun," she said. "With ammunition ..."

There was a faint click. "I'm afraid the fabber is operating under counter-suicide protocols," X's voice said. "You cannot order anything that might prove dangerous to either of us. I suggest you don't try."

Pandora glowered at the fabber. If it was programmed to prevent her from killing herself ... she was sure the programming could be evaded, given time, but she had no idea where to begin. There were horror stories about people who had accidentally ordered something lethal, or somehow reversed the polarity of the neutron flow and created antimatter ... she had no idea how *that* had happened, or why the programmed safeguards hadn't stopped it before it was too late. She tried to think, wishing she'd spent more time poking and prodding at the protocols worked into the fabbers back home. She'd never seen the point of pushing the limits, when it couldn't get her anything she wanted. In hindsight, learning how to work her way around the programming would have been very useful indeed.

She turned and headed into the bathroom, stepping into the shower to wash herself clean. The water was hot and very welcome, she kept running the shower in hopes of using up all the water supplies even though she knew it was probably pointless. The waste water would be cleaned and pumped back into the tanks, and no matter how long she kept the water running it was unlikely to bother him in any way. Hell, he could just mine a passing comet or create water out of pure energy if he ran short. She cursed, tasting her own helplessness as she stepped out of the shower, a drying field sending an uneasy tingle through her body as it lifted every last water droplet from her skin. The fabber refused to give her clothes, but bedding *was* on the menu. She altered the parameters until it gave her a blanket she could turn into a makeshift dress, covering her nakedness. It had never bothered her on Clarke, but now ... it was just another sign of her vulnerability. She wondered if he'd order her to strip naked again.

X said nothing as she ordered herself a meal – the cutlery was plastic, blunt to the point of uselessness – and ate it quickly, experimenting with the limits as much as possible. She couldn't order alcohol, let alone poison, and the system balked at providing her with a frozen leg of lamb. It puzzled her until she realised it could serve as a makeshift club, although she doubted there was any point in keeping it from her. The datacore could and would stop her before she even picked it up, let alone bashed it over his head. She made a mental note to try throwing something at him, as she poked around to see if she could order anything hard enough to do real damage. The protocols were alarmingly good. She couldn't get anything that could be used as a weapon, nor could she find a selection of items she could put together to build something dangerous. She had wondered why X hadn't tied her up, or put her in stasis, but she knew now.

He doesn't need to bother, she thought, numbly. *I'm trapped.*

She clambered into the bed and closed her eyes, trying to reach out with her mind. Her head spun the moment she tried to send her awareness back to Clarke, her own thoughts reflecting back on her as if she were directing them at a mirror. She felt alone, utterly trapped in her own head … a flash of panic shot through her, a sudden thought that he had somehow managed to switch off her abilities. It couldn't be true and yet … she opened her eyes, picked up the remains of her dinner with telekinesis and …

The air hardened around her, again. "I should add, any attempt to use your abilities will be harshly punished," X said. "Don't try."

Pandora groaned as the air let go of her. She was being watched, of course. There could be hundreds of nanotech sensors hidden in the bulkheads, or simply floating through the air … or even in her bloodstream. She had never had any privacy on Clarke, but neither had anyone else. She had never been unaware of her peers, or how much she shared with them and vice verse … she understood, suddenly, why the Children disconcerted the researchers so much. X was watching her, his datacore scanning constantly for any use of her powers, while she couldn't watch him. She was alone, and naked … the sensors could see through the blanket as if she really *was* naked. Every shift in her body, every flicker passing through her mind … he'd see it. For all she knew, he really *was* reading her mind.

It wasn't technically impossible. Just unethical.

She drifted off to sleep, her mind a leaden weight as she fell back into darkness. It was hard to be sure she really was asleep, her mind so confused she thought she was dreaming she was asleep. Her memories spun around in confusion, flickering images of people she knew and loved clashing with faces she didn't know … she cursed, inwardly, as she realised she truly was alone. The nest was hundreds of light years away, if it still existed. X could have destroyed Clarke effortlessly, if he'd wished. It was just … she might be alone. She thought she sensed someone sharing the bed with her, but when she opened her eyes she was alone. She wasn't sure how long she'd slept, or even if she'd slept at all. The terminal refused to tell her anything useful. It wasn't even loaded with games, or VR sims, or something – anything – she could use to distract herself, to forget she was a prisoner.

X's voice crackled through the air. "You will join me in the lab."

Pandora scowled, looking around for a speaker. She saw nothing. "And if I don't?"

There was no answer. Instead, her body started to move of its own accord, walking into the lab. X was standing beside a table, two sealed orbs resting on the top. Pandora felt her body come to a halt, the force that had taken control of her withdrawing as effortlessly as it had come. She gritted her teeth, trying to hide a new wave of helplessness. She'd known, intellectually, that the datacore could puppet her, but she hadn't wanted to believe it. She couldn't help herself now.

X tapped the orbs. "What do you think these are?"

Pandora glowered. She felt too rotten for guessing games. She doubted there was any point ion even trying. "Why don't you tell me?"

The orbs turned transparent. Pandora sucked in her breath as she saw the brains, floating in a translucent liquid. It was a sickening sight, all the more so ... her head spun as she stared at the cloned organs, suddenly convinced she *knew* they were hers. X had taken her blood and used it to clone and force-grow a pair of brains, her brains. It was ...

X passed her a headband. "Put this on."

Pandora wanted to tell him to go to hell, but it was pointless. The datacore would just puppet her again. And again. The headband felt light against her hair, yet there was something about it that pressed against her mind. It felt as if the universe was holding its breath, waiting for something to happen.

"Let us see ..."

Pandora felt a tickle, a moment before a surge of pure terror shot through her. She staggered, feeling warm liquid between her legs; she would have collapsed, again, if the datacore hadn't caught her and kept her upright. The terror vanished as quickly as it had come, replaced by red-hot fury; she lurched forward, intent on wrapping her hands around his neck and squeezing as hard as she could. The urge to murder was overpowering. It was gone too, a second later … she gasped as a wave of pure orgasm ran through her body, her hips spasming around an imaginary penis. She was coming physically and mentally, sharing her lover's sensations …

The feeling vanished too, leaving her cold. And ashamed. She had never felt so ashamed before.

"It's interesting what happens if one tickles the brain's emotional centres," X observed, calmly. "It's quite easy to become lost in the sensation."

Pandora felt her legs buckle. This time, she was allowed to sit down. A handful of drones swooped around, cleaning up the mess. She felt … she couldn't be sure how she felt. If he could make her feel what he liked, he could break her …

"I think we're going to make a piece of art," X told her. The heavy satisfaction in his voice chilled her to the bone. "Shall we see what we can do?"

Pandora shook her head. But she knew it was pointless. He'd already made up his mind.

CHAPTER

Sixteen

It was just a matter of time, according to the Confederation's last survey of the system, before the natives of Jorlem Prime developed warp drive and started to explore the star systems surrounding their homeworld. They had successfully passed through the nuclear age and started their space age, developing colonies right across their star system while researching possible ways to reach the nearest system in a reasonable timeframe; the files stated they'd have warp drive, and be ready for contact, within a decade. The Confederation had already withdrawn most of the observation platforms it had deployed when the system had first been charted, just to make sure the locals didn't discover them, before it was too late. The younger races rarely understood that their older and more mature neighbours needed to keep an eye on them, to ensure they didn't accidentally destroy themselves before they matured and reached for the stars. It would be difficult for such a race to accept the existence of far more advanced races, but it would cope.

X smirked to himself as he guided his ship into the system, his passive sensors soaking in data as he watched for the sensor platforms. There was no reason to fear detection from the locals, and the sensor platform wouldn't be able to summon help in time to keep him from turning the system into a new work of art, but he hadn't remained free for so long through being careless. The locals – the file stated they were an avian race, calling themselves the Jorhasha – were expanding rapidly, driven by a nervous energy the human race had left behind long ago. The Jorhasha knew they had a destiny and couldn't wait to meet it. X supposed they were right. It just wasn't the destiny they had in mind.

His lips twisted as he studied the flow of data. The system was developing rapidly, giant asteroids being pushed into orbit around the homeworld and mined for raw materials for colony ships and exploration vessels. Their industrial base was puny compared to the fabbers on his ship, let alone a planetoid or star-spanning megastructure, but still remarkably advanced for their technical development. The cities on the planet below looked cleaner than they'd ever been, as the governments and corporations moved more and more power plants and factories into orbit, where there was no need to worry about pollution. The files suggested they were moving past the limits of their biology too, their females gaining rights and freedoms as they no longer *had* to remain tied to the nest.

"Got it," he muttered. The Confederation sensor platform was invisible to the locals, but his sensors were far more advanced. It might as well have been broadcasting its location on all frequencies. He took careful aim with his railgun and fired a stream of pellets at near-light speeds. If the Confederation was keeping a real-time eye on the system, it would look like a tragic accident rather than hostile action. "And now, let us see."

He turned back to Pandora. The young girl was lying on the examination table, held in the datacore's cold and merciless grasp. Some people *liked* being controlled, liked the sensation of being at someone else's mercy, but Pandora was clearly not one of them. X wasn't one of the few who liked controlling others either, although he had no qualms about doing it if it was the simplest way to keep her from escaping. Or killing him. X could envisage quite a few ways to use her abilities to hurt or kill him, without alerting the datacore until it was too late. Could she?

"What are you doing?" Pandora's voice was harsh. The drugs were taking their toll, even though there were limits to how much he could give her without risking real harm. Her genetic tweaks were designed to flush intoxicates out of her bloodstream as quickly as possible. "What are you …"

X ignored her as he examined the brain tissue. Pandora could push her emotions at him … and with cloned brain tissues he could boost the effect, even steer it. The abilities didn't seem bound by the inverse square law, which was interesting and very worrying, but … he shrugged and checked the headband. It was easy enough to simulate her brain to produce the right emotions, although it ran the risk of inflicting permanent damage. Thankfully, the cloned brains seemed to pick up most of the strain.

And they're drawing power from somewhere, he mused. It defied belief that a human brain could generate a core tap, a device designed to suck power from hyperspace itself, but … where else could the power be coming from? He'd tried to simulate it and drawn a blank. Half his assessments suggested it was impossible and the other half insisted she would have blown herself and much of a star system to atoms if she'd tried. Core taps were deadly dangerous. *What is she doing?*

"Please," Pandora said. "Don't …"

X keyed a command into the terminal. Her face went red with rage, her body twisting unnaturally as it fought the datacore's control. She wanted him dead and she didn't care if she got killed in the process … not, he knew, that she had enough of a clear head to think so rationally. Her body struggled, the emotion reaching through space and brushing across the planet below. His drones were already in place to record every last detail of the apocalypse to come. It was going to be one hell of a work of art.

He couldn't wait.

***

Junior Flock Leader C'North clacked his beak angrily as he made his way back to the nest, feeling dull resentment and irritation bubbling at the back of his mind. The training program had been expanded to bring in a number of females, because the government wanted to make a big show of how it was opening up opportunities for young females too selfish to find a mate and raise his chicks, and the men who had objected had been told they were no longer welcome to attend unless they begged the females for their forgiveness. It was madness! The females weren't qualified for the program – the males had worked their tails off for their posts, each successful entrant jumping ahead of countless males who hadn't quite made it – and the best anyone could hope for was that they'd wash out very quickly. He knew better. The government would rig the results, put an imperfectly-trained female in command of a spacecraft, and swear blind the disaster had nothing to do with their foolish politics. No doubt they'd find a way to blame it on the males.

The anger burned at his mind as he reached the nest and opened the door. His wife was nowhere to be seen, even though she should be keeping the nest warm and welcoming for him. His anger surged as he strode through the chambers, cursing his mate savagely as he hunted for her. She had a good life – a loving mate who brought home enough money to ensure she could put food on the table – and yet, she couldn't be bothered to stay home? Where was she? His anger bubbled and boiled, overflowing as he heard someone at the door. He hurried down to meet her, his thoughts aflame. Had she been cheating on him? If she had …

She stood just inside the door. She was angry too … why was *she* angry? He heard a distant explosion, and a scream, and paid them no heed. How dare she look him in the eye, as if she were the male and he the female? How dare she …?

He lunged forward, claws extended, as the rage blinded him. She screeched and charged, rather than bowing her neck in submission. The lack of repentance enraged him, all the proof he needed that she was cheating on him. Or something ... his claws tore into her, even as hers slashed deep into him ...

(At some level, he was scared, unsure of what he was doing or why he was so angry. But he was too lost in himself to care.)

***

X watched, feeling the cold satisfaction of an artist watching his artwork take shape, as chaos washed over the alien world.

The rage had been building slowly, but effectively. Bird-like aliens grew angry and infected others with their rage, the madness expanding with ever-greater speed as it raced around the planet. Happy couples tore themselves apart, drivers slammed their cars into pedestrians, policemen and soldiers drew their guns and opened fire, seemingly at random. X was sure there was a pattern, although he couldn't parse it out. Not yet. The first sparks of anger had latched onto real grievances, he guessed, and then exploded outwards as the emotion drove its victims to violence. The Confederation was generally very good at meeting the needs of its people, but it *was* a post-scarcity society. There was enough for everyone. That couldn't be said of the Jorhasha.

His lips twisted as the rage built. Some orbital miners shoved asteroids into the planet's atmosphere, their madness driving them to the point they could no longer think clearly. A world leader was trying to launch a missile strike, although one of his subordinates was refusing to give the authorisation codes the system needed to let the missiles fly. Several others were launching coups on the fly, the different sets of plotters running into each other and opening fire. It was completely and utterly mad. And he loved it.

Pandora's face cleared as he deactivated the headband. Her eyes went wide with horror. It was hard to tell if she was horrified at what she'd been made to feel, or how others had been forced to share her emotion without the restraints, but it hardly mattered. X ignored her as he studied the sensor feed, the rage dying away in places but remaining strong in others. Some victims were collapsing, overcome by the horror of what they'd done; some were still fighting, unwilling to admit that their civilised veneer had been stripped away and the blood-red monster underneath allowed to roam free, with neither conscience nor mercy. The aliens had started beating each other to death with their bare hands …

"You monster," Pandora managed. She could barely talk, her breath coming in fits and starts. Blood trickled down her lip and pooled underneath her head, staining her hair. She'd bittern herself in her desperate desire to be free, to murder him with her bare hands. "You …"

X keyed the keyboard. Pandora's eyes rolled back in her head as a wave of sexual excitement washed over her, the emotion so strong it drove away all conscious thought. He studied her body dispassionately, then turned to study the live feed once again. The Jorhasha were consumed by their own waves of excitement, some couples making out on the bodies of their victims and others – less affected than their peers – being hunted down and raped. X's lips thinned in distaste as the nightmare spread, although he knew the horror was going to destroy what remained of their society. Their orbital infrastructure was already badly damaged. The asteroid impacts had killed hundreds of thousands, perhaps millions. The rest would die soon.

His hands danced over the terminal, simulating wave after wave of different emotions. The planet was overwhelmed by fear and terror, then rage again, then a sense of desperate helplessness that left the survivors unable to move. The drones started reporting odd little glitches, hiccups in the sensor readings that made little sense … he wondered, just for a second, if someone was trying to hunt down his drones, before realising it was impossible. The Jorhasha didn't have the technology to detect his nanotech drones, let alone block their signals. And if the Confederation had tracked him down …

He pulled back, allowing his sensors to roam across the system. The madness was spreading, destroying colonies and spacecraft … he couldn't even *begin* to guess at the death toll. Some deaths were odd: a fusion drive bending and twisting in a way that should have been impossible, even if the crew were suicidal; a colony dome shattering for no apparent reason. He turned his attention back to the planet and sucked in his breath as the sensor readings continued to glitch. It was as if reality itself was breaking down.

"You monster," Pandora breathed. X glanced at her, alarmed. She seemed to be changing, growing bigger … somehow larger than life, even though his sensors insisted she hadn't changed at all. "You …"

A surge of *something* brushed against his mind. The brains amplified it, pushing it across the system. A tidal wave of … X snapped a command and the datacore put Pandora to sleep, shutting down all her higher brain functions long enough to let him rethink his approach. She twitched, as if she was somehow fighting the impossible fight, then relaxed, her face smoothing into an almost child-like peacefulness. X clenched his fist, feeling a flicker of naked anger, then caught himself. The surges of emotions were threatening to overwhelm even him …

He sucked in his breath, again, as the drones started to recover. The planet was devastated. The population either dead or unconscious, bodies lying on the ground as if they were nothing more than puppets whose strings had been cut. The sheer scale of the disaster awed him, even as he sucked in all the data he could for later transmission to the darkweb. Here and there, things had happened that defied analysis. Explosions and disruptions … he blinked at a report that a fusion plant had gone into meltdown, the core sinking deep beneath the earth before coming to a halt. A *fusion* plant? He'd thought that impossible. And yet, it had happened.

"Curious," he mused, deploying more drones. There wasn't much time to get a complete sensor recording, before what remained of the alien civilisation faded away. It would raise all kinds of interesting questions on the darkweb, once it got free. "Very curious."

The scale of his artwork continued to take shape and form in front of him. An entire civilisation gone, the population either dead or wishing they were. It was glorious, a work of art that would be remembered for the rest of time. He reached out and patted Pandora's head, silently thanking her for her involuntary assistance. It wouldn't have been possible without her. The data kept flowing into the datacore, the chronicles of a dying world ... a world that had been forced to destroy himself. His eyes lingered on Pandora's head for a long moment. He cared nothing for her body, but her mind ...? If he could take out a system-wide civilisation with her assistance, what couldn't he do?

He ordered her transferred to a stasis tube, then guided his ship out of the system. There was no way to tell just how far the effects had spread, or who – or what – might have sensed them. If the telepathy moved at the speed of light, it would be years before anyone noticed ... but it moved a great deal faster than that. It was hard to be sure, yet ... judging by the sensor data, the effect had washed across the system virtually instantly. How far had the wave spread? The nearest Confederation outpost was several hundred light years away, according to the last update he'd downloaded, but there could easily be a ship or station that had been left off the charts. Or someone might have noticed the missing sensor platform and sent a starship to investigate. Or ... who knew?

A drone vanished. Two more flickered and died, the odd sensor readings sending a chill down his spine. The landscape below was twisting, becoming something truly alien. He stared for a long moment as several more drones vanished, then snapped a command into the datacore, wheeling around and launching his ship into hyperspace. The last of the sensor records could be collected later, then carefully edited and uploaded into the darkweb. Or …

He stared at the cloned brains, thinking hard. How far could he go? The idea of a tidal wave of madness overrunning a Ring or a Sphere was awesome and yet … could he make it work? Or … what else could he do? If he used the cloned brains to manipulate the world around him … what if … what if *that* was how it worked? The researchers had assumed telepathy and telekinesis involved moving things with one's mind, but what if it was *really* the manipulation of reality itself? What if …?

That might explain some of the oddities, he thought. *She doesn't seem to have any more trouble lifting heavier weights than lighter ones … why? Could it be as simple as manipulating something on a display?*

The thought seemed odd and yet … it hung in his mind, refusing to go away. Humans had been building tools to manipulate the world around them for centuries. Perhaps – just perhaps – the Darius Children didn't need tools, they just used their brains. And their parents, the ones who had cast magic spells and turned their enemies into frogs … perhaps their abilities were being boosted by the Darius Machine. It was impossible. It violated all kinds of physical laws. And yet it had happened, until the machine had been destroyed. The Confederation had the sensor records to prove magic and magicians had really existed.

And the Children had different abilities. They'd been raised after the machine's destruction. They had inherited something from their parents … psi powers? Was it possible that magic was just boosted psi? And that meant …

His lips curved into a smile. *If the Darius Machine can boost their powers, I can do it too. And who knows what I can do then? What can I do to reality itself?*

CHAPTER SEVENTEEN

Henri screamed.

Mari started awake as the datanet alarms howled through her head, rolling out of bed and hurrying to the hatch. Henri could not be hurt, he couldn't be in any danger … they were in hyperspace, inside one of the most powerful starships in the known galaxy. He couldn't have been attacked and yet … the hatch to his bedroom opened, revealing Henri bucking and kicking and trying to claw his eyes out. Mari grabbed him instinctively, gritting her teeth as he struggled against her. He was strong. If her body hadn't been enhanced long ago, she would have had real trouble holding him still. Even so, it was still a struggle.

"Hold still," she said, ordering the internal sensors to scan his body. Was she wrong? Was he under some kind of mental attack? Or was he trapped in a nightmare? He didn't look to have been using the VR headset, let alone accessed a bootleg or black-market simulation without all the safety features, but … she held him as he staggered, wondering if she should sedate him. "It's alright. I've got you."

Henri turned, his eyes wide and staring as they met hers. He looked blank, as if he didn't know who she was. Mari would have smiled – there had been quite a few times in her career when she'd gone home with a stranger, for a quick fuck and a hasty departure the morning after – if it hadn't been so serious. She'd never freaked out so badly after a night of passion and she didn't recall any of her partners doing the same, not ever. Henri was young, she reminded herself, and lacked the maturity of an older person. He didn't even have the experience of someone raised in the Greater Confederation.

He sagged. "I felt anger and fear … *her* anger and fear," he said. His voice was weak, as if he could barely keep himself together. Mari gently lowered him onto the bed, keeping a sharp eye on him, then ordered a cup of hot milk from the food processor. "He did something to her and …"

His eyes narrowed. "It's still going on. I can feel it."

He pointed. Mari felt her eyes narrow as she ran a projection. If he was pointing to Pandora's current position, they were slightly off course … her mood darkened as she realised there was a primitive world – interplanetary spaceflight, but not yet interstellar – further down the line. *Right* down the line. The odds of *that* were incredibly small, given how tiny even something the size of a planet was on an interstellar scale. It was too great a coincidence to ignore, not when X was involved. He'd come very close to ruining one primitive world – the last update suggested he'd succeeded, with the entire population trapped in full-blown Outside Context Problem derangement – and there was another along his flight path. She hadn't considered it as a possible destination, but perhaps that had been a mistake. He might assume he was too far from Clarke to be traced.

"I'm altering course," she said, sending the command to the datacore. "If he's there, we'll get him."

"And Pandora," Henri said. "You have to get her back."

Mari nodded, watching as he staggered to his feet. His body was as fit and healthy as the average teenager, although she couldn't help noting that he'd avoided the urge to give himself muscles on his muscles or craft a face so handsome it was literally inhuman. She cringed inwardly at the remembrance of how *she'd* been as a teen, experimenting with everything from changing the size of her breasts to fiddling with her gender and sexuality. She was surprised Henri had avoided it, although it was possible being part of the nest ensured he knew he was accepted for who and what he was, rather than needing to change himself to fit in. She almost envied him, despite the downsides of sharing his thoughts and feelings. Who knew? If all humans *knew* what their peers were feeling, there would be far fewer misunderstandings that could lead to grudges, resentments, and all-out war.

"Go shower," she advised. The automated systems were already scrubbing the sweat out of the compartments, but a shower would make him feel better. "I'll be in the main cabin."

Henri managed a tight smile. "Not the bridge?"

Mari shrugged, then headed outside. She'd said it before, time and time again. There was no *need* for a bridge on a starship that was controlled by a combination of neural links and datacores. Henri had been watching too many dramas, no doubt ones set in the era before the Confederation had risen to unite the human race and take it to the next level of development. She rolled her eyes at the thought – the people who romanticised the past had never lived in it – as she downloaded the files on Jorlem Prime. They were too advanced to be ignored and too primitive to be contacted, at least until they broke the FTL barrier and started advancing into interstellar space. The idea of X playing his games with them was maddening. They would have been safer, perversely, if their tech had been a little *less* advanced.

She sent a quick update back to Clarke, then leaned back in her chair and waited as the Archangel neared the system. Henri joined her, looking pale and holding a second mug of hot milk as though it was a life preserver. Mari nodded to him, then linked her mind back into the datacores, her awareness expanding to sweep across the entire system. There were no contacts in hyperspace, not even a lone ship running as fast as it could. She hoped that meant X was still somewhere within the system, watching the chaos from a safe distance. His ship might be mindbogglingly advanced, to the natives, but to her it was just another target. She'd be on top of him before he knew she was there.

"Here we go," she said. The eerie lights of hyperspace twisted and gave way to the inky darkness of realspace, broken only by the blue-green orb dead ahead of her. "I … shit!"

The system unfolded in front of her, so utterly chaotic her datacores couldn't even begin to process what she was seeing. The entire system seemed to be locked in war, a war so erratic that even her best tactical analysis programs couldn't tell who was on what side … or even if there *were* sides. Ships and weapons seemed to switch sides at random, some even shooting *themselves* … her eyes narrowed, sharply, as she noted the sheer number of incidents that defied any sort of rational explanation. She could understand how a fusion torch could be used as a weapon – humans had done the same, back in the early days of spaceflight – but how the hell had a spacecraft managed to warp and twist the flame to melt their own hull? It was impossible …

Henri whimpered. "He did something to them."

Mari nodded as her awareness swept over the high orbitals. The last survey had noted thirty-seven asteroids orbiting the planet, all gone. The rest of the orbiting infrastructure hadn't survived either, leaving nothing but wreckage drifting down into the gravity well. It looked like a bizarre combination of enemy action and suicide, as if the entire system had suddenly been overwhelmed by a death wish. Ice ran through her blood as she realised that might well have been *exactly* what had happened. It was rare for mimetic warfare to spread so quickly, even on a modern datanet, but the Children were telepathic. If X had somehow forced Pandora to broadcast her feelings into the entire system …

"She wouldn't do that," Henri said.

Mari felt a hot flash of anger. He was reading her mind!

"I don't think he gave her a choice," she said, suppressing her irritation. "Given the right sort of technology, and a complete lack of scruples, he could make her do almost anything."

Her mind raced, considering possibilities that went so far beyond the ethical they were almost unthinkable. Could X subvert Pandora's mind completely? Or trap her in a VR sim so perfect she would react as though it were real? Or simply plant post-hypnotic suggestions into her mind? Or ... given time, it was possible to reprogram anyone. Hell, for all she knew, he'd copied his own personality and played it into her mind, overwriting her personality with his own. The technique wasn't reliable, even with modern technology, but he could just keep trying until it worked. Or he accidentally blew himself up.

"She's not here," Henri said. "I can't feel her thoughts."

Mari nodded curtly, allowing her awareness to sweep over the planet. It was ... it was incredibly wrong, as if someone had taken a dozen different disasters on a dozen different alternate worlds and merged them together into one nightmarish whole. There were cities that had been torn apart by violence, millions upon millions of dead bodies lying on the ground, torn and mutilated; there were disasters, both natural and man-made, that made no sense. A fusion core had gone into meltdown ... how the hell had that even happened? She checked to be sure it wasn't a fission core and drew a blank. It had definitely been a fusion core ...

The list of irregularities grew longer, and stranger. An asteroid had come down in the ocean, drenching the landmass on one side of the water ... but not the other. Some cities were gone completely, others warped and twisted into nightmares that didn't obey the laws of physics. Her onboard sensors noted that one city was roughly twenty kilometres from one side to the other, but her drones insisted the city was several times bigger – as if it were bigger on the inside – and failed completely when she directed them to fly into the city. She cursed under her breath. Foldspace and quantum communications links were supposed to be impossible to track, let alone jam, but no matter what she tried the drones didn't last past the moment they crossed the city limits. She launched a second spread with radio and laser communications packages, yet they failed too. The radio channels were teeming with howling nonsense. She couldn't stand to listen to it.

"I don't understand," she said. "What did he make her *do*?"

The list of irregularities just got longer. Time itself appeared to have run backwards in some places, in others there were fewer – or no – bodies. A city that had been noted by the last survey team was missing, missing so completely she wondered if it had ever existed. Her sensors tracked a number of animals that had died out a long time before the planet had given birth to an intelligent race, their existence only uncovered through archaeological research; there was no way the locals could have resurrected them, not without the technology the Confederation had used to bring the dinosaurs back to life. The ones she was seeing shouldn't have existed at all.

"Something bad," Henri said. He sounded shaky, as if whatever had happened was making him physically unwell. She checked his life signs and swore under her breath. There was no physical trace of anything wrong, but his vital signs were dangerously unstable, his heart beating so rapidly it would have burst without the genetic tweaks that were part of his heritage. He was afraid, afraid in a manner so primal it was poisoning the air around him. "It all feels wrong …"

Mari pulled back from the planet as the last of her drones failed. Whatever was loose on the surface reminded her of Darius, although in a very different way. Her scans suggested that most of the planet's remaining infrastructure was offline, disabled in a manner that chilled her to the bone. Once, centuries ago, an elder race had trapped a particularly dangerous race on its homeworld, using an energy absorption field to prevent the development of anything more dangerous than steam power, something the locals had never been able to understand, let alone counter. The Confederation *had* understood both the technology and the motives behind it, but this … this was inexplicable. It was as if parts of reality itself had been damaged beyond repair.

Henri swallowed, hard. "Is there anyone still alive?"

"I don't know." Mari had the most advanced sensors in the known galaxy at her disposal, but it was hard to locate any survivors. The results were odd, as if someone was deliberately screwing with her readings … odd in more ways than one, when they were doing it in a manner calculated to tip her off. Most spoofing tech worked by putting together a convincing image, accurate in all details but one. This was … weird. There was no discernible pattern. "I can't find anyone."

Her heart clenched as she took in the scale of the atrocity. There had been billions of natives, scattered across the system. They had had a bright future ahead of them, as they cracked the secret of warp drive and began their expansion into interstellar space. And X had destroyed them … she swallowed hard as she realised it was out of character for him. He could have killed everyone on Parnassus in an instant, if he had wished, but instead he'd set out to convince them to destroy themselves. It had taken years and he'd come very close to success … here, he'd blotted out billions of lives, in a terrifyingly short space of time. A species that successfully climbed into interplanetary space was effectively immortal, once it no longer had all of its eggs in one basket. If nothing else, it took time to hunt down each and every colony and slaughter their populations. But that certainty was gone now …

"Point me to her," she ordered, tersely. There was nothing she could do for the locals, if indeed there were any left. They had to get moving and fast, to track down X before he did it again. "Now."

Henri's hand shook as he pointed. Mari sent a command into the datacore and the ship flew back into hyperspace, pushing the drives to the limit. X couldn't be that far ahead of them, she was sure. If the atrocity had begun when Henri awoke, screaming ... she ran through the calculations, considering all the possible vectors. Four hours. He had four hours lead on them. At most ... her heart sank as she considered the implications. The disaster – the atrocity – had taken less than four hours to sweep across the system. Whatever he'd done, it had moved faster than the speed of light. If it took over four hours to send a radio signal from Earth to Pluto ... no, judging from the damage she'd seen, the signal had propagated instantly. Or close enough to instant to make no difference.

It couldn't have spread beyond the system limits, she thought. *Could it?*

She cursed under her breath as she sent a pair of signals to the peacekeepers, requesting an immediate recovery mission to Jorlem Prime and a check on every known inhabited world near the system. The closest was nine light years away, a planet settled by a race that had never quite grown accustomed to the idea there was *anyone* more powerful than themselves, something she supposed they had in common with the human race. They tended to resent any contact with the Confederation ... not, she supposed, that the Peacekeepers had to make contact to determine if their system had been effected. A single fly-through under stealth would make it clear.

Henri looked worried as she disconnected from the datacore. "If there's no one left alive ..."

"There will be someone," Mari said, with a confidence she didn't feel. A telepathic command to commit suicide would be quite bad enough, but whatever X had unleashed had damaged reality itself. It was completely without precedent, so bad none of her projections were anything more than guesswork. The sheer scale of the disaster made a full-scale interplanetary war look insignificant. "The Peacekeepers know what to look for …"

And how important it is to keep the planet under quarantine, she added, silently. *Whatever he unleashed, we don't want it to spread.*

She scowled, recalling an old – very old – story about a fool of a boy who had owned a star. A small star, but a star nonetheless … a star he had kept feeding with raw matter until it had turned into a black hole and destroyed the entire world. Not a real threat in the Confederation, where gravity beams could direct a microscopic black hole into interstellar space, but lethal to a pre-space world. She wasn't sure why the concept had popped into her head, except … the boy in the story hadn't understood what he was doing, or the danger of the forces he was playing with so casually. What sort of idiots would let someone like that have his very own star? What next? Antimatter? Or whatever power had been used by the Darius Machine?

The locals thought it was magic, she mused. *Was that a way of naming something they didn't understand, or was it a way to actually* limit *their understanding of how the world actually worked?*

She frowned as she accessed the files again. She'd grown up in a universe where shouting bastardised words in a long forgotten tongue was pointless, but if that hadn't been true … if the world had changed, when she chanted certain words, what would she have learnt from the experience? And what conclusions would she have drawn?

Henri cleared his throat. "What now?"

"Now?" Mari eyed him thoughtfully. He hadn't grasped the full scale of the atrocity. It wasn't uncommon, but still … "We track them down, get her back and kill him. Before he does anything worse."

"Like what?"

"I don't know," Mari said. "But *he* does."

CHAPTER EIGHTEEN

Pandora felt sick.

It was something unknown to her, unknown to anyone who wasn't a purebred human. There was little she could eat that would make her feel unwell, nor would her tweaked body be unduly bothered by changes in velocity or localised twists in the gravity field. And yet … she felt sick, a churning rolling sensation that washed through her mind, a feeling that she was nauseous on a level so deep and primal she could never rid herself of it. It was impossible to think clearly, impossible to move … she was drowning in her own mind, pulled down by something so vile she could feel it pervading her every thought … she knew, somehow, that she was trapped, held in place on the very verge of drowning. Or death. It was impossible. It was impossible …

And yet, it was happening.

She jerked awake a moment later, sitting upright in the tube and dry retching painfully. There was nothing in her stomach, nothing to throw up … she knew, without knowing *how* she knew, that the nausea had nothing to do with her stomach, but something worse. Something part of her … she doubled over, the compartment seeming to spin around her. It was just … wrong.

"Interesting," X said.

Pandora felt a surge of pure anger, an emotion so

strong it felt almost alien. She had never felt anything so intense on Clarke, even when she and her peers had gone through puberty and they'd discovered the joys of sex. She wanted him dead. She wanted to reach out with her mind, with the telekinesis that had effortlessly picked up and carried objects far larger than a single human, and crush him like a bug. The air rippled around her before the thought could lend itself to action, a grim reminder the datacore was watching. She wouldn't be able to crush him before it stunned her.

"You were in stasis," X said. "And yet, you were awake and aware."

He cocked his head. "How much do you recall?"

Pandora scowled. "I thought that was impossible."

X's eyes gleamed. "It should have been. You should have been in stasis, utterly frozen, unaware of time passing. And yet, despite the stasis field, you were clearly awake and aware on some level. What do you recall?"

"It was a nightmare," Pandora said, shortly. If she had been in stasis ... how could she be both in stasis and out of it? It wasn't as if she had been in cryogenic suspension, her mind held in a dreaming web while her body waited to be taken out and brought back to life. "I don't recall much beyond ..."

Her stomach heaved. "You destroyed an entire world!"

"You make it sound like a bad thing," X said, dispassionately. It wasn't a joke. He genuinely believed it. "Their lives are meaningless on a cosmic scale, while their deaths taught me many interesting things about how your powers truly work."

"Abilities," Pandora snapped. "How many did you kill?"

X shrugged. "Their files insisted there were around nine billion sentients in the system. All dead."

Pandora couldn't wrap her head around the sheer scale of the atrocity. It was ... she swallowed hard, recalling history lessons about people who had denied the horrors of the Nazis, the Righteous Minds, the Thule ... and many others, nightmares the human race tried to forget.

Some had denied for political reasons, but others had done so because they simply couldn't grasp the sheer scale. The death of one person was a tragedy, the death of millions was just a statistic. It was impossible to wrap her head around the idea of so many people as anything other than a number, let alone grasp the meaning of their lives … and their deaths. It was …

"You are a monster," she said.

X shrugged, again. "You can take care of yourself, I am sure," he said. "We'll do a few more experiments later."

He turned and left the compartment, the hatch hissing closed behind him. Pandora forced herself to stand and clamber out of the stasis tube, eyeing the autodoc with some interest before tapping a command into the terminal. The system was locked. Of course. She leaned against the tube for a long moment, cursing her wobbly legs, then staggered to the other hatch. It hissed open as she approached, revealing her bedroom. The sense of being watched grew stronger as she walked to the food processor and ordered water, then something to eat. X had eyes everywhere, of course. She wondered, sourly, if he was learning anything useful from her bedroom habits. It wasn't impossible. There were datacore analysis programs that could learn a great deal about someone by studying their habits, no matter what they were. She made a mental note to do things that were a little out of character, just to confuse him. It might not work, but she couldn't think of anything else …

It hit her a moment later, the tidal wave of emotion driving her to her knees. A race had died, screaming in horror, because he'd used her abilities to broadcast her feelings right across the system. It should have been impossible – she had been able to feel her peers' emotions, yet she'd never mistaken them for her own – but it had happened. Flickers of memory, images she'd tried to block out of her mind, clashing impressions of a world dying in a manner horrific beyond words. The impressions were jarring, human features contrasting oddly with humanoid forms that were very far from human, but … how far had the effect spread? She didn't know, couldn't even guess at the answer. It was unthinkable.

She closed her eyes for a long moment, too drained even to cry. X was a sociopath. To him, no one else was quite real. Even *she* was an object in his view, too minor to be of any real importance beyond what he could get for her. But to her, the aliens had been real. They had lived and laughed, loved and cried, their minds understandable even as their bodies had been different enough to make them seem inhuman. She knew that if she'd met them mind-to-mind, they would have been friendly … there would have been no distraction caused by physical forms. It would have been …

It wasn't going to happen. They were all dead.

Pandora rubbed her eyes, feeling … too drained to feel anything. Except … there was something scratching at the back of her mind, something pressing lightly against her mentality. She had the sudden mental impression of a mouse on the far side of a wall, scratching the plaster for weak spots while watching and waiting for the cat …

… She recoiled, her mind slamming back into her body without any real awareness it had been somewhere else. She found herself lying on the deck, her eyes open and yet unseeing … she blinked hard, catching her hands as they reached for her eyes. She wasn't sure what had happened, or why, but … she no longer felt safe. She laughed at herself a moment later. She hadn't been safe since X had killed at least three people and kidnapped her.

The professors can be resurrected, she thought. Professor Exurban would have backed himself up, she was sure, and Peter would have been strongly urged to do it himself. They'd be lacking some memories, when their recordings were played into a clone body, but at least they'd be alive. Probably. Centuries of philosophical arguing over the question of whether or not a cloned and resurrected personality was the same person as the original had never produced any definite answers, and there was little hope it ever would, yet ... she felt her heart sink. *The aliens he killed will never live again.*

She forced herself to stand up and finish her meal, then make her way to the bathroom as her mind puzzled over just what had happened in the stasis tube. X was right. She should have been suspended in a moment of time, her thoughts as unmoving as the rest of her. She'd read stories of people who had gone into suspension for a century or two, moving forward in time to see how the galaxy had changed. They had never been aware of time passing, and rightly so. But she had been aware, in a sense. It made no sense. She washed thoughtfully, then clambered into bed. She was bone-wrenchingly tired and yet sleep didn't come easily, not after everything she'd done. It hadn't been her fault and yet ...

Her dreams were nightmares, visions of alien lives that had been snuffed out by a rogue human sociopath. Aliens in human form, living and dying ... she swallowed hard, aware she was dreaming, as she realised the rage had fed on thoughts and feelings already there. It was no consolation. Few of the Darius Children ever lost themselves so completely to their emotions – she couldn't help thinking she'd given an entire planet a childish temper tantrum – because their feelings were public, and could be addressed. The aliens had been overwhelmed so quickly that they hadn't stood a chance. Guilt gnawed at her as she saw the memories of a young female – a young girl – who had been looking forward to a life of sexual equality, without the chains that had bound her mother and grandmother ... dead now. An older man's memories brushed against hers. He had been restrictive, from her point of view, and yet he'd been a person. He hadn't deserved to die.

She tossed and turned, feeling torn between horror and the sense she was on the cusp of a breakthrough. The pattern nagged at her mind, something she was seeing – sensing – without quite understanding. It was weird and inhuman and yet ... it was there. It was ...

The rage spread in patterns, she thought. Horror

washed through her, again, as she realised the true scale of the disaster. *It spread into minds with latent telepathic abilities and used them to amplify them.*

It was impossible to be sure, but she knew she was right. It was …

A shiver ran through the air, a wave of coldness that jerked her out of her nightmare. "You may awake," X's voice said. It was so close that she thought, for a horrified moment, that he was right next to her. "We have much to discuss."

"Oh." Pandora forced herself to sit up and look around. The chamber was empty. The voice was coming from a terminal. And yet, she still felt as though he was looking over her shoulder. "We do, do we?"

There was no answer. She sat back in bed, crossing her arms under her breasts, and gritted her teeth. If he wanted her, he could damn well *make* her come to him. Nothing happened. She forced herself to wait, something she knew was her weakness. There had been very little, in her early life, she'd needed to wait for … except freedom. She stood a moment later and made her way out of the chamber, picking up and pulling on a robe in passing. Nakedness didn't bother her, but … she had no idea what he might have in store for her.

X was sitting in his research lab, drinking from a cup. Pandora could smell the alcohol as she entered, although it wasn't much of a danger to someone who presumably had the same genetic tweaks as herself. He could drink a wine so strong it was practically nothing more than alcohol without suffering any ill-effects, unless he chose to feel them. She gritted her teeth as she took the proffered chair, wondering if he was trying to mess with her mind. The fact he wasn't playing power games wasn't a good sign. It suggested he felt very secure in himself.

And he's right, she reflected. She wasn't sure how long she'd spent on his ship – it was hard to get a real sense of time, and the datacore refused to tell her anything useful – but she hadn't been able to figure out a way to kill him or take control without being killed herself. She told herself she wouldn't mind if they died together, although it wasn't wholly true, yet ... it was unlikely she could kill him before the datacore got her. And he probably had himself backed up too. *He has me in the palm of his hand.*

"You didn't have a restful night," X observed. "What did you dream?"

Pandora kept her face blank. He was monitoring her body ... she wondered, numbly, if he'd shot nanotech into her bloodstream or inserted a regulatory implant into her cortex ... or something, anything, that would let him monitor her emotional state. The bastard didn't see any need to be bound by the normal moral constraints ... hell, for all she knew, he'd already copied her personality, downloaded it into a datacore, and torn her thoughts and memories to bits. It was unethical beyond words, but a man who had sentenced an entire intelligent race to death was unlikely to care about ethics.

"I saw the dead and dying," she said, bluntly. She kept her insight to herself. "All killed. By you."

"A work of art," X breathed. The surge of emotion from him was soft and warm and welcoming and *completely* at odds with the horror he'd unleashed. Human emotions could be mixed and contradictory, yet ... she gritted her teeth. It was a seduction, intentional or not. He was trying to convince her that he'd done the right thing ... the hell of it, she thought, was that he wasn't actually trying. It was how he truly felt. "The art will live on forever."

Pandora shook her head. "You're mad."

"There are worlds out there that are completely dead, trapped like flies in amber in a moment of timeless wonder," X told her. "They are *completely* dead, drained of every last flicker of life, so completely drained there is *nothing* left on those worlds. Not even a single microbe. And those worlds will be circling those stars for centuries, utterly unchanging. Works of art."

"No," Pandora said. Some instinct was telling her he was wrong, and not for the reason she thought. She kept that to herself too. "How many did you kill?"

X shrugged, as if the topic bored him. "Answer me a question. Why are some of the records from Clarke so weird?"

Pandora shrugged back, affecting an air she *knew* irritated the researchers. "Because you don't understand the key to putting them together?"

X smiled. "I think I do have the key."

"Really?" Pandora felt a flicker of alarm. "You think you can succeed where the greatest minds in the Confederation have failed?"

She'd hoped to irritate him, just a little. But it didn't work.

"The records show you lifting small weights with your minds, easily," X said. "When you lift bigger weights, you have trouble … or do you? The records suggest that you have more problems when you can see the weight …"

"We know that," Pandora said. "That's not exactly new."

X cocked his head. "Why is it that you have more trouble when you *can* see what you're doing?"

Pandora considered it for a long moment. It made little sense. Not being able to see where she was going could end with her walking off a cliff or straight into a wall, but not being able to *see* the weight she was trying to lift somehow made it easier to lift it? The oddity had been noted before, yet … no one had managed to explain it. It was just one of many.

"Tell me," X said. "What do you do? When you use your telekinesis, what do you do?"

"I lift something with my mind," Pandora said. She had said it before, to researchers who had wondered if she was playing dumb. It had annoyed her at first, if only because trying to explain how her abilities worked was like trying to explain how she breathed. She just *did*. "That's how it works."

"Is it?" X leaned forward. "How does that work?"

He shrugged. "Logically, you should have the same level of difficulty with two objects that weigh the same, even if you can't see one of them," he said. "Why isn't that true?"

"If we knew, we would be a great deal happier," Pandora snarled.

X ignored her tone. "Imagine I have a cat in a box. You can't see the cat. Is the cat alive, or dead, or somewhere in between?"

"I have no idea," Pandora said, dryly. She had the odd sensation his thoughts were going in precisely the *right* direction. "What does a possibly-dead cat have to do with me?"

"The cat's status remains indeterminate until you open the box and look at it," X said. "The quantum wavefront doesn't collapse into something real until you look, binding it to reality."

"And ...?"

"I think the researchers approached your abilities from precisely the wrong direction," X told her. "They thought of them as ... extra arms and legs, things you can use to manipulate the world around you, when instead they affect reality itself."

Pandora felt ice prickling down her spine. "And your point is?"

"On Darius, sorcerers transformed people into animals and objects, and then back again," X said. "Impossible, right? What happens to the rest of the mass? Where does it hide? Why does it come back? Why does it even fall into the same pattern? And why does the transformed person, with a brain incapable of hosting human thought patterns, still have a human brain? It's ... magic."

His eyes gleamed. "But all is explained if your power is *really* tampering with reality itself."

Pandora shivered. "And ..."

"And I think I have had an idea," X said. "A wonderful idea."

CHAPTER NINETEEN

In a galaxy of wonders, the Life Sphere stood out.

No one knew who had built it, but they had clearly been masters of their art. The Life Sphere was a colossal structure, a Dyson Sphere on an unimaginable scale, constructed around not one but two stars, both carefully restructured to ensure they would keep burning brightly for millions of years to come. The shell itself was oddly fractal, the giant plates crafted to orbit the stars and the installations in the barycentre without completely enclosing and hiding the stars; the plates so vast they had gravity fields of their own, each one with a different biosphere. The Builders had taken samples from countless worlds – some identified, others still a mystery – and seeded them across the sphere, creating a realm suitable for nearly every known form of intelligent life, from humans and humanoids to things that dwelled within gas giants or the airless vastness of interstellar space. They hadn't brought any intelligent life, as far as anyone could tell. The inhabitants had arrived later, after the Builders had passed on. They had been welcome.

The Confederation had been perplexed, when it had first discovered the Life Sphere, to note that the giant megastructure was ruled by an AI that was both incredibly powerful and yet disturbingly primitive. It didn't seem inclined to interfere in matters that didn't threaten the sphere itself, nor to be anything other than a distant observer of matters within the sphere, yet it had welcomed successive arrivals of settlers and colonists, helping them to find places to set up their new homes, and aided them to integrate with their neighbours. A handful of races had attempted to seize the Sphere from time to time, only to discover that the AI was perfectly capable of defending itself and – afterwards – that it was better to leave the Life Sphere as neutral ground. It was a place to trade, a place open to all who could reach it; a place where secret negotiations could be conducted, and the last survivors of doomed races spend the rest of their lives. The datanet teemed with conspiracy theories about the true purpose of the Life Sphere, from interstellar diplomacy to secretive voyeurism, but nothing had ever been established. The Life Sphere had been in existence millions of years before humanity and it would likely be around for millions of years after humanity passed on.

X couldn't help feeling a flicker of awe as his ship dropped out of hyperspace, on the edge of the powerful hyperspatial currents surrounding the system. FTL travel was strictly forbidden within the region, and anyone who tried was attacked by hyperspace cannons of immense power, a reasonable precaution given the dangers of a lone starship slamming into the sphere at several times the speed of light. It was big enough to be seen with the naked eye, glowing faintly even though logically the entire structure should have been as dark and silent as the grave. Hundreds of starships – some human, some very inhuman – orbited the megastructure, or made their way in and out of the interior. The sheer scale of the sphere was mindboggling. The nearest entrance – a chink of light, dead ahead of his ship – looked small, but it was easily large enough to accommodate a whole *fleet* of planetoids. It was true, he reflected, that the sphere was 'just' a shell enclosing a pair of stars, and an incomplete shell at that, yet it was still an astonishing accomplishment. Even for him.

His mind raced as the ship fell into line, making its way

towards the entrance. There was little in the way of traffic control, beyond a handful of stations controlled by races living on the nearest plates of the sphere. The AI didn't seem inclined to intervene unless the visitors did something that threatened the sphere itself, a surprisingly high bar to clear. X had no idea what the Builders had used to build the shell, but it was tough enough to shrug off an antimatter strike. He kept the thought to himself as the line moved closer to the entrance, his eyes flickering over the nearest ships. Were they dangerous? Did they know who he was? Or …

Pandora stepped into the compartment and stopped, dead, as she saw the holographic display. X glanced at her, wondering if someone of her limited experience could truly comprehend what she was seeing. The sheer immensity of the Life Sphere was just … All she was seeing, without knowing it, was a tiny fraction of the whole, a skin cell belonging to something much larger than herself. The Confederation had built a handful of Dyson Spheres of its own, but none had encompassed more than a single star. The Life Sphere was an order of magnitude more impressive. And utterly alien.

She shot him a sharp look. "Are you planning to destroy that too?"

X smiled, as if the thought hadn't occurred to him. It had, although he had no idea what the AI would do if he started playing his usual games. The majority of civilisations on the sphere – some isolated, some integrated – belonged to races more than advanced enough to notice and counter his subtle manipulations, although in his experience that didn't mean they were any better prepared to face them. *That* only came with maturity, and far too many races lacked the maturity they needed to walk into the future. Perhaps the AI would do nothing, or perhaps it would swat his ship like a bug. It was impossible to tell. The Confederation had accessed records from races that had been living in the sphere for millions of years, and noted all the times the AI had intervened, but there was little in the way of a consistent pattern. The only thing they all had in common was that there was a threat to the sphere itself.

"We'll see," he said. He waved a hand at the display. "How does it make you feel?"

Pandora shook her head. "It's just … there."

X shrugged. "There are people who think the Builders enjoy watching the immigrants, as if their lives are just a giant soap opera," he said. "And others that think the sphere is just the bait to lure intelligent life forms into their clutches. What do *you* believe?"

"I don't have an opinion," Pandora said, stiffly. "Why did you bring me here?"

"All in good time," X told her. "All in good time."

He leaned back as the starship passed through the entrance, the horizon shifting weirdly as the interior of the sphere blotted out the night sky. The entrance looked tiny to the naked eye, and disturbingly thin, but it was still big enough for an entire fleet to pass through in relative safety. He spotted a number of structures that had clearly been added to the gate by some later settler, their spacedock looking crude and unfinished compared to the disturbing smoothness of the sphere; he wondered, despite himself, if there would be a price to pay, one day, for making so free with the sphere. The original owners might want their property back, if they ever returned.

The sphere unfolded in front of him, a megastructure so vast it was hard to even *begin* to grasp it all. The plates themselves, surrounded by a swarm of space stations, starships, and everything a civilisation needed, on a scale that would awe even the Confederation. There were megastructures within the megastructure, stations so large they could pass for planets and gas giants floating around the system as though they *were* planets. His communications node reported an endless barrage of signals, everything from friendly invites – some races enjoyed meeting newcomers – to datanet spam, advertising products and services from the comprehensible to the bizarre. It was hard to believe no one had ever cleaned up the local datanet, but it was such an old system it was probably beyond repair. It was a miniature representation of the Galactic Net, both isolated and yet part of something greater.

Pandora sounded faint. "How many people *live* here?"

"Millions. Billions. Quadrillions. Quintillions." X essayed a black joke, "I may have to make up some new numbers."

"Really."

X shrugged. "The average Confederation Dyson Sphere holds around five or six quintillion humans," he said, thoughtfully. The population density could be several orders of magnitude higher without pushing the ecosystem to breaking point. "The largest known to exist is supposed to host fifty quadrillion, although it is difficult to be sure because the builders of *that* sphere tolerate a population density high enough to drive humans mad. Here? I don't think anyone has ever managed to carry out a proper census, certainly not one that can be considered reliable. The total could be anything from several quintillion all the way up to several million quadrillions. We may never know."

Pandora sagged. "It feels ... wrong."

X raised his eyebrows. "As though we are being watched?"

He smiled at her expression. He'd spent the last two days testing her and she *always* knew when she was being watched, even if she didn't know *how* she knew. She had tried to hide it, but the sensors he'd had watching her couldn't be fooled so easily. Oddly, the surveillance system – a range of devices, from primitive cameras to hyper-advanced nanotech spies – watched her all the time, but she only reacted when he accessed the live feed personally. She didn't seem to notice when he accessed the recordings, as long as they weren't close to real time. It was interesting that she *did* notice a time delay of a few seconds ...

Which confirms my theory, he told himself. *Her abilities react to the quantum foam itself.*

His lips twisted. The observer affected the observed ...

it was why so many research stations were designed to make it hard, if not impossible, for the observed to realise they *were* being watched. He'd gone to some trouble to eliminate *everything* that should have given her a clue, only to discover she could still tell when she was being watched. It should have been impossible, yet … perhaps she could sense his eyes when he looked through the sensors, as if he were breathing on the back of her neck. It was happening. There was no point in trying to doubt it. He needed to figure out how to take advantage of it.

"So," Pandora said. "Why are we here?"

X ignored her as they glided further into the sphere, practically crawling towards a giant station that looked to have been put together from the remnants of countless alien starships. He wondered if they'd been abandoned long ago and dragged into the structure, or had originally been crewed by society's rejects and only later become part of the galaxy's black market. The Confederation had been founded on the principle of making sure everyone had everything they needed – and a post-scarcity society could meet every need its citizens had and then some – but other civilisations were not so enlightened, even if they were a technological match for humanity. He could name a dozen hyper-capitalist races, their languages shaped by corporate jargon that puzzled the universal translators, and others who gloried in their conquests and loudly insisted the weak had to be destroyed, for the good of the universe. His lips twisted darkly as he recalled the latter. It was funny how they changed their tune, when they came face to face with someone far more powerful than themselves. Their devotion to their ideals rarely lasted past that point.

Pandora glanced at him. "What's so funny?"

X smirked. "You can't read my thoughts?"

"I try not to," Pandora said. She held herself bravely, but X could hear the fear in her voice. His sensors picked up on it too. "What's so funny?"

"The big secret of the universe," X said. He made a show of whispering. "There is *always* someone bigger."

Pandora flinched, as if he'd slapped her. Again. "The Confederation is big …"

"Yes," X agreed. "And if we run into someone bigger, our fleets will be nothing more than scrap metal."

"No."

"Yes," X mocked. "There were hundreds of thousands, perhaps millions, of warships fighting the interstellar wars. Enough firepower to vaporise planets, or even snuff out stars. How long do you think those fleets, if they were gathered in one place, would last against a single modern starship?"

"Not long," Pandora guessed.

"Seconds," X agreed. "Maybe a few minutes, if the modern ship doesn't *want* to slaughter millions of crew who can neither see their enemy nor strike back. We're at the top of the galactic power structure, the most advanced material civilisation known to exist or have ever existed, and yet … there is always something bigger."

He turned his attention back to the alien structure. It was growing rapidly, a mishmash of ships thrown together seemingly at random. There were ships that appeared to have been welded to their neighbours and others that looked completely isolated, although that meant little when teleporters could be used to move around the structure. He keyed his console, transmitting the IFF code Loki had given him. It took surprisingly long before there was a response, welcoming him to the station and pointing him to a docking port. He wasn't fool enough to take his entire ship so close. If the aliens decided to cover their tracks by killing him, he had no intention of making it easy for them by taking his ship into point-blank range.

"Let's go."

Pandora's voice shook. "You don't have to hand me over to them," she said. She'd clearly been reading his mind, or the surrounding quantum foam. It might very well be the same thing, if his theory was correct. "I'll do anything …"

"On your feet," X ordered. He signalled the datacore at

the same time. It took control of her body, directing her to stand in a jerky, almost robotic, manner. "Let us be off."

He could *feel* her anger and helpless rage poisoning the air as he led the way down to the shuttlebay. He'd never cared for shuttles that lacked FTL drives, if only because they were easy targets for most advanced races, but right now there was little choice. He activated a direct foldspace link, constantly backing himself up, as he stepped into the shuttlebay itself, then directed her to sit down. Her eyes glared daggers at him as her body betrayed her, steered by an external force. X almost smiled. In a sense, her body was an apt metaphor for the Confederation itself. The average citizen had access to wealth and resources on a scale their ancestors would have found unimaginable, but they were controlled by forces beyond their ken. Pandora knew it. She could feel her body moving to the beat of an unseen drummer. Others were not so lucky. They couldn't see the bars of their cage.

X could. It was why he had chosen to leave.

The shuttle wobbled slightly as it lifted from the deck, then flew through the forcefield and out into open space. The control blinked a warning, the local command network was trying to take control of the craft. Not an unexpected precaution and fairly common, but still irritating. X allowed it, bracing himself as the alien structure came closer. Up close, the sheer age of the starships was all too evident. They looked as if they'd been drifting in the void for thousands of years.

Reality flickered, as if the universe itself was shifting. X *felt* it.

"Calm yourself," he ordered, without looking round. He had considered simply knocking her out, but he wanted to know how she'd react to the sphere. That might have been a mistake. "I don't want to shut you down completely, but I will if I have to."

There was a long, eerie pause. The shuttle's internal sensors twitched, sounding so many contradictory alarms that the self-checking systems joined the frenzy, insisting the sensors *had* to be in error. X braced himself, ready to shut her down, before the effects faded away. The data was hastily relayed back to his ship. It was proof, if he needed it, that his theory was correct.

The shuttle flew into what had once been a cargo hold and was now a makeshift shuttlebay, landing neatly on the metal deck. A forcefield flickered into existence behind them, an oddly primitive arrangement for such an advanced structure. A modern starship was perfectly capable of projecting a forcefield that would allow shuttles to pass whole keeping the atmosphere safely inside. Pandora whimpered. X ignored her as the shuttlebay slowly pressurised, the sensors reporting the air was safe to breathe. *That* was a relief. It suggested the buyers knew how to keep a human alive.

He stood as the hatch opened, Pandora following like a puppet on a string. The air smelt of nothing, a very specific nothing that suggested it had been carefully cleansed to remove any betraying emissions. A hatch on the far side of the chamber hissed open a moment later, revealing the buyers. X sucked in his breath. He'd expected to face one race, one of humanity's more covert antagonists … instead, there were three. Three buyers, three different races …

Pandora swallowed, and spat as the force holding her body weakened. X almost felt sorry for her. She had never met a single alien before, an experience that could be disconcerting even if the meeting was held under carefully-controlled conditions. It wasn't easy to cope with a being that wasn't remotely human, let alone three *different* beings. Even *he* felt some qualms as the buyers advanced.

Her voice was weak. Faded. "What is this place?"

X allowed himself a smile. "This is a research lab," he said. It was true, as far as it went. Not very far. "And it is also an auction house. You will be tested, then sold to the highest bidder."

CHAPTER TWENTY

Pandora struggled, helplessly, as the aliens advanced.

There were three of them, utterly alien. A giant spider-like creature, with tentacles and mandibles that sent chills down her spine; a sluggish creature that looked like a moving pile of slime, growing manipulators out of its oozing body to handle everything from a terminal to a device she guessed was a weapon. She recalled covering both in her lessons, covering alien entities from the primitive to the terrifyingly advanced, but she'd never seen either race in person. The third was humanoid and yet managed, with a weirdly thin body, a bulging head and giant inky-dark eyes, to be the strangest of all. Her head spun as she eyed the creature. It appeared to be naked, as far as she could tell, but there was no hint of sexual organs or gender. It's body was a smooth grey, unbroken by orifices and undaunted by age. She didn't recall seeing anything like it, in the files, but it's mere presence bothered her on a very primal level. She had the oddest feeling humanity had encountered the race before, a long time before it climbed into the stars and left the darkness behind.

"The payment has been made," the spider said. It spoke through a voder, the voice stripped of all emotion. The race called itself something humans couldn't even begin to pronounce, Pandora recalled, and was fully a technological equal to the Confederation. Contact had been limited, from what she'd read. They found humans as disturbing as humans found them. "You may surrender your test subject and leave."

"I thank you," X said. He sounded unbothered by the three aliens. Pandora wondered, sourly, if he was an alien himself. It would certainly suit her to believe he was an outsider, rather than one of the worst monsters the human race had ever produced. "I do trust you will have fun with her."

Pandora's body jerked as he passed the control terminal to the grey alien. She gritted her teeth mentally, struggling against the invisible bonds, hoping and praying the aliens intended to reward X as a traitor deserved. The two races she knew might be dangerously advanced, but the human race had the numbers. They were risking war by purchasing her from her kidnapper and they had to know it, although … she felt her heart sink. The galaxy was a vast place, so vast that even the Life Sphere was tiny. The Peacekeepers could look for the rest of time and never come close to finding her.

She found herself walking forward, beside the grey alien. It moved in a manner that was somehow *more* alien than its companions, its arms and legs bending in odd and unpredictable directions. She wondered, as the hatch slammed closed behind them, if it was some manner of artificial being. Humans had spent thousands of years improving themselves, but they still had sexual organs and orifices to eat and expel waste; the grey alien didn't seem to have a rear, let alone an anus or anything other than two large eyes and a tiny mouth. It wasn't impossible. There were quite a few races who had been uplifted by long-gone patrons and then left on their own when their creators went elsewhere. And this one certainly felt eerie …

The air shifted as they passed through more hatches, the crude systems contrasting oddly with the hyper-advanced technology that had built the sphere. Her nostrils wrinkled as she smelled a handful of scents, some alien and others disturbingly familiar. She hoped her biology could adapt to whatever was in the air, if the aliens didn't breath a standard atmosphere mix. They didn't look like methane breathers, but it was impossible to be sure. The genetic tweaks in her body could handle a different oxygen level, yet there were limits. Her captors could kill her entirely by accident.

She kept walking, passing through a maze of corridors that had clearly been designed for different races. Some were tall and thin, others low and wide … the hatches were strange, as if the designers had been trying to accommodate as many races as possible. The bulkheads varied between spotless and scarred, some marked by rust and others covered in a blackish material she feared might be mould. It gave her an odd sensation, when she looked at it, and it took her a few moments to realise why. It looked like the nanotech X had used to attack Clarke and kidnap her.

A wave of despair washed over her as they walked onwards. She was utterly alone, countless light-years from friendly space. Her mind hurt every time she tried to contact the nest, leaving her without even a vague sense it still existed. X had deployed nanotech … had he turned the entire planet into grey goo, or simply dropped enough antimatter to turn the world into nothing more than a cluster of radioactive asteroids, or even snuffed out the sun? She didn't know and yet she feared the worst. If she were alone in the universe, effectively unique, she would fetch a much higher price at the coming auction.

She plodded on, trying to look around as they steered her into the lab. There was no sign of anyone else, not even a single lone alien. The entire complex felt deserted and yet … she thought she could sense someone watching her, unseen eyes studying her with a cold calculating gaze. It was hard to be sure. The aliens forced her to walk into the centre of the chamber, then left her standing there as they talked. She couldn't make out the words. It sounded like one of the trade languages, artificial tongues created to facilitate communication between different races, but she didn't know it. She cursed mentally as the implications sank in. If she didn't know how to speak to the locals, how could she get back home even if she managed to escape?

Her body jerked again, then walked through a hatch and into a smaller chamber. A weird-looking cross structure greeted her, surrounded by more of the grey aliens. It puzzled her for a long moment, before she realised – too late – that it was an examination table. Her body kept moving, clambering up and onto the structure; the grey aliens snapped manacles around her wrists and ankles, then altered the table's position until she was lying flat on her back. A flicker of light danced over her body, tickling her. Her outfit fell to pieces, leaving her naked. The grey aliens showed no reaction as they worked, moving in eerie unison. A chill ran down her spine. It reminded her of the nest.

She gritted her teeth and reached out carefully with her mind, trying to ignore the towering pieces of utterly alien machinery being pulled into view. The grey aliens were driven by *some* kind of telepathic field – she couldn't tell if they were individuals, a hive mind or biological robots – that felt as alien as their faces, a whispering that was completely beyond her understanding. It felt as if ... it was different, somehow. A flash of disappointment ran through her. She had always thought she'd be able to touch alien minds as easily as their human counterparts.

Her body twitched again, the controlling force letting her go. She tested the bonds as subtly as she could and discovered, not to her surprise, that they were unbreakable. The grey aliens kept fussing around her, their fingers brushing against her bare skin in ways that sent shivers down her spine. There didn't seem to be any purpose to their touches, unless they were gauging her reactions. She turned her head and saw the other two aliens, standing by the wall and staring at her. She thought. The spider had eyeballs on stalks, some seeming to be peering in her direction, and it was impossible to tell with the slug. How did it even see? A sense of perception? Or ... something akin to astral projection? If ...

She reached out again and brushed her mind against the slug's. A torrent of thoughts and feelings overwhelmed her, so different and yet so familiar. It was strange. She had seen the world through the eyes of her peers, male and female alike, but this ... a strange thrill ran through her. The researchers had speculated that all intelligent life was the same deep down, once the chains of their biology were removed, and Pandora thought she knew – now – that they'd been right. She had nothing in common with the slug, and yet she did.

The torrent of thoughts and feelings grew stronger. It had been hard to understand how Henri had felt, when he had played with his penis, but Henri had practically been identical to her and the slug ... was not. The alien was alien, driven by a biology she knew little about. And yet ... the more she made contact, the more she saw within the alien mind. A hint, a worry ...

She forced herself to speak. "Why have you brought me here? What do you want?"

The aliens didn't answer, not verbally, but the question brought the answer into the forefront of their minds. They were scared, badly so, of something called the quantum foam and humanity's new ability to manipulate it. It was something so fearsome that they were prepared to risk war with the human race, just to nip it in the bud. She didn't understand. It was a theoretical danger and yet it was also very real. She wanted to ask more questions, to trick them into thinking of the answers, but the grey aliens were pushing more machinery into place. A wave of warmth ran through her body as they turned on their machine, followed by a burst of pain. She felt as if every last atom of her body was on fire, the pain so absolute she couldn't think clearly. Her mind ran away ...

... And found itself in a dark chamber.

Pandora felt her mind spin. Where was she? Had she somehow teleported out? Escaped? No. She could feel her body, writhing in agony ... she'd somehow left her body behind, protecting her mind from the onslaught the only way she could. She had withdrawn from reality itself

... and she wasn't alone. There was something behind her. She could *feel* it. Him.

She turned, slowly. The presence moved too, remaining behind her. She could *feel* it breathing down her neck, something she couldn't see and yet knew all too well was there. It was ...

"Who are you?" Pandora's voice felt weak, even to her. "Why can't I see your face?"

"You couldn't see my face," a voice said, quietly. It seemed to come from all around her. "It would shatter your mind."

The world turned white. Pandora squeezed her eyes shut as the light burned into her eyes, burned into her very soul, even as she felt the world twisting around her, reshaping it into something she could handle. Her eyes snapped open a second later, revealing a simple office ... Professor Gerang's office, right down to the comfortable armchairs, the tea set on the table and the aroma of freshly-baked biscuits in the air. One of the chairs was empty. The other was occupied by ... she thought, for a crazy moment, it *was* Professor Gerang, but the more she looked the more she knew it was something very different. Very inhuman. The face was just something thrown over the true self, the smile on the face of the tiger. The professor's features became more and more indistinct, the more she looked at them. It was impossible to see him clearly.

"Who ... what ... are you?"

"Now, that's not very polite," the figure said. The voice was surprisingly animated, as if there were levels to the tone she couldn't quite here. "Did you say that, the first time you encountered a non-human intelligence?"

"I didn't, until today," Pandora said, trying to reach out with her mind. The entity was a brooding presence: huge beyond comprehension, solid and yet composed of hundreds of thousands of components that blended together to form one whole. "And you have been reading my mind."

"I haven't, actually," the figure said. There was a hint

of a smile as Pandora waved a hand at the fake office, built from her memories. "I really haven't."

The smile grew wider. "Call me Loki, if you like. The old jokes are still the best."

Pandora shivered, despite the warmth. The name meant nothing to her, and yet she had the oddest feeling it really *should*. She didn't know why. One of the Children was called Luke, and there'd been a researcher called Saki ... somehow, she didn't think *that* was why the name was so familiar. It was ... something old, something buried so deeply in humanity's racial memory that it was all but forgotten, save for a flicker of naked fear.

Loki leaned forward. "Tea?"

"Is it real?" Pandora recalled the tea the professor had served, very much an acquired taste. "Is it?"

"Yes. No. Does it matter?" Loki shrugged. "Reality is a very flexible thing, as you are coming to realise."

"X said my abilities tampered with reality itself," Pandora said. A thought crossed her mind. "You didn't read my thoughts to get this ... this place. You read reality itself."

"Yes," Loki said. "I drew a mental picture and reality drew it for me. Or maybe it was the other way round. Or both."

Pandora scowled as she sat down. The armchair *felt* real. "Do you *have* to talk in riddles?"

"Could you explain a starship to an ant?" Loki passed her a cup of tea. "Could you explain the colour blue to a man born blind?"

Pandora took a sip. It tasted perfect, just right. Too perfect. She closed her eyes and reached out with her mind, trying to understand just where she was. She'd thought it a VR sim or a perceptual reality ... and in a sense, that was *exactly* what it was, only one born out of reality itself. A sub-universe, only one created in the real universe ... no, it was both part of reality and something altogether different. Her eyes widened, just slightly, as her awareness drifted towards Loki. The humanoid form in front of her was little more than a protuberance, a tiny fraction of the whole extended from some unknowable higher dimension into the material world. It was an iceberg … she felt cold as she realised Loki had been pulling the strings all along, steering X into kidnapping and delivering her to her new captors. It had been him all along.

"You brought me here," she snarled, opening her eyes. Loki no longer looked *remotely* like the kindly professor she'd known, his face too … *real* … for her to get a good look at it. She felt as if his mere presence was pressing down on her, a light so bright she wanted to turn away. "Why?"

Outrage ran through her. "He killed millions! Billions! For you!"

"A minor matter," Loki said. The dispassion in his voice was worse than X's glee over his brand new work of art, a nightmarish structure built on the corpse of an entire sentiment race. "It is all for the greater good."

"The greater good?" Pandora stared. She had always been told that an advanced life form would be capable of empathy, yet … "Why? What is the point?"

Loki seemed to lean forward, his presence looming even though his body didn't move. "I am helping to push the human race, and everyone else, in the right direction," he said. The sheer assurance in his tone was shocking. "The greater good must be served, above all else."

Pandora swallowed. "And the greater good is served by killing billions?"

"Your Confederation made the decision to avoid contacting newborn races until they developed warp drive, and started to expand into interstellar space," Loki said, as if they were debating a minor point of law instead of the destruction of billions of lives. "In doing so, you chose not to assist primitive races as they developed technology, condemning trillions to die of disease and injury, injuries that your people regard as fads and fetishes rather than serious matters, and to let them die in wars or unjust societies rather than helping them out. You could have made contact with Parnassus or Jorlem Prime long ago, uplifting them to your level. Instead, you let them struggle and die."

"That's different," Pandora argued. "If they were introduced to the Confederation, it would destroy them. The cultural inferiority complex would shatter their minds and …"

"And so you leave them to suffer," Loki said. "For the greater good."

He pointed a finger at the wall, which was slowly blurring into an inky mass. "Seven hundred light years away, as we speak, a male is being beaten to death by his wife, because her society treats males as property. Nine thousand light years away, a species is on the verge of dying out because a radical faction released a virus they thought wouldn't affect them, because they were convinced of their genetic superiority. A universe of horrors you could avert, and yet you do nothing. For the greater good."

Pandora shook her head. "It isn't like that …"

"No," Loki agreed. "It's worse."

The office came apart, shattering into atoms. Loki was gone. Pandora felt her mind spin, her body reaching up to draw her back down, the pain tearing through her soul a moment later. She opened her mouth to scream, her eyes meeting a grey alien's dark orbs and recoiling in shock. There was nothing human there, just a cold dispassionate determination to undercover the truth and …

And Loki was watching. She could *feel* him.

The pain grew worse, daggers stabbing deep into her soul. She blacked out.

CHAPTER
TWENTY-ONE

"Do you want to have sex with me?"

Mari blinked at the question, honestly shocked. Henri had spent the last two days moping, accessing VR sims or trying to sleep in between pointing Mari towards Pandora so she could adjust her course accordingly. Mari hadn't minded, in all honesty. She had never been particularly sociable and cared little for the relationships that so delighted her peers, to the point she was quite satisfied with the occasional tryst during downtime, or a few hours with a sexbot or even immersing herself in an erotic VR sim. Henri wasn't bad company – she had had worse guests on her ship – but she had no objections to him keeping himself to himself.

And to be honest, she'd never considered having sex with him.

He was old enough – true – and handsome ... but he lacked the maturity of someone with a few more decades of experience, the understanding the relationship wouldn't last forever no matter how intense it felt. Mari mentally cringed every time she recalled *her* teenage years, the belief her first partner would remain hers forever followed by tears when she realised that wasn't remotely true, and silently thanked the universe that she had grown old enough to understand that nothing truly lasted. What was a handsome face and a perfect body, weighed against an older man who could have all those for the asking *and* had the maturity to understand their relationship would never last? Perhaps if he'd had a few more years of lived experience …

She frowned, inwardly. "What sort of question is that?"

Henri looked irked, although the irritation didn't seem directed at her. "The kind I wouldn't normally have to ask," he said, sourly. "I know if someone is interested …"

Mari snorted. There was a fashion, amongst youngsters in their second or third decades, to wear bracelets signifying everything from relationship statuses to gender preferences and just how far they were prepared to go for pleasure. They could state what they enjoyed, everything from vanilla sex to heavy metal bondage or mental domination, secure in the knowledge they'd have no trouble meeting someone who shared the same tastes. She supposed the Children had an even easier time of it, given their awareness of each other's thoughts and feelings. Henri would know if his peers wanted to have sex or not, and he wouldn't need to waste his time on courtship. It would be … she wasn't sure. She liked the idea of plain speaking, or of *knowing* without speaking, but she also liked her privacy.

"You're too young for me," she said, finally. She doubted Henri was particularly interested in *her*, although his mental abilities probably meant he really *did* see her as a person as well as an attractive body. Maybe not the latter. She had tweaked her body with an eye to her duties, rather than attracting potential lovers, and if there had been anyone else on the ship he would probably not have looked twice at her. "And we have a job to do."

"We're still following her," Henri said. "What'll we do until we find them?"

Mari shrugged. "We have a job to do," she repeated. She'd been checking her files, trying to determine where X might take Pandora. Did he *know* he was being followed? He had taken out the sensor platform keeping an eye on Jorlem Prime, which would certainly attract attention even if the Peacekeepers didn't know who had killed the platform or why, and it was vaguely possible *someone* would have followed him from the dead world. She still didn't know why he'd fled Parnassus so quickly, before she could bring him to justice. "There isn't time for fun and games."

Henri looked down. "But ..."

"You're young," Mari said, dryly. She recalled being a teenager with painful clarity, her thoughts lingering on the exact moment sex had turned from something disgusting beyond words – her parents had done *that?* How *could* they? – to something she and her peers had sought with a passion their younger selves would have thought shocking. "I know you feel deprived, but ... go enjoy a VR sim."

"It isn't real," Henri said. "You don't feel the other person."

Mari had to smile. She'd never considered *that* implication. A VR touchy-feelie could convince someone they *were* having sex in real life, but they weren't designed for telepaths. Henri wouldn't be able to convince himself his partner was real ... she supposed he'd have the same problem with a sexbot, no matter how carefully it was designed and programmed. Not that most took them seriously, anyway. The programmers often came across as teenage virgins and the less said about their dialogue the better.

She considered it, briefly. Sex was a learned skill and it had taken her time to learn how to please her first partners, just as they'd needed time to learn how to make her body sing. Henri would have an unfair advantage. He'd *know* what she liked; he'd know what made her feel naughty, or awkward, or disgusted. If he hurt her, he'd know before she could even grunt in pain. It would be a fascinating experience, and perhaps ironically disappointing for him. She wouldn't be able to tell what *he* was feeling.

Her lips twisted. Henri was a teenage boy. He'd be satisfied with practically anything.

"No," she said, finally. It was tempting, but it wouldn't end well. "We have a job to do."

Henri looked morose. "That's the third time you've said that."

"Is it?" Mari pretended to be surprised. "Why are you counting?"

"I just …" Henri shook his head. "It's easier on Clarke."

"You knew the job was dangerous when you took it," Mari said, bluntly. The danger wasn't the real problem. It was the cramped confines, so tiny compared to a planetoid or even a real planet. "I'm sorry your quarters are not living up to your standards, but …"

Henri looked down. "How long can he keep running?"

Mari had no answer. There were a multitude of possible destinations along their flight path, including several more primitive worlds. She had signalled for backup, asking for Peacekeeper cruisers to be redirected to cover possible targets, but she feared the cruisers wouldn't get there in time and even if they did, could they stop an attack that shattered reality itself? The recovery team that was scanning Jorlem Prime, hunting desperately for survivors, reported that the damage to reality hadn't gone away. It was like probing through a radioactive wasteland, they'd noted, only worse. Radioactivity wasn't a problem. An unseen force that interfered with the most advanced technology at humanity's disposal *was*.

"We'll catch up," she assured him. "Given time …"

Henri frowned. "Is there nowhere we can stop, just for a bit?"

Mari cocked her head. "Do you want to find your friend, or do you want to give her captor a chance to commit a second genocidal atrocity?"

Henri flushed. "Sorry."

Mari reached out and patted his shoulder. "I do understand, but it can't be helped. Read a book. Go study engineering. Go do something …"

"I …" Henri looked up. "Why are people so scared of us?"

"I thought you were telepaths," Mari said. "Don't you *know*?"

"No." Henri shook his head. "It just makes no sense. Why?"

Mari stepped over to the food processor and ordered two mugs of coffee. "You know what happened in the bad old days?"

"I know history," Henri said, taking the mug she offered him. "Some of it, at least."

"Back in the dark ages, men didn't understand women and vice versa," Mari said. It had sounded odd to her, when she'd reviewed the early years of humanity's existence, and she'd been older and more mature than him at the time. "Men had a lot of silly ideas about women, women had a lot of silly ideas about men; both thought the other was like them, at base, and that when the chains of society were removed the two would be identical. It didn't work that way. True equality only came when it became possible to change sex, and even then it didn't always work out."

Henri frowned. "And your point is?"

"Men have no instinctive simpatico for women and vice versa," Mari said. "You have the same problem. You don't have any understanding of how they feel, because you don't share the same ... things. The same abilities. You ... I knew someone who once asked why they didn't abolish racism on Old Earth by giving everyone the genetic tweaks that would allow them to change their skin colours. Can you guess the answer?"

Henri frowned. "It makes sense ..."

"Only if you have the ability to do it," Mari pointed out, dryly. "The early humans weren't able to change their skin colours at will, let alone change sex or even something as simple as their facial features. It took a great deal of effort and resources, if it could be done at all. The option of waving a magic wand and simply fixing all the problems by giving everyone such abilities simply didn't exist."

She leaned forward. "And you don't really understand it. You don't need money, or to work for a living. None of us do. You have never known a day's illness in your life, and never will unless you choose to infect yourself with something minor, just to see what it is like. You can heal from minor wounds that would kill a pre-space human without a doctor's assistance, and modern medical science can repair almost anything that isn't immediately lethal. And even if you die, you can back yourself up and be resurrected. You are effectively immortal. How can you understand what life was like, back on Old Earth? An alien world would be more comprehensible."

Henri frowned. "And …?"

"You are a telepath. The general population is not. You can sense thoughts and emotions, and you have very poor control over your abilities; the general population cannot, and doesn't believe you can't control it. You understand your peers very well, and don't keep secrets from each other; the general population often doesn't, and feels the need to keep secrets even when the secrets are very silly. You …"

"And so they're scared of us," Henri said. "Why?"

"People have always feared the unknown," Mari said.

She looked down, feeling a twinge of guilt. "There's a race. It considers – considered – itself to be the most advanced in the known galaxy, because it stagnated too quickly to discover more advanced and powerful races. It was a highly ritualised culture, too lost in itself to think outside the box. They knew there *were* other aliens, but … none as advanced as themselves. The fact they were at least a thousand years behind *us* … well, they didn't know it.

"There was another race, even more primitive. They made first contact with the stagnant race and it went horrifically wrong. War was declared, a war that only lasted as long as it did because the first race was quite adaptable, even though they were grossly outmatched. They would have won effortlessly if the technical balance had been even. As it was, they were only slowing down the inevitable. The stagnant race congratulated itself on its superiority as it steered its fleets to the enemy homeworld, ignoring their pleas for mercy."

Henri swallowed. "And then what?"

"We intervened," Mari said. "They had no concept of hyperspace weapons. We had no trouble disabling their ships, knocking them out without killing a single soul. The engagement was so one-sided that calling it an engagement is giving it credit it doesn't deserve. We proved our superiority ...and it broke them. They might have been able to handle faster missiles, or more powerful ray guns, or better warp drives, but technology that might as well be magic? They couldn't cope."

She frowned. "And your abilities? It will take a long time for the general population to get used to the idea, and stop being scared of shadows."

"Oh," Henri said. He looked down for a long moment, then looked up. "Would you like to go to bed now?"

Mari blinked, then realised she was being teased. "Yes," she said. "Alone."

Henri pouted, and then froze. His face twisted in pain, his mouth opening slightly ... soundlessly. The internal sensors sounded the alarm a moment later, noting he was in pain while being unable to find the source. Mari reached out and caught him as he buckled, lowering him gently to the deck. His body felt almost absurdly light.

"She's in pain," he gasped. "They're hurting her!"

Mari felt cold. X had a new toy, and he was experimenting to see what he could do with it. She could imagine another world being driven mad ... or worse, now X knew how to make better use of her abilities. If he understood that reality itself had broken down in places ... the reports were frankly absurd, the kind of statements that wouldn't be believed under almost *any* other circumstances. What could he do, if he understood what he was playing with? What *couldn't* he do?

Henri shuddered against her, his entire body convulsing as if someone had hit him in the groin. His mouth was wide open, yet there was still no sound ... she summoned a hypospray and shot a powerful sedative into his bloodstream, one that should have put him out within seconds. It didn't work. A quick scan revealed the sedative had vanished, as if the hypospray had been empty. She summoned a second and tried again, monitoring him closely. The sedative appeared to disappear the moment it entered his body. It defied everything she knew about medical science.

"She's in pain," Henri managed. His body was jerking, his eyes wide and staring. "I can *feel* her."

"Point me to her," Mari ordered. The odds were good they weren't heading *straight* to Pandora, even if they were travelling in the right general direction. "Hurry!"

Henri raised a hand and pointed, barely managing to hold it upright for a second before dropping it again. His body was twitching violently, as if he were being beaten up by an invisible enemy. Mari scanned his body and cursed under his breath as she realised the nanites were gone, as if they'd never existed. Henri didn't have a communications implant or a datanet neurotransmitter … it was rare for children to be granted such devices, but the researchers should have offered them to the Children when they reached physical maturity. Why not? Had they tried and discovered they didn't work? Or …

"Crap," she muttered, as she projected the flight path forward. Pandora was somewhere along that straight line, and so was the Life Sphere. She wanted to believe it was a coincidence, but she knew better. There was almost no better place in the galaxy to hide a prisoner, or hand her over to the highest bidder. The Peacekeepers couldn't throw their weight around there. "If he took her there …"

Horror washed through her. Was X attacking the Life Sphere? It was out of character for him, but so were his actions at Jorlem Prime. The idea of wrecking such a vast megastructure, and driving so many advanced peer-power sentients insane, had to be fascinating to him. The fact it would mean war on an unprecedented scale would mean nothing, not to a man who was responsible for the deaths of countless intelligent beings. The nightmare *had* to be stopped before it was too late.

It isn't too late, she told herself, as she altered their course and pushed her FTL drives to their limits. She wasn't sure it was true. *It isn't*!

Henri shuddered, then lay still. "They're hurting her."

"We're on the way," Mari said. She ran a quick calculation

and cursed mentally. Even if she ramped her drives up to the point they might suffer significant degradation, even failure, it would take nearly a day to reach the sphere. "Can you make contact with her? Direct contact?"

"I keep trying," Henri said. "But I don't think she can hear me."

If she's in agony, she might be unable to think straight, Mari thought. What the hell was X doing to her? Was he making her hurt and broadcasting her pain across the sphere ... how? The Darius Children had never had that sort of power, had they? It just made no sense. They were missing a puzzle piece, the biggest of all. What *was* it? *Or he might be blocking the connection somehow.*

She frowned, thinking hard. X had no sense of ethics, no scruples ... and access to some of the most advanced technology in the known galaxy. Could he have inserted control implants and taken direct control of Pandora's abilities? Or used a mind-twister to steer her thoughts in the right direction? It wasn't easy without knowing how the abilities actually worked, and that was the one thing the researchers had never been able to figure out, but X could have made it work through sheer dumb luck. Or he might just be torturing her and hoping for the best. Why not? It had worked once before.

Henri staggered to his feet. "She's alone, alone in her head," he said. His face was drenched with sweat, marred by scars that had no discernable cause. "Is that what it's like for you all the time?"

"I suppose." Mari knew, intellectually, what it was like to live in a society that wasn't post-scarcity, but she didn't really understand it. The habitats kept at a low-tech level had escape hatches, for anyone who found they couldn't hack it and wanted to leave. A person who lived on a genuinely primitive world wouldn't have that way out. "We learn to cope. Somehow."

Henri looked at her, his boyish eyes somehow both young and naive and yet pitying. "I'm sorry."

"Don't be," Mari said. The depth of his emotion was just another reminder of his youth. "It isn't your fault."

CHAPTER TWENTY-TWO

X was mildly surprised the alien researchers hadn't found his sub-nanotech spies.

Or, he reminded himself as he kept one eye on the livestream and the other on his personal research, they simply didn't care enough to remove them. Two of the researchers came from races that could give the Peacekeepers a fight and the third was a complete unknown, his scans suggesting a biological robot put together by someone who wanted to keep their involvement an absolute secret. They might well succeed. There were quite a few races that used biological technology, and what little his scans had noted hadn't provided any clues leading back to the maker. The drone would have been programmed to self-destruct if it fell into enemy hands, wiping out what little evidence there was. It was what *he* would have done.

He dismissed the thought as he studied the brains taking shape in the bioreactor tank. The human brain was an incredibly complicated piece of biological machinery, but in the end it was *just* a piece of machinery. X was not prone to being humble and yet even *he* found it hard to accept that his body was a machine, his brain influenced by hormonal fluxes and reactions he couldn't even *begin* to overcome. He had never felt the urge to upload himself into a datacore, to become a human personality within a machine, but he thought he understood it now. A personality within a datacore lacked many of the weaknesses of a biological human, even as it developed newer and potentially worse weaknesses of its own. It was galling to think his personality could be reprogrammed, if he fell into the wrong set of hands, but then that was true of both biological and electronic humans. It was unethical to reprogram someone without their consent, yet far from impossible.

His thoughts darkened. The brains were already being reprogrammed to his specifications, their intellects forced into the correct line well before they developed any sense of their own personality. Reprogramming was tricky, and it wasn't uncommon for the victim to realise something was wrong even if they couldn't do anything about it, but these brains would never know there was anything wrong with their existence, that they could be something more than boosters for his own formidable intellect. He had the mental image of his brain being linked to a swarm of others, as if he had donned an enhancement suit, and felt his lips curve into a smile. It was true, in a sense. The brains *were* intended to enhance his own abilities.

If only because I managed to think outside the box, he told himself, mentally congratulating himself on his own perception. The researchers had wasted a great deal of time looking for something that simply didn't exist, even though they really should have realised there was *something* odd about the way the psi abilities worked. Where did the energy come from? Why couldn't it be detected? *Why didn't they consider the truth?*

His lips quirked again. The average person wouldn't *like* to consider that someone was reaching down from high above and rearranging the scenery, an invisible force adjusting the world around them. It was like a cartoon in which the main character was at the mercy of the artist, who could change everything except the character's personality ... funny, like so many of the old entertainments that had gone in and out of fashion time and time again, yet strangely horrific in the real world.

The researchers – and the Darius Children – had been blinded by their own preconceptions, but also by a refusal to look an unpleasant truth in the face. X was not so limited. He *knew* the truth.

A console pinged. X turned away, checking it thoughtfully. The first and second layer of sensors had picked up nothing, but the third – more of a self-checking routine rather than actual sensors – had picked up an oddity, a set of contradictions in the live feed that could not be reconciled. X leaned forward, feeling his lips curve into a tight smile as he studied the results. The aliens had put Pandora in a research lab, twenty metres by twenty metres, but now some sensors were insisting the lab was smaller and others that it was much bigger on the inside. Other sensors had failed completely, the natural laws that let them function breaking down as the aliens carried out their tests. X wondered if they'd realised the problem, realised their results were unlikely to be helpful even if they managed to record them properly; it was quite possible, he reflected, that they hadn't realised their data was skewed. Even if they had … he shrugged. It wasn't his problem. The fewer who worked out the truth, the better.

He left the data flowing into the datacore, for later analysis and sale to the highest bidder, and returned his attention to the bioreactor. The brains appeared to be merging together, the clones forming into a fleshy mask that sent chills running down his spine, his imagination granting it an eye, and other forms of sensor input, that simply didn't exist. The brains were isolated in liquid, deprived of all sensation … a form of torture banned, for good reason, although the brains lacked the mental ability to appreciate the lack of input. Or did they? His sensors reported a complete lack of higher functions, the intellectual patterns that turned an animal into a sentient being, but was that actually true? The researchers had never been able to detect the brain patterns that linked the Children to their abilities, which suggested he might not be able to detect true intelligence either. Another chill ran down his spine, hastily banished. He was on the verge of a great discovery.

Turning away, he triggered his implant and backed himself up again. The Life Sphere's datanet was vast, including datacores from nearly all known spacefaring civilisations, and it had direct hyperwave links to the Galactic Net. His backup would make its way through a handful of relay stations, eventually finding rest and resurrection at his secondary base. If something went wrong, if he lost control or died in the experiment, he would live again. Unless the Peacekeepers stumbled across the base … it wasn't impossible. The base *couldn't* be completely isolated without making it impossible to send his backup there. If they got lucky …

He shook his head as he sat down, facing the brain-mass and reaching for the neural link. The brain matter was a fusion, grown from cells harvested from both Pandora and himself, and it was hard to know how it would react to him. There were some humans who duplicated themselves constantly, even though it was frowned upon to resurrect a living person, through cloning their bodies and uploading their personality backups into the cloned minds. The rejection rate was very low, but the uploaded personalities were uniquely suited to the cloned brains. They were, in a sense, the same person. The fusion construction was a mix, one that might just as easily reject as accept him. If the latter, he would have to find a way to rewrite the DNA without erasing the psi abilities.

A stab of pain shot through his mind as he gently pressed the neural link against his forehead. He gritted his teeth and pulled it away, carefully adjusting the settings a little in hopes of making the contact a little easier. Neural links rarely malfunctioned, but when they did the results were almost always lethal. The fact it hadn't killed him suggested that *something* was working as planned, even if it wasn't working perfectly. He finished adjusting the neural link and tried again, this time feeling a dizzying sensation of being in two places at once. A normal link would draw his mind into the datacore. This one ...

This one doesn't. This one doesn't. This one doesn't. This one doesn't.

X caught himself, his head spinning as the safety interlocks, carefully programmed to ensure they only intervened when he was on the verge of brain-death, snapped into place. His head pounded, his brain feeling as if it had been punched repeatedly, the blow somehow manifesting inside his skull. His mind staggered, the pain making it hard to think clearly. He guessed it was his brain trying to comprehend what had happened, translating the sensation into something he could understand. Or something that might be actively misleading. The human mind was so limited. Even *he* lacked the true understanding of an immortal being.

He cursed under his breath as he realised what had happened. He had been reading his own mind, his thoughts reflected back at him in an endless cycle that had come alarmingly close to damaging his brain permanently. He checked the safety interlocks again, adjusting their settings, and tried again. The uneasy sense he was about to step right through the looking glass washed over him as he plunged forward, the brains bubbling as they channelled ...

The universe exploded around him, a torrent of new sensations slamming into his brain. It should have hurt and yet, this time it didn't. It was more like finding himself trapped in a holographic maze, the walls and inhabitants nothing more than insubstantial shapes that weren't truly *real*. But they were ... He was suddenly very aware of his surroundings: his body, his ship, the alien structure and the sphere beyond ... he saw them all with one flash of insight, saw all their imperfections hidden to the naked eye. To look was to comprehend ... his ship, the most advanced starship available to the average civilian, was a rattletrap, a creaky piece of junk. The sphere was crude, so poorly designed the AI needed powerful gravity beams to hold it together ... it would come apart within seconds, he thought suddenly, if the AI failed. A structure so big it defied the imagination, yet so fragile … it could be destroyed with one single perfectly placed blow. He was almost tempted to try.

Focus, he told himself.

He had to fight to narrow his eyes … his mental eyes. The brains were drawing him onwards, bombarding him with sensations he couldn't begin to understand. Everyone was shouting, their words echoing through the airless void … the sheer impossibility helped him to concentrate, to realise he was reading the minds of *everyone* on the sphere. It was hard, so hard, to narrow his perceptions, to tune the intrusive thoughts out of his mind. He wasn't sure why his brain hadn't melted under the impact, unless his own certainty he would survive had kept him alive. If one had the power to tamper with reality itself, why would one *not* ensure one's own survival?

His perceptions narrowed further, focusing on his lap. The imperfections bothered him at a deep, almost primal, level. The bulkheads were solid … except they weren't. Not really. His entire ship was on the verge of coming apart … he bit his lip hard, using the pain to focus his mind before his thoughts started affecting reality itself, making his perceptions reality. He had planned to let himself die before falling into Peacekeeper hands, committing suicide to ensure his backups were never found before he was resurrected, but killing himself by *accident* would be humiliating as well as deeply ironic.

Pandora is too limited in her outlook, X mused. She was a bright girl, according to all his tests, but not *that* capable of thinking outside the box. Perhaps that was a subconscious act of self-defence. She was far more powerful than she knew. *I could kill myself with a thought.*

He focused on the metal block he'd placed on the table. His awareness swept *through* it, noting the gaps between atoms … to his senses, the block was almost as solid as the air surrounding it. He pushed the thought out of his head and focused, trying to pick up the block with his mind. It didn't work. The block remained unmoving. He cursed and tried again, willing it to work. It didn't.

Fuck, he thought. Pandora had done it. He'd seen her. *Why ...?*

Understanding clicked. He shaped his thoughts carefully, forcing them into a pattern he could use ... a user interface, one that allowed him to alter the world around him as if it was just something within a datacore. The block wasn't picked up so much as its location was altered, time and time again. X giggled as the block rose into the air and flew around the chamber, then fell to the deck as he let go. It was suddenly more real, and then less real, and then ... his head spun as he reached out again. Did he dare try transmutation? It would be a risk.

X couldn't stop himself. He tried to change the block's internal structure ... and failed. He kicked himself a moment later, realising his mistake. The trick wasn't to change the structure atom by atom, but to change its *whole*. The world spun again as he tried, the block changing in the blink of an eye ....

He fell back into his own body, the safety interlocks cutting in as the neural link threatened to overheat. X removed the link – it felt warm to the touch, even though logically it shouldn't have been – and then forced himself to look around. Reality felt thin and translucent, the lab equipment and even the bulkheads somehow not quite real ... he wasn't even sure how his chair was holding his weight. It felt soft and not quite there, as if it were almost transparent ... he stood quickly and pressed his finger against the seat, frowning at two contradictory results. His finger felt solid material, but it also felt something insubstantial, something disturbingly like jelly. The world around him felt ... wrong, skewed like a poorly-designed perceptual reality. It was not a pleasant thought.

Charming, he thought, numbly. He bit his lip hard, tasting blood in his mouth. It was quite easy to get lost in a fantasy, to believe the perceptual reality around him was truly real ... it was how the Peacekeepers treated sociopaths who refused personality reprogramming or didn't want to be locked up in a secure cell. A flash of paranoia ran through him, despite the taste. Had he been captured years ago and put in a computer-generated universe, a cell he couldn't escape because he couldn't even see the bars? Had everything he'd done been nothing more than a fantasy? *If it is true ... if it isn't true ...*

He rubbed his forehead. No. The world was real. It had to be.

His body hurt as he staggered to the hatch, aching in places he hadn't known he had. He wasn't sure why he was hurting, although he had a handful of theories. He made a mental note to test them one by one, after he backed himself up again, and see which one was closest to the truth. The hatch hissed open, revealing a block of ice on the deck. It was weirdly shaped, as if it had been allowed to partly melt and then flash-frozen again, but it was very definitely there. He reached out to touch it lightly, sucking in his breath. It had been a block of solid metal a few minutes ago.

He checked the internal sensors. They were worse than useless. The block of metal had been there one second, then there had been a moment of utter distortion, and then there had been a block of ice. The distortion had been so complete that *none* of the sensor records could be trusted, the results so insane he was tempted to wonder if his ship's datacore had developed intelligence and was screwing with him, rather than demanding immediate passage to Calculus. It was supposed to be impossible, but stranger things had happened. The block of metal turning into a block of ice was also supposed to be impossible.

His mind raced. It was technically possible to transmute iron into gold, or base metals into rare and precious ores, but the energy demands were staggering for most races. It was far easier to search asteroid belts for raw metals, and cheaper too. But if it could be done cheaply ... the possibilities were endless. He could imagine a dozen ways he could use the ability to change the entire universe.

He studied the sensor records thoughtfully. They were a little skewed, as if the universe had been taken apart and put back together in a manner that was almost, but not quite, perfect. It hadn't felt a long time, yet the sensors insisted he'd been linked to the brains for four hours. Perhaps longer. Half the clocks disagreed, some suggesting he'd been in contact for bare seconds and others insisting it had been days. Even the direct link to the local datanet was faintly skewed. It made him think of the phase-shift experiments, back in the day. They hadn't worked out too well either. No one was quite sure why.

He yawned, suddenly. His mind was tired. He needed sleep.

I could become something more, he thought, as he stumbled into his cabin. There was no time to undress, no time to do anything but close his eyes. The exhaustion was total. *I could become a god.*

He awoke, what felt like moments later. He'd been dreaming … but he couldn't remember the dreams. There had been something scratching … he wasn't sure why. He forced himself to sit up and order food, before resuming his experiments. Perhaps it was time to leave …

An alarm pinged, a moment later. X leaned forward, cursing under his breath. He hadn't expected company, not so quickly. The Peacekeepers shouldn't have been able to track him down, not when they had no way to predict his destination. But he had been wrong. The proof was right in front of him.

An Archangel had arrived.

CHAPTER
Twenty-Three

Pandora had lost track of time.

She had moaned, back on Clarke, about the researchers poking and prodding at her and her peers, conducting endless experiments intended to determine how the Darius Children did the things they did. She hadn't precisely *hated* it, but she had found it annoying, particularly when she'd found herself sensing the irritation and frustration surrounding her as the researchers slowly lost their faith in their ability to solve any problem. She understood their feelings – they had the finest sensors in the known galaxy, access to human and alien scientific research dating back millions of years, and a firm belief that anything could be explained through science – and yet they irritated her. Science was an endless process, a series of steps leading from the dawn of the human race to the spacefaring civilisation surrounding her: it was a story of discoveries, of tiny advancements; of certainties that were disproven and replaced with new certainties, which would be disproven and replaced themselves in time. The idea the mystery could be solved so quickly ...

The alien researchers were much nastier, their experiments pushing her to the limit. She could feel their minds buzzing around her, their thoughts surprisingly familiar and yet strikingly alien, as they moved their machines up to the table, carried out their tests, and then moved them away again. The machines were very alien; some leaving her unmoved, others sending nasty little feelings running through her body as they scanned her, time and time again. She wished, with a passion that surprised her, that she was back on Clarke. The worst of the researchers, the one who had suggested a handful of more invasive tests, was sweetness and light incarnate compared to the alien researchers. Even X had been preferable, despite everything he'd done.

She cringed back as the grey aliens pushed another device into place and shone a blinding light into her eyes. She tried to close them, only to have the aliens hold her head firmly in place and open her eyelids with their eerie alien hands, their mere touch sending shivers down her spine. It was hard to see their thoughts and what little she could feel was cold and calculating, a dispassionate mind that cared nothing for the finer things in life. Her earlier thoughts returned to haunt her as the light pulsed into her brain, the pain reaching breaking point very quickly. The aliens were biological robots, and the true masters had yet to show themselves.

Her entire body twitched painfully, her muscles spasming. A stab of pain shot through her, a needle pressing against her abdomen ... pushing into her body. Her muscles locked a second later, keeping her still ... the pain grew and grew, then vanished as quickly as it had come. A shimmering light surrounded her for a moment, pressing against her mind ... a series of emotions ran through her, from helpless anger to sexual arousal, followed by fear and dread ... they weren't real, she realised numbly, but flashes of feeling caused by their probes brushing through her mind. They clearly didn't have solid data on humanity, she told herself, although she doubted it was true. The human race had been around for a *long* time. The odds were good the aliens knew precisely how her body worked. It wasn't exactly a state secret.

Except it might be, she thought, as the grey aliens stepped back. *Am I human?*

The thought nagged at her mind. She had seen the medical records, the researchers using everything from simple x-rays to biological scans and nanotech probes to study every last atom of her body. She was human to ten decimal places, the few deviances easily explained through her ancestors having lost touch with the rest of the human race centuries ago. She certainly lacked the technopathic implants favoured by human cyborgs, or altered internal organs used by humans experimenting with life on very hostile worlds or interplanetary space. And yet, she had psi powers. Abilities! Abilities that had never been satisfactorily explained.

Am I human, she asked herself, *or am I something else that* thinks *it is human?*

The grey aliens came closer, their machinery humming loudly as they focused their devices on her body. Pandora closed her eyes and tried to let her mind wander free, to escape the nightmare around her. It felt as if something was pressing down on her, trying to keep her trapped … her mind shifted and changed, tendrils of thought exploring in all directions. The sensation of being watched was strong, powerful eyes studying her … Loki? She wasn't sure what he was or even if he existed at all, her mind flinching away from considering he might exist … she gritted her teeth, telling herself he did. And …

Her mind fell forward … fell upwards. The contradiction confused her, until she realised she was thinking like a human. A *limited* human. Her mind wasn't bound by the limits of her body, the pressure holding her down couldn't affect an astral presence that was little more than a ghost. She floated up and *through*, passing through the barrier as if it wasn't there. Her lips twisted into a smile as she saw threads of power reaching through the world, through the *worlds*. She followed one of them and …

… Her perspective shifted, her mind struggling to comprehend what it was seeing. Loki towered over her, but he was also *below* her. He was staring at her, yet he was somehow also looking down … she thought she understood, just for a second, that both things were true at the same time, before the understanding faded. The realm wasn't a place for humans, no matter their abilities. It wasn't for her …

… And she wasn't alone.

It was hard to even perceive the entities surrounding her. Giant figures darted through the background, existing only at the corner of her eye. She couldn't look at them directly. Every time she tried, they moved without actually moving. Some were humanoid, some were so strange that they had nothing in common with humanity … she realised, at some level, that they were both alike and very different. They were something greater than a material person and also firmly rooted in the physical … she had a sudden impression of how humanity had climbed into space to stay, eventually leaving most planets fallow and choosing to live in megastructures. Perhaps she was looking at the next level of existence, beings that had left the material world behind.

And yet they are still interested in us, she thought. *Why?*

"THE HUMAN IS TOO CLOSE TO THE QUANTUM FOAM."

Pandora flinched. The booming voice was all around her … no, it was *inside* her. It was so much *more* than just a voice that it threatened her very being, as if it was somehow designed to compel her to believe, to obey. She had the strangest sense, as her emotions spun around her, that it *wasn't* designed to influence her, that it was a by-product of carrying far more than just words to the listener's ears. It was inflection and tone, carried so profoundly it was impossible to misunderstand the meaning behind the words. It was …

She tried to look around for the speaker, but saw nothing. It was there – she could *feel* it – and yet there was nothing. A thought flashed through her mind, an old-fashioned big game hunter swaggering through a forest, bemoaning the lack of any game to hunt … while the viewer, eyeing the tree trunks, noted that some looked suspiciously like legs. If that were true ... she kept her thoughts under tight control as she realised what she was seeing. The entities around her were so big, so massive, existing in dimensions humanity couldn't even begin to comprehend ... they were so big that they literally *couldn't* intervene on the material plane, not directly. She supposed it explained why Loki needed X, if he couldn't meddle directly himself. Perhaps the grey aliens were *his* creations, tools he could use to manipulate the material world. And yet, if that were true, why would he need the other aliens?

"You are upsetting yourself needlessly," Loki said. His tone was flat and yet Pandora thought she heard a hint of amusement, as if he were taking a quiet pleasure in the booming voice's irritation. "The matter is well under control."

"IT IS NOT. THE HUMANS ARE EXPERIMENTING WITH THE QUANTUM FOAM. IT IS ONLY A MATTER OF TIME BEFORE THEY LEARN TO MANIPULATE IT. DISASTER WILL RESULT."

Pandora staggered. The sheer *conviction* running through the words was impossible to deny, a truth-teller proclaiming the truth so definitely that it could not be questioned. Or ... a liar lying with such power it was difficult to suspect the truth, let alone try to prove it. The sheer force of the words was just too strong to challenge, not openly. A thought ran through her mind. Was magic nothing more than the ability to lie to the universe itself, and make that lie stick?

Her mind raced. She had studied history. She had watched the psychohistorical analysts as they pointed out how one minor change could alter everything, their models shifting as the effects of the change percolated through history. If you somehow developed the power to go back in time and kill a vitally important figure, hero or villain, the changes would develop naturally from that point, as the world around them struggled to cope with their absence. Was magic the same thing? Make one small change and watch the greater changes take effect, as the world responded to the first change?

"YOU HAVE ALLOWED THE HUMANS TO LEARN TOO MUCH. THE DISASTER IS IMMINENT."

Loki looked up. For a moment, his eyes met hers. And he winked.

"Relax," Loki said. "The matter is fully under control."

"YOU WILL DEAL WITH THE INFECTED HUMANS."

Pandora felt a wave of disgust that nearly threw her out of the mental plane. The intensity was so strong that … she'd never felt anything like it, not even through the nest. The voice was repulsed on a very primal level and …

"Relax," Loki repeated. The words were the same but the tone was different, changing the meaning in a way she didn't understand. "The matter is fully under control."

Pandora blinked. Loki was suddenly standing in front of her. She recoiled. His human seeming was nothing more than a façade, a way of presenting himself as something she could understand … she wondered, suddenly, if there was some message in the way his outfit kept changing before her eyes. He was a researcher and a doctor and a soldier and an interested bystander and … she forced herself to peer forward, under the shroud. He was so big …

He smiled. "Do you like what you see?"

It was hard to think clearly. "Why … why are you doing this?"

Loki shrugged. "It is not something you will ever comprehend," he said. The sheer force of his disdain shocked her. None of her peers, or the researchers, had ever looked down on her with *quite* so much … the feeling was so intense she couldn't put it into words. Loki had a superiority complex that dwarfed anything she'd sensed from the researchers, one that was fully justified by his sheer power. Perhaps he did have problems operating on the material plane. They weren't problems he couldn't overcome. "For now, all that matters is the great work."

He made no visible motion, but Pandora felt herself picked up and shoved back into her body by an irresistible force. The pain slammed into her a moment later, the sudden shock almost overwhelming. Cold black eyes met hers as the aliens tested her, their needles digging deep into her flesh. The enhanced healing spliced into her genome was actually making it worse, she realised numbly. Her skin was trying to heal and not succeeding ... she wondered if her body was actually trying to dissolve the needles, to break them down before they could pose a threat. If so, it was too late. She was a prisoner.

"Let me go," she managed. Her voice felt harsh, as if she'd forgotten how to speak properly. How long had she been in their hands? She couldn't remember ... a few hours? Days? Weeks? Months? The pain rose again, up and down; she shuddered helplessly, her mind struggling against the force holding her in place. "Let me go."

The grey aliens showed no visible reaction. The light was so bright she couldn't see the other aliens, if indeed they were still there. Perhaps they were watching from a safe distance, perhaps they had outlived their usefulness ... the ruthlessness it took to destroy even a handful of lives was alien to her, but not to X. Perhaps he was dead too, or perhaps he'd escaped before they destroyed him ... Pandora knew, with a certainty that could not be denied, that she was completely alone. If there were any other humans on the giant alien megastructure, they didn't know about her ... she tried, once again, to contact the nest. There was no response. She couldn't even sense its existence.

She was alone.

Something twisted in her head. It had been unthinkable, in so many ways, to use her abilities to hurt someone. On Clarke, she had been all too aware of just how much her abilities frightened the junior researchers, how much fear they caused just by existing; on the ship, she had known that even *trying* to use her abilities would get her stunned or killed. But now, if she was truly alone, the rest of the nest and the researchers murdered by X … she reached out with her mind, trying to work her way out from under the trap and into the quantum foam. The gods were scared of her touching the foam? Good. She would use it.

The world seemed to shift around her. She sensed flickers of panic darting through the air, not from the grey aliens … the others had to be still there, watching with their naked eyes rather than using the sensors. She wondered if that was a mark of bravery or foolishness, then dismissed the thought as she reached further. The world around her grew thin and translucent, almost insubstantial. Something jabbed into her arm, the pain both excruciating and yet … nothing, as if it wasn't truly there. She heard sounds in the background – she knew, somehow, they were alarms – and ignored them. Loki was above her, metaphorically speaking. She would go sideways.

Her mind expanded, taking in the sheer size of the alien station. She saw it in all its glorious imperfections, tasted the despair of the first aliens to pull the scrapped ships together to make a home, followed by their growing awareness that it would never be enough. She saw the scum of the galaxy coming to make their mark, the original settlers leaving in dismay as their makeshift home fell into darkness. She was almost disappointed by the sheer mundane criminality of the new arrivals, criminals no better than thieves or pirates … lacking, in so many ways, any true vision. She had been told that a truly advanced society would have no such criminals, but her tutors had been wrong. There were races out there that had never solved their problems. They still hadn't.

She sucked in a breath as her awareness kept going, taking in the sheer size of the sphere. It was all around her, a simple and yet infinitely complex megastructure. The AI wasn't a true AI, part of her mind noted. It acted within a set of guidelines laid down by its creators and lacked the intellect to consider itself an intelligent being, or the imagination to think of a way to evade the limitations its designers had worked into its structure. It was odd, both greater than any human and yet smaller, almost nothing. It lacked even the *hint* of a presence in the quantum foam.

The difference between a sentient being and a dumb beast is the ability to touch the foam, she thought, numbly. Her thoughts were echoed onto the foam ... in a sense, they were part of it. She could sense others, hundreds of others, all around her. They were millions of miles away ... no, in a sense, they were right next to her. All points were one, in the foam. *And the difference between me and the average human is that I can actually* manipulate *the foam.*

Another thought ran through her head. It wasn't hers. *The quantum foam is the base matter of reality itself, and psi is the ability to manipulate it at will.*

Another stab of pain shot through her. The grey aliens were trying to shut down her mind. The drugs weren't working ... she wasn't sure why. No, that wasn't true. She had determined she would stay awake and reality itself was bending to her wishes, keeping her conscious even as they pumped her with enough sedatives to put a dozen humans to sleep. Her awareness spun, pulses of unreality spinning around her, as she found herself caught between her body and the quantum foam. A grey alien held a gun to her head, silently daring her to take a chance. Could she survive a headshot? She didn't know ...

Madness howled at her mind, her thoughts twisting in eerie directions. She could see the walls of reality, hear *things* scratching at the edge of the world. Hungry things, wanting in. The pain grew worse and yet, it wasn't true pain. It wasn't real. Nothing was, not even her. And nothing really mattered.

Quite calmly, she reached for the *things*. All she had to do was touch them.

And then she would let them in.

CHAPTER
Twenty-Four

"Wow!"

Mari couldn't disagree as she exploded out of hyperspace, dangerously close to the Life Sphere. The megastructure was so vast she knew she could see it with her naked eyes, if her ship had an observation blister allowing her to stare into the inky darkness of space. Henri would have to cope with the holographic display, as she stared through her sensors. The sheer size of the sphere was mind-boggling, even to her. On one hand, it was an exercise in engineering rather than something supernatural; on the other, it was built on such a scale that it was simply impossible to dismiss as anything other than a true wonder. The Confederation would be hard-pressed to build its like, if it had wanted to try.

"Try and find her," she ordered. The Life Sphere *was* the most significant structure along their flight path, and it was an ideal place to hand Pandora over to her buyers, but she might already be on her way elsewhere. "Hurry!"

She sucked in her breath as more data poured into her sensors and pooled in the datacore. There were hundreds of thousands of starships orbiting the Life Sphere, including at least nine thousand warships from a multitude of different races. Peer powers ... the ships alone weren't that much of a threat, if only because vast numbers of automated vessels could be thrown together very quickly, but if they were backed up by modern weapons and datacores they could pose a serious threat. The remaining ships couldn't be dismissed either. They could easily be armed with something dangerous, something that might give their crews an edge. And …

Ice crawled down her spine. The Life Sphere was technically neutral. Most races honoured it and the few that didn't were driven away by the rest, in hopes of preventing the local AI from intervening. There was no reason for so many warships to be dispatched, certainly not from so many different races. Unless … she had the nasty feeling their arrival wasn't a coincidence. If Pandora's buyer was amongst the crowd … why? They had to know the Peacekeepers wouldn't just let the matter go.

Unless they are powerful enough to give us pause, she thought. The majority of the known peer powers were badly outnumbered by the Peacekeepers, but there was no reason they couldn't put together a modern battle fleet fairly quickly, one that lacked the weaknesses of an automated force. *Would we let the matter go, if the alternative was a galaxy-wide war?*

Her mood darkened. Outright war amongst post-scarcity societies was rare, if only because there was no *reason* to fight. The history books humanity had found on the Galactic Net, archives so old their creators had been gone millions of years before the human race discovered fire, spoke of ancient conflicts on unimaginable scales, but no one knew for sure what had really happened. The Peacekeepers had gamed out such wars, and concluded they would be utterly devastating beyond words, the sheer scale of the destruction difficult – if not impossible – to grasp. Stars would be sent supernova, megastructures would be melted or destroyed … millions of starships would be lost, in engagements so vast no one could truly determine a victor. If that was the threat, would the Confederation concede defeat and let the kidnappers go? She feared the worst.

Henri gasped and choked, retching helplessly. "I can

feel her," he said, his voice weak. "She's ... she's mad! Or on the verge of suicide! She's ..."

He pointed. Mari allowed herself a moment of relief as she realised Pandora was somewhere inside the sphere, rather than on one of the warships. It didn't mean she'd be easy to find – the sphere was vast, big enough that searching for a lone human would be like searching for a needle on an entire planet – but with Henri's help they could get a lock on her exact location. It wouldn't be easy to get to her, yet it would be a start.

"She's doing something," Henri said, between retches. "It feels like ... like the ruined planet!"

Mari swore under her breath. Whatever Pandora was doing, or why, it would be on a far greater scale than Jorlem Prime. There were warships orbiting the sphere that would pose a genuine threat to her, and their neighbours, and if they started shooting randomly ... the devastation would be immense even if the AI intervened at once. No one was quite sure what the threshold for intervention was, according to the files, but *everyone* knew the AI rarely bothered to separate the innocent from the guilty. If it opened fire, hundreds of ships and millions of people, human and alien, were likely to die.

She shot a handful of enquires into the local network, trying to determine what – if anything – the local authorities knew. The answer came back a moment later. There were *no* local authorities, certainly none with authority over the entire sphere. The few local governments listed as such didn't appear to have any awareness of what was really going on, although Mari knew better than to take that for granted. The Confederation couldn't hack datacores produced by peer powers. The truth might be locked in a database she couldn't access. And that meant ...

"I can't talk to her," Henri said. "I ... I can't tell what's wrong."

Mari thought fast. If she broadcast a warning, would it be believed? The news about Jorlem Prime *had* to have reached the Life Sphere, but ... if the locals knew what had caused the early disaster, would they try to kill Pandora? Or take her into custody? Or start fighting over who got her? Mari could normally make decisions in the blink of an eye – she normally operated alone, unable to contact her superiors for orders – but for once she had no idea what to do. There were just too many starships flying around, some from races that disliked the Confederation. What would they do if they knew the truth?

"I'm sending a warning," she said, finally. Her datacores put a broadcast together at speed, something precise enough to be hopefully convincing without giving away too much. Her files suggested the galaxy didn't know much about the Darius Children, but she dared not assume that was true. They could easily have been monitoring the public datanet and downloaded copies of everything that entered the public domain. "And let us hope they listen."

She kicked in her drives a moment later, zooming towards the sphere. It grew closer with terrifying speed, the lattice of metal growing and growing until it became a flat wall blocking her flight. Centuries ago, humans had believed their world was flat; Mari knew, staring at the sphere, why they hadn't realised the truth. The sphere was a sphere, true, but it was one on so great a scale that a person living on the surface wouldn't have a hope of seeing a curve. The horizon would be as flat as a pancake. She wondered, suddenly, what sort of conclusions anyone living inside a Dyson Sphere would draw about their world, if they hadn't been the ones who'd built it. Would they suspect the truth? Or would they think the megastructure was the way the world was meant to be?

Her flight path altered, skimming across the surface and heading straight to the nearest entrance. The gap was both astonishingly large and yet terrifyingly small, a spaceport structure somehow resting within the gap even though it really shouldn't be there. It looked weirdly crude, both part of the sphere's interior and yet somehow separate from it ... she thought, suddenly, of a hermit crab, finding an abandoned shell on the seabed and turning it into a new home. The original builders were gone. Countless others had moved in, taking over the sphere. She wondered if the builders would be pleased, if they returned, or if they'd order the newcomers out. *That* would put the cat amongst the pigeons.

Henri gasped as she aimed for a gap between the spaceport struts, a space that looked tiny on the holographic display and yet was strikingly large in realspace. Mari paid him no heed, her awareness filling with urgent signals from the nearest alien stations, from demands she identify herself to traffic control – such as it was – to requests for more information about the scale of the crisis. Her communications subroutines monitored the traffic, noting hasty signals being exchanged between the fleets outside the sphere and smaller formations within, the latter making a mockery of the sphere's claim to neutrality. Her tactical subroutines drew up an ever-changing list of alliances, trying to determine who was on what side, and worked through possible tactics for escaping or evading if – when – the aliens opened fire. There were at least nine possible sides, she noted coldly, most of whom would be working at cross-purposes. Thankfully, their best chance of stopping her was already behind them. If they'd had time to get organised, they could have blocked her passage through the entrance and forced her to come to them, narrowing the range sharply. Now ...

"I think they're angry," Henri said. "And confused."

Mari grinned. "Can you read their thoughts at this distance?"

"I can feel their minds," Henri said. "They're different, and yet ... they're just like us."

"Oh." Mari frowned, thoughtfully. The display made the sphere look small, and the enemy ships look within spitting range, but there were millions of kilometres between her and the nearest potential target. If Henri could read thoughts at *that* distance ... she shook her head slowly. There would be time to worry about it later. Right now, she had to get past them before they decided to open fire. "Can you find her?"

"Yeah." Henri pointed. "She's thataway."

Mari plotted the course. Pandora was somewhere near the barycentre ... something of a relief, in a sense, given just how much damage she'd done on Jorlem Prime. There were two stars inside the Life Sphere and she dreaded to think what would happen if reality started to break down inside even *one* of them. Supernova bombs worked by creating gravitational eddies that triggered off a supernova, even in stars that were too small to go supernova naturally, and her sensors had insisted there were places on Jorlem Prime where the gravity field was strikingly, and impossibly, variable. For once, she hoped the sensors had been spoofed. The alternative was worse.

She ran a quick simulation, but she already knew the answer. Some local settlements *might* have forcefields that could protect them against a supernova, most wouldn't. The sphere itself might survive, but the interior would be largely swept clean of life, killing an uncountable number of sentient beings. The devastation would be beyond anyone's imagination, the simulation presenting numbers she couldn't mentally translate into anything resembling reality. It would be the greatest single catastrophe in the history of the known galaxy, perhaps killing more people in a moment than the Thule Wars had killed in ten years. If Pandora did it, accidentally ...

Not that she can't do a great deal of damage even without detonating a star, she thought. *If she really is on the brink of madness.*

"Hold on," she said. "Here we go."

There was no point in trying to blast *through* the alien ships, not if it could be avoided. She dared not fire the first shot, nor could she risk getting close enough to let them hit her before she knew she was under attack. Hyperspatial weapons could strike her ship well in advance of any warning, and she had no idea if the blocking force would risk using them. She was following an evasive course, just to make it harder to target her, yet if they used a scattershot pattern there was a very good chance they'd score a hit. Hell, if the range closed too rapidly, they might hit her with a sublight weapon. Instead, she altered course, skimming over the atmosphere at a respectable fraction of the speed of light. The enemy altered course themselves to keep blocking her. The fleet commanders seemed to have some difference of opinion about the right thing to do.

Henri cleared his throat. "Some are unsure if they believe us," he said. "Others know we're telling the truth."

Mari felt cold. "Can you point out the ones that know it?"

Henri hesitated, then pointed. Mari frowned. Four possible warships, three belonging to the slug-like race with an unpronounceable name. They were one of humanity's most persistent opponents, amongst the peer powers, never hesitating to put the human race down even as they did nothing to help the poor and downtrodden, or even to stop the human race. The fourth wasn't listed in her warbook, which suggested it belonged to someone new – or, more likely, that it had been carefully designed to alter its true origin. The Slugs were a major threat, at least to her, but they wouldn't risk outright war. Would they? If they weren't alone …

Her thoughts darkened as she altered course again. Sheer numbers wouldn't determine the outcome of any war with a peer power. It would be technology, ruthlessness, and a certain willingness to strike first. If the Slugs had put together an alliance to contain humanity … they had been talking about it for decades, but as far as the Peacekeepers had been able to determine it had never got any further than talk. If that was inaccurate … she frowned as the tactical patterns continued to develop. The Slugs were resting on the least-time course to Pandora's likely location. The other ships weren't. That suggested they didn't know what was really happening.

But they have to try to stop us before the AI intervenes,

she thought, grimly. *If they keep moving, I can isolate them from the Slugs.*

She kicked the drive to full power and blazed away from the surface, flying further into the sphere. The Archangel was the fastest thing in realspace, but if the enemy risked using hyperspace weapons or warp missiles they might well score a hit … particularly if they threw caution to the winds. She sent a series of commands into the system, launching a spread of decoy drones right at the Slugs while pulling a cloaking field around her own ship. It wouldn't fool them for long, but it might just be enough to force them to make some hard decisions. If they opened fire … it was hellishly risky, yet if it gave her clear proof the Slugs were hostile …

The Slugs opened fire, vaporising four of the drones. Their detection systems were better than projected, she noted coldly. Intelligence had missed something … either that, or they'd recently obtained the tech from someone else. Not impossible. The human race had copied a great deal of tech from other races, during its early years of spacefaring, and there was no reason the Slugs couldn't do the same. It was a challenge, but not one they couldn't overcome. Their active sensors pulsed, searching for her. She cursed under her breath, dropped the cloak, and flew forward, closing the range with terrifying speed. There were bare seconds to get through before it was too late …

Her subroutines flashed up an alert. The starships behind her were flash-charging their weapons, a clear threat to open fire … she tried not to roll her eyes as urgent signals came in a second later, ordering both her and the Slugs to stop firing … cheeky, when she hadn't fired a single shot. The drones weren't weapons and they had to know it. The Slugs widened their targeting locks, the space-combat version of pointing a loaded gun at someone's face, aiming at both her *and* the other starships. Her sensors noted a torrent of signals being exchanged, all so heavily encrypted that there was little hope of deciphering them in a reasonable timeframe. She suspected she could guess their meaning.

"They're going to fire," Henri said.

Mari didn't hesitate, throwing her ship into an evasive pattern as the Slugs opened fire. They weren't using any sort of FTL weapons, but that was meaningless when she dared not cross the FTL barrier herself. Instead, she projected false sensor images around her ship and dived closer, closing the range fast enough to engage with sublight weapons herself. Energy pulses flickered between the fleets, gravity-bombs twisted space; her datacores swept the enemy hulls, trying to upload aggressor programs into their datanets. Mari doubted they'd be able to take full control of even a single enemy ship, but a few seconds diversion might buy her enough time to get through and past. Might ...

Alerts flickered, behind her. Starships – warships – were entering the sphere. Dozens ... hundreds ... she couldn't tell who was on what side, or indeed if there *were* sides. There was too much firepower too close for anyone's peace of mind ...

"They're mad," Henri breathed.

"I got that," Mari said. Which side were the newcomers on? How many sides *were* there? The Slugs were altering course, coming around to chase her ... she hoped that was proof there wasn't another blocking force between her and the barycentre. The forces behind them seemed uncertain what to do, some chasing the Slugs and others heading to the entrance. She guessed they were planning to get out before it was too late, before they found themselves on the wrong side of a war. "I ..."

She broke off as more alarms sounded. She hadn't managed to get a good look at the structure near the barycentre, the structure that looked like hundreds of starships had been welded into one, but it was changing, warping and twisting, the struts bending in directions that made her head hurt ...

Henri screamed. "They're coming!"

Mari threw caution to the winds and dropped into warp drive.

But she knew it was already too late.

CHAPTER
TWENTY-FIVE

X had never seen anything so beautiful.

He had never dared play his games with a peer power. An advanced race would have no trouble spotting his agents, as they were inserted or corrupted, nor would be naive enough to fall for tricks that would have fooled a primitive and inexperienced race that barely understood the concept of life on other worlds. Getting caught might have triggered a war between humanity and his would-be victims, but there'd be no pleasure in watching two almighty civilisations burning if he weren't alive to see it. He'd often regretted his inability to convince an advanced race to destroy itself. It would be one hell of a show.

Now, he watched in awe as a dozen alien factions fell into combat. He'd seen hundreds of warships enter the sphere, and he'd known there were thousands more outside, but he hadn't really believed they'd actually start shooting at each other. The winning bidder would have more than enough firepower to keep Pandora, once they took possession, and everyone else would probably give up and go home, and scheme to kidnap a Darius Child of their own. The Archangel didn't change the situation that much, not when the bidding war had barely begun. He had wondered if it was time to leave …

Instead, hundreds of warships were clashing, exchanging blows in a manner unseen since the last major war. They were limited to STL weaponry, for fear of drawing the AI's attention, but that didn't stop them from devastating each other. Phasers and antimatter disrupters, microscopic black holes and nanotech weapons … he grinned, despite himself, as a giant five-kilometre starship vanished into a black hole, the mass dispelling a second later as it ran out of matter to eat and evaporated back into nothingness. The starship's allies retaliated with weapons of their own, seemingly-crude energy beams that rotated through frequencies until they found a weak spot and struck right *through* their target's defensive shields. The target staggered under their fire, launching smaller craft to defend their hull as the crew tried to withdraw. It was too late. Their shields went down and a spread of antimatter torpedoes vaporised the ship. It went on and on and …

An alarm sounded, one he'd tied to his cloned brains. X started, hastily rotating the display to look at the alien station. It was warping and twisting in front of him, so dramatically that he thought – for a moment – that the station had been struck by a black hole weapon and was dying in glorious slow motion. He realised his mistake a moment later. The station wasn't crumpling into a singularity, but warping and twisting in ways he couldn't even begin to comprehend. It was like gazing into a distorted mirror, a holographic funhouse where nothing was ever quite where it seemed. He keyed a switch as a distress beacon activated, the standard message replaced by something so distorted it was impossible to make out the words. And yet, just listening to it, he felt a chill running down his spine. The words were impossible to make out, but the meaning was clear.

Something is coming.

X stood and hurried to the brains, donning the neural link with complete disregard for his own safety. The impression of imminent doom grew stronger as awareness crashed down on him, confronting him with a reality he couldn't deny. His eyeballs hurt as he stared at the station, as if they were being forced to turn in several different directions at once. The starships were bending and twisting, some internal passageways leading in ways he couldn't comprehend and others elongating in a manner that was flatly impossible. The structure should be coming apart at the seams and yet it wasn't, as if it were a computer projection rather than a physical form. He wondered, a moment later, if that was what it was, in a sense. If they were messing with something really dangerous …

His mind darted forward. Pandora was trapped in the lab, local space warping and twisting around her and … something was scratching at the edge of reality, forcing its way through. X got a glimpse of one … and found himself back in his body, his nanotech working desperately to fix his eyeballs. It had been like staring directly at a star … no, it had been far worse. He felt as if someone had reached into his eye sockets and wrenched out his eyes, leaving him forever marked by contact with something utterly inhuman. The things on the other side were incredibly dangerous, and the researchers had let them in. Or perhaps it had been Pandora. Who knew? The data he'd downloaded before everything went to hell was inconclusive.

He gritted his teeth as the nanotech finished its work. His vision returned … it should have been perfect, yet instead it was blurred. He knew, at some level that could not be denied, that his vision would remain that way for the rest of his life, even if he cloned himself another body and uploaded himself into a brand new brain. The change was more *real* than the surrounding world … his sensors, trying to study the changes to the station, were giving up one by one. He didn't need them to know that something was coming, something scratching and tearing at the walls of reality. He could *feel* it.

His lips drew back in a snarl. The universe was going mad. The natural laws were breaking down, as he'd seen before, but this time he was right next to the epicentre. How far would it spread, he asked himself, as he swept his sensor focus over the station? The inhabitants were already going mad, fighting each other savagely; his tactical programs couldn't pick out any rhyme or reason, sides changing so randomly it felt as if something was constantly flipping a switch. Would the madness reach across the sphere? Or even further? Something was waiting to be born …

And Pandora was right at the heart of the madness.

X keyed his terminal, bringing his systems online. He'd wanted a tool to bring down almighty civilisations and he'd had one all along, before hanging her over to her buyers. He could take her back now, in all the confusion, and turn her into a weapon, the most powerful weapon the galaxy had ever seen. His imagination ran wild, coming up with all sorts of schemes for triggering wars and devastation on an unprecedented scale. Perhaps he could detonate stars, wipe out whole civilisations … he could play his games with everyone, after becoming a god in all but name. He could even challenge Loki …

His mind raced. Getting to her would be difficult, even if the station's inhabitants offered no resistance …and they were fighting each other so savagely there was a very good chance they'd take him out without knowing what they'd done. Teleporters were unreliable … or were they? The matter stream would be warped and twisted, scattering Pandora's atoms across hundreds of light years … he checked anyway, just to be sure, and cursed under his breath as the results popped up. His sensors were insisting Pandora was already hundreds of light years away. The sphere was big, immense beyond words, but not *that* big. He couldn't tell if the eerie distortion was getting to the sensors, or if the gap between the ship and the station was somehow bigger on the inside. It didn't matter. He had to hurry.

His fabber produced a simple combat suit. Simpler would be better, he thought, if everything was breaking down. Some of the station's systems were glitching, seemingly at random … he didn't have time to worry about it, as he snatched up a cloned brain and tied it under his arm. If his hunch was right …

He didn't bother with the shuttle, as he hurled himself into space. The craft would likely glitch – and besides, if his plan worked, he'd have to leave it behind. The suit's propellers pushed him forward, towards a station that now looked as if it were sharing space with something else, as if two structures had merged into one. He had to force himself to concentrate on the nearest airlock to the lab, just to get close to it. The distance he had to fly seemed impossibly long, but ... the airlock nearly came up and hit him. He opened it gingerly – the power had failed completely, something else that should have been impossible – and made his way into the structure. The lighting had failed too, yet the air was pulsing with an eerie reddish glow that made his head hurt. The corridors were twisted and warped, some leading in directions his instincts told him he couldn't go. He had seen some horrors in his time, but this ...

The corridor widened suddenly, revealing a handful of bodies on the ground. X studied the nearest one, a humanoid alien he didn't recognise, and sucked in his breath as he realised the alien had clawed out his eyes. They all had ... some were splattered with their own blood, which was developing mould ... X eyed it warily, all too aware it might be something far worse. There were some very nasty pieces of biological technology that started life as something akin to mould, consuming everything they touched and turning into something far bigger. He scanned it rapidly, but drew a blank. The results were so crazy they were impossible to believe. He hoped that meant the sensors were failing. The alternative was worse.

He kept walking, his audio sensors pinging wildly. Someone was screaming ... he could hear the sound inside his helmet. Pandora, broadcasting telepathically? Or someone else? He didn't know. His sensors started to fail, his internal guidance system going crazy ... he concentrated on the scratching, the sound always at the back of his head, and let it lead him onwards. The station appeared to be changing in front of him, the corridors shifting and twisting; liquid ran *up* one bulkhead and vanished into the shadows, liquid with no visible source … it was hard to remain focused, to keep going. The temperature rose sharply and then fell again. He wasn't sure if his suit's internal systems were failing too, or if it was all in his head. Or both.

A howl rent the air as he entered the next compartment. A seething mass of flesh greeted him, dozens – perhaps hundreds – of sentient beings, fighting so savagely it was beyond all reason. The aliens were tearing desperately at each other, their shouts and screams blending together into a single nightmarish sound … he couldn't tell if some were trying to escape or if they were all trying to kill each other, before they were killed themselves. It was … the mass just stopped, as if someone had flipped a switch, and looked at him, their faces going blank in eerie unison. The scratching grew louder. X gritted his teeth. If any sort of contact with the others was enough to drive sentient beings insane … oh, the possibilities were endless. He couldn't wait.

He aimed his machine guns and opened fire, spraying the crowd with primitive bullets. He'd thought the glitches wouldn't affect something so simple and he was relieved to find he was right, although some of the aliens started to move even *after* being sprayed with bullets. He shot one's head off, only to see the body keep advancing towards him. He had to practically riddle the bodies with bullets to keep them from moving, then hurry past them into the final section. If his plan didn't work, if he had to drag Pandora back again …

The scratching grew louder. He could hear voices, loud enough to be sure someone was talking and yet too quiet for him to make out the words. The corridors seemed to straighten, even though he had the uneasy sense he was plunging downwards. The bulkheads were lined with runes drawn in blood, the liquid gleaming wet and yet somehow remaining in place; he memorised them for later analysis as he hurried onwards, pushing open the final door. The lab was dark and yet he could see clearly.

An alien was sitting on the deck, rocking back and forth as blood poured from its eyes; a sluggish body was lying beside it, little more than a pile of slime. The darkness pulsed with alien life, *things* brushing against the material world. He stepped forward and blinked in surprise. The grey aliens seemed unconcerned about reality breaking down around him, unheeding of the damage to their supposed comrades. They were *still* poking and prodding at Pandora.

They really are biological robots, X thought. It was the only explanation that made sense. His research suggested that intelligence meant a link to the quantum foam, which also meant vulnerability to attacks that came from beyond the foam. A sighted man could be blinded by a strong light, aimed into their eyes, but a blind man couldn't be harmed by mere light. *And their master is far away enough not to be affected by the breakdown in local reality.*

The grey aliens ignored him. He took careful aim and opened fire, putting a bullet through the closest alien's head. It exploded into a greenish mass, degrading the moment it hit the atmosphere. X twisted his lips in disgust and shot the remaining aliens, one by one. They made no attempt to stop him, or even to escape. More proof, if he'd needed it, that they weren't really alive. Most life forms would fight, if there was no other choice; there were only two known races physically incapable of violence and they'd both wound up slaves to others that could and would use force at the drop of a hat. He stepped forward, scooping up a sample of the biological matter for later study. It was degrading at remarkable speed, destroying the evidence of who'd created them, but ... it hardly mattered. He wanted to create his own, not track down the creator.

He gritted his teeth as he reached the table. The scratching was all around him now ... it was *in* him. He dared not raise his head and look behind him, or even widen his eyes, for fear of what he might see. The whispering was growing louder too, promising him everything he'd ever wanted ... the sound was more *real* than anything else, growing and growing until it was the only thing in the universe. Something was crawling inside his eyes ... he held himself still with an effort, feeling as if he were holding reality together by sheer force of will. He looked down at Pandora, her body so pale it shocked him ... she'd been tanned, only a few short hours ago. Her skin was red raw around the straps holding her in place, as if she'd been mindlessly struggling; her eyes were wide, staring at nothing. His sensors refused to pick up anything under her skin. They seemed unsure if she were even there.

What if our universe is the hologram, X asked himself, *and she's slipping into the* true *reality?*

He wasn't sure if it was his thought or something else, something alien, but it refused to go away. He touched her lightly and frowned. She felt real and *alive* and also cold and dead. It made no sense ... he shook his head, reaching for the cloned brain and linking his mind into the neural net. Reality was twisted and warped ... he forced it to straighten, as if he were catching and tying a boat a moment before it plunged over the waterfall. Pandora moaned – he wasn't sure how he heard her – as the world calmed, the tempest retreating into nothingness. X didn't hesitate. He triggered the teleporter, bracing himself ... if his gamble failed ...

The teleporter was normally a tingle, the world dissolving into light and rematerialising into something different. This time, it was a long slow process, his body frozen in a beam of light and yet itching, an itch he couldn't scratch. His thoughts were sluggish, each moment of thought inching through his mind ... a process that was flatly impossible. He thought he saw *things* in the teleport beam, *things* that shouldn't have been there ... it was impossible, in theory, to be trapped forever in a pattern buffer, but so many impossible things had happened in the last few days that he no longer believed *anything* was impossible. The air itself seemed to crawl around him as the teleporter put him back together, his body staggering as gravity took hold once again. Pandora's body hit the deck hard, her hair spilling out in a manner that suggested it no longer needed to care about the laws of physics. X slapped a control nanotech hypospray against her skin and shot the nanomachines into her, then ordered a pair of plastic ties from the fabber and used them to bind her hands and feet. The nanotech was no longer reliable. He dared not assume the datacore could keep her under control. The distortion was getting worse.

And the Archangel was inbound. He had no more time.

X activated the cloaking field, then steered a hasty course around the station and away, relying on the sensor distortion to cover his path. The Archangel shouldn't be able to even get a sniff of his presence, although now Pandora was removed from the station he had no idea what would happen to it. The shifts in reality might undo themselves and everything might flow back into place, or several parts of the structure might try to occupy the same place at once, resulting in a colossal explosion. Or … who knew? All that mattered was that he had Pandora …

And the power he needed to set the galaxy on fire.

CHAPTER TWENTY-SIX

Mari felt her head hurt as she neared the alien structure.

Her sensors were amongst the finest in the known galaxy, certainly the best the human race could produce. She could track a tiny starship halfway across a star system, locate another that had powered down completely and was pretending to be an asteroid, perhaps even track a lone human on a planet and scoop him up with her teleporters before he realised his cover had been blown and he was about to be taken away. And yet, the results were maddeningly contradictory, to the point she was running a constant series of self-checking subroutines. The station appeared to be changing in front of her, as if several different structures were trying to occupy the same space and time. *Nothing* made any sort of sense.

"They're coming," Henri moaned. "I can hear them!"

"Can you find her?" Mari didn't mean to snap, but her sensors couldn't dig more than a few metres into the structure. The few results she had were maddeningly inconclusive ... she couldn't help wondering if someone had hacked into her network and was currently feeding her a stream of lies. It was supposed to be impossible, but so was an entire planet being driven mad by a human sociopath. The irony was that a hacker somehow cracking her datacores would be a lesser threat than the twists in reality itself. "Is she on the station?"

"I can't tell," Henri said. "The … something is coming. Something bad."

Mari found herself, once again, unsure what to do. She had a thousand hostage-rescue programs in her datacore, from the use of covert force and infiltration to hasty assaults that took out the kidnappers and recovered the hostages before they knew they were under attack, but they all relied on full access to her ship's weapons and intelligence-gathering capabilities. Right now, the probes were failing and she had no idea where to even begin looking for Pandora. There was no way to take down the shield generators either, not when she wasn't sure they even existed. A standard distortion field had an epicentre, where the generator had to be located. *This* one was weird, ebbing and flowing in a manner that suggested there were multiple generators or none. She feared the latter. The effect was just too strange, too uncanny, to be the product of known technology.

She launched a spread of drones towards the station, keeping them under close observation through a foldspace link. It should have been impossible to disrupt the links, let alone break them, but the drones started to drop out of the network the moment they entered the station and started making their way through the corridors. The handful of images they sent back were far from reassuring, scenes of horror that chilled her to the bone. They were distorted too, in a manner that puzzled her. She couldn't recall who had first pointed out that whatever was half-seen was all the more disturbing to the imagination, but it was true. The images scared her on a very primal level.

"I'm trying to reach her," Henri said. "But the noise is so loud …"

Mari nodded. Two of her drones had landed on the station's hull and were trying to hack the local network. It should have been easy. Most of the local datacores were primitive. But instead … the data was heavily scrambled, the files wiped or somehow randomised, leaving very little behind. Some of the programs were even actively dangerous, pulsing out a series of patterns that threatened to infiltrate her defences. The entire system would have to be physically destroyed at some point, she noted coldly. Whatever it was storing in its datacores, it was too alien to be countered and too dangerous to be kept around for study.

"There's only a handful of minds left on the structure," Henri reported. "I ... I don't think she's there."

Mari frowned. "Dead?"

"I ... I don't *think* so," Henri said. "I think I would have felt her die."

And how would you know? Mari asked herself. None of the Darius Children had ever died. They had no way to know how it would feel, when one finally did. *She might have died somewhere in the distortion and ...*

"Tell me where they are," she said. "If we can get a proper lock on the survivors, we might be able to teleport them out."

Henri hesitated. "I can't determine the exact location," he said. "But ..."

He cleared his throat. "We could go to them."

"No," Mari said, firmly.

She ignored his gasp of dismay. There was bravery, and then there was suicide. She had no idea what awaited them, inside the warped and twisted structure, and no backup. The fighting fleets couldn't be relied upon, even the factions that seemed more interested in restraining the Slugs than helping them. If she'd had a crew, even a handful of Confederation Marines, she might have taken the risk ... or perhaps not, not when the Marines controlled their remote units through foldspace links that should have been impossible to jam. The system made sense normally – it didn't matter how many jarhead remotes were destroyed, when the operator remained well clear of any fighting – but now it was an actual liability. Henri didn't have the training or implants he needed to go in alone, nor could he operate the ship while she went in ...

A thought crossed her mind. She sent a series of instructions to the fabbers, commanding them to push out a wired control system, backed up by radio and laser signals. Primitive, compared to modern technology, and lacking the bandwidth she was used to, but it might just survive the maelstrom where modern technology glitched and died. She didn't dare go much closer, not until she had a better idea of what she was dealing with, but ... she breathed a sigh of relief as she launched the first set of modified drones. The datalinks failed the moment they reached the interior. The radios were disrupted. The wires remained intact.

Unless they can be distorted too, she thought. Primitive societies such as Parnassus never realised their communications cables could be hacked from a distance, if the hacker had the right technology. *Whatever we're dealing with, it is far beyond us.*

The thought chilled her as the drones advanced slowly into the station. The images were clearer now, but they were so improbable she honestly wondered if they were being spoofed. A stream of greyish water was heading *up* a bulkhead, with no visible source; she couldn't tell if it was bubbling up from under the flooring or simply appearing out of nowhere. Bodies lay everywhere, many injured at their own hands ... she shuddered as she realised just how many aliens had torn out their own eyes, rather than see whatever they were seeing for one second longer. Others had clearly fought to the death, dealing out and taking immense damage as the bloodlust overwhelmed them. She felt her heart twist as she spotted a Sarnia, a representative of a race that was normally gentle and utterly civilised ... the alien had died with his hands around another alien's throat, his placid features frozen in a rictus of snarling rage. The nightmare had killed nearly everyone ...

She cursed under her breath as the images started to flicker, even though the wires remained intact. Some bulkheads were twisted and broken, as if some angry god had picked them up and put them back in the wrong order; some corridors looked out of proportion, as if they were far longer than they should be. She pressed onwards, using maintenance drones to add extra wires ...

she realised, too late, that the disruption was stronger when there *wasn't* a mind controlling the drones. It made no sense. Why did it matter?

Henri spoke into the silence. "Perhaps the observer affects the observed."

Mari felt a hot flash of anger. "Don't read my mind!"

"I'm sorry," Henri said. "But ..."

"Be quiet," Mari said. The drones were inching into a chamber, the distortion almost painfully strong. The network was threatening to collapse completely, even though she was controlling the links directly. The floor was covered in slime and ... a lone alien was sitting in the liquid, rocking back and forth like a child. "I wonder ..."

She took a breath, locked the teleporter onto the alien, and kept a firm eye on the system as it beamed the alien onto the ship. The laws of physics had changed ... perhaps they'd been rewritten completely. A high-gain signal like a teleporter shouldn't work, but if she watched everything herself ... would that *make* it work? Her old tutors had talked about the power of positive thinking, something she'd thought was silly at the time. There were some odds that simply couldn't be defeated, no matter how positive you were. But here ... she breathed a sigh of relief as the alien materialised on the pad, a forcefield snapping into place to contain him. It had worked. Cold logic told her it shouldn't, yet it had. It was just ...

The alien started, his hands coming away from his eyes. Henri retched. There was nothing left, but ... Mari tried not to recoil as she scanned the alien's body, silently relieved she had a baseline for his species loaded into her datacore. The results were odd. Some of his implanted hardware had failed, with no apparent rhyme or reason ... her eyes narrowed as she realised there *was* a logic to the glitches. The implants that were practically part of him had survived. The rest were dead and gone.

She frowned as the scans dug deeper into his body. He was wounded, in ways that made no sense. He looked to have suffered internal injuries, yet there was no trace of anything passing through his body. If he'd had nanites in his bloodstream, there was no trace of them either. There didn't seem to have been any repair efforts or medical treatment ... some of the wounds were oddly *real*, perplexing her sensors. It made no sense.

The alien spoke in a common trade language. "Who are you?"

"You are onboard a Peacekeeper starship," Mari said, in the same tongue. It had been designed for inter-species communication and lacked a great deal of finesse, but it would suffice. The alien being blind worked in her favour, as much as she hated to admit it. If he knew how few humans there were on the ship, he might do something stupid. She dared not assume he couldn't hack the datacores. Half his implants were still working and some had functions she couldn't work out without removing them. "What were you doing on the station?"

She frowned as she reviewed the last of the footage. There had been a table in the chamber, an examination table ... not proof of anything, not in itself, but suspicious. The alien had been there ... she sent the last of the drones forward, trying to find proof Pandora had been there. A proper DNA sweep was impossible, but the primitive sensors should be able to find traces of a human presence ... she sucked in her breath, sharply, as the results came in. Pandora had been there.

"You were experimenting on a human prisoner," she said, carefully. The baseline data she had wasn't good enough to pick out a lie, but hopefully the alien wouldn't know it. "What were you doing with her?"

The alien said nothing for a long moment, then spoke with desperate intensity. "I demand you return me to my people at once."

Mari scowled. "You were captured in the middle of an illegal operation, conducting experiments on a kidnap victim," she pointed out. Some races thought nothing of kidnap and rape or even murder, but most understood that others disagreed with them and kept such tendencies firmly within their own societies. "We have more than enough proof to detain you."

"I know nothing of such matters," the alien said. "I demand you return me to my people."

Mari briefly considered her options. There was no easy way to force the captive to talk. The rules for treating POWs were very clear: they could not be compelled to talk, nor could they be subjected to anything from torture to direct brain scanning. There were some exceptions, but she wasn't sure if the courts would agree with her interpretation of the rules. The simple fact that the alien came from a peer power meant that it wouldn't be easy to dismiss their objections, if indeed they took offense. Mari wouldn't hesitate to cheer if an alien race killed X in cold blood and, for all she knew, the POW's government would feel the same way. But it was rarely so simple. X was human and the Confederation had a duty to humans …

Henri stepped forward. The alien flinched, although he couldn't see Henri. Mari felt cold as she realised what Henri was doing, scanning the alien's mind. It wasn't illegal … not technically, if only because there were no recorded incidences of cross-species telepathy. She wondered, numbly, if it would be counted as brain scanning, if the alien government filed a formal complaint. It wasn't going to end well.

"You …"

Mari reached out to stop Henri before he committed a genuine crime. "Did you get everything."

"Yes." Henri sounded shaken. "I …"

"Good," Mari said. She triggered the stasis field, trapping the alien in a moment of suspended time. The alien's implants were frozen, but … there were some oddities around its mind. There shouldn't be any patterns, yet they were there … as if the stasis field had only slowed down time rather than stopping it completely. It was just bizarre. She ordered the manipulators to transfer the captive to a tiny cabin and lock him in, just in case he somehow escaped the field. "Now. Tell me."

Henri looked pale. "He's a top-secret government agent, who was sent to study a human captive" – he grimaced – "he never knew Pandora's *name*. His government was given a chance to verify the captive's abilities, then bid for permanent possession. The war fleets were dispatched to ensure the bidding was fair and above board, then transfer her back home if his government won the auction."

Mari scowled. "Does he know that for sure, or does he merely believe it?"

"He thinks he's working for his government," Henri said. "I think ..."

"He may be," Mari said. Deniable assets were common, and so were false-flag operations. So too were deception ops, designed to convince angry enemies that it really *had* been a false-flag and the true culprit was someone somewhere else. "Go on."

"Pandora was brought here and handed over to the research team," Henri said. "There were some creepy grey aliens in charge of the tests, but he watched the experiments until everything started to break down. Until ..."

He staggered, as if he'd been hit. "Everything is blurry at that point, impressions and *things* at the back of his mind ..."

Mari reached out and held his arm. "Why did he tear out his own eyes?"

"There was something ..." Henri broke off. "There was something so terrible he couldn't bear to look at it. It was so bad he ..."

His hands twitched and clawed, reaching for his eyes. Mari darted forward and caught his wrists, a second before he could jab his fingers into his eye sockets. She would have thought the pain would be enough to stop him, but it was difficult – almost impossible – to resist an implanted command. Had the alien been commanded to blind himself? Or had he found himself staring into the face of the medusa? Mari had never felt so convinced she had to destroy her own body and mind, or even erase some of her memories, and she'd certainly never done it ... but the alien clearly had. What had he seen? Did she even want to know?

"The next thing he remembers clearly is being here," Henri said. "I ..."

He relaxed. Mari didn't let go of his wrists. "Why ... why did he think his government could help? Would help?"

"Because governments don't like other governments pushing their people around," Mari growled, thinking fast. "They have to defend their people, even if they are utter bastards, for fear of setting a dreadful precedent. And if that happens ..."

She shook her head slowly. "Can I trust you not to claw out your own eyes? Or should I tie you up?"

Henri managed a bleak smile. "You're into bondage?"

Mari rolled her eyes. She was perfectly familiar with raw and inexperienced officers using humour to distract themselves from their fears, but there were limits. And she had no idea if she *could* trust him. If he'd somehow picked up a piece of alien conditioning ... Henri might mean well, but if there was something lurking in his mind his promises meant nothing. His free will could be overridden at any moment.

"I'll program the datacore to grab you if you try," she said. She hoped to hell it would work. The eyes could be regrown, given time, but the oddities surrounding the alien's eye sockets worried her. If she couldn't replace Henri's eyeballs, would he be blind for the rest of his life? It made little sense, but what did now? "Now, can you find her?"

Henri hesitated, closing his eyes for a long moment, then pointed. Mari projected the course ... past the station and heading towards the closest star. Her heart sank, then hardened.

"Tell her we're on our way," she said, sending orders to the datacore. X was close. He wasn't going to escape this time. She would fly through an alien battle fleet to grab him. "It won't be long now."

CHAPTER
TWENTY-SEVEN

Pandora came back to herself slowly, painfully.

Her head hurt. Her eyes hurt. Her vision was oddly blurred, as if she were trapped in a chamber of fragile translucent holograms. She was lying on a cold metal deck, her arms bound behind her back and her ankles tied together. The deck was solid and yet, in a sense, it wasn't. The entire world felt faintly skewed, as if it had been taken apart and then put back together in a manner that was just a tiny bit wrong. Her head echoed with pain, her memories a jumbled mess. Where was she? What had happened to her now?

She reached out with her mind and regretted it, instantly. The astral plane was *boiling* with … *something*, something so alien she couldn't force herself to look at it. She had the uneasy sense she would die if she tried, or that she'd bring something back into her mind that would overwhelm her and flourish into the mortal plane. It was … she felt sick, twisting her head as she dry-retched helplessly. She had no idea how long the little grey aliens had kept her in custody, but they hadn't bothered to feed her. It felt as if she was on the verge of starving to death.

Her wrists hurt. Someone had tied her tightly, too tightly. She had to force herself to wrap her head around it, in a universe where nanotech could operate her body on remote control someone had bound her hands? It made no sense and yet ... she felt an odd flicker of hope. The ties were solid and yet, they were also translucent. She pushed at them, twisting her head in a manner that was practically at right angles to reality, and pulled her hands *through* the ties. They crumpled to dust behind her. The ankle ties followed a moment later. She rolled over and sat up. She was alone in the chamber.

She looked down at herself. Her skin was strikingly pale, too pale. Her wrists were bruised, the dark marks standing out against her unnaturally pale skin. There were faint marks all over her body, suggesting the grey aliens really *had* been randomly stabbing her with needles. She forced herself to stand, reaching out carefully with her mind. The astral plane was still boiling, but ...

... She was suddenly aware of a dark sun hanging in her mind ... no, in the astral plane ... shedding dark light over the scene ...

Her legs wobbled. She caught herself and staggered forward, unsure what she hoped to find. The world was thin and translucent, the display pad on the side of the hatch dark and cold. It felt more like a dream than reality, even though she knew she was awake. The hatch hissed open and she saw ... she recoiled, suddenly unsure *what* she was seeing. X sat in a chair, facing her, but his head was overlaid by a giant pulsing brain. It throbbed as she entered ... she had the oddest sense it was looking at her, even though X was staring at the deck and there were no visible eyes on the brain. She wasn't even sure it was real ... no. It was real. It was the realist thing on the starship.

And X was right in front of her, helpless.

She lunged forward before she could stop herself, bent on smashing his skull. He was probably backed up somewhere, but she no longer cared. She just wanted him dead. The pain and suffering and ... and something she couldn't quite remember, something her mind had blacked out for the sake of what remained of her sanity, demanded revenge. She wanted to kill him and ... her body stumbled as it was suddenly frozen, her heartbeat halting even as her thoughts raced on. X raised his head and stared at her. She had the weirdest sensation his head was bigger, far bigger, than it looked ...

And something was wrong with his eyes.

X had been dark and handsome, in a vague kind of way. His eyes had been part of his charm, perfectly sculpted to complete the impression he wished to make. Now ... his eyes looked as if they were no longer part of him, as if they were balls that had been pushed into his eye sockets and declared eyes, as if declaring something was true was enough to make it so. Her blood ran cold as she realised that might be true, if one could manipulate the quantum foam. She had the feeling he was doing it too now ...

She allowed her perceptions to rush around the chamber, even as he held her body firmly in place. The chamber was surrounded with brains, bubbling in liquid and linked to his mind through a complicated nightmare of biological tech and neural links. They felt oddly familiar and yet alien ... horror ran through her as she realised he'd kept cloning *her* brain, using it to give him comparable abilities ... without, she noted grimly, the empathy that was part of her birthright. Reality itself was shifting around him and that meant ... she didn't want to know. The researchers had held her back, simply because they'd believed the psi powers had to be governed by the laws of physics. X was not so burdened, and that made him powerful. Powerful ... and dangerous.

"Well." X spoke directly into her mind, his thoughts cold and hard and threatening in a way none of her peers had ever been. "How did you free yourself?"

"I just did," Pandora lied. She didn't want him to know what she'd done. "It just worked."

X didn't move. It crossed her mind, too late, to wonder if he could read her thoughts. He didn't appear to have the empathy that defined the nest, but that didn't mean he couldn't look into her mind. She wasn't used to lying either ... had he been able to tell? Or had he decided she knew little about how her powers worked ...

Her body jerked. "You may order something to eat in

the next chamber," X said. "The datacore will watch you. You will not be permitted to hurt me."

Pandora scowled. "What did you do?"

X smiled, although there was no humour in the expression. "What did *you* do?"

Pandora shuddered as her memories unlocked. Something had been scratching at the edge of reality, demanding in … she'd *let* it in. She wasn't sure what had happened afterwards, but …

"There were nearly thirty thousand sentients on that station," X said. He sounded amused at her dismay. "You drove them mad. Many killed themselves. Others killed their fellows, or clawed out their eyes because they couldn't bear their glimpse into the fundamental nature of reality. You did that."

"I didn't," Pandora protested. "I …"

"You changed reality itself," X said. "And you have unleashed something great."

Pandora closed her eyes. The dark sun was behind her, behind them, but she could *feel* it and …

She shuddered. The aliens were fighting, great warships manoeuvring to strike deadly blows at their enemies. She could *see* them. She could sense the minds controlling the mighty ships, some intent on victory at all costs and others trying to figure out how to disengage without being stabbed in the back; she groaned, bitterly, as a starship exploded, a thousand sentients evaporating into nothingness … she had the eerie sense their souls were going somewhere she couldn't follow. She felt tears prickling at her eyes. Millions had died, and millions more were going to follow, and it was all her fault.

"We're coming," a voice said, into her mind. The rush of personality traits nearly drove her to her knees. Henri! It was Henri! He was alive. "We're coming!"

X started. "The Archangel has locked onto us!"

Pandora followed his thoughts. His ship was racing across the sphere, but another ship – a faster ship – was giving chase. X had a cloaking device, yet it seemed useless … she couldn't keep from smiling as she realised Henri had sensed her presence. The cloaking device couldn't hide her thoughts from her friend! And that meant …

"You're doomed," she said. Taunting X was hardly safe, but she no longer cared about her own safety. "That ship will destroy you."

X held her eyes. "No, it won't," he said. "Because I have you."

Pandora gritted her teeth as the translucent brain pulsed, daggers of hostile thought stabbing into her brain. He was trying to use her, she realised numbly; he was trying to trigger her powers, to cause another series of disasters that would take out the new ship – and Henri. Pandora didn't know if Henri would fight her, or even if he could … if he realised he'd have to try. The Children had never fought, never set out to hurt each other … he wouldn't see her as hostile and he wouldn't defend himself, not until it was too late. Her telekinesis could rip the oncoming ship to atoms …

No, she thought. Her power tampered with reality itself. There were limits … or were there? It didn't matter. She told herself it wouldn't happen and it didn't. He could control her body. He couldn't control her mind. *I won't let you use me any longer.*

X muttered a word she didn't recognise, but sounded vile. "Open your mind."

"No." Pandora was suddenly more aware of herself than she'd ever been. He hadn't risked tampering with her mind, not on a major scale, but … a flash of horror ran through her as she realised he *had* managed to implant at least one suggestion into her mind. A simple suggestion that kept her from making contact with her peers … "I won't."

She tasted his sudden flicker of desperation, his mind racing as he grasped for options. There were none. There was no way he could get out of the sphere and escape into hyperspace and, even if he risked going to FTL *inside* the sphere, the newcomer was close enough to give chase and follow him all the way to his destination. He couldn't outfight the newcomer and he couldn't outrun her and …

he couldn't even threaten to harm Pandora if he wasn't allowed to leave freely. There were so many lives at stake that the needs of the majority equation was far too easy to solve. Pandora was entirely sure she would be considered disposable and … she didn't mind. Not really. It wasn't that she wanted to die, and there was no backup of her as far as she knew, but in truth she no longer cared.

"Give up," she urged. What could he do? Fly into a star and hope his shields would let him survive long enough to escape? Even for the Confederation, star-diving was a dangerous sport and its players had been resurrected multiple times. "This is the end."

X closed his eyes for a long moment. Pandora stared, suddenly convinced he was doing something … but what? She forced herself to reach out to Henri, to channel as much information as she could into his brain. He had to understand the danger, if X used his abilities to damage reality around the oncoming starship. If he couldn't keep reality on an even keel …there was no end to the list of potential disasters, each one worse than the last. X had an active imagination and a complete lack of scruples, of anything that might make him think twice about what he was doing. Hell, his lack of precise scientific knowledge might be an advantage. He had fewer preconceptions about what might be impossible.

The universe shifted again, as if it was on the verge of sneezing. Something thrust its way into reality, from above … a process that was both incredibly fast and terrifyingly slow. She opened her mind … and then rapidly shut it again as a presence slipped down the link, materialising in the middle of the chamber. Loki stood there … he had always been there, as if reality itself had pulled back to make a space for him. Pandora's head hurt. He was there. He had always been there. He *would* always be there …

"You appear to be in something of a pickle," Loki observed. His tone was light, as if he was more amused than concerned by the whole affair. It was hard to look at his form directly. The more Pandora looked, the more blurry he became. "There's an Archangel on your tail."

"You wanted me to hand her over to a bunch of alien researchers," X snapped. Pandora didn't need telepathy to *hear* the desperation in his voice. "And now the researchers are dead."

"They are?" Loki pretended surprise. "What a bore."

"You promised me a reward if I delivered her to the researchers," X said. "I want to claim it now."

"I told you that you would *name* your reward," Loki corrected. It was impossible to make out his lips, but Pandora was *sure* he was smiling. "And you will."

X looked as if he had been punched. "You ... you said I could name my reward!"

"I said you would," Loki agreed. "I never promised I would give it to you."

Pandora couldn't help herself. She giggled. It was a childish argument, a loophole that would shame a grown adult ... and a near-omnipotent being, who had named himself after a trickster god, was using it to refuse to help his pawn? X rounded on her, then stopped himself with an effort. He didn't have time.

"I need your help," X said. "If they catch me ..."

"I told you that I could not offer you supernatural assistance," Loki reminded him. There was no doubt about the smile now: cold and cruel and utterly inhuman. "I cannot be seen to intervene."

"I'll tell them all about you," X threatened. "I'll tell them ..."

Loki shrugged. "So what?"

He vanished. Reality snapped back into place, as if he'd never been there at all. Perhaps he hadn't, in a sense. Pandora felt her head spin ... the body they'd seen had been little more than a glove puppet, an avatar operated by someone – something – far away. Loki wouldn't have noticed, or cared, if X destroyed his puppet, any more than the Confederation cared about the loss of the foldspace-controlled drones it used to talk to aliens living on gas giants. She wondered if he'd even feel it, if someone attacked his puppet. And yet, the link between his true self and the drone had been obvious to her.

She giggled, again. "What are you going to do? Sue him?"

X glared, his eyes bulging in unnatural directions. "You think the Confederation will let you go back to Clarke, after this? You're as responsible for the deaths of countless billions as I!"

Pandora hesitated. In truth, she wasn't sure. The Peacekeepers might understand that she had been kidnapped, her abilities used against her will, but would the general population? The Darius Children frightened the Confederation by existing, and *that* had been before Jorlem Prime and ... and whatever she'd unleashed, the protuberance that took the shape of a dark sun. The aliens were still fighting ... would she be blamed for that too? Or ...

"It doesn't matter," she said. She would take her knocks, if that was what they felt she deserved. She would submit herself to their justice, accept their right to judge her ... even if it meant her death. Would it? The Confederation didn't use the death penalty, but other races did. If she was handed over to one of them, she would be killed before she had the chance to back herself up somewhere safe. "It wasn't my fault."

"They won't believe it," X said. He turned away, his hands dancing over a console. The display changed, showing the starship ... and a second ship, closing from the rear. "How many people did you kill? Do you think they'll let you go free?"

"I don't care," Pandora said. She could feel reality shifting around her. Henri was coming ... but would he be in time? She didn't know what was going to happen and yet ...she knew something was. The dark sun was still glowing, its presence casting a long shadow through the collective unconscious of each and every intelligent race. "If I die ..."

She drew herself up, as best she could, and tried to put a dignified expression on her face. "If I die, at least I'll take you with me."

X snorted. "I have backups, somewhere so well hidden

that if you had a billion years you would never find it," he snapped. "The data I took from you, the data I stole from the researchers, has been sent onwards, to an equally secure datastore hidden on the darkweb. I will be resurrected and live again, learning from the mistakes of my past self and turning the knowledge I gained into something practical."

He poked a finger at her. "You will just die. And that will be the end."

His voice hardened. "Do you even *have* a backup?"

"Of course," Pandora said.

X smiled, cruelly. "Liar."

Pandora tried not to flinch. She didn't *like* lying. It was pointless back home and here … it was worse than useless. She hoped X hadn't seen through her earlier lie, but … he probably had. A wave of helplessness washed through her, a grim reminder she was still his prisoner. He had one last card to play.

His gaze hardened. "But seeing you won't do anything to help, I suppose I'll have to take care of it myself."

Pandora's eyes narrowed. "What do you mean …?"

X tapped a switch. In unison, the brains started to thrum …

And Pandora realised, too late, what Loki had wanted all along.

CHAPTER
TWENTY-EIGHT

Mari couldn't hide her anticipation as the range closed.

X had a big ship, bigger than she'd realised, but it was almost painfully slow compared to the Archangel. Lacking an effective cloaking device or a head start, the odds of a successful escape were low to the point of non-existence. Unless Pandora somehow came into play … Mari had no idea what had gone wrong on the alien structure, and the records she'd stolen were hopelessly distorted, but it seemed unlikely that her abilities could be used as a targeted weapon. There was certainly no evidence to suggest otherwise. Jorlem Prime had been a planet, an easy target, and Pandora had been inside the alien station. She kept a wary eye on her sensors anyway, checking for the first sign of distortion. She wanted to recover Pandora alive, but if all hell broke loose she'd blow X's starship away and to hell with the consequences.

Henri cleared his throat. "Shouldn't we be demanding their surrender?"

"I can try," Mari said, doubtfully.

Her eyes narrowed. X *had* to know he'd be spending the rest of existence in suspension, after his backups were tracked down and eradicated. She was mildly surprised he hadn't committed suicide, although sociopaths were so self-centred they rarely regarded anyone else – even their own resurrected clones – as true people in any sense of the word. Besides, he might not have been able to back himself up after departing on his mission. It was possible to send a message through the local network onto the human datanet, even something as data-intensive as a personality back-up, but that would be noticeable. X had to fear it might be tracked back to his secure base. If his clones were destroyed before they were fully activated ... he would know true death. To a sociopath, there was nothing more terrifying.

She sent the signal anyway. There was no response.

Mari glanced at Henri, splitting her attention between him and the enemy starship. "Can you contact her?"

"I'm trying," Henri said. "It's ... I don't understand what I'm feeling. It's just ... *wrong*."

Mari gritted her teeth. Was X trying to lure her close, so he could blow her away? She had no idea what sort of weapons might have been loaded onto his hull, and his mysterious patron almost *had* to be a peer power. His ship shouldn't have been carrying anything capable of threatening her, but if he'd been given something that actually could punch through her shields and atomise the ship ... it wouldn't end well. The Archangel's small size normally worked in her favour, yet if she was damaged her destruction would follow quickly. Something a planetoid could shrug off would vaporise a ship her size. And if X really did have a weapon provided by a peer power, there would be very little warning – if any – before it hit her.

"Keep trying," she ordered, launching a spread of drones. If she could open a channel through his screens, she could teleport Pandora off the ship and then destroy it. X could die in fire, giving the Peacekeepers time to track down his secret base before he was resurrected. If not ... her mind raced, searching for options. There weren't many. If she had to open fire, she might accidentally kill Pandora. "We don't have much time."

She cursed, again. The alien fleets were shaking out, several formations racing towards her – pushing their drives to the limits – and others cutting and running, as if they'd decided the prize wasn't worth the candle. Her tactical subroutines ran through a hundred simulations, concluding that direct conflict with thousands of starships would end badly. Mari could have worked that out for herself, she reflected darkly. The aliens could fill space with enough firepower to guarantee a hit, unless the AI intervened. There was a possibility of working with one or more of the factions to take down the rest – her communications subroutines were noting dozens of signals being aimed at her, from offers of alliance to outright attempts to hack and subvert her datacores – but she doubted she could make it work long enough to grab Pandora and escape. The long-range sensors were reporting even *more* alien ships coming in from the opposite direction, suggesting her time was shorter than she'd thought. She might have to destroy X's ship – and Pandora – before they got into firing range. If that happened …

Henri coughed, violently. "Something is happening …"

Mari sent the signal again. There was still no response, but … her sensors were starting to go … she sucked in her breath. She understood sensor screens, and jamming, and even cunning attempts to spoof her sensors, tricking them into reporting misleading data, but this … it looked weird, as if someone was trying to mislead her sensors in a manner that was blatantly obvious. It was strange. Most sensor spoofing technology was designed to be as subtle as possible, to keep analysis subroutines from noticing discrepancies and taking the data apart to determine what was hidden under the façade. *This* was utterly absurd. The readings made no sense. Ice ran down her spine. Reality itself was breaking down. Again.

"I'm sorry," she said. She *had* wanted to recover Pandora. The poor girl hadn't asked to be kidnapped, or to be turned into a living weapon. Mari was sworn to protect Confederation citizens and Pandora very definitely *was* one. But … she couldn't let X threaten the entire sphere. There were billions upon billions of intelligent beings living on the surface or orbiting the two suns, all now at risk. "I truly am."

She triggered her weapons array. It was too late.

***

X felt reality itself boiling around him as he plunged his mind into the network of brains and reached out, his perception gliding through the starship hull as though it didn't exist and spreading out across the sphere. He felt a flicker of dark satisfaction at how well he'd tied the brains together, using them to cushion the sudden impact of being aware of literally *everything* around him, and reached out carefully to locate his target. It wasn't easy to organise his thoughts into a coherent pattern, not when distance was suddenly meaningless. There was an alien on the far side of the sphere, nearly a light-hour away, whose thoughts were bombarding his mind … it was hard to shut him out, him and all the others who were linked to the quantum foam. He had to struggle to narrow his perception, to locate the fleets approaching from two different directions. Their minds were an open book. They wanted Pandora and they didn't care if they had to take her over his dead body. X smirked in dark amusement. They had no idea what they were dealing with …

He narrowed his mind still further, his amusement growing as he sensed Loki. The entity was far superior to any material mind, yet forced to operate at one remove … his mere presence on the material plane, X noted, threatened to cause untold devastation if he tried to cram too much of himself into his glove puppet. X made a mental note of the potential, rolling his eyes at the sheer *lack* of involvement. Loki could do all sorts of wondrous and terrible things, yet he was content to watch. X hoped he would enjoy the show, as his mind kept expanding into the quantum foam. Given time, he would be powerful enough to challenge even a god.

His mind kept expanding. He was suddenly very aware

of Pandora, her thoughts a bright spark within the quantum foam. X *looked*, and suddenly knew *everything* about her, from her very first memories to thoughts and feelings she'd tried to hide from him. She was truly a pathetic creature, reliant on her nest for everything from validation to emotional support. He tasted her very first kiss, experienced her first experimentation with sex … the memory was so strong he could *feel* the penis slipping into her … he shook his head, dismissing her. She lacked the strength to stand on her own, to shape the universe around her; she couldn't even claim the rights of a citizen, the right to leave her homeworld and explore the galaxy. X had never depended on someone else, not like that. His ship was all he needed to cover the galaxy in his art.

Pathetic, he thought.

The Archangel was a tiny little ship, but the thoughts of its pilot and passenger were easy to detect and track. The passenger was just as pathetic as Pandora, more desperate to escape his homeworld and yet unwilling to use the power at his disposal to see it done. The Darius Children had barely scratched the surface of what they could do, prattling about telepathy and telekinesis without understanding the true nature of their power. X felt his lips curve back into a snarl as he explored Henri's mind, rolling his eyes in disgust. He was slightly more driven than Pandora, and the average citizen, but hardly enough to work for what he wanted. Or to find a way to take it.

Henri recoiled, in shock, and tried to fight. X laughed. It wasn't enough.

His mind kept expanding. There were no limits to his power, nothing stopping him from doing whatever he liked … no, that wasn't quite true. His personality was spreading through the quantum foam, but it was still linked to the network of cloned brains he'd devised to generate and bolster his abilities. He could do anything within their sphere of influence, nothing outside it … not directly. It was deeply frustrating, yet … the more his mind inched into the quantum foam, the more his sphere of influence grew. Given time, he would be able to do anything to the Life Sphere ... and beyond. His mind reached out to brush against the alien spacers, plotting to betray each other as soon as Pandora was within their grasp. Idiots. They had no conception of what he'd become.

The Archangel fired. X was almost impressed. The pilot had given up hope of recovering Pandora and was trying to kill her, along with him. A smart move, under the circumstances, but far too late. X could see every passing nanosecond, the light-speed weapons crawling towards his ship ... it wouldn't have worked, he noted coldly, if the enemy pilot had risked using superlight or hyperspatial weapons. A hundred thousand possibilities ran through his head, from the simple to the bizarre. He could stop the beams before they reached his ship, or bend them around his hull, or even aim them back at the shooter. He could warp and twist space around his ship, widening the gap between the two vessels to the point they would never meet in realspace, or ... he was almost overwhelmed by the sheer scale of his own omnipotence. It didn't frighten him. It just made it hard to decide what to do.

He focused, and bent the beams around his ship, pointing them at the nearest alien warship. It was the sort of targeting feat that was tricky even with modern technology, but easy for him ... in a sense, he hadn't aimed the beams so much as he'd told them what they were going to hit, drawing a mental picture that rewrote reality to suit himself. A hundred files ran through his mind, records from Darius. The magicians had cast spells using voodoo dolls, or blood samples, or even pictures of their targets ... the Confederation hadn't understood, but X did. Now. The distance was immaterial. All that mattered was that the spell focus and the target were linked together.

His lips curved back in a snarl as the Archangel fired again. It was time to have some fun.

***

Mari stared in disbelief. She'd fired a full antiproton burst, rotating the frequencies so rapidly that her beams *should* have cut through his shields and done real damage to his drive section and power cores. Even if the blast wasn't enough to destroy his ship, it should certainly have crippled him to the point the second blast would have vaporised both the vessel and its occupants. Instead … the beams had somehow curved *around* the ship and raced onwards, somehow transcending the speed of light to strike an alien warship. It staggered under the blow, then exploded. It shouldn't have happened. It was a big alien ship.

Henri screamed. "He's coming …"

The world seemed to fade around her, the entire ship threatening to crash so completely her mind was nearly thrown out of the datanet. She'd never seen anything like it, not since basic training. A total power failure was almost unknown. Anything powerful enough to take out the entire power generation and distribution net would also take out the entire ship. And yet … her head spun rapidly. It was strange. The aspects of the datanet she controlled personally were fine; the ones she normally left to subroutines were collapsing rapidly, as if they no longer existed. It was an incredibly powerful subversion, and yet it wasn't. It was something else.

Her sensor readings were so bizarre she almost hoped they *were* being spoofed. Her interior was suddenly impossibly big, yet also infinitely small. Henri was alive, and dead, and somewhere in between. Her hull no longer existed … no, it was made of paper … her weapons were firing madly in all directions and also powered down … she gritted her teeth and forced herself further into the datanet, trying to control as much as possible with her mind. It was …

"He's doing this," Henri breathed. The sensors insisted he was literally headless … and that he was somehow breathing vacuum. The contradiction was impossible to resolve. Alarms howled as the ship appeared to dissolve like a sugar cube in his tea, while remaining simultaneously intact. "I can feel him!"

Mari shuddered. There were few reports of contacts between humans and entities so advanced they might as well be gods, and most were difficult to believe. The few that *had* been verified ... she shuddered, again. Could she fight a god? Could she ... she bit her lip hard, reminding herself that defeatism almost always led to defeat. Whatever X was doing, it was curiously limited. If her own mind was holding it together ...

"Fight him," she urged. She thought it made a certain amount of sense. If her mind shaped local reality, she could keep him from influencing it through observation. Perhaps ... she wasn't sure of anything at the moment. "Try and keep him out!"

She fired, again. The weapons lashed out ... and did nothing. It was impossible.

But what *wasn't*, now?

***

Pandora sat on the deck, hugging herself, as she *felt* the nightmare spreading through the air ... no, reality itself. X was losing himself to his own creation, his mind poisoning the universe around him. It wasn't the *things* she'd seen on the other side of the quantum foam, she realised numbly, but something far worse. X was becoming a higher-entity, drunk on his own power and ... no, he was becoming a cancer. A cancer on reality itself.

That's what Loki wanted, she thought. It was difficult to wrap her head around the sheer scale of the impending disaster, but she was mortally certain it had been his intention all along. *He wanted a colossal disaster to give him an excuse to intervene.*

She shuddered. The Confederation had one exception to the non-inference rule and that was when a primitive race was on the verge of destroying itself. A species that was embarking on a nuclear war that would leave the world dead could be saved, even though the intervention would destroy their conviction they were alone in the universe and threaten them with an inferiority complex that would destroy them mentally, if not physically. Perhaps Loki intended to intervene – she could feel him watching, even now – or perhaps he *didn't*. The cancer was spreading, assaulting the very foundations of reality itself. Pandora could imagine stars exploding or simply being snuffed out, as the laws of physics changed around them; she could imagine technology failing on an unprecedented scale, the Confederation collapsing in a flash as the power went out once and for all. It would be the end …

He's scared of us, she thought. In the end, X and Loki had much in common. They both set up primitive races for self-destruction. *Scared enough to risk unleashing a holocaust on the entire universe.*

Her mind reached out. X was battering at Henri's ship … his power so vast, now, that it was actually hard to focus on such a tiny target. No … he was playing with it, tossing the ship around as if it were nothing. Henri was trying to fight, but he was a fly caught in a hurricane. Pandora tried to help, to offer him everything she knew, yet it wasn't enough. The pilot was no better. She couldn't keep her ship intact, past the moment X decided to destroy it. The possibilities were literally endless. He could turn the hull to antimatter, trap the ship forever in a single moment of time, even toss it so far across the universe that the pilot would never be able to find the way home. She could sense all kinds of twists in reality erupting across the Life Sphere, the side effects of X's grasp for supreme power. They were minor to him, yet utterly devastating for anyone nearby. She wondered, suddenly, what would happen to the sphere if the power failed. Would it remain habitable? Or would it freeze? Or fall into the stars?

She closed her eyes, unwilling to witness the end, and then stopped. X *hadn't* had abilities of his own. He wasn't one of the Darius Children. He'd stolen hers …

And that meant there was one last card to play.

CHAPTER
TWENTY-NINE

"Hold on," Henri said. "*Think* with me!"

Mari gritted her teeth as his mind thrust into hers, drawing on the raw power of her neural net as well as his own abilities. It was incredibly disorientating and if she hadn't been so used to linking her mind to the ship's datanet she suspected she would have pushed back, refusing to allow him to slip into her mind. Flashes of memory shot through her, memories that weren't hers ... her head swelled, a sensation that was both oddly pleasant and yet also very painful. It was suddenly very hard to think straight.

And yet, she had no choice.

She could *see* reality around her, see the underlying bedrock of the universe. It was as hard as stone and yet also flexible, if one had the right sort of abilities. X was a pulsing presence within the quantum foam, a nightmarish monster in human form ... limited, she realised grimly, only by his inability to comprehend his own abilities. He might be a sociopath, yet he was used to thinking of himself as human. That would change, as he grew more used to his new abilities. His mere presence was poisoning space, reaching out to poison her. She had the uneasy sense she was watching a star collapse into a black hole, close enough to make out every detail ... close enough to be sucked in, when the event horizon formed and started drawing everything else towards the black hole. Henri was beside her … no, he was inside her. Her lips twitched humourlessly. They were practically one person now, fighting desperately to maintain a stable grasp on their own reality. She had the nasty feeling they'd built a sandcastle on shifting sand and now the tide was coming in, threatening to destroy everything they'd built. And X was playing with them.

Mari shuddered. She could feel him too, the reality behind the pretence. He was no noble artist, no brave man discarding the restraints of lesser men and striding boldly into a brave new world; he was a twisted monster, caring nothing for anything save himself, a manipulator who wouldn't hesitate to play his games with humanity, if he thought he could get away with it. In the end, he was no better than any other sadistic edgelord, cloaking his true self behind an aura of being true to himself, of transgressing to prove that some rules existed only to be broken. Mari wondered if his fans understood his true self, or if they simply didn't care. The façade he projected was nothing more than an attempt to justify his crimes, and give his fans a degree of legitimacy. And in the end, it was just a lie.

She gritted her teeth, feeling his tendrils pulsing through the void, reaching out towards them. Their mere touch threatened reality itself, pushing them around as X laughed … his madness poisoning the universe around him. Mari drew on her datanet to support Henri, trying to hold reality together, all the while feeling her efforts being overwhelmed by X's sheer power. He had more than enough imagination to kill them instantly, if he wished, but he was playing with them instead. She could practically *see* ideas darting through his mind, ideas that would have been impossible – once – to even the most sadistic of sadists. She knew sociopaths who had locked themselves in perceptual realities or private universes of blood and pain and death, creatures so perverse she didn't want to acknowledge them as human. X would become worse than all of them put together, she realised grimly, if only because it would be real. You could use a safe word in a perceptual reality, if the reality proved to be worse than fantasy. There was no such thing as a safe word in the real world.

"Hold on," she said. Or Henri said. She couldn't tell. "We have to hold on."

Her weapons fired, beams lancing through space and stopping – dead – when they hit his shields. They were impossibly strong ... no, she knew now, he had twisted reality to ensure she couldn't hit his ship. It was now a law of nature, a localised law that was nonetheless unbreakable, that nothing could get through the invisible wall. She could feel his mind holding it in place, a subroutine that was somehow not a subroutine. If they could hack it ...

If they couldn't, they were doomed.

***

X hadn't had so much fun since he'd manipulated an entire planet into unleashing a hate plague and watched them destroy themselves.

It had been tricky, back then, to make it happen without intervening openly. The aliens might have been primitive, but they were rational, and their instinctive reaction to his subtle prompts had been to question what they were being told, rather than accept it unquestioningly. They'd been smarter than humans, he'd reflected at the time, and it had taken decades to put all the mental dominoes in place, ensuring that when they crossed the line the plague would spread too rapidly to be countered and defeated. A handful had even survived ...

Now, he could twist reality itself. The Archangel was a bubble of the old reality trapped within the new, a wooden sailing ship caught in a storm so powerful it was just a matter of time before it capsized and sank, the crew dragged below the waves and drowned. His awareness flashed through the bubble, sensing the desperate thoughts of Henri and Mari as they struggled to hold themselves together long enough to destroy him ... pointless, of course. Mari was admirably ruthless for a Peacekeeper, and she'd certainly been prepared to kill Pandora if it meant killing him too … he tasted her gritty determination to do just that and smiled to himself, appreciating the shift in her mind as one might appreciate a fine piece of artwork. It was nice to know that barbarism lurked beneath everyone, no matter how evolved and civilised. The Peacekeepers as a whole wouldn't kill him, but Mari would. It was very human of her.

The more things change, he reflected, *the more they stay the same.*

His mind kept expanding, brushing against the alien warships. Their crews exploded with rage and hatred, some firing madly in all directions and others collapsing on the decks, their minds shattered beyond repair. A handful of tiny glitches in reality spread rapidly, some disrupting antimatter storage facilities and others tearing through tiny singularities that served as alien power sources, destabilising them and destroying their host warships. Only a handful of aliens remained sane and coherent, their thoughts spinning in circles as they tried to understand what was happening to them. They were as blind as a pre-hyperspace race under hyperspatial attack. Even if they worked out what was happening, there was nothing they could do about it. Not yet.

Fear, X thought. He hoped Loki was enjoying the show. *Fear us.*

He turned his attention back to the Archangel. It was running out of power, the two humans under such immense strain it was difficult – if not impossible – to tell what was going to break first, leaving them at his mercy. He hoped it was the machinery, if only because the humans would be helpless without it. He could snap Mari's brain, unleashing the barbarian within, or turn Henri into a psi bomb that could be turned against the sphere, or even pointed at Loki himself. Or he could bring them down to normal, removing their implants; he could even turn them into animals, or objects, or *anything.* The possibilities were endless …

***

Pandora reached out carefully, very carefully, with her minds.

She'd thought of the cloned brains as something separate from herself. In hindsight, that had been a mistake. The brains might not have been inserted into her skull, nor might a copy of her personality have been downloaded into the grey matter, but they were still connected to her mind at the quantum level. The thought caused a brief flash of awareness as she linked herself to the nearest brain, a sudden reflection that the resurrected person really *was* the person … the body and brain might be new, yet at the quantum level they were the same. It was oddly reassuring and yet worrying. If the backups were real, X could resurrect himself after he died.

She put the thought aside as she felt her own thoughts and memories being reflected back at her. It was like being in the nest again, yet … a nest of one, a mind that existed in multiple bodies and yet was truly only one. Not even that, she suspected, as her mind continued to expand. The brains were tied to X's own brain tissue, and to the quantum foam beyond. She understood, suddenly, how the Darius Machine had worked. It had boosted the abilities of her parents, and others with low-level psi potential, and done it in a manner that made it very hard to apply any form of scientific study. The Confederation had assumed it was a trick … and, in a sense, they'd been right. It was a forgery that was so close to the real artwork that it was a work of art in its own right.

Her mind continued to expand. X was a looming presence, a giant stamping across a wooden floor; his footsteps echoed across reality itself. His thoughts were becoming corrupted, a whirlwind vortex of madness that was slowly and steadily consuming him. She wondered if he realised he was becoming a monster, then asked herself if he even cared. His existence might not last long, once Loki intervened, but even a few seconds of unrestrained power would be long enough to rip the galaxy apart. The sheer scale of the power around her was terrifying, all the more so because it *wasn't* brute force. It was the ability to make a microscopic change and watch the rest of reality fall into line.

No wonder they're scared of us, Pandora thought, numbly. *We are so much more powerful than we know.*

She sensed Henri, just for a second, then drew on the brains – her brains – as much as she dared. A shockwave ran through reality as X was suddenly aware of her, his mind lashing out in fear and rage ... Pandora cursed mentally, realising she'd left it too late. She'd hoped she could take control of the brains he'd cloned from her and cut him off, but he'd already connected his own mind to the quantum foam. He hadn't even done it deliberately. He just had. His body was still on the ship, yet it was no longer vulnerable. He'd altered reality to ensure he could never be killed. Not by any physical force.

Her mind staggered as he gathered his power and lashed out at her, trying to erase her from reality ... the universe heaved around her, blinking as reality tried to give him what he wanted without causing a paradox. He wasn't trying to kill her so much as he was trying to wipe her entire existence, to ensure she never existed at all. Flickers of a hundred alternate reality blinked in front of her – X had kidnapped a different Child, X had been a Child, X had stolen tissue samples and used them to turn himself into a Child – and then snapped out of existence, the paradox vanishing before it could truly take form. She felt reality start to crumble underneath her, the first hint of an avalanche that would eventually destroy a chunk of reality ... she understood, suddenly, why reality had started to break down on Jorlem Prime. The changes in reality had been unsustainable and the whole edifice had collapsed. They might have been lucky, she reflected, that the collapse hadn't spread much further ...

"You're not God," she said. Or thought. "I won't let you go."

X screamed something incoherent, a wave of madness slamming into her mind. He was becoming a true cancer, a nightmare … she cursed mentally as she felt the telepathic waves spreading across the sphere. It was doomed, if he wasn't stopped … she drew on the brains, trying to overpower him, and realised it was impossible. His madness gave him strength.

But she wasn't alone.

She reached out to Henri and … a torrent of personality traits blasted through her mind. *Mari's* personality traits. Pandora split her attention in two, drawing on their support – Henri's stubbornness, Mari's grim reluctance – and reached out again, holding X in place. Their abilities clashed, the fabric of reality heaving as they grappled … he had the edge, except he didn't. She didn't have to let him think himself stronger, and besides … it didn't matter. She let him think her weaker, as she undid his protections. His ship – his body – was suddenly vulnerable.

Now, she thought.

Mari fired, one final time. This time, there was nothing blocking her beams. X screamed as his body died, his links to the brains severed … Henri took advantage of his distraction long enough to hold reality in place, undermining the basis for his new existence. The laws of reality no longer allowed him to exist … power boiled around them and Pandora took full advantage, drawing on the power to erase X from existence. Everywhere. Her awareness picked out his hidden bases, and his stored backups, and wiped them out. He was gone …

Her mind spun. Her body was gone. She was dead. Except she wasn't … her mind grabbed hold of her body, yanking it out of the exploding starship, and deposited it on the Archangel. Her awareness followed a second later, landing within her own body. It was dizzying. It was …

"Pandora!"

Pandora opened her eyes and looked up. Henri was there, running towards her. She opened her arms and grabbed him and … she could feel him physically, but not mentally. Her mind had been changed, altered … she was no longer part of the nest. Panic echoed through her thoughts as he hugged her tightly, his eyes going wide as he realised she was cut off. His grip tightened and ...

"You're alive," he managed. "I ..."

A trickle of power bubbled at the back of her mind. She shivered. It wasn't over yet.

***

Mari had to react at lightning speed to keep the internal defences from frying Pandora.

The girl had just appeared on Mari's ship ... her sensors were completely confused, unsure if she had teleported or if she'd been there all along. Mari couldn't make head or tails out of the sensor records and she didn't have time to try. Pandora was Pandora and yet ... there were oddities inside her body that defied analysis. There was no time to worry about that either. Her head was spinning, the mental contact between Henri and her had been broken, and two alien fleets were closing on her. The brief burst of fighting was over. They wanted blood.

She took a moment to scan the remains of X's ship. Local reality appeared to have broken down once again, leaving nothing but a stain that baffled her sensors. The more advanced the sensor sweeps, the more confusing the results. Telescopic scans suggested there was nothing left ... she cursed under her breath, all too aware X would have backups somewhere. He'd be resurrected sooner or later and then he'd start his old tricks again. She might never be able to track him down in time.

"We need to get out of here," she said. "And quickly."

It was hard to think clearly. The alien fleets were picking up speed, their tactical sensors locking onto her hull. The smaller warships were spreading out, ready to engage her no matter which way she moved. Her tactical subroutines suggested they'd put aside their differences and resolved to destroy her, something she understood better than she cared to admit. She was picking up distress calls from some parts of the sphere and ominous silence from others … she had no idea what X had done, to races fully as technologically advanced as humanity, but the silence spoke for itself. She didn't want to think about how many had died, or how many would follow them into the fire if the incident led to war. X might have the last laugh after all, when he resurrected. He might come back to life to see a galaxy in flames.

Desperation roared through her mind as her drives came online. The ship was damaged … in a manner that made no sense. What did, these days? She wasn't sure she could trust her sublight drives and even if she risked jumping into hyperspace, she'd have to evade alien ships that would likely be faster than her damaged vessel. There was no one who could help her, either. They were trapped.

"That isn't true," Pandora said. There was something oddly distant in her tone, as if she'd been pushed too far and could no longer force herself to care. "I can …"

The world blinked. Mari started in shock. The sphere was gone … no, they were somewhere else. She brought up position-fixing subroutines she hadn't used since the very first day and ran them hastily, swallowing hard as she realised they were near Jorlem Prime. They'd crossed nearly five thousand light years in the blink of an eye. New alerts flashed up in her mind. The Peacekeeper squadrons dispatched to do what they could to help the stricken world were trying to raise her, confusion evident in their signals. From their point of view, the ship had popped into existence from nowhere.

Henri grinned. "I can hear you!"

Mari smiled as Henri and Pandora kissed, then felt cold. There was no escaping the implications, not now. The mission might be over, but …

After everything that had happened, the galaxy would never be the same.

CHAPTER
THIRTY

"And you can feel the nest again?"

Pandora nodded. She wasn't sure if it was giving up the last of the power to save the Archangel from the alien fleet that had saved her mind, or if she had simply needed time to adjust to being back with Henri, but she could definitely feel the nest again. And Mari. It was odd to realise that Mari was now technically part of the nest too, although it wasn't clear if she'd be joining them on Clarke or not. The Peacekeepers didn't seem to know what to do with them.

Professor Jasmine leaned forward. "And X is dead?"

"Yes." Pandora had felt him die. "More than that. I wiped out his backups."

Jasmine seemed unconvinced. "How can you be sure?"

Pandora hesitated, unsure how to explain what she'd done.

"Imagine the universe as being nothing more than a giant database," she said, finally. It was as good a metaphor as any, although it didn't come close to conveying everything she'd seen in the final desperate seconds before X's death. The whole experience felt like a particularly vivid dream, one part of her wanted to forget. "Everyone is tagged within that database. I hacked the database and erased everything tagged with his name, wiping out every last backup as well as everything else.

He isn't just dead. He's gone."

"I see." Jasmine frowned. "What do you want to do now?"

Pandora shook her head. She'd spent the last week making love to Henri, being debriefed and doing what she could to relax. There was no shortage of things to do on a planetoid, from extensive VR simulations to exploring the habitation caves and all the other distractions the designers had installed to make the giant starship feel like home, and it had kept her from thinking too much about the future. The power she'd touched, if only briefly, was a constant temptation. The Darius Children really were more powerful than they knew.

"You need to think about Loki," she said, instead. "He wanted to cause a disaster."

Jasmine looked unconvinced. Pandora didn't need to read her thoughts to know the older woman didn't believe *that* part of her story, even though the room was closely monitored and the sensors should have been able to pick out a lie. No one was sure, though. Pandora's body felt normal, and reacted normally, but the sensors had problems studying her. The results were twisted, *wrong* … as if something inside her was trying to spoof them, in a manner that made no sense. If Henri hadn't vouched for her, she wondered if she'd be allowed anywhere near the Confederation. The Confederation didn't like mysteries.

"If an advanced entity chose to meddle," Jasmine asked, "why?"

"He wanted to cause the disaster," Pandora said. She wasn't sure *why*. Loki had made no attempt to intervene, as far as she could tell. She wasn't even sure when his awareness had pulled back, although that was meaningless. A being of such power could be watching her at any moment and she wouldn't have the slightest idea … probably. There were too many unknowns. "I don't know why."

"We will consider the matter," Jasmine said, finally. "Until then, amuse yourself."

"I'll try," Pandora said.

She watched Jasmine leave, then sat back in her chair. The planetoid was comfortably solid, a starship built on a colossal scale, and yet part of her mind saw it as nothing more than an insubstantial *thing*, something that wasn't quite real. It was almost as if she could push her fingers against the bulkhead and *through*, without resistance. She was almost tempted to try … except she didn't dare. She wanted to go back to Clarke and spend the rest of her life chasing pleasure, yet the thought appeared pointless. Worse than pointless. She was a butterfly who could not climb back into her cocoon, could not reverse her transformation.

And Loki was still out there, waiting. She had to be ready for him.

They all did.

***

"So far, there has been no clear consensus on just what happened on the Life Sphere," Admiral Roger said. "The various governments involved in the incident appear confused about how their researchers were recruited to examine the kidnap victim – they appear to have no idea of her name – and why their fleets were dispatched to ensure safe passage, if they won the bidding war for Pandora. It's possible they're telling the truth."

"Yeah," Mari said. "And I'm the Queen of Sheba."

"Sheba doesn't have a queen," Admiral Roger said. "No, you're right. I don't believe them and nor does the Security Council, but they *have* covered their tracks very well. The combination of plausible deniability, and the devastation unleashed on the Life Sphere, will make it harder for us to press for any sort of retribution. Whatever they were planning to do, it cost them dearly."

"Maybe," Mari said. She wasn't convinced. "They may continue to work against us."

She shuddered. She hadn't believed Pandora when she'd claimed to have erased X from existence, not at first. The statement had been absurd. And yet, it appeared to be true. The Peacekeepers *had* noted a handful of his secure datacores, monitoring their locations in hopes of shutting them down when he died, before he could resurrect and inflict himself on the galaxy once again. Those datacores were now gone, with nothing beyond the records to suggest they'd ever existed at all. The power was just too great for her to comprehend.

"They were scared of us before, but their tech level was high enough to give us a fight," Mari added, after a moment. "This is different."

She paused. "And if Pandora is right about Loki ... we have a new and immensely dangerous enemy."

She wasn't sure she believed that, either. *Someone* had helped X, but that someone didn't *have* to be an extra-universal entity. It was far more plausible it had been one or more peer powers, perhaps an alliance of criminal factions or deniable assets. The bidding war might have been rigged from the start, just to get other races involved without sharing anything beyond the basics. And yet, there were a great many oddities about the whole affair. She didn't believe a peer power could have hacked the datanet so effectively, or given X the tools he needed to insert himself on Clarke and kidnap Pandora. And ... and Pandora believed it. She'd met Loki.

"We will consider the matter," Admiral Roger said, finally. "If we really do have such a powerful enemy ..."

"I think we have to assume we do," Mari said. "And act accordingly."

Admiral Roger raised his eyebrows. "And where do you suggest we begin?"

"We know what X did, to raise his mind and boost his abilities," Mari said. The experience had been nightmarish. "We also know what we did to counter it. If we put the two together, we might be able to evolve. Or at least develop a defence against a transcendent being."

"There are ethical issues," Admiral Roger pointed out.

"None of which will matter if the next attack wipes us out," Mari said. "X did ... *something* ... to Jorlem Prime and there are parts of the planet where reality itself has broken down. The tests the alien researchers carried out on Pandora triggered another eruption, shattering the station in a manner beyond repair. Advanced tech failed, in ways that should have been impossible. Even primitive tech had problems. If that happens again, on a Ring, we will lose billions of lives. And that's not getting into what will happen if someone else duplicates what X did, in a bid to become a god. We have to prepare."

"And we will," Admiral Roger said. "Carefully."

Mari nodded, reluctantly. She had the feeling they were running out of time.

***

The edge of the universe, the ever-expanding wavefront of the explosion that had brought the material realm into existence, was surprisingly crowded. A race had discovered, billions of years ago, the advantages of opening wormholes and using them to station observation platforms at the very edge of creation itself. They had vanished long ago, but others had followed in their footsteps, creating a cluster of ships and stations that had been passed down from owner to owner, existing so far from any inhabited galaxy that even the fact they existed had little bearing on the affairs of the material races. Those who could find them, let alone join them, rarely cared for politics, or war, or anything other than the greatest question of all.

Some found their answer. Some stagnated. Some died.

Loki, incarnate in human form, stood on the hull of a starship almost as old as himself and stared towards the distant galaxies. A human would have seen nothing more than a faint hint of light; his senses, far more capable than any material being, had no trouble picking out the Milky Way, even spotting individual people in realtime. The holes in reality left behind by X – and the cancer he'd tried to spread – were noticeable, but hardly fatal. The true threat lay elsewhere.

"You have failed," a quiet voice said.

Loki didn't turn. The entity behind him was a multitude, a creation that was composed of the essences of many different creators. It had a name, in human myth, but to use the name was to limit one's understanding, to cripple one's self before one could come to terms with what it truly was. It was both an agent and yet, in a sense, an aspect of its creators.

"I didn't fail," Loki said.

"The human cancer has been destroyed," the multitude said. "Your plan has misfired."

"No," Loki corrected, mildly. "The true fire is yet to burn."

And he smiled, coldly, in anticipation of the apocalypse to come.

The End

A Brief Introduction to the Inverse Shadows universe

The universe is a very strange place.

As it became aware of the possibility of life on other worlds, the human race was increasingly baffled by the absence of apparent alien civilisations. Logically, humans reasoned, any species capable of intelligence would eventually develop spaceflight and even if they were restricted to slower than light spacecraft they would have spread across the universe well before the human race discovered fire. A number of theories advanced to explain the lack of intelligent races, ranging from humanity being truly unique to a hostile force that tracked down and destroyed intelligent races as they developed technology. It was not until the human race developed warp drive, and later hyperdrive, that the truth was finally uncovered.

Intelligent races, it was discovered, generally fell into three categories. Some races never developed technology, never developed scientific methods they needed to understand the universe around them and therefore never progressed beyond the stone or iron age. Some races fell victim to their own technology, fighting a nuclear war or accidentally creating antimatter or black holes on their homeworlds, wiping themselves from existence. And still others developed socially as well as technologically, passing through the singularity and developing post-scarcity societies, and never felt the need to settle vast regions of interstellar space. It was surprisingly rare for a spacefaring species to colonise more than a handful of star systems, before they reached the point that further expansion seemed pointless. Their maturity led them to isolate themselves from other developing worlds, when they encountered them, and eventually to seek fulfilment by transcending physicality to become a higher order of life. In doing so, they effectively removed themselves from the universe.

The human race was unusual in that it developed faster than light travel before it was mature enough to handle it. Instead of a slow and steady settlement process, humanity exploded in all directions, expanding so rapidly that hundreds of planets were settled within a few dozen years and a number of races, trapped in technological bottlenecks, found themselves introduced to the wonders of interstellar civilisation. Humanity rapidly discovered dozens of worlds that had been left behind by races heading into the higher orders, and artefacts that veered from understandable to the completely incomprehensible; they stumbled across the Galactic Net, the creation of a long-gone race that allowed sufficiently advanced aliens to converse with their peers, and developed their own, often bootstrapping human technology on the remnants of alien civilisations. It was a time of great heroism, of pushing back the boundaries of the possible, but it was also an age in which some of humanity's worst traits were allowed to roam free. Humans dreamt of a universe in which everyone was equal, but others dreamt of a galaxy ruled by the human race – or nightmares in which a handful of genetically superior humans would rule the rest of the race for the rest of time. In some ways, humanity's vast expansion made it extremely difficult for the human race to mature, pass through the singularity, and develop a post-scarcity society. Even now, humanity has not quite faced up to the past and prepared itself to walk into the future.

It is often said that the Confederation is the last

survivor of the wars for supremacy over the human race. It is a post-scarcity society in the truest possible sense; it has no trouble meeting the reasonable or often unreasonable demands of its human inhabitants, from simply ensuring they have more than enough to eat to churning out everything from private starships and fabricators to entire pocket universes and de facto immortality. The average inhabitant can live pretty much as they please, as long as they don't infringe on the rights of others, and in consequence there has been a great flowering of technology, artwork, and everything else that gives the human race meaning. Crime is almost nil, with the exception of sociopaths (see below), and a combination of freedom of expression and very few laws have ensured a certain degree of maturity for the human race.

The Confederation has almost completely abandoned planets, choosing instead to build megastructures, pocket dimensions and planet-sized starships to house its population. The vast majority of humanity's former colony worlds have been restored to their pre-discovery state, as much as possible, and left fallow in the hope they will one day produce a native race of their own. Earth herself is one of the handful of planets that remain inhabited, cleansed of the pollutants of early technological development and turned into a tourist attraction. Most humans will make a pilgrimage to Earth at least once in their lives. It is generally expected that the remaining worlds will be abandoned in the next few thousand years.

The average human child is born into a luxury their predecessors would have trouble comprehending. Most humans spend their first decades developing a basic understanding of their society, then indulging themselves until they develop the maturity to realise that pleasure is not the be all and end all of their existence. At that point, they start to search for meaning in their lives: they join the Peacekeepers (the *de facto* Confederation Navy), lose themselves in research, or join one of the uplift programs designed to assist races trapped in technological bottlenecks without destroying them through contact with a vastly superior species. A handful request private starships and set out on their own missions of exploration, although the Confederation generally maintains a careful watch on such missions and forbids unsupervised contact between humanity and races that have not reached interstellar space on their own merits.

The Confederation is a representative democracy, with each habitat electing a council that makes local decisions and a representative who speaks for the habitat in the Confederation Senate. Most matters are debated endlessly on the datanet, before referendums are held, and everyone is allowed to have their say (although there is no requirement for everyone else to listen). Politics are normally low stakes, which does tend to make debates more intensive. The few matters that are genuinely serious – contact with peer aliens, for example – are treated with more caution.

The Confederation's medical science is second to none. The average human has been genetically improved to render them incredibly adaptable, to the point they are immune to almost all known diseases; it is child's play, to the Confederation, for a human to change sex, skin colour, or even basic bodily form (or upload themselves into a datacore/android body/nanite cloud) and indeed most citizens will spend some time experimenting with such matters until they discover one they find comfortable. The average human is also effectively immortal, their cells regenerating automatically and in the event of actual death, most humans can be resurrected from their backups (although some humans choose not to have backups).

The Peacekeepers are the closest thing the Confederation has to a proper Navy, and they are – to all intents and purposes – the most powerful military force the human race has ever assembled, with weapons that can atomise planets and trigger supernovas. Service is strictly voluntary, with a training period followed by a first deployment; promotion is strictly on merit, and – unlike the rest of the Confederation – there is a firm chain of command. The majority of Peacekeeper starships are cruisers, capable of handling most operations alone, but backed up by planetoids if they face a more significant threat. Their ancestors would find the Peacekeepers disturbingly lax, when it comes to matters of discipline, but they are well trained and most discipline is internal (a consequence of most volunteers being constantly older than their ancestors were when they joined up).

Crime is relatively low within the Confederation, a natural effect of living in a post-scarcity society. There is no need to steal food, for example, and most human desires can be met quite easily without infringing on someone else's rights. However, the human race has not yet managed to expunge all of its demons: sociopaths, humans who get their pleasure through hurting others (or playing games with other races), remain a constant headache. Most tend to be extremely adaptable and innovative, which makes them incredibly dangerous because they lack the morality of the mature human race. If they are caught, they are normally given a flat choice between personality reconstruction or permanent exile to an asteroid that has every luxury save one: the right to leave. It is often claimed that the Peacekeepers sometimes recruit sociopaths for dangerous missions, but that is simply untrue. The Peacekeepers have no trouble finding someone capable of handling nearly any mission, without the downsides of having to deal with a known sociopath.

Perversely, the simple fact that the sociopaths are willing to transgress so blatantly against the laws of their society gives them a kind of disturbing glamour. Some take advantage of this, broadcasting recordings of their crimes into the datanet and revelling in their infamy: others, perhaps driven by demons they do not fully understand, try to stay as undercover as possible.

The Confederation attempts to maintain friendly relationships with peer powers (alien civilisations advanced enough to give the Peacekeepers a fight). This isn't easy. Some races are too alien to be easily understood, others resent or fear the human race; some are so distant, on their way to join the higher orders of life, that they are beyond all contact. A surprising amount of contact occurs at lower levels, meetings on neutral territory (such as the Life Sphere), or through the Galactic Net. By contrast, the Confederation attempts to keep its distance from less advanced races, fearing the disruption direct contact will cause to their societies. The possibility that the more advanced peer powers feel the same way, about humanity, is one the Confederation chooses to overlook.

Despite being one of the most advanced (and certainly the most populous) societies in known space, there are still mysteries that baffle the Confederation. A handful of inexplicable alien artefacts have been discovered, their mysteries beyond human understanding; several hundred worlds are dead, so dead they appear to be wrapped in timeless space and modern technology, no matter how advanced, is disturbingly unreliable on such worlds. The ancient sections of the Galactic Net whisper of godlike beings, and wars fought so long ago that they have passed into legend, and races that were actually designed by elder races, their origins long forgotten. It is rare for an archaeologist to stumble across something really dangerous, but isn't unknown. The Confederation attempts to keep a watch on all potentially-dangerous alien artefacts, yet even the Confederation cannot keep an eye on all of them.

In some ways, the sheer scale of humanity's advancement makes such mysteries harder to tolerate. But the quest to solve them may lead the human race into some very dangerous places indeed.

Elsewhen Press

delivering outstanding new talents in speculative fiction

Visit the Elsewhen Press website at elsewhen.press for the latest information on all of our titles, authors and events; to read our blog; find out where to buy our books and ebooks.

Sign up for the Elsewhen Press InFlight Newsletter at elsewhen.press/newsletter

Iaen series by Terry Grimwood
INTERFERENCE

The grubby dance of politics didn't end when we left the solar system, it followed us to the stars

The god-like Iaens are infinitely more advanced than humankind, so why have they requested military assistance in a conflict they can surely win unaided?

Torstein Danielson, Secretary for Interplanetary Affairs, is on a fact-finding mission to their home planet and headed straight into the heart of a war-zone. With him, onboard the Starship *Kissinger*, is a detachment of marines for protection, an embedded pack of sycophantic journalists who are not expected to cause trouble, and reporter Katherina Molale, who most certainly will and is never afraid to dig for the truth.

Torstein wants this mission over as quickly as possible. His daughter is terminally ill, his marriage in tatters. But then the Iaens offer a gift in return for military intervention and suddenly the stakes, both for humanity as a race and for Torstein personally, are very high indeed.

ISBN: 9781911409960 (epub, kindle) / 9781911409861 (96pp paperback)

TOR

Tor Danielson
Saviour of humankind; Participant in genocide;
Puppet President of a corrupt government

Mi
Near-mythical planet of refuge; Both Heaven and Hell
Killer and comforter; Yet sanctuary for Tor…
…until he is confronted by an unwelcome visitor who brings the past in his wake
and drives Tor towards a desperate act of redemption.

Tor – both standalone novel and sequel to Terry Grimwood's British Fantasy
Society award-nominated *Interference*
ISBN: 9781915304780 (epub, kindle) / 9781915304681 (126pp paperback)

THE LAST STAR

Beware god-like aliens bearing gifts

Stasis and inorganic self-repair, new spacefaring technologies for humankind, yet more gifts from its closest extra-terrestrial ally, the Iaens. There are, it seems, no limits to humanity's outward journey.

Then Lana Reed, Mission Commander of the interstellar colony seeder, *Drake*, awakes from her own stasis to discover that all but three of the vessel's other tanks are dark, their occupants suffocated, screaming yet unheard in their high-tech coffins. But the stasis tanks are not all that is dark. The sensors return no readings from outside. The external vid-feeds show only unending blackness.

There are no stars to be seen. No planet song to be heard. No galaxy cry. No echoing radio signals that proclaim life.

The *Drake* and its surviving crew are adrift and alone in a lightless, empty universe.

From Terry Grimwood, another taste of the human realpolitik alliance with the Iaen, begun in *Interference*

ISBN: 9781915304377 (epub, kindle) / 9781915304278 (144pp paperback)
Visit bit.ly/Iaen-series

ABOUT THE AUTHOR

Christopher G. Nuttall has been planning sci-fi books since he learnt to read. Born and raised in Edinburgh, Chris created an alternate history website and eventually graduated to writing full-sized novels. Studying history independently allowed him to develop worlds that hung together and provided a base for storytelling. After graduating from university, Chris started writing full-time. As an indie author he has self-published many novels, this is his latest science fiction novel to be published by Elsewhen Press, the long-awaited second book in the epic *Inverse Shadows* Universe. Chris lives in Edinburgh with his wife, muse, and critic Aisha and their two sons.

* 9 7 8 1 9 1 5 3 0 4 8 8 9 *